Aubrey McKee

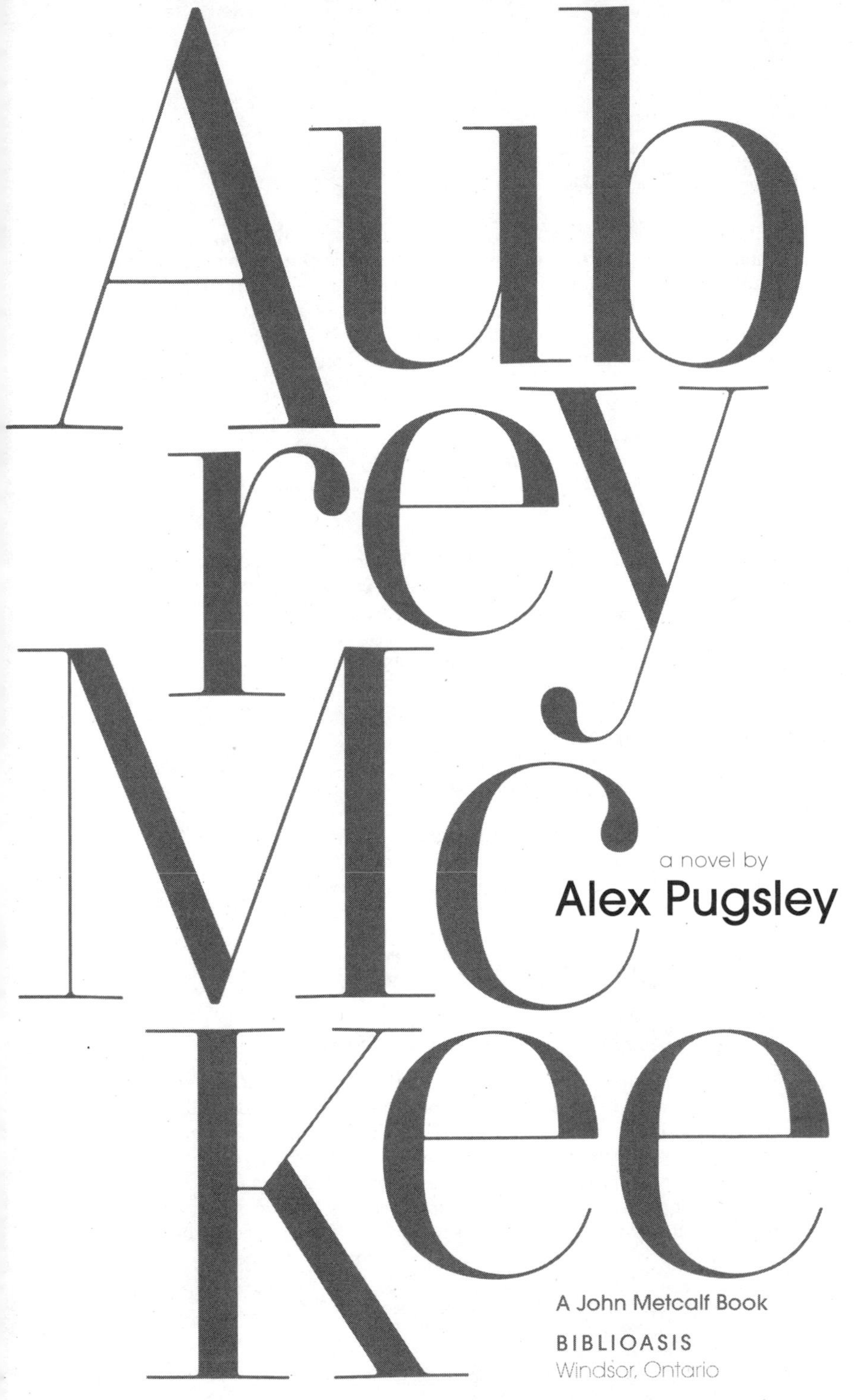

Aubrey McKee

a novel by

Alex Pugsley

A John Metcalf Book

BIBLIOASIS
Windsor, Ontario

Copyright © Alex Pugsley, 2020

All rights reserved. No part of this publication may be reproduced or transmitted in any form or by any means, electronic or mechanical, including photocopying, recording, or any information storage and retrieval system, without permission in writing from the publisher or a license from The Canadian Copyright Licensing Agency (Access Copyright). For an Access Copyright license visit www.accesscopyright.ca or call toll free to 1-800-893-5777.

FIRST EDITION

Library and Archives Canada Cataloguing in Publication
Title: Aubrey McKee / by Alex Pugsley.
Names: Pugsley, Alex, 1963– author.
Identifiers: Canadiana (print) 2020017813X | Canadiana (ebook) 20200178164
ISBN 9781771963114 (softcover) | ISBN 9781771963121 (ebook)
Classification: LCC PS8631.U445 A68 2020 | DDC C813/.6—dc23

Simultaneously published in a hardcover limited edition of 300 copies, signed and numbered by the author.

Edited by John Metcalf
Copy-edited by Martin Llewelyn
Text and cover designed by Ingrid Paulson

Much of the material in this novel originally appeared in the following magazines: *Brick*, *The Dalhousie Review*, *Descant*, *Eighteen Bridges*, *The New Quarterly*, *Prism*, *This Magazine*, and *The Walrus*.

Canada Council for the Arts | Conseil des Arts du Canada

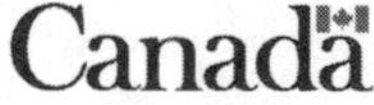

Published with the generous assistance of the Canada Council for the Arts, which last year invested $153 million to bring the arts to Canadians throughout the country, and the financial support of the Government of Canada. Biblioasis also acknowledges the support of the Ontario Arts Council (OAC), an agency of the Government of Ontario, which last year funded 1,709 individual artists and 1,078 organizations in 204 communities across Ontario, for a total of $52.1 million, and the contribution of the Government of Ontario through the Ontario Book Publishing Tax Credit and Ontario Creates.

PRINTED AND BOUND IN CANADA

*To those people I've met in my life,
this book is most ardently dedicated.*

Contents

Ten Recollections of Theo Jones / 3

Dr. B / 13

A Day with Cyrus Mair / 40

Action Transfers / 60

The Pigeon Lady / 73

Crisis on Earth-X / 93

Fudge / 125

Wheelers / *159*

Karin / *189*

Gail in Winter / *258*

The Return of Cyrus Mair / *283*

Death by Drowning / *337*

Tempest / *355*

Aubrey McKee / *381*

WHAT FOLLOWS IS OF MY OWN MAKING. Of course in all parts and ventures I am indebted to those spirits who have gone before—as well as some who move before me now—words and turns of theirs my pages will darken and light up. I am from Halifax, saltwater city, a place of silted genius, sudden women, figures floating in all waters. "People from Halifax are all famous," my sister Faith has said. "Because everyone in Halifax knows each other's business." So those who follow were in our tabloids, our splash pages, and on the covers of our magazines, stories true in every detail to my remembered life. I live with each even now, very now, but as I am reminded that my stay here is only provisional, that someday I may melt into the air, I have decided to make good on a promise once made, to give expression to the lives I encountered, and to make sense of some of the mysteries that seemed to me the city's truths. Much of this was put in motion before my own appearance and some set in play by me. For on a warm September afternoon, once upon a time, I ran away from my sister's birthday party and met a kid named Cyrus Mair—

Ten Recollections of Theo Jones

IN THE LIBRARY of my last school there was a little room that sold second-hand books. It was a pet project of one of the English profs at the university, a German dude who taught a course in Renaissance poetry. He had an office upstairs full of too many books and he used this downstairs room to sell off his doubles, his unwanteds, his overflows, as well as to share his shy love of books and book collecting. Wandering around on an afternoon, I often went in to browse and check new arrivals. The room was organized into expected divisions like British Fiction, American Fiction, Philosophy, Poetry, Drama, Sci-Fi, but on the bottom shelf of the bookcase near the cash box table was an uncared-for section labelled Antiquarian. These were very old books, falling-apart books, and I remember thinking there was something tawdry about this old German trying to fob off volumes missing pages or covers. When I got around to looking through the Antiquarian shelf, I was stunned to see that some of these books were hundreds of years old, that they were artifacts escaped from the sixteenth and seventeenth centuries. Most were published in Latin and Italian, but I was intrigued by a coverless third folio of the works of Shakespeare dated 1664. The prof wanted six hundred bucks for it and because five hundred was all I had until end-of-term, the purchase was beyond me. So I put it back on the bottom shelf. But, as I stepped outside into the November afternoon, piles of leaves orange in the sunshine, undergrads tossing Frisbees, an idle, generous idea glimmered in my brain that I might return to this bookshop when I was a millionaire, and that I would buy the folio and give it to the person who introduced me to Shakespeare, a guy who was, in a symbolic way, my first English teacher. As I walked away from that library, I thought of Theo Jones.

THE FIRST SCHOOL I WENT TO was a private school in Halifax known variously as the brain school, the fag school, the snob school. When I arrived as a six-year-old it was newly co-ed and my class was twenty boys and four girls. Like all first classrooms, it smelled of pencil shavings, forgotten apples, leftover milk in little milk cartons, and was home to rusty scissors, the crusting rubber tip of a LePages's school glue. Behind the school was a not-quite regulation soccer field and here the teachers and big kids were a mass of groups and games and incomprehensible enthusiasms. I had a young uncle at the school (my mother's little brother, eight years older than me), and he allowed me into his recess soccer matches. He and his classmates ran around with their white shirttails flapping out of their regulation grey flannels, their regulation blue blazers hung up in a line on the pointy chinks of the wire-linked fence. My uncle had a rapport with Mr. Jones because Mr. Jones was the coach of the middle school boys' soccer team. As a preschooler, I'd seen black-

and-white photographs of my uncle's championship team in the yearbook. In the back row, in the centre, surrounded by smiling kids, that was Theo Jones. With his youthful skin, short hair, dark-framed glasses, and skinny mod suit, he looked like the singer in a British Invasion band. But he was for me just another of the mysterious faculty for the older kids, a faculty of eccentric Nova Scotian indigenes—an Acadian lesbian who taught French, a PhD dropout from Dalhousie who taught Physics—and a splurge of Commonwealth types: four Australians, three Scots, but just one Englishman, which was Mr. Jones. "Wait'll you get Theo," my uncle said, coming off the soccer field and inflecting the name with a sarcasm beyond my understanding. "He's a freak-master."

I HAD TO WAIT SEVEN YEARS to get Theo Jones. Because of family finances and my own personal delinquency, I switched in and out of three other institutions before returning to the brain school. But come eighth grade, or Middle Four as it was called, I was sitting at a desk, waiting with my pubescent classmates for the first English class of the year to begin. It was a square room, with high windows along one wall, small student desks facing the bigger teacher's desk—a desk exactly normal except for the somewhat curious piece of homemade sculpture behind the teacher's chair. Which was: a pinned-up scholar's gown topped by a cow's skull. To me, the installation was gothic, corvine, purposely theatrical, though my memory might have been influenced by what happened next, which was Mr. Jones's English-accented voice floating into the class as he walked down the hall. "Now my charms are all o'erthrown," he recited. "And what strength I have's mine own." And on, the entire epilogue from *The Tempest*, the first text of the year, committed to memory and performed for us as he walked in with a manic, gleeful smile—a smile which, even then, seemed slightly inappropriate. He was a sudden and nervous laugher.

MUCH WAS COMMITTED to memory. Each Thursday afternoon, when English class was held in the wall-to-wall carpeted audiovisual room and called Drama, a student would be marked on his or her memorized recitation. "Little Gidding," "Kubla Khan," "Upon Julia's Clothes," "The Tyger"—all of these are in my brain today because of Mr. Jones. Drama class was itself memorable, not only because of a dance made locally famous by Sarah Lorcan—Lorcan's pork and beans dance—but because Andrew Pulsifer, a shy, goofy-toothed student, refused to "sell his chair" to anyone else. For a full twenty-two minutes we sat hopeful, restless, listless, and finally gloomily resigned as this kid, Andrew Pulsifer, his forefinger twitching at his lower lip, stared at the floor, terrified, unable and unwilling to comply with Mr. Jones's suggestions. Andrew Pulsifer! A stutterer who had only one close friend in class, Ewan Gruber, with whom he devised a race of Zulus they cartooned on scribblers at lunch hour. Andrew really only talked with Ewan, only lost his stutter with Ewan. With everyone else, teachers especially, he was dumbfounded with stage fright. "Andrew," Mr. Jones said. "Just say, 'Anybody want to buy a chair?'" Silence. "Andrew? Did you hear me?" Andrew staring at the floor. "Andrew!" And so on. We all recognized a battle of wills. By the end of the class, Andrew endured only to autistically thwart Mr. Jones's wishes. We, of course, hated Andrew Pulsifer for ruining a class that was on its way to real entertainment—one that had started with the pork and beans dance!—and we would forever begrudge him for not even trying ("Remember Andrew and the chair?"). But after that class we all wondered at Mr. Jones. He was vexed. He was intense.

BY THIS TIME THE SCHOOL'S dress code had relaxed into hippie outfits. The regulation blue blazers and tunics had given way to tie-dyed shirts, corduroy bell-bottoms, overalls. Mr. Jones now had wavy growing-out hair, frizzy sideburns, turtleneck sweaters, jeans, Chelsea boots. His face was still youthful, but puffy, as if he'd been out drinking with Van Morrison the night before. He looked a bit like Van Morrison, actually, or—as my uncle's class liked to pass him off as—Tom Jones's brother. For a while, teenage girls would surprise him, singing choruses from "What's New Pussycat?" before running down the stairs, ponytails flouncing, their voices vanishing in a Doppler effect of dwindling giggles. In class, his mind was keen with rhyme royals and anapests, sonnets and sestinas, and after school he could be found alone at that teacher's desk, writing poetry of his own. One winter afternoon, I find him like this, staring out the windows at the darkening sky, underneath his gown and skull. He is working, he tells me, on a long poem. "Miranda," it's called. He keeps his drafts and fragments in a wooden box on his desk. The box, as I contemplate it now, seems like a piece of his own personality, so confidential it is, so worn with care. "I've been working on it for eight years," he adds. I nod appropriately but privately I think: *Eight years*? To a thirteen-year-old it's more than half a lifetime. On one poem? A poem was homework you did between TV shows. What was it doing taking eight years? I walked away reverential, astonished at Mr. Jones's conception of his own poetry, yet to my young mind there was something odd and flawed about the enterprise. I didn't understand Mr. Jones. He was a swaggerer. I had seen him roughhousing with the soccer team and his movements, the way he tried to swipe the ball away from you, his body language suggested that sooner or later we would all relate to him as if he really *were* a lead singer or rock star. He bugged me.

HIS HANDWRITING WAS LIKE the handwriting of genius. Quick italic printing with delicate flourishes on the stems of the h's and d's. One year, instead of being typed, all the poems in the yearbook (including one of my uncle's) were handwritten by Mr. Jones and photographically reproduced page by page. His remarks on report cards seemed poems in themselves. I still have a report card from that winter term. The French teacher: *"Bien! Mais Aubrey doit travailler un peut plus."* The Physics teacher: "Acts up in class." And Mr. Jones, the English teacher, in his fluid, precise calligraphy: "A vivid mind slowly coming to grips with itself—Theo." I was so gladdened. It meant much—that he would think to communicate that to me—even though, as I knew, I was not one of his favourites. He noticed me, liked me, was kind to me, but I was not one of the inner cabal as Jim and Jack Von Maltzahn were, as Sarah Lorcan was. These students converged in the school's drama club and, under Mr. Jones's direction, presented plays—*Arsenic and Old Lace, Our Town, Under Milk Wood.* Play readings and weekend rehearsals were at Mr. Jones's flat, the top half of a Victorian clapboard house six blocks from the school. There, he and the kids would rehearse and eat hot dogs. That year Sarah Lorcan was cast as Gwendolen Fairfax in *The Importance of Being Earnest*. She was a modest kid, an ash-blonde of demure looks and storybook smiles. How can I say this next part? For a kid, the world seems full of too many people and not enough stories. Mr. Jones's world was full of stories and poems and he looked to you, as he looked to me that day after school, with one of his smiles, to see how many stories and poems you knew and if, possibly, you might come to know others together. That almost says it right. I could say he believed in the wizardry and collaboration of literature, but that sounds different from what it was.

Anyway. What exactly happened next no one knows, except, perhaps the feature players themselves. But on a Monday morning in March, two weeks before *Earnest* was supposed to open, the school got a call from Dr. Lorcan, an orthopedic surgeon in the city. He wanted to discuss Mr. Jones's rehearsals. It seems Mr. Jones had invited Dr. Lorcan's daughter to what she'd understood to be a group rehearsal but which was, in Mr. Jones's mind at least, an opportunity for something more intimate. Before noon that same Monday, the entire school knew about it, talked about it, joked about it. It was a gasper. "You hear about Mr. Jones? He chased Sarah around his apartment. She had to fight him off." Another girl, Didi Fitzpatrick, came forward with a story of her own. So did a girl on the volleyball team. There seemed to be a girl in every grade. Mr. Jones disappeared from school that Wednesday afternoon. For the next week, English class became a reading period invigilated by a depressed gym teacher in a red Adidas tracksuit, who frowned into a crossword puzzle book. Another week went by. Then a mimeographed memo was tacked up on the empty bulletin board beside the doors to the audiovisual room. "A Celebration of Mr. Jones," it read, and detailed the order of events for Mr. Jones's retirement service.

WHAT A STRANGE ASSEMBLY it was. The senior class boycotted the event. So did the class above mine. But I sat on the carpet in the same spot where, just two months before, I'd watched Andrew Pulsifer refuse to sell his chair. This time I listened as Mr. Dodds, the Irish headmaster, a portly smiler and a fake, improvised unbearably garrulous remarks about Mr. Jones's legacy at the school. Mr. Jones sat—fidgeting, exasperated, tortured. "Oh no, Mr. Dodds," said Mr. Jones, his voice becoming complicated with grown-up emotions.

"No, no," he said, standing up and waving his hands to stop the proceedings. "I'm not going to do this. Not this." And he left the room, his once tremendous laugh strained, weakened, not equal to the situation. It was horrible.

AND SO THE BRAIN SCHOOL, the fag school, the snob school lost an English teacher. We were confused and slightly panicked, and in our panic we allowed Mr. Jones to become a joke. We were cruel. "Never guess who I saw at the movie." "Who?" "Theo." "Who was he there with?" "By himself." "Oh Theo. Poor Theo. What a Theo." The very name became a quip, a punchline, and Mr. Jones a bozo. A few years later, I went to a public high school and became a dope dealer. I was a stoner kid with a pencil case full of joints I sold three for five. The summer of Grade 11, me and another kid are drifting through the old campus of Dalhousie University when we see a sign, *Auditions Today*, on a chair bracing open a door. For a laugh, as a joke, because we're high, we descend into a basement room. Mr. Jones and a gypsy woman in a head scarf are behind a makeshift table holding tryouts for a Shakespeare play. We ask if we can audition and, appropriately, zingingly, I recite "Kubla Khan" as if I am a hallucinating weirdo. That night, a woman calls my house and leaves a message. I am invited for a callback. But I do not go and I never call back. My mother, however, a professional acting type herself, sneaks out one rainy October to see the closing night of Pier One Theatre's production of William Shakespeare's *The Tempest*. "Uneven," is her one word review, adding later that Mr. Jones was "most impressive." He both directed and starred in the show and I imagined him as Prospero, his sideburns immense, his hair powdered white, in the wings watching with excited eyes that first storm scene, Ariel flaming amazement, the fly loft full of thunderclaps. "What cares these roarers for the name of king?"

"IT'S A SHAME," my mother would say afterwards whenever Mr. Jones's name was mentioned. "A tragedy in a way. He really was a fine English teacher." In the next years, Theo Jones fell away from the life of the city. There were rumours he was supply teaching in Cape Breton, that he'd returned to England, to Leeds or Yorkshire or someplace, that he'd there procured a manual labour job or some gig as a groundskeeper. One night, when my family is watching a favourite British TV show, *The Rise and Fall of Reginald Perrin*, we see Leonard Rossiter in disguise as a sewer worker. In one long, soundless sequence, he filtrates a sewer for dead rats. "Look," I say to my family. "It's Theo." And we laugh, for the guy *does* look like Theo, in the exaggerated wig and fake teeth, and it seems condign to our minds that an Englishman in a torpor would derelict into a job as a rat catcher.

HALIFAX IS A CITY OF BARS—taverns, clubs, cabarets. The taverns close near midnight, the clubs at one. But last call in the cabarets isn't till three-thirty so the university kids, the secretaries, the sailors on shore leave, the divorcées, the Caper Bretoners in town for the weekend, and anyone who doesn't want to go home is pulled, like ions in a tractor beam, to the big cabaret on the side of Citadel Hill, to a pleasure dome called The Palace, a live-music venue and last-chance saloon. "Two people enter," as one of my sisters jokes, "one couple leaves." The last year I live in Halifax, the winter I decide to leave the city for good, I arrive at the Palace much more drunk than sober. I am twenty-two years old and grief-struck by the recent death of a friend. So I stare at the giant video screens on the walls. I am watching the music video for The Police's "Wrapped Around Your Finger," sort of trying to figure out how Sting can be dancing in slow motion in a maze of tall candlesticks while his lips are in sync with the song, which is not in slow motion, when I become aware of someone beside me also watching Sting. It's Theo Jones, holding a beer to his chest, and swaying slightly. He is past forty now, but looks roughly as he once did, though puffier and shorter. "Mr. Jones," I say, companionably, raising my beer toward him. But my gesture of respect and goodwill does nothing. Theo Jones only stares at me with a mean, contemptuous smile, as if he has heard all the things we have said about him, as if he has heard all the jokes. He stares at me as if to say, "You don't fool me, McKee, you smug little punk, smoking your drugs and mocking your betters, but when it gets rough you'll retreat into the coze and comfort of your South End family." And I was ashamed. Because in my heart I knew he was right.

Dr. B

GAIL'S FATHER CAME from Bydogoszcs. I don't know how to pronounce Bydogoszcs. I asked him more than once to say Bydogoszcs, but I was perplexed when, after a number of repetitions, I couldn't mimic the sound perfectly. My Polish back then was limited to a very few irrelevant phrases—*Jak się masz? Dobrze! To jest bloto*—that I would sneak into conversation with Dr. Benninger as I could. It was part of our standing joke, our banter, our back-and-forth.

The first time I saw him, I was six years old—a surly, tangled-haired kid, unsure of my parents' recent reconciliation, accompanying my father on Saturday morning errands. We were in a delicatessen called Astroff's on Dresden Row. Glass display cases of mainly adult foodstuffs—dark salamis, queer-looking pâtés, stinky yellow cheese in waxed paper. With my finger tapping on the glass, I listlessly examined the few items I liked, hoping for a subsequent stop at the Candy Bowl or the French Pastry or even the Downtown Bookmart, which at least sold comics. It was this moment of kid-abstraction that Dr. Benninger interrupted, asking Mrs. Astroff if she wouldn't mind giving a slice of smoked meat to the little boy in the red hat. I was unnerved that a stranger would talk to me, or about me, and peeked up at a man with curly hair and wavy sideburns in a tilted, grey astrakhan hat, who watched me with a charming but distant smile. Of course my father came over straightaway to greet Dr. Benninger, with an obliging cheerfulness mixed with surprise, and I could tell from this exchange that the stranger was known somehow to my dad—in the way that everyone in the city was known somehow to my parents.

In the car going home, nibbling at the slice of smoked meat, which my father had allowed me to keep and which I decided I was going to like, I saw Dr. Benninger driving away in a blue Volvo station wagon with round headlights. I wondered where he was going—for certainly I didn't know who he was. I knew nothing about the guy, as I knew next to nothing about any of the adults in the city. Adults, especially adult men, were impossibly remote and complicated entities. They seemed the result of a thousand decisions made in the generations before I was born.

But my father talked of Dr. Benninger as if we had met him before (and maybe I had), letting me know he was a doctor at the hospital, that he was from Europe, that he spoke four languages. At home, I stared at the compact countries of Europe on my uncle's Risk board, intrigued but worried by all the capital cities. From how my family talked, Europe seemed a place of sadly marshalled peoples, border checkpoints, gloomy hotel lobbies, decrepit basements and disintegrating canals in which ebbed and flowed heads of state, adulterers, gypsies, concert pianists, misfit suicides. Dr. Benninger was the first real person I knew from Europe and this explained, what were by Halifax's standards, his many idiosyncrasies. It was why he drove a Volvo, why he was president of the Bordeaux society, why he wore an astrakhan hat in winter or a straw boater in summer. And it was why he didn't care if people thought him a showoff or a peacock. Although my father greeted him jovially at Astroff's, I felt he didn't quite trust Dr. Benninger—mainly because my father didn't quite trust any man whose ski hat matched his ski jacket *and* his ski gloves. Or whose tennis wristbands matched his visor and socks. Or who went jogging without a T-shirt. Which is how my mother and sister and I saw Dr. Benninger one autumn evening a year or so later. Waiting at the traffic light at South and Robie Streets, we spied Dr. Benninger on the sidewalk, also waiting for the light. He was topless in tight black shorts, a house key safety-pinned to his waistband, running on the spot, knees bouncing high, hands on hips, head flung back—acting as if he thought he were by himself, as if he thought he wouldn't be recognized.

"Hm," my sister said. "That's a little different. Don't you know that guy, Mom?"

"He looks," said my mother, driving away, "like a perfect asshole."

To my father, she said: "We saw your pal on the street today." This in itself did not mean that much. Everyone was a pal to my parents. It was one of their diversions to refer to any recently seen acquaintance—colleague, nephew, adversary—as a pal.

"Who's that?"

"Dr. B. That man is really stuck on himself. He has such stubby little legs he wears these little hot pants to make his legs look longer. He runs around jogging everywhere in them. It's such vanity. Honest-to-God, you've never seen such vanity."

My father, in a we-don't-have-to-keep-talking-about-this way, said, "Well, Mumsy, old Stan's an eccentric."

"Eccentric?" said my mother. "In my life, I've met a hundred people who *want* to be eccentric. I've met maybe two real eccentrics. And Stan isn't either of them."

IT WAS NOT EXACTLY anomalous for my mother to offer judgements about people she saw in the neighbourhood. As a rule, she was very free with her appraisals of character, conduct, possible imperfections. Why exactly she attached herself to a conclusion was sometimes hard to pinpoint—for, as we kids intuitively understood, her own biases shifted over time, so that someone who was a perfect asshole last week might be an absolute saint the next. After an evening out, a fundraiser for Neptune Theatre, say, or a reception for the Scotia Music Festival, I would hear my mother in the breakfast nook, sitting at the table with one of my sisters, debriefing the evening, trying to make up her mind if someone was Good or Bad. Dr. Benninger, as a subject, occupied her more than most. "I'm telling you. He sashays around, acting like an I-don't-know-what, the Byronic hero, I suppose. Bit of a darb. Bit of a darb. Walking around the Burrs' house in a paisley ascot, talking about the mystique of a Frank Lloyd Wright house. Yuck. It's enough to make you want to throw up. He thinks he knows something about Frank Lloyd Wright? Let me tell you something. He doesn't know shit about Frank Lloyd Wright. He doesn't know shit about Anne of Green Gables! But you can't tell Stan anything, you know what I mean? He thinks he knows it all. I'm telling you, children, there is nothing more unattractive in someone than self-interest. And the older people get, the worse they are like that. Self-absorbed. I tend to measure people by how much they reach out to others, you know. And that man, he's full of himself." But even on this she would flip-flop. From Dr. Benninger's wife she learned he gave a hundred dollars to a Polish exchange student who was stuck in Halifax over Christmas. ("It was a woman, mind you," said my mother, holding up a finger, making sure this detail was not lost.) Less easy to explain was Dr. B driving home a male hospital porter all the way to Tantallon during a snowstorm. Or donating a set of Balzac to Hope Cottage, a men's shelter, or, what almost stopped my mother cold, his offer to pay a teenager's way through college. "You know that red-haired boy at the express check-out at Sobeys? With the over-bite? From Musquodoboit Harbour? He got to talking to Dr. Benninger because he wants to go to med school. And on the way to the car with the groceries, Dr. Benninger said he would give him the money. The tuition. Not lend it, but *give* him the money. And the kid doesn't have to pay it back. He just has to do the same for someone else when he's older. If he can. Can you believe it? I have never heard of anyone doing that at the express check-out at Sobeys. And I have heard a lot." I could tell my mother was dissatisfied with these new developments because she preferred definitive verdicts. I would see her sometimes, maybe after a phone call with Mrs. Benninger, thinking about that family, looking as if she'd just swallowed sour milk, but she didn't speak so rashly about Dr. Benninger anymore. For the moment, his actions were rather outside her purview, contravened her laws of thermodynamics, and her analyses began to subside. I think they would have lapsed entirely had it not been for two further plot-points—me falling in love with Gail, the Benninger's younger daughter, and my mother becoming the closest of real pals with Sophie, Dr. Benninger's wife.

SOFYA BENNINGER was merely one of the most charming persons known to the city. To see this woman as she was in 1973—when she drove a bunch of ten-year-olds to Lunenburg on a school trip—was to see the most charismatic woman imaginable, certainly she was for me, sitting directly behind the driver's seat in that same blue Volvo station wagon, peeking as I could at the fluent eyes and nose reflected in the rectangle of the rear-view mirror. I'd seen her before, scanning the school parking lot for her own children, and felt at that time her sense of responsibility toward kids. Most moms were like that—even Mrs. Burr, the glamorously blonde, crinkly-smiley matriarch of a family of boys, was like that—but Mrs. Benninger *was* a little different. She had a tacit, relaxed affinity with children and even shy kids ordinarily uncomfortable with physical contact, even the hypersensitive Cyrus Mair, did not mind being touched or finger-poked or grabbed by Mrs. Benninger. She had a genius for it and seemed to mean by it only kindness, amiable provocation, fellow-feeling.

The school trip was on a muggy Saturday morning. Six kids and a mom caged in a car, lost trying to find the highway back to Halifax. Careening around the twisty, inclined streets of Lunenburg, Mrs. Benninger invented a game called Carp Shorners wherein all her passengers went into the back seat and allowed the centrifugal force from the Volvo's turns to propel them from side to side—aided by a well-positioned foot or extending arm. We stacked up on each other, cramming elbows into ears, fogging the windows, screaming for them to be lowered so we could breathe, kids bouncing around the back seat like ball bearings in a wagon. But, as we approached the on-ramp to Highway 103, she pulled over onto the gravel shoulder, and had us quiet down and put on our seatbelts again. After games of Buzz and My Grandmother Packed My Bag, Mrs. Benninger said we should go around the car, that each of us could tell a joke. I don't remember my contribution but I recall Mrs. Benninger's to this day. "So it's my turn?" she said. And then, colludingly, as if she too were on the run from the adult world, she asked me to draw on my fogged-up backseat window. Under her supervision, I diagrammed an overhead view of a house, a stick-woman in a bed, a red light in the front window, the street outside—and four stick-men, three inside the house and one across the street.

"Is this a puzzle?" a kid asked.

"Sort of," said Mrs. Benninger. "It's a whorehouse. And those are four different men. Can you guess their nationalities?"

Pause. Kids looking at each other in bewilderment. What kind of joke was this? And did she just say *whorehouse*?

Starting to giggle, Mrs. Benninger pointed at the four stick-men. "He's Finnish. He's Russian. Himalayan. And that's a Newfie waiting for the light to change."

Jolted, we were, that a joke could be so involved, that adults actually told dirty jokes, that Mrs. Benninger would repeat one to us, a bunch of kids in grade school.

She invented Carp Shorners. She told us a dirty joke. She said *whore*. I was in love with her. We were all in love with Mrs. Benninger.

I NEVER SAW MY MOTHER laugh as much as she did with Sophie Benninger. Just helpless, pee-your-pants, that-woman-is-a-riot hysterical. For my mother, Sophie was a brunette counterpart, an accomplice, a sister. Whether working on the board of Neptune Theatre, organizing a fundraiser for the Halifax Trojans Swim Team, or just flirting together at a cocktail party, they touched off something in each other's sensibility and between themselves, developing a giddy, feed-backing party personality. They would laugh-talk in a way that made everyone feel involved and scandalized and delighted—and wanting to participate in the froth of that delight. No one knew what they were going to be excited about, no one knew how far they would go. I see them from those years, in the slide show of memory, in white tennis dresses with green trim, arriving at the Ottway's tulip party, clutching Dunlop racquets and fluted glasses of champagne. Then at my sister's wedding reception at the Lord Nelson Hotel, hiding from their husbands and sharing a Cameo Mild cigarette, Mrs. Benninger politely swishing her exhales upwards as if this method dispensed the smoke faster (I thought it looked European). Preparing sangria in our breakfast nook, Mrs. Benninger dropping orange slices into a pitcher, her slacks unbuttoned because somehow the "dryer had shrunk the waist five inches." Then, later in the rec room, the two of them in their stocking feet, watching *The Producers* on TV, laughing harder than I thought women could laugh.

My sisters were cautious of Mrs. Benninger's high spirits, thought her uncontrolled, too hotsy-totsy, called her Mrs. Dubonnet—then later Rhoda after *The Mary Tyler Moore* show, a TV program my mother and Mrs. Benninger debated long after it ended. Wasn't Georgette fantastic singing "Steamed Heat," why did Rhoda leave the show, what was she doing with that husband? Of course as I grew older, my crush grew with me, and to my pubescent imagination Mrs. Benninger was the fantasy older women *sans pareille*. With her dark, somewhat slanted eyes, straight nose, pale complexion, and full, dark hair, she had the concupiscent feminine presence of an Italian movie star. In those years, the very words *bosom, zaftig*, and *camisole* excitedly implied Mrs. Benninger. I remember Digby Lynk on Jubilee Road, returning from a party at the Benningers, turning to me somewhat unbelieving, somewhat embarrassed, speaking in a whisper of hushed admiration, "Gail's mom's fucking *hot*." And sure she was—she was *la femme la plus séduisante du ville* and, years later, reading my way through *War and Peace*, I thought of her when I read about Hélène Bezukhov: "'So you have never noticed before how beautiful I am?' Hélène seemed to say. 'You had not noticed that I am a woman? Yes, I am a woman, who might belong to anyone, might even belong to you,' said her eyes."

"OH SOPHIE'S SOMETHING ELSE, I want to tell you," my mother would say, as though Mrs. Benninger were someone she knew only vaguely. "She knows what she's doing. Never met a woman so sure of her effect on a man. At every moment.

Could have anyone she wants. So what's she doing with that old thing? She is *fifteen* years younger than Stan. What's she going to do when he's old?"

Together, as husband and wife—actually I never saw them when they thought themselves alone. But in front of others, Stan and Sophie Benninger carried on a kind of vaudeville routine. She would touch at him, act as if she were unable to keep from touching him, stroking his shoulder or absently fingering the hair at the nape of his neck as she sat next to him at a dinner table. He would wince, affect extreme displeasure, slap at her fingers: "Stop playing with my hair, woman!" (His nicknames for her were Woman, Frauenzimmer, Sophalina; she called him Ivan Skavinsky Skavar.)

My mother detected animosity in these performance pieces. "He's always got to have her under his thumb. You watch him. He's threatened by her. Sometimes he doesn't even *like* her. Maybe that's why he's always going on those trips. I mean, if that guy isn't fooling around on his wife, meeting other doctors at conventions and whatnot, I'll give him a thousand dollars."

"Mackie," my father would say, concerned the topic was hardly child-suitable. "What kind of talk is this?"

"And why in the name of God would he? He's only married to the most vibrant woman in the city. If you ask me, that man needs help."

And perhaps he did. But much of this came later. I am free-ranging over many years and details here. In Halifax, priorities are not always obvious.

I WAS AWARE OF GAIL BENNINGER and her exquisite-looking sister Brigid my whole Halifax life. I have tried elsewhere to give an account of Gail's character—and her very persevering sense of justice—and faltered, because truthfully I don't know, and I'm a little afraid of, what drifts in the deep end of my ideas and feelings for her. TWO QUICK NOTES: on a first day of school, in kindergarten, Gail pulled the fire alarm in the gym. On the last day of high school, she gave our valedictory address and refused the Edith Cavell Award ("awarded to a girl in Grade 12 who excels in personality and in possession of high womanly qualities") on ethical grounds. That goes a little way to indicating the virtuoso contradictions inside Gail and some of these manifested in her relations with her father—a man to whom she often did not speak for weeks on end. "Could you tell my daughter, Charles," Dr. Benninger would say to me, deliberately getting my name wrong. "Could you tell my daughter that she is not to use the front door, indeed any door belonging to this family, until she apologizes to her mother for what she said this morning." Or: "It's very simple, Charles. Your friend, my daughter, has been sent home from her convent school for, if memory serves, calling Sister Irmgard 'a fascist hog.' So she will remain in her room until she writes a letter of explanation and apology." In these instances, he did have a kind of Mitteleuropean arrogance that bugged me and which I found burdensome and distracting. Then I would resent the melancholy and disdain which floated in the air after his yellow-voiced remarks. I never talked back to him but I did hurry out of the car one afternoon a few years later, in Grade 11, when Gail and I were in the back seat talking about applying to MUN, the Memorial University of Newfoundland. Dr. Benninger pulled over, switched off the engine, and turned very slowly to Gail. With imperious self-regard, he said, "You are not enrolling in some glorified fish school just to spite me."

But before all that, back when Gail and I were just ragamuffin youths, during our teenage years, we were both loose in the city. My parents had separated again, for three years this time, and I was running with disparate kids who wrecked beater cars on the weekend and chugged vodka and Lemon Tang behind the bubble of the Halifax Junior Bengal Lancers—delinquents who knew Gail. One afternoon, rolling joints in her basement, she guided me to a second-floor bathroom—it was the first time I'd been upstairs—and in my spaced-out reverie the rooms and furniture had the faultless, presentational splendour of an art gallery, a vibe it retained all the years I knew it.

The Benninger house on Robie Street, like so many in the South End, was a three-storey Victorian. I do not know who occupied the place before them, though my mother remembers. "I used to go with the boy who lived there," she said. "Before I met your father. His bedroom was in the attic. The whole place was this god-awful olive colour. But Stan and Sophie, I got to hand it to them." In the Benninger house, the normal paraphernalia of comfortable middle-class life was apparent—the Persian carpets, the recent magazines, brass fire-pokers beside the fireplace, the porcelain figurines posed on a shelf in the front porch—but everything was on display, museum-quality, eerie. *Zum Beispiel*—if you were to yank open a drawer at our house, you'd find a blue Christmas tree lightbulb, a disembodied Barbie head with the hair hacked off, a baffling postcard from Uncle Lorne, a rusting Double A battery, one of my father's yellow legal pads, an unrinsed dental retainer, a capless red Flair marker, a school photograph of a kid caught mid-blink, a muffin recipe torn from a cereal box, traces of a broken Pringle's chip, a shriveled carrot. But slide open a drawer at the Benninger's and see only a clean stack of mint-condition *Architectural Digest* magazines. Or a silver cigarette box. Or a single brown dreidel on its side, just now settling to a stop, its rolling prompted by the drawer's gentle movement.

MY OWN FAMILY WAS NOT JEWISH. Our surname was McKee. We ate fish sticks with frozen peas and canned corn. We drank Kool-Aid. Our house smelled like Tide laundry detergent. We were perceptibly Protestant in outlook and sensuality. That Gail and her family were Jewish or Hassidic or Lubavitcher entranced me. They had challah bread and Bibb lettuce and salmon. They went to Shaar Shalom Synagogue. They went to Hebrew School. I wanted to know about the kabbalah, whether women really couldn't shake an orthodox rabbi's hand, about the holes in the bridal sheets. Learning how many tummlers and writers were Jewish, my interests dilated proportionally and I became impulsively pro-Semitic—which alarmed my parents, especially my father. At first, I thought it was because he felt thinking too much on the differentness of Jewishness would lead inexorably to rampant bigotry and spray-painting swastikas; later I realized it was because he was concerned my faddish interest would be construed as representing the views of my sponsor, i.e. him and Mom. But the Benningers more than abided my naive enthusiasms. They lent me books. They told me jokes. I learned a Catskills accent and did voices. I made side-curls by stapling my oldest sister's hair into my grandfather's top hat. One night, over the basement phone, I recited the entire Duddy Kravitz monologue from *St. Urbain's Horseman* to Gail, barely able to get the words out, giggling so hard the bones behind my ears hurt.

There was one book, though, I never read and couldn't read. In the Benninger house, in the white bookshelf beside the phone on the upstairs landing, was a hardcover copy of *My Name Is Asher Lev* by Chaim Potok. This book used to stare out at me from the middle of a row. I must have glanced at it three hundred times, the title horizontal on the dustjacket spine, the words arranged in an orange Arabic-looking script. I didn't know why, but the book more than half-frightened me, belonging as it did (in my mind) to some abstruse world of adultishness that Dr. Benninger conveyed, some Cyrillic or Jewish sense of self he had (and which I would feel whenever I encountered the words *mishpocha* or *tzedakah*). I remember turning the corner on these stairs, on a summer weekend when Dr. and Mrs. Benninger were away and Gail and I had sex for the first time, my foot touching bare on the plush throw rug of the landing, and knowing the book was there, but unable to look at it directly, because I felt so starkly blameworthy, as if I were a filthy interloping Gentile, a piggy goy-goy mucking inside a temple.

SCENE: AN EVENING IN JUNE. I arrive at the Benninger house in a lime-green tuxedo, holding a box that contains a purple wrist corsage. I spring up the stairs to the front door. I ring the doorbell three times to let them know it's me. Dr. Benninger opens the door an inch or two, and leaves it like that, to let me know it's him. I shove the door open. Dr. Benninger stands six feet back, squinting at me with distress. "Uh-oh," he says. "Oh dear God. Look who it is."

Mrs. Benninger's voice glides in from the pantry. "Who is it, dear?"

"It's Shadrach, Meshak, and Charles."

He continued to call me Charles for reasons I don't remember or never learned. This intentional mistake and the arch tone both belonged to Dr. Benninger's mock-patrician manner, a kind of overly civilized comedy character—as if he were carrying on for an audience much more sophisticated than either of us. It was very funny to me, when I understood it. Other times it could be wearing.

"His name's *Aubrey,*" says Mrs. Benninger. "Try that on your Steinway. Come in, dear. Don't mind what's-his-name."

I step in, holding out my hand. "Doktor Professor Benninger, I presume?"

He does not move, regarding me with confusion, as if unsure of the situation's possible danger. Finally there is an indignant wifely noise from the pantry, the moment is broken, and he swiftly conducts me into the living room. "Guten Abend, Charles. What's the good word? Perhaps you would like to see the new Tabriz. Cobalt blue. What does Mr. Cecil Edwards say about this one, hm, Charles? Ah. Here we are. Yes. Have a look at this eight-pointed star in the inner guard border."

Tonight it's antique Persian carpets, which he collected and fetishized, trying them out in different rooms, but it could just as easily have been the Dreyfusards or glass paperweights or Charlemagne. Many of his references I didn't follow, and felt threatened by the possibility that someone like Kierkegaard mattered in a world outside my own. So I would have to say, "Uh, Dr. Benninger? We haven't learned that in grade nine biology yet." And he would stare at me, as if puzzled by such freak gaps in my learning, as if to say, "You don't know that? But of course you know that. Yet for some reason you're pretending *not* to know it—but why? To tease me? *Answer* me, boy!"

In other moods, I would emphasize my teenage doltishness, purposefully mispronouncing Yiddish words (chuts-pa) or replying to him in an exaggerated backwoods accent: "Boys oh boys, I don't know too much about that end of the deal there, Doc, with Mr. Kookaburra there, but sounds good. Real good. Yes sir, I'll have a little of this, a little of that, thank you very much, no pun intended."

My antics made him laugh, he liked escapades, though he often thought me funnier than I was. And that could trouble me. It was as if he needed me to be funny, or as if teenagers were there for his amusement; I was also a little uneasy with the claims of intimacy our joking implied.

But on this evening, the night of Gail's prom, he continues in a tone of deadpan seriousness. "No pun taken. But tell me, as my wretched daughter busies herself upstairs with thoughts of insurrection, where are you two planning to go tonight? It's a local ritual of some sort, this convocation?"

"That's it, Doc. Graduation. Make a few bonfires. Sacrifice a few ponies. Maybe a nun."

"Maybe Sister Irmgard. But truthfully now, Charles, Mrs. Benninger and I wanted in a small way to congratulate you and Birdy for surviving the last year." And, after this brief preamble, Dr. Benninger produces a demi-bottle of champagne as a gift. I think he is going to pull it away when I reach for it, but he sets it on the dining room table in front of me. A little card taped to the neck reads *Gratuluje!*

AFTERWARDS, MY FATHER had to be told twice. "Was it real wine?" he asked.

"No, it was a bottle of champagne. With a real cork."

"Sparkling wine or champagne?"

"It had a red label with 'Mumm' on it."

"He gave you a bottle of Mumm's? Mumsy? Did you hear this? Stan gave Baby-boy a bottle of Mumm's for his graduation. I've never heard anything like it."

"Uh-huh," said my mother. "Figures." She was rehearsing for a play at the time and shut up in what used to be my uncle's bedroom but was now the upstairs den and sewing room—it was the place she went to memorize lines.

"How old are you, Baby-boy?"

"I'm forty-five."

"You're fifteen years old and you're drinking champagne? Mother, did you hear any of this? Come down here and get your son off the bottle."

"Go watch your hockey game. I'm trying to do this."

But my father, who took note of gestures of magnanimity, began to think Stan was a different sort of person than had been previously understood. He began to see him as a terrifically humorous, somewhat misunderstood gentleman given to unpredictable generosity. He now admired Dr. Benninger's quizzicality, his off-point sarcasms, his nonchalant patience. He started calling him Stanny. He would say: "Stanny's wonderful! Fantastic fellow." Or, if he had to, he might say: "Well, yes, Stanny can be peculiar. Some days he has no sense of humour at all. But most of the time it's marvelous."

My going out with Gail inaugurated a time when the two grown-up couples were inseparable best friends and some of the slides shown earlier really date from this period. The McKees and Benningers coincided on surprise birthday parties, New Year's Eve dinners, theatrical premieres, wine, children, trips, and gradually, inescapably, as always happens in Halifax, the lives of the two families interinanimated in a thousand explicit and ambiguous ways. That's the wear-you-out thing about the place. One's sexual, familial, and personal and professional lives all complicate with connection, alliance, and shared secrets, so much so that the citizens seem to be participating in some Grand Dysfunction. Lives leak in and flow out of each other like a human version of the water cycle. Apart from fleeing the ecosystem, it is impossible to withstand it, impossible to stay aloof. Everyone who lives in Halifax is absorbed. "Life in the fish bowl," as my sisters would say. "Halifax, the evil village," as Gail says. Of course the village had different denizens, some more powerful than others, and it was toward the village elders that Dr. Benninger became drawn.

"Why Stan is so gaga on Tiggy's crowd I will never know," said my mother. "All he wants is to be invited into the best houses. He's like a court jester. Talking about Salvador Dali to a bunch of orthodontists from Bedford, give me a fucking break." Tiggy's crowd was a stratum or two above our own. Although my father was a lawyer, he had no inherited dough and did not own one of the nicest homes in the city or a Dutch Colonial house in Chester's Back Harbour. In Tiggy's ionosphere were eight or nine recurring families, including the Ingrams, who ran National Ocean Products, the Ottways, who developed the Halifax downtown, and the Bugdens, who owned the newspaper. Some of these families were very impressive. Many were not. They were just rich. But Dr. Benninger was fascinated by all of them, attracted to all of them, even if, at the same time, he could be contemptuous of what they represented. On the steps of the newly built Park Lane, an upscale mall built on Spring Garden Road, he once took a breath to say, "The bourgeoisie always win, don't they, Charles? No matter what we do." By this time I knew enough of Karl Marx to know that Dr. Benninger and I *were* the bourgeoisie. That mall, with its chichi clothes stores and movie theatres and jewelry shops, was built for people exactly like us. Didn't he think he was one of them?

TIGGY WAS MARRIED TO GREGOR BURR, a senior partner in the law firm Merton Mair McNab, and a man unimpaired by intellectual complication. The father of three boys—Brecken, Bunker, and Boyden—Mr. Burr was a jumbo preppy boy himself. He called everyone Tiger, wore purple golf shirts and scarlet Bermuda shorts. In my few excursions to the Royal Nova Scotia Yacht Squadron, I saw him there each time, variously tottering along the breakwater, playing the bagpipes, crunching beer cans in his fists, tossing the water taxi girl into the sea. He skippered a thirty-foot C&C sailboat called *Sun Dog* and made the boat a recreation for his boys and their girlfriends—and anyone else who wanted to show up. One of my sisters was a friend of a girl who went out with Brecken Burr, in the way that girls are friends with people they loathe, and one September she crewed the Labour Day races with the Burrs. "Mr. Burr's a pig," she said afterwards. "It's *disgusting*. All the sons' girlfriends are on the sailboat in bikinis and he's slapping their bums, telling them to take off their tops, and trying to get them to sit on his lap. The man's a big-time slime." My mother dismissed Gregor Burr with a one-liner: "A stiff prick hath no conscience—and not a lot of clues either." An articling clerk at the law firm, a page at the legislature—these were two of Mr. Burr's liaisons I knew about. I'm sure there were more. Tiggy Burr wore an undaunted, enlightened smile throughout. That is, if she knew. But how could she not? She responded to her husband's carousing by joining the board of the art gallery and becoming an aerobics instructor at the YMCA. In a few seasons, she was one of those gaunt, over-exercised women who look more sorrowful the more they perspire. She also developed a heart problem. From all her four-more, three-more, two-more work outs, the muscles in the left ventricle of her heart had become enlarged and obstructed her blood flow. It was July, I think, when she had open-heart surgery to remove these ventricular muscle bundles, the insides of her very heart exposed and remedied by Dr. Stanley Benninger, FRCP.

Are you starting to feel the claustrophobic connectivity of the place? And I haven't sketched any of the hospital politics themselves, which were often riven with feuds and factions, grievances and power plays. It was, of course, a whole other Theatre of Operations for Dr. B—hundreds of surgeries on Maritimers who needed septal-defect repairs, coronary artery bypass grafting, aortic valve replacements, rib resections. A nurse once brought an action against him for kicking a metal bucket of sponges against the wall of the O.R. ("What does he expect," said my mother, "operating when he's too tired?"), but besides this one incident he was said to work himself into long-term weariness, doing as many as four bypasses in one day. From the hospital, he would come home depleted, pass out on the sofa, or collapse into *Weltschmerz* and take to his bed for days at a stretch, watching war documentaries downstairs, his feet hidden in black-soled slippers, the floor strewn with medical journals and echocardiograms. In these moods he was unreachable by word or gesture, the whole house subject to the glooms of his depression. It was as if he understood too much, saw too much, knew too much. And yet he didn't really know his own daughters—whose damage and instability were linked, I felt, with their father's sporadic autisms. These situations would excite an orange-coloured rebelliousness in me that I was at pains to disguise. But what could I do? I had only a limited experience of the guy, saw him mostly from my own or my family's point of view, and I knew there were angles I would never encompass. I guess my core confusion was this: he was either a preoccupied connoisseur with a true and painful exposure to mystery or an immensely pretentious mugwump who messed his Einstein hair on purpose. But I cannot in good conscience continue such explorations because, let me say here, Dr. Benninger emerged as a child from true Second World War horror. He was born in Poland, as noted, but he and his parents were in Germany when war broke out, when the Panzer divisions rolled across the border. They lived with friends, in hiding, they were in Dresden when the Allies fire-bombed that city and, posing as Germans, helped find bodies in the rubble and shovel buried corpses of German soldiers. His parents died when he was six. A relative got him to England.

"Mmm-hmm, yes," said my father, who evidently knew about Dr. Benninger's childhood, in that way my father seemed to know about everyone. I thought my mother would be good for specifics, but she didn't have the same energy for the subject anymore. She liked Stan now, was touched by the stories of kindness his patients ascribed to him. No, it was Sophie who occupied her, especially when she learned, through Sophie's sister, what she'd suspected for six months: that Mrs. Benninger was ill.

"LUNG CANCER," said my mother. "There's two types. Big cell and small cell. If it's small cell, you have a chance. If it's big cell, she's had it. She might have a remission, but if it comes back, you go pretty fast."

I didn't know what kind it was. Mrs. Benninger was in and out of hospital for the next eighteen months undergoing chemo and radiation therapy. She went from being one of the most visible of citizens to essentially vanishing from the shops and theatres and living rooms of the city. It got so I was afraid to ask Gail how she was doing.

One day in December, my sister walked into my room. "You going to the Dubonnets?" she asked. "We're all invited. It's a Christmas party. Well, Hanukkah."

"I thought she had cancer."

My sister shrugged. "She's really healthy now, apparently. She's starting to get her hair back. But just in case, Mom's giving her the wig from her play."

Gail, for reasons I won't go into, chose not to attend. But I went. In a show of solidarity, all the female guests wore wigs from Neptune Theatre's wardrobe department. Except Tiggy Burr, who arrived late and hadn't heard about the arrangement. But there was Mrs. Ottway in Nora Helmer's loose upswept bun, Mrs. Ingram in grey Blanche DuBois ringlets, Gail's Aunt Tova in *The Gingerbread Lady*'s fright wig, and, in a majestic return to form, Mrs. Benninger in a Marie Antoinette-style pompadour from Congreve's *The Way of the*

World. The women were transformed by their outfits and the men by their transformations. The gathering had an effervescence and unpredictability I didn't associate with adult parties. Sophie's older brother Morrie was there from Montreal. So were her mother and father from Cape Breton. A soprano from the Canadian Opera sang "There Is Beauty" from *The Mikado* accompanied by Dr. Benninger on piano. Bottles of wine everywhere. Birch logs settling in the fireplace. A cousin fiddling in the kitchen. A nephew step-dancing. My mother in the living room playing side one of the soundtrack from *Saturday Night Fever*. Everywhere platters of brie, cherry tomatoes, goose liver pâté, fresh baguettes. Adults goofily dancing in the dining room. The Benninger house, which for so long seemed an airless exhibit, was warm with conviviality and release. Years later I would wish I'd stayed longer, but there were three more parties to go to that night, with people my own age, and near midnight I decided to make my exit. I was the last young person there. Searching the house to thank my hosts, I found Dr. Benninger elegantly two-stepping with Mrs. Burr in the pantry. He wore a blue blazer, a white shirt with French cuffs, an orange silk tie bought in Italy.

I told him I was leaving.

"But Aubrey," he said, in an odd tone of voice, at once impatient and casual. "Aubrey, you can't leave. Mrs. Benninger will be heartbroken if you go without dancing with her. Please. Dance with my wife. Come follow me."

Admittedly it was a daydream I'd had for nine years (a long time in boy years), to share a romantic moment with Sophie Benninger—a moment when I would be taken as a proper, full-grown dance partner and not a kid on a school trip. So we danced. With one hand on my shoulder, the other steadying her wig, she and I waltzed about the Persian carpets. But as I looked evenly into her eyes, I saw that she was far more weakened and frail from the radiation therapy than anyone was saying. Her face was grey, there were spooky blotches on her neck and thin colourless lines tracing away from her eyes. Whether she recovered or not, I could tell she would never be as abundantly lovely as she once was. I could also tell this didn't matter to her. When the song ended, she saw me to the front door and searched for my duffel coat in the hall closet. And then I began a sequence of doofy, clownish actions which makes me blush to recall even now, many years later. Flustered by so many incidents—that I'd danced with Mrs. Benninger, that I'd found Dr. Benninger and Mrs. Burr together, that Gail had decided not to come, that I was drunk—and seeing that Mrs. Benninger had sorted past my duffel coat three times already, I reached over her shoulder and grabbed my coat off its wooden hanger, bumping her off one of her high heels. Covering for this, I threaded my arm over-efficiently into my coat sleeve and spun myself sideways to better pull on my coat. As I was rotating, my shoulder knocked the porcelain figure of a dancing woman off the shelf in the front porch. It fell and broke into three chunks on the floor. I despised that I could be so clumsy as to break something the Benningers valued, especially something from Dresden, something that might have belonged to Dr. Benninger's lost family. I blurted that I would pay for it, that she must let me pay for it. Holding the pieces in her hand, Mrs. Benninger was very calm. She checked the stability of the surviving figurines on the shelf, then kindly smiled at me, her pompadour wig askew, sagging a little. "Aubrey, it doesn't matter. Don't even think about it. I'm glad you could come to our party. Take care of your parents for me, won't you? And thank you for being so kind to my daughter. Happy Harmonica."

"But I'll pay for that. I want to—"

"Aubrey, dear—" And she finished the thought with a little spin of her fingers that made me understand I shouldn't talk about it again.

"Okay, Mrs. Benninger," I said. "Happy Harmonica to you, too. And see you next year. You take care of yourself, too."

"I'll be fine." And then, in one of the movie-moments of my late childhood, Mrs. Benninger kissed me on the lips, a loose moist kiss, redolent of red wine, swoony perfume, and a deeper, unhealthy organic under-smell that I did not allow myself to register. "Good bye, dear."

I stepped outside into a snowstorm. She closed the door. Inside, someone turned up the stereo and "Night Fever" by the Bee Gees burst again from the living room, shaking the front windows. Standing on the top step, trying not to cry, snowflakes stinging my eyes, I watched a ginger cat tear across Robie Street toward Gorsebrook Hill. Then I slipped on the wet steps and fell to the sidewalk, breaking the pint bottle of bourbon in my back pocket.

MRS. BENNINGER WENT BACK into the hospital for treatment the day after New Year's. There was good news. A second course of radiation therapy was going well. Then it wasn't. She got pneumonia. Then kidney failure. My mother was in Tampa visiting Nan when my father called her. While my mother was in the air, Sophie Benninger, born Sofya Anna Schwartz in New Waterford, Cape Breton, in 1944, expired on the seventh floor of the Victoria General Hospital in Halifax. She was thirty-eight. My sunburned mother sat up all night in the breakfast nook, her head in her hands, sobbing, her voice breaking with grief. "She was such a loving mother and loving wife," she said. "Oh what a cruddy business. That such a woman could perish." Thinking of her in later life, my mother would fall silent, then say softly, "That was the last time I was ever young, the day Sophie died."

THREE WEEKS AFTER the funeral, Dr. Benninger moved into an apartment in Summer Gardens with Tiggy Burr, astounding the city not least because she was still married to Mr. Burr. It was a development that strained and ended diplomatic relations between our families. My father did not talk about it. My mother tried out a number of explanations. "Stan always had to be liked. And he was. He really was. Mostly. All the doors of Halifax would open for Stan and Sophie. 'It's Stan and Sophie, Sophie and Stan. Come on in. Have a drink. How've you been?' But he misjudged everybody. When he took up with Tiggy. It was too soon. We were at a party at the Ottways, Stan and Tiggy walk in and everybody got their coats and left. Just left. Well, Hal and Issie won't have them in the house anymore. Neither will the Fingards. I don't think the Goodmans will. Even the Jacobsens." All the families that my mother swore Dr. Benninger wished to impress and befriend—the Ingrams, the Lordlys, the Buckles, the Ottways—they cut him and Tiggy. The invitations to the summer houses in Chester stopped. The phone calls ceased.

Perversely, Gregor Burr, the careless alcoholic and careless womanizer, never seemed in danger of losing social position. Maybe he had too much money. Or his affairs had gone on so long people were used to them. Or maybe his dalliances were tolerated because they never jeopardized his marriage to Tiggy. Dr. Benninger and Tiggy, however, were not tolerated and, if there is such a thing as Halifax Society, Dr. Benninger fell from it. He was seen as a culprit. Whether this ostracization contributed to Tiggy's decision, after four months with Dr. Benninger, to return to Mr. Burr, I don't know. Maybe it would have happened anyway. Tiggy Burr is a strange woman guided by criteria I will never understand. But gradually, over a year of community correction, during which time even Mr. Burr made a show of understanding, or, at least, a show of trying to appear as if he were capable of understanding, Tiggy was rehabilitated to the community of the South End.

But Dr. Benninger was not. Nor did he wish to be. He returned to the house on Robie Street, lived there by himself, got a spaniel named Boot. I would see him walking this dog around Black Rock Beach in Point Pleasant Park, a park where once he ran cross-country races. He moved with a prominent limp now (the years of jogging ruining one of his knees), and kept to himself, as if he were in exile from a distant kingdom, an outcast among pine trees and sea spray. I was puzzled he stayed in Halifax. Why wouldn't he escape to Tuscany or Provence—some country of sun-spangled vineyards? Why would he choose to end his life in this isolated saltwater city? Why would he choose at all to end his life? This was, of course, the question on which the whole city wanted a final verdict. Even his suicide became a spin on his mystery. I decided to see it as a convergence of many impulses—a refuge, a surrender, an escape—a final ending to all the contradictions and documentaries. In later years, I could resent his death. I felt that in passing into the next world he was somehow passing on to us his sense of mystery—as if he knew that his death, the question of his death, would become part of *our* mystery. And I didn't want it. Once on a crosswalk in Montreal I began furiously talking to him, swearing at him, but of course he wasn't anywhere except in my memory.

A year after he moved back to his house, I heard through my sisters that Dr. Benninger was remarrying. He'd met a woman, whose name I never learned, who taught at the med school and who had a young daughter from a previous relationship. They purchased one of the new condos at the bottom of Jubilee Road but, as my mother pointed out with a wistful smile, "He should have sold the Robie Street house first." It was one of those capricious buyer's markets that occur in Halifax from time to time, when properties stay on the market for years, dissipating spirits and savings. Nevertheless, Dr. Benninger and his fiancée were determined to go through with the move. And this is how I saw him for a last time in front of the Robie Street house. It was one of those sunny April days when weeks of Atlantic fog and sleet are spectacularly expelled by a high-pressure system, clarifying the city, illuminating bare tree branches, making forsythia seem possible again. The sky was high and cloudless, the sun radiant on the front yards of snow, and I could see from as far away as University Avenue that same blue Volvo parked in front of the white house. The back seats were bent forward, the doors open. Dr. B was loading into the car some rolled-up Persian rugs, a few paintings, wine boxes packed with silver—possessions, presumably, he did not trust to the movers. I saw him put down a box in the snowmelt of the sidewalk then re-enter the house. I stood on the sidewalk, beside the *For Sale* sign, wondering if I should keep walking. I was pretty sure he hadn't seen me. My parents had no dealings with him, neither of his two daughters spoke to him anymore, I knew he wasn't really choosing to acknowledge people so much himself. But watching the trickles of snowmelt stream under the cardboard box, and remembering who had given me my first glass of champagne, and Courvoisier and Calvados, who had given me a slice of smoked meat more than twenty years earlier, I picked up the box and waited. It was a Riesling box hastily packed with galoshes, an unpolished menorah, an art book on Matisse. A few seconds later he came out, locking the front door and placing the key in a metal box that hung from the door knob. He turned and saw me, his hand on the wooden railing of the front steps. "Charles, yes, I thought it was you." He composed a smile and it pained me to see how difficult it was for him to make this smile. All the quips and charms his smiles anticipated, all the little jokes he used to tell himself, they were gone. It is always disquieting to see that people have aged, but Dr. Benninger looked elderly now, his hair gone white, his face loose, shoulders stooped.

"Doc!" I said, brightly. "New digs? Onward and upward? Shall I put this box in the Volvo?"

"Yes, Charles. That would be good. Put it next to the Sauvignon Blanc." And without too much difficulty we had a chat: what was I doing in Toronto, did I see so-and-so. I congratulated him on his marriage. Standing there in front of the house, he had that ephemeral but persistent Frenchness about him and reminded me, in his resigned civility, of a character out of Proust or Turgenev. I wanted to ask about Boot, the piebald spaniel I liked so much, but was worried that, like so many other things, Boot didn't figure in the story anymore. So I didn't. And neither of us mentioned Gail. I don't remember our last words. As I had twenty years earlier, I watched him get in his car and drive away. Three months later, on July 12, the day that would have marked his and Sophie's thirtieth wedding anniversary, Dr. Benninger went back to the empty, unsold house on Robie Street and hanged himself with a rope on the upstairs landing. Rumours were that he was in financial trouble, that he had sunk into another depression, that he was ill with a terminal disease. His body hung there overnight until Marni McCafferty, the Century 21 real estate agent, opened the door to show the house to a young couple from Calgary. By six o'clock that afternoon, everyone in the city knew what had happened. My family called me in Toronto as I was going out the door to a play. "Survivor guilt," said my mother.

A Day with Cyrus Mair

ALL MY LIFE I'VE BEEN THINKING about Halifax—generally as it is expressed by its families, somewhat specifically by the Mair family of Tower Road, and super-specifically by Cyrus Mair, a friend and rival whom I met one afternoon when I was exactly five years and two days old. Of course the old Mair house on Tower Road is no longer there. The remains were demolished long ago to make way for two apartment buildings. But the final ruination of the family was set in motion years before, on the day I met Cyrus Mair, when his father's body was found floating in Halifax Harbour, on this side of McNabs Island, the first in a series of bizarre events that would conclude with a house fire on the snowiest night in a century. But what of Cyrus Mair—whiz kid, scamp, mutant, contrarian pipsqueak, philosopher prince, pretender fink, boy vertiginous—where was his matter and how was he formed? Cyrus Mair came into my life on the afternoon of my sister's ninth birthday, on a day of gifts and escapes and inventions, the drama beginning with me ringing and ringing at my own front door, waiting to be let in, idly probing with my tongue a front tooth newly loosened. Inside, my sister Bonnie came to the door in her sparkle dress—I could see her distorted through the stained glass of the door's windowpanes—to ask what I wanted.

Now Bonnie was smart. She knew how many seconds there were in a year, that blue and yellow made green, and she could count up to forty in French. Once we'd been happy allies, the two of us venturing nude and hatless into our parents' cocktail parties, but in the past months a coolness had prevailed between us, and now that she was nine she assumed an officious attitude toward younger kids, acting as their *de facto* guardian, and in these moments she became the Big Sister who wiped your nose and reminded you to use the basement door—which is what she was doing now, her eyes scolding, her finger circling. By parental decree, children were supposed to use the back or basement door unless there were special circumstances but I *was* special circumstances. I understood we could use the front door on our birthdays, and a mere two days earlier, when it had *been* my birthday, I'd proposed the idea of moving my front door privileges from my birthday to any other day in the year—and I was choosing today. Bonnie, I saw, had conveniently forgotten this amendment. But I was used to being misunderstood. I was something of an exceptional child, to tell the truth, and from the age of four and a half on I had the uncanny and somewhat underappreciated ability to repeat the "Witch Doctor" song for hours at a time without stopping. My performances didn't win over all my audiences, true, but nonetheless I persevered—just as I persevered now in ringing the front doorbell. Bonnie appeared again, this time with my oldest sister, Carolyn, both tying off helium birthday balloons, and in a burst of tandem head-shaking and hand-waving, they conveyed the instruction to go around to the basement door.

I stood on the porch, furious, knowing that many of the world's mysteries eluded me, but starting to understand better and better that my older sisters wanted to destroy everything I held to be important. Slamming my fist against the glass of the door, and perhaps not really knowing exactly what I wanted, I left off ringing the doorbell and ran in madness to the end of the block, where, contrary to family rules, I ran across Victoria Road. Farther up the street, past the crazy Pigeon Lady's house, and safely distant from all birthday festivities, my shoulders relaxed and I shifted into another of my personas, which was *Aubrey McKee—Boy Detective*. I started memorizing passing license plates for possible future reference and attempted what was known in my trade as a forward tail. This was a sidewalk surveillance technique that involved tracking a subject who was actually *behind* the operative. I'd noticed, for example, on the other side of the street an unknown, fair-haired kid, and as he went about his way, following a single sheet of coloured paper down Tower Road, absorbed in the little world a child has, I was giving him enough time to draw alongside me. But looking across the street now, the boy in question was gone, the sidewalk empty save for a few rain puddles, so I simply crossed South Street and made for the Halifax School for the Blind. This was an enormous stone building, a remnant from another century, and setting foot in this territory was always iffy because it meant one might encounter, as my sister Bonnie described them, "a bunch of blind albino kids from P.E.I." I'd sometimes seen sightless children waiting on the school's front steps, and one winter afternoon I'd heard floating out of open windows the sound of piano lessons, but I'd never seen a blind albino kid, not even from any province. All the same, as I snuck toward the school's playground, I was mindful of Bonnie's cautions and, panicked that I would be randomly chased by creatures with pink gogs of bloodied flesh where their eyes should be, I slunk under the black wrought-iron fence and into the green and sun of the playground. Once inside, I resumed my maneuvers. Some weeks before, I'd lost a Hot Wheels Batmobile in this playground, and since then I tended to line-search under the swings, kick at dirt-clumps in the sandbox, and scowl at the happy kids playing on the teeter-totter. The playground's perimeter I investigated in Boy Detective fashion, planning to work my way into the centre as I went, but this idea I abandoned in favour of the monkey bars, from the top of which I was soon hanging by my knees—my head low-drooping—and noting the traces of sun on the nearby Victoria General Hospital, the wrinkle pattern of the crumbling black asphalt at the edge of its parking lot, and a deep puddle directly below the monkey bars superb in its facility to reflect the upside-down sky. Turning the other way, I noticed a green seed pod, from a maple tree, tumbling in the wind, and I was staring at it some moments before I saw, out of focus in the background, the fair-haired kid I'd seen earlier. He was waving from a softly rotating merry-go-round. I'd not seen him come into the playground so it was as if he had teleported from coordinates elsewhere in the galaxy. He looked about five years old. His hair was corn-silk blond and he was costumed miscellaneously. He wore a silk pajama top, pale blue with navy trim on the collar and cuffs. Over this was an adult's black dress belt, so big it went round him three times, cinched very tight, causing the pajama top to flare out like a skirt below the waist. Completing the ensemble were grey jodhpurs and Oxford shoes, untied with no socks. All this he sported without a trace of self-consciousness, not for a moment considering that his clothes were anything but regulation. He was shy, forward, joyously alert, and within his blue eyes shimmered a quick originality. I'd never seen the kid before—and I knew a *lot* of people from nursery school, the bookmobile library, and even the Public Gardens—and asked where he was from.

He made no answer—he seemed to be holding his breath—and I was wondering if he were one of those semi-autistic kids who stare for hours at a green eraser when he finally exhaled to say, "I'm not even here!" His eyebrows, I noticed, were sun-bleached to whiteness. "I'm supposed to be somewhere else, but I'm not there either because—because I'm an escape artist!" He was English or at least spoke with an English accent. In later years, when I remembered this moment, I would think of him as one of those hyper-articulate British schoolchildren whose accent is so fluty, and whose syllables are so precisely enunciated, you want to thump them in the head with a rubber fish. I ran to the merry-go-round and grabbed the handrail closest to me. Giving it an almighty heave, I spun the boy as fast as I could. The contraption revolved twice and I timed my next push for maximum acceleration.

After a few unstable rotations, the boy jumped off, woozying a few steps and bringing his fingers to his eyes. "Oh my lumbago," he said, dropping to the grass. A small eyedropper bottle tumbled from his pajama pocket. The boy picked it up, wiped away some dirt, and showed it to me. "This is one of my newest inventions," he said. "A potion of many ingredients!" He gave me the bottle. I held it to the sun. Inside its blue glass was some sort of liquid, a small key—as if from a lady's jewelry box—as well as some shifting blobs of oil. "All I need to complete it," said the boy, taking back the bottle and looking at me wildly, "is a drop of human blood."

I asked why he needed the potion.

"I'm making it," he said, shaking the bottle, "in case a sea pirate comes home to find that I've been abducted by a goliath. This is the potion that can bring you back to life. This is the potion that can grant you one wish!" He looked at me, conspiratorial. "I've also invented a word—shropter."

I asked what it meant.

"I don't know yet." He searched for something in a front pocket of his jodhpurs. "My first invention was a treasure map of many escape routes." He brought out the sheet of coloured paper I'd seen him chase along the sidewalk. It was marked up with several scribbles and diagrams. I liked it straightaway and immediately wished it were mine. "Probably it will fall to me to escape. But it may do for my father as well. Do you have a father? I have a father. I've only met him twice. But I'm going to see him again, I should expect. That's why I've become interested in inventions. And you?"

I had four sisters, I told him, and made a shrugging reference to Bonnie's birthday party, adding that I didn't much want to go.

"Why? Is she a biter? I've known some biters. Is she younger?"

My sister was older, I said, and wasn't much of a biter. Then, on impulse, I opened my mouth to display my wobbly front tooth.

"Ooh," said the boy. "May I?" He touched at my tooth with his fingertip. "Yes, that will come out directly." He made a strange sort of smile, exposing his own front teeth. "I still have mine. See? But yours will grow back. They do grow back." He glanced down, as if searching for something lost in the grass, then looked at me to confide, "There's a skeleton inside you, you know. A complete and utter skeleton. Beneath your skin."

This news I received with some confusion for I connected skeletons with ghouls and graveyards and scary cartoons—and I couldn't be sure if this kid was telling the truth or if he was merely, and this impression had been building over the past few minutes, indulging in a form of slapdash free association. What kind of person would tell you there was a *skeleton* inside you?

Giving the merry-go-round a last shove, I said I was going back to my sister's birthday party but he could come if he wanted.

"A party?" He winced. "Maybe. But I don't like ice cubes. I don't like to taste them and I don't like the sound they make in my teeth. One second—" He put a hand on my elbow, conspiratorial again, and evaluated me. "You know, you could grow a moustache if you wanted. And no one would recognize you. Except French people. There's a seagull!"

I looked up—only to realize he was pointing at the shadow of a fleeting bird, a shape that was presently ribboning across the grass and puddles of the playground, gliding past the curb, and unfolding into South Street...And so this boy, this unexpected child, this curious young party, this was Cyrus Mair. There was something incomprehensible and quivery and completely recognizable about him. He reminded me of the imaginary kid, a character in my own private mythology, who ran along the side of the highway, keeping pace with my family's car on road trips—a fantastically swift boy who hurdled over cement culverts, slipped under fallen trees, never tripping, never tiring—and as I watched Cyrus Mair in the playground of the Halifax School for the Blind chasing a seagull's shadow, on the way to the rest of his life, passing his fingers along the posts of the wrought-iron fence, trying to touch every one, now going back to tap the post he missed, I thought him reckless and exuberant and smart. He was fabulously weird. I wanted to know what he knew. I couldn't really guess what he was dreaming up in his mind, nor what games and inventions occurred there, but I liked him. His world was in a constant state of becoming, and this September afternoon was the beginning of a fascination that would last a sort of lifetime for me because, even if I didn't know what I wanted, like everyone else I would not be able to stop paying attention to the creature known as Cyrus Mair.

"DO YOU LIKE JOKES? I like jokes. Did you hear about Napoleon?" Cyrus turned to me. "Josephine sucked his bone apart!" It was probably the single-worst joke I'd ever heard. His jokes made no sense at all. I didn't get them. I didn't get them the *third* time he told them. But each joke went over huge with Cyrus Mair, his giggles bursting into the air like birdsong. I did not share his high spirits at first. But, at a later juncture, around the time we were sneaking into my backyard and toward my family's basement door, the phrase "Coat-Cheese" arose in our conversation, an example of the usage for which might be "Coat-Cheese, Coat-Cheese, you're a fat Coat-Cheese," or "Coat-Cheese, Coat-Cheese sitting in a pie," or even "Coat-Cheese, Coat-Cheese stuck inside a toilet seat, Coat-Cheese, Coat-Cheese pooping in your eye," all of which formulations seemed astonishingly relevant to our developing understanding of the afternoon, and by the time we were tiptoeing up the basement stairs, Cyrus bent over with laughter, slapping his thigh to keep himself from falling, we were sweaty and gleeful and manic with intrigue. The birthday party was in full fling—a dozen teenybopper girls hopped up on peppermint cupcakes and cream soda. Cyrus was happily assimilating all the details of the party— the girls in their swishy party dresses, helium balloons bouncing against the ceiling, the table of wrapped gifts—assimilating these details but perhaps not processing them. "There's a lot going on in this house," said Cyrus. "I think we need a drink." He moved somewhat instinctively to the living room and my parents' liquor cabinet where he fetched out a bottle of Rose's Lime Juice Cordial. "Ah." He twisted off the cap. "The good stuff." He brought the bottle to his lips and glugged off several swallows. "That's the spot," he said, tightly shutting his eyes. "I think I'm drunk already."

I asked what he was going to do when he had the last ingredient for the potion, the drop of human blood.

"Good question," he said, passing me the bottle of lime cordial. "My plan is—Wait. Before we go any further, I need to know something." He took a step back and put his hands on my shoulders, much in the manner of a captain steadying the nerves of a young recruit. "Are you a Crab or an Anti-Crab?"

I asked what he meant.

"Well," said Cyrus, puzzled. "It's quite simple, really. I'm an officer in the Anti-Crab Army. Like my father. And the world is either Crab or Anti-Crab. Which are you?" He peered into my eyes. "I think you're Anti-Crab."

Swigging from the bottle of lime cordial, I made a few nods to show I was inclined to agree.

"Good. That's all you have to tell them. That and your serial number. Remember that when you're being tortured."

"When I'm being *tortured*?"

"Exactly!" said Cyrus, racing back into the party, his pajama top coming loose from his belt and billowing like a sail.

THE CAKE WAS BEING SERVED—a special in-house recipe my sister Carolyn made for each of us on our birthdays—a vanilla sponge cake embedded with store-bought candies and coated with milk chocolate icing. Carolyn was handing out plates of this delicacy to the last guests when, seeing Cyrus and me, she sliced off two more pieces. "Ah," said Cyrus. "Chocolate Thermidor." He spun toward me. "But maybe you shouldn't."

"Why not?"

"You know—" He tapped at his own front tooth. "The wiggler."

I said I'd use the other side of my mouth to chew and this seemed to reassure him. Focusing his attention on his own piece of cake, he took a large bite and chomped the cake experimentally—before spitting a mouthful to the linoleum floor. "Just as I suspected!" He made an odd smile. "Raisins." He kicked at the offending gob with one of his Oxford shoes—which was loose on his foot now, the laces free from the top eyelets. Carolyn assured him there were no raisins in the cake, and Cyrus, seeing his blunder, for he had mistaken a red jujube for a raisin, bent to the floor to pick it up. He was popping this in his mouth, to the fascinated horror of at least three of the girls present, when my sister Bonnie returned from a bathroom break. "Who the hell is that kid?" She pointed at Cyrus. "And who invited him to my party?"

I was explaining I'd invited him, that he was my guest, when, rather as if he'd been waiting for the appropriate moment, Cyrus stepped to the centre of the room to say, "I'm the world's best escape artist!"

Bonnie looked at him, skeptical. "Um," she said. "No, you're not."

"Oh, yes I am," said Cyrus, swallowing the red jujube. "I can escape from any ropes or shackles you devise for me. And—" He flung his hand above his head to point at the ceiling. "I throw down the gimlet!" He was beaming at the girls, daring to be contradicted. "You could tie me up and I shall escape anything!"

A small girl in a turtleneck dress, her name was Alice Gruber, produced a pink skipping rope and Bonnie took it and thrust it at Cyrus. "Prove it."

Taking the skipping rope, he wrapped it around his left wrist three times. "I wrap it like this and you"—he offered his hands to Alice Gruber, who seemed shyly delighted to be participating—"you tie it nice and tight on my other hand."

Alice Gruber tied a simple bow knot firmly around his right wrist. He offered his tied wrists for inspection. "See? So I shall go behind these drapes." He walked to the windows, where my mother, because of our too-close proximity to the next-door house, had installed floor-to-ceiling curtains. "And

I shall escape and disappear by a count of ten. Ready? On your marks—Go!"

Cyrus's small outline, and especially the heels of his shoes, showed in contours and creases in the fabric of the curtain. The girls looked at one another, uncertain, so Carolyn started loudly counting, the rest of us joining in and finishing—noting, of course, that Cyrus's shoes were exactly where they had been when we started.

Bonnie pulled the curtains open, revealing the skipping rope fallen into Cyrus's empty shoes. For two or three seconds we were fully amazed, as if the laws of the universe had shifted without us understanding why, until Bonnie jerked the curtains all the way open, revealing Cyrus giggling, barefoot, and triumphant at the end of the window. "Yes!" His face flushed pink as he took back his shoes from Alice Gruber—who had picked them up in her new capacity as magician's assistant. "My second greatest escape today! I told you. I can escape from wire cages or torture chambers or anything at all." The birthday guests were certainly amused and so was I but not so the birthday girl. My sister with narrowing eyes was rethinking the wrapping and tying of the skipping rope, correctly deducing that Cyrus had made sure the skipping rope crossed on the underside of his left wrist, allowing for a quick release when he twisted his hands *away* from the criss-crossed rope. Once free of the rope, he slipped out of his shoes and slunk along the window to hide flattened within the curtains.

Keen to continue the challenge, Bonnie brought a chair from the dining room. She asked if Cyrus could escape if he were tied to the chair and blindfolded and locked in the hall closet. Cyrus studied the door to the hall closet. It was an antique-looking door with a skeleton key resting in its lock. "It would be my third great escape today," he said, considering.

After procuring a fold of newspaper, which he positioned on the floor beneath the lock, and making us promise we wouldn't tinker with its placement, he raised his hand to point again at the ceiling. "I accept the gimlet!" Bonnie then went to work, securing him to the chair, tying his hands behind his back with the pink skipping rope, binding his ankles to the chair legs with kitchen twine, and using the sash from her sparkle dress as a blindfold. All through this procedure, Cyrus held his breath, quietly smiling, and flexing his shoulders to make himself bigger. With Carolyn's help, Bonnie bumped Cyrus and the chair over to the hall closet, dumped him in, and turned the key in the lock—just as my parents came through the front door. They were confused to see the birthday party gathered around the hall closet, and more than this, I could tell from their posture and solemnity that Something Complicated had happened in the outside world. It was only now I realized how irregular it was that neither of my parents had been home to direct the events of Bonnie's birthday party—it was a tribute to Carolyn's abilities the party's proceedings had gone so smoothly. So we dispersed, innocently returning to balloons and loot bags in the kitchen, and leaving five-year-old Cyrus Mair chair-tied and blindfolded on the hardwood floor of the hall closet.

A NOTE OF CIVIC HISTORY—Howland Poole Mair, K.C., known popularly in the province as H.P. Mair, served as the fourteenth premier of Nova Scotia many years before Cyrus and I were born. Most of the Mairs were given to highly variable and eccentric vanishing acts, but the disappearance of H.P. Mair was bold even for them. On the day he vanished, H.P. Mair was senior counsel to one of the city's oldest law firms, Merton Mair McNab, and the circumstances surrounding his disappearance, and the convergence of inward meaning and outward implication these circumstances provoked, would generate speculation for years to come. I saw him only twice, the first time when I was four and he was eighty-three, outside St. Matthew's United Church one winter morning when my father made a point of introducing to his children an approaching older man, elegantly dressed, sharply stern. Tall and bald, to me H.P. Mair most resembled a stretched-out version of the Banker in the board game Monopoly. I remember singing for him the first verse of my newly composed "Extravagant Yogurt" song, a routine to which he gave a quick and single roar of laughter, and I remember my father treating him with uncharacteristic deference—a consequence, I would later learn, of my father having articled with H.P. Mair when he first graduated law school. My father would accept a position with a different firm, but his debt and connection to H.P. Mair he always respected. Not so my mother. "The Old Grey Mair," she said. "He ain't what he used to be. *Such* a peculiar fellow. We'd be at some party. He'd walk in, speak to no one, watching from the corner. You try to talk to him, he'd just shake his head and walk away. If you ask me, he needed help. But your father loved H.P. Mair. Thought he was brilliant. Sure, if brilliant means drunk. If brilliant means stumbling home drunk from The Halifax Club, then he was a genius. H.P. used to show up soused at our front door. I'd give him the vacuum cleaner and tell him to start in the living room. The man was just sozzled. Juiced to the gills. Alcohol ruins so many families, Aubrey. And at the end he didn't know where he was. At the end he sort of knew he was yesterday's man. The last year of his life, he was calling your father at all hours. In the morning, the middle of the night. The man was over-billing, double-billing, he needed money something terrible. Had a wife with expensive tastes, for one, plus this young girlfriend, and drinking all the time. That once-brilliant mind, all that booze. The month he disappeared, he came to see if your father would represent him because he was about to be disbarred and God knows what else."

My father was president of the Nova Scotia Barristers' Society at the time, a member of the same disciplinary committee that was investigating H.P. Mair, and so was obliged to recuse himself from acting for him. H.P. Mair went missing three weeks later. He had lunch at The Halifax Club near noon and was later seen purchasing a bottle of Veuve Clicquot at the Clyde Street liquor store, the cashier giving a statement to the police that, the last she saw him, H.P. Mair was walking down South Park Street. Officers found his house with its doors open, his purple Mercedes-Benz in the driveway. His disappearance would become the talk of the province. There were theories he'd been murdered, that he'd run off to Bermuda to avoid prosecution, that he'd committed suicide in Maine. For a while he was the missingest man in Canada and seemed destined to become one of those figures, like Judge Crater or Captain Slocum, who simply evaporates from the twentieth century. But twenty-one days later, on the morning of Bonnie's ninth birthday, a body was glimpsed in the ocean off Black Rock Beach by two Waegwoltic kids in a Sunfish sailboat. The authorities recovered the drowned man, finding on the fully clothed corpse no identification except, in a sodden suit-pocket, my father's business card. My father was asked in for questioning later that day. After identifying the body as the remains of H.P. Mair, my parents went along to relay the news to the widow—a peripheral family friend. Vida Mair, who had been estranged from her husband for some years, lived alone and alcoholically on the seventh floor of the Hotel Nova Scotian. Not only was she vexed to learn of her husband's death, but she was out of her mind with worry that one of her extended family, her husband's son with another woman—a five-year-old who had been placed provisionally in her sister-in-law's care—had gone missing the night before. Phone calls were made, a search party rallied, and another Missing Persons file opened.

It was with somber and serious worry for this errant child that my parents walked in the front door of our house on Tower Road somewhat surprised to find the very object of their concern tied to a dining room chair, sideways on the floor of the hall closet, blindfolded, and thrashing like an animal in a trap. "What in God's name is that noise?" asked my mother. Speeding to ground zero, I spun the key in the door, yanked it open, and bent down beside Cyrus Mair. I pushed away the blindfold. Although he was on the verge of liberation, his expression did not change. His eyebrows were tense with concentration and, now that I was this close to him, I could see three of his eyelashes had gone white—or started white—and I noticed, too, a spiral of absolutely white, de-pigmented hair swirling out of the crown of his head. He was silent, sullen even, as if he suspected he had misjudged the situation—or the situation had misjudged him. "If you help me escape," he whispered, struggling against the pink skipping rope. "If you help me out of this booby trap, I'll help you escape from anywhere. And I will remember. Will you?"

"Remember what?"

"Everything!"

I said I would help him if he showed me all of his escape routes. "You promise?"

"I promise," said Cyrus Mair, his blue eyes very wide. "I do."

HALF AN HOUR LATER and the party was in the breakfast nook among some softening-but-still-airborne balloons, second helpings of cake, and Bonnie's haul of birthday gifts.

Cyrus had very easily integrated himself into the gathering and babbled intimately with everyone—as if he'd known each of us all his life. Bonnie, feeling contrite over his imprisonment, and sensing my parents' distant but frank interest in this child's welfare, tolerated his presence. The other girls accepted and approved of him, especially Alice Gruber, who, in a tizzy of overexcitement, had begun applying chocolate icing to the tip of his nose. "That's dis*gust*ing!" said Cyrus, wiping his nose and straining to make the word as emphatic as possible. He turned to Bonnie, who was opening and reading a birthday card. "I think you should always keep a present you don't open," Cyrus said, moving his piece of cake away from the groping fingers of Alice Gruber. "That way you can always go back to open something you don't have." Alice Gruber let out a squeal of laughter at this remark, then right away covered her mouth with both hands, shutting down any further noises. Bonnie opened the beautifully wrapped present anyway, displaying to the table a page-a-day pocket diary. I thought it very splendid with its gilded pages and royal blue binding, as well I should, for I remembered it was my gift to Bonnie. My mother and I had charged it at Mahon's Stationery the week before, my mother deciding that the gift of a diary would encourage Bonnie to read more. Bonnie remarked casually that she already had three diaries, that I could keep this new one, and flipped the gift back to me. She went on to the next present and so did everyone else. Everyone except Cyrus Mair, who stared at the diary as if spellbound, as if he'd never imagined such an invention could exist.

Finishing my own piece of cake, I became aware of my parents talking in the kitchen. I was not really sure of the topic of conversation, but sifting into my vicinity was the sense that Something Complicated was ongoing, and overheard in my mother's side of the conversation were phrases such as "heart flutter" and "shock of the water" and "the whole thing is unthinkable." This last phrase was delivered as she stared out the window at a favourite tree, a Japanese maple, which was always first to turn in autumn and the phrase acted on Cyrus's imagination with great force and meaning. The boy, even as kids go, was tremendously suggestible and in another moment he'd wandered out of the breakfast nook. "The whole thing is unthinkable," repeated Cyrus, touching at his pajama pocket and his potion of many ingredients. "But if you can't think it, how can you say it? How do you even *know* it?" My mother came over to warmly smile at Cyrus, saying she was glad he'd had some birthday cake, he was welcome to another piece, perhaps some ice cream, and he shouldn't worry because arrangements had been made to get him safely home. She sent a look to me to show she was happy with my own conduct and then joined my father, who in quiet tones was speaking into the black rotary telephone in the dining room.

"There really *is* a lot going on in your house," said Cyrus, following my mother into the hallway. There seemed to be too many ideas fizzing at the brim of the moment, mostly beyond a kid's immediate ability to sort or commit to understanding, and Cyrus, standing in front of the telephone desk beside a wicker chair, was choosing simply to register the desk's sundry details—a white wooden golf tee, the Halifax-Dartmouth Yellow Pages, a stapler, a hardcover copy of *Tom Swift and The Visitor from Planet X,* as well as a box of envelopes for the Sunday offering provided by St. Matthew's United Church. He studied the cover of the Tom Swift book and said, to no one in particular, "Every book is the same book. That's why you read them. Unless it's a mystery book. And then it's eponymous." Holding the eyedropper bottle as if it were a wand, Cyrus passed it over the desk's effects.

"This could be a church," he said. "And all these bits its candles. But you have to be careful because people will turn you into a bob." He looked at me with real purpose. "People will turn you into a *fact*."

The front doorbell rang. After a furtive look into the hallway, Cyrus turned to me. "I'm getting curious again. I can feel it. And when I get curious, I'm supposed to breathe and count to twelve. But I can't because I'm feeling—shroptered." The word seemed to make perfect sense to him now and I nodded to show I understood. The doorbell rang again and I stepped into the hallway to see what kind of oddity would be ringing and ringing the front doorbell. There on the porch, framed through the doorway, was a giant of a man. He wore a heavy black raincoat and a brimmed, flat-topped hat. He was, I would learn later, a driver from Regal Taxi. But in form and demeanour he reminded me ominously of Bill Sikes from the movie *Oliver!* seen by me a few weeks before. So frightened was I of Bill Sikes, and so scared to see this fellow staring into our house, that a cold shiver spread across my shoulders. While I was perturbed to see this man, Cyrus was absolutely horrified. Whether he recognized him as an actual enemy or simply guessed at possibilities darkly perfidious, I wasn't sure, but Cyrus's nervousness quickened toward an almost epileptic intensity. As he backed against the wall, scanning the rooms for alternate exits, I felt something peculiar happening to the ground floor of the house. Cyrus's jumpiness was making me triply aware of my surroundings and their causes and effects. Items within his awareness began to resonate with newfound, probable energies, and so the stapler on the telephone desk seemed to vibrate, the wicker chair seemed to teeter and slide to one side, and my very thoughts seemed to variously spin, as if the merry-go-round of my mind had been pushed in new directions. "Just after my best greatest escape," said

Cyrus, his eyes leaky with anxiety. "*That's* when he starts staring all over me?" He tucked his pajama top into his jodhpurs and readied himself for a getaway. But I could tell he was worried. He had that skeleton-inside-you look again. "But if it's unthinkable," he whispered, "then I'm not even here. So how could anyone find me?" His questions were frightening for me to consider and as I thought over the scenes of the afternoon I felt I couldn't be sure I hadn't dreamt all the days before this, the small world where I had my own life and times, my Batmobile and Boy Detective games. The moment was oddly emotional for me, and for some reason, I picked up and pressed into his hands the gift of the page-a-day pocket diary, explaining my sister Bonnie had three other diaries, she preferred pink diaries anyway, and he should take this diary for his own inventions.

Cyrus turned to me, touched to be given such a souvenir. There was a glisten of perspiration on his forehead and he blotted this moisture with his pajama sleeve. "But I don't have anything in return because—wait a minute." He gazed at me with open eyes. "Say! I don't know your name."

I told him.

"Aubrey McKee," he repeated. "I don't have anything. Except perhaps—" From his pajama pocket he took out his potion of many ingredients. "Except this. There's enough for one sip. Would you like to make a trade?"

THE PROGRESSION OF EVENT that follows I still have trouble sequencing. I remember opening the eyedropper bottle, squeezing the bulb pipette, and stealing a swallow of the potion—tasting the ferrous bitterness of the key—just as the late-afternoon light streaked through the stained glass of our front door, creating a gleam of rainbow on the hardwood floor, and the Regal Taxi driver stepping inside our house, my mother turning to greet him with perfect charm when Alice Gruber, kicking at a deflated red balloon, ran to my mother to ask if Cyrus Mair had to escape again could she at least keep his shoes? Whether it was my mother's murmur or Cyrus's shriek that came next, I'm not sure, but I recall Cyrus sprinting barefoot into the front hallway, clutching the blue diary, aiming for the still-opened front door but in his panic running smack into the newel post of the staircase. Then I was in the hallway myself, watching him bounce backwards through the air and rear-end my sister Carolyn and Cyrus sprawling on the floor, his right leg twitching, only to spring up straightaway and dash under the sweeping arms of the taxi driver toward the puddles of the sidewalk. I was appalled. Shouldn't this kid have *told* me when he was going, how he was going, where he was going? It seemed to me then that everyone was deliberately betraying their promises to me and with a sense of berserk purpose I put my head down and made for the front door, planning to catch up to Cyrus Mair. The door was swinging shut, and I saw I would soon crash into its stained glass window, but I chose to persevere, my upper lip hitting first, my nose squishing, the door-glass shattering, my loose front tooth detonating out of my mouth, and as my tongue touched at the gap in my gums where once my tooth had been—a trickle of warm blood mixing with the residue of the potion's bitterness—I saw through the smithereening glass Cyrus Mair escaping down the sidewalk, pajama top blousing out of his jodhpurs, and I closed my eyes, swallowing a drop of the completed potion, but knowing finally what I wanted, for I wanted to *be* Cyrus Mair.

Action Transfers

THE SUMMER MY PARENTS DIVORCED the first time, the summer I turned seven, I was no longer able to walk. Something happened to my super-speed. The flash of quickness I once relied on to propel me past any other living kid left me and I began to limp from an ache localized at the top of my left leg. This progressed into a sharp and steep pain, preventing me from walking, from hobbling, until finally I simply hopped everywhere on my right foot. My older sister said it was because I had an undigested carrot lodged in my hipbone and explained I should have listened to her about properly chewing my food, but another diagnosis pointed to a form of idiopathic avascular osteonecrosis and a bone disorder called Legg-Calvé-Perthes. So I was hospitalized for the months of that summer and spent my days and nights in orthopedic traction—that is, with pulley weights dragging my legs away from my pelvis.

Even though I had brought with me a pencil case of precious effects, and even though my parents had spoiled me with a number of new Letraset Super Action Transfers—acetate heroes that could be rubbed on to cardboard panoramas—my stay in hospital was a strange time for me. I was so surprised by my new situation that I mostly pretended it wasn't happening, that I wasn't in a hospital, that things were the same, and that I would soon be returned to my family's life, delivered from whatever mythical creatures this place contained. But morning after morning, I awoke in the Izaak Walton Killam Hospital for Children, unable to walk away from my hospital bed, unable to use my legs, unsure what would happen.

I REMEMBER THE SMELLS of the place, the green reek of the industrial cleanser used on the tile floor, the blended odours of a lunch cart's undelivered meals—cubes of processed ham congealing into cheese macaroni, softening tapioca pudding, snack-size cartons of souring skim milk. By the end of the fifth day, I developed chafed elbows and bed-sores, my skin a mess of raw crosshatchings, and I was forced finally to pass a bowel movement into a metal bed pan. I buzzed for a nurse to come empty this pan but nurses were often busy and no one came right away. So the smell of my feces, my just-lying-there-on-the-stainless-steel poop, spread through the air, slightly sickening me and very much embarrassing me, for I was not alone in the room. I was in a double room and over the eight weeks of my stay behind the curtained partition was a succession of other kids—tonsillitis kids, appendix kids, car accident kids. A new patient might come in the middle of the night, host a crowd of visitors that morning, have surgery that afternoon, and be gone the next day.

Small talk with other families depleted me—fake smiles, hopeful waves, promises to stay in touch. I was happiest when I was alone and the other bed was empty, a stack of laundered sheets tidy on its bare mattress. All day I would occupy myself with my pencil case of precious effects—a much-loved Batman figure sprung from a toy Batboat, a green terrycloth wrist band, a newly received Yellow Submarine. For hours I played with this Yellow Submarine, tremendously impressed with the cast-metal permanence of such an artifact, its revolving periscope, and the hatches that opened to reveal pairs of psychedelic Beatles. At the end of the day I watched the black-and-white television mounted on the ceiling, each evening wondering at *Truth or Consequences* and the lives of people who lived outside hospitals. I awoke sometimes to screams at night—kids wailing, adults sobbing—and sadder adults you will never see than those pacing a children's hospital at three in the morning. The hallway outside my room was mostly quiet with moments of sudden, shrieking calamity.

MORE TERRIFYING FOR ME was the attempt at recreation and diversion on weekday mornings. Day after day I would be wheeled toward the elevators in my hospital bed, the hallway's perspective telescoping wildly like the dolly-zoom in a spooky movie, where I would share the rising car with a Perpetually Smiling Porter. Arriving at the top of the building, I would be steered down the hallway toward the fifth-floor play area. From inside my bed, I watched the walls go by, queasy at the sight of the cheerful posters that featured, say, a photograph of two kittens dangling from tree branches beside the jokey caption "Hang In There!" or a school of cartoon minnows happy to be reading from the same storybook. For the fifth floor was full of extremely ill and not-healthy-at-all children: cancer kids, burn victim kids, paralyzed kids in wheelchairs. But my attention that first morning was drawn to a purple-faced boy in a hospital bed.

I say purple-faced boy because that's all he seemed to be—I had no idea the world held such problematics. He was a Thalidomide child who, God knows how, had survived into puberty and adolescence, and the purpleness of his complexion, which under the fluorescent ceiling lights looked positively saurian, was the combined result of teenage acne and steroid medication. The purple-faced boy was one of fifty Thalidomide cases born in the city and he was, like the jokes I would later hear in the school playground, a Guy with No Arms and No Legs. He was mostly just a head and I felt so humiliated and sorry for this purple-faced boy, who was living an existence he hadn't chosen but which he must have known was about as wretched as a human life could be—and I am ashamed even now as I write this—that on that first morning I couldn't look him in the eye and was too afraid to talk to him. Because he could speak, of a fashion, making glottal noises in his throat to indicate a direction or that he wished returned to his bed a fallen book. I was embarrassed by this purple-faced boy—wondering how on earth he had happened and could what happened to him happen to me?—and I was sickened to feel such embarrassment and this first moment has stayed with me and stayed with me and stayed with me, because of all the kids in the fifth-floor play area, the cancer kid, the burn victim kid, the paralyzed kid in the wheelchair, or me, a kid in traction, we all knew we were better off than this purple-faced boy, who was a horrendous fuck-up of a human. With his misshapen head and squiggly appendages—one arm stumpy, the other a fin with a crab claw—he seemed a sort of whelp and not a sure bet to be anything but dead. I had never met a kid so marked for death. I could sense he knew this, his eyes were grey and grim and guarded, he probably knew he was not going to get out of that children's hospital and that his possibilities for life were diminished and diminishing.

We happened to be the only kids in hospital beds that morning and the Perpetually Smiling Porter put our beds together, so that we were side by side, our bed rails bumping. A nurse assigned to the fifth floor, this was a formidable woman from Herring Cove named Patty Oickle, suggested I share my Super Action Transfers with the purple-faced boy. But in my panic I feigned discomfort, as if I were in pain from my traction weights, and stared instead at the bald cancer kid who was loose on the floor, playing with a golden Hot Wheels car I recognized as Splittin' Image.

From the nearby nurse's station, an eight-track played a release from that year, *Bridge Over Troubled Water*. Though I had loved the first side a few months before, especially the jubilant "Cecilia," the tape's second song became for me a small eternity of suffering. This was "El Cóndor Pasa," an odd, despairing folk tune, full of faraway sorrow. The singer's existential musings—he'd rather be a sparrow... than a nail... or a hammer... if he could? Who would want to be either? I didn't *understand* the guy—preyed on my sense of insecurity and looming dread so that when recreation time was over and I was finally free of the fifth-floor play area, I was fantastically grateful to be delivered back to my room, regardless of its screams and smells and possible roommates, content in my diversion of Letrasets and comic books and my pencil case of precious effects. I'd rather stay in my room for the entire two months by myself if I could—if I only could, I surely would.

But each weekday morning on the polished floor I would hear the shoe-steps of the Perpetually Smiling Porter and I'd be wheeled again to the fifth-floor play area. The first day of my second week, my middle sisters brought me a care package (Twizzlers, Maltesers, a Green Lantern–Green Arrow comic), and, not finding me in my room, went searching. They came exploring down the fifth floor hallway, my sister Faith softly humming "See See My Playmate," and then—and I remember this moment so exactly—they were completely bewildered by the sight of the purple-faced boy. Both reacted by staring at him, hardly blinking, gazing in a sort of simple fascination, not because of any prejudice but because of a lack of all reference for what they were seeing, which in turn provoked wild curiosity and disbelief. They were having trouble identifying the purple-faced boy as a person, as something less than monstrous, as a creature recognizably human. I felt in that moment that completely ignoring him was not the sort of example I should be setting for my sister Faith, who was four years old and quite an impressionable young girl, and so I turned to the purple-faced boy and said hello and told him my name. He did not have a lot of motor control over his neck and his pupils tended to quickly shift and re-adjust, often straining to the limits of the eye-socket. But he made a sort of smile, his eyes sympathetic to me, and through the bars of his hospital bed I touched at his crab claw.

After Bonnie and Faith left—for the fifth-floor play area was off-limits to civilians—I showed the purple-faced boy the Letraset I was working on, which was a space adventure called The Red Planet. Letraset was about finding the right place in the landscape for the action figure as well as cleanly transferring it to the panorama. Sometimes in my haste the figure, especially if he were in a pose I considered humdrum, would only partially come off the acetate, forcing me to line it up again and to try to match, say, a sentry's hand with a disembodied ray-gun. The purple-faced boy examined my handiwork, noting the split-level choreography I'd achieved around a cliff face, and glanced at the sheets of acetates. I passed him the last sheet and the teaspoon I'd been using as a transferring implement. He accepted the acetate but made me aware that he didn't need the spoon, producing from the bed-sheets a pencil, sharpened at both ends. He held this double-pencil in his crab claw and penciled the acetate figure into the landscape with surprising authority and concentration. His handiwork was superb and glitch-free, his effort very genuine, and, as I nodded to him, the mutual enterprise involving us, bonding us, I understood I had a colleague in the fifth-floor play area.

THE PURPLE-FACED BOY was steady and studious and resolute—he took nothing for granted, ever watchful, noting everything for himself—and he had a superpower. He had an ability to read fast, very fast, there's-no-way-he-read-it-that-fast fast. His hospital-bed was home to an improvised library and book after book vanished into his eyes and the systems of his brain. I saw him put away *Tintin au Congo*, André Norton's *Witch World*, and *The Fellowship of the Ring* in the space of a day. He would use his double-pencil to guide his eyes along a line of text and, when reading a newspaper, he arranged his bed-sheets on either side of a column so his gaze wouldn't bounce around. Because he didn't really speak, I guessed his reading was swift and free of any subvocalization, fields of text moving wholesale into his nervous system. One quiet Wednesday in the fifth-floor play area, Nurse Patty Oickle rolled over to our purlieu one of the hospital's book trolleys. This was a collection of sorry-looking children's books within which had been stashed some adult hardcovers like *King Rat*, *Valley of the Dolls*, and *Papillon*. The purple-faced boy was fascinated by *Papillon*. I saw him read it three times, and, though I could be baffled by the tedious sameness of the pages of an adult book, I scanned through it myself, understanding it was a true-life adventure about criminals escaping some place called Devil's Island. But I was busy finishing

General Custer, my next-to-last Super Action Transfer. The remaining Letraset was some jungle-themed piece I didn't care for called Animals of the World, all elephants and peacocks, and I offered it to the purple-faced boy. His eyes spun to their furthest extreme, bloodshot with strain, indicating I should return to him the hardcover *Papillon*. He pressed down and held the book still with his stumpy left arm. In the top right corner of the book's first endpaper, he placed the image of a bull elephant and rubbed it perfectly into the book. He turned the page and positioned a second elephant on the next recto page, again in the top corner, so the images would align. He turned the page and began another, in this manner filling up the book's first quire, one end of his double-pencil whittled down to a nubbin. I said nothing, watching the acetate animals emerge glistening on each page corner. Then, in a moment that revealed to me an intricate genius, he fluffled these first pages, making the animals move in a flicker of animation. He'd made a flip-book.

"We can do this," I said to him, excited, raising myself off my bed. "We can do the whole book. I'll help you. Wanna do it?" The purple-faced boy looked at me, his own eyes shining a moment, their grimness replaced by curiosity. I asked him again and slowly, because the movement was onerous, he nodded his heavy head—yes, yes he would do it.

I'M NOT SURE WHY, exactly, it became crucially important for two bedridden boys to transfer an acetate figure to every other page of a book called *Papillon*. The venture was ours, it was attainable, it was perfectible, and I liked that we were giving new and vivid meaning to a contraption already in the world. I suppose the project was our *plan*, our jubilation, our method of escape, and there was for me something so inexplicably right about it. My days in the hospital, which had once seemed never-ending, an infinity of bedsores and decomposing lunches, became fraught and finite. To inscribe every other page of the book would require 228 figures—elephants, eagles, lions, gladiators, wild-west cowboys, I didn't care as long as they were transferred in the mint-perfect style he'd established.

In mid-August, there was a visitation from my mother, distracted in a floppy hat and peasant skirt. I put in my request for more Letraset then asked her about the purple-faced boy. How long had he been in the hospital? How long would he stay in the hospital? "He can stay till he's eighteen," said my mother. "And then he'll have to go to another hospital." Then where—where would he go then? But my mother, who was suffering from the lingering effects of a yearlong postpartum depression, who had spent a few weeks that summer in another hospital herself, who would shortly leave my father for some months, was not able or interested in pursuing an unknown child's possibilities. She shrugged to show there were contingencies in the world she neither controlled nor understood. I didn't push the subject, opting to simply re-emphasize my requisition order for Letraset. And to my deepest pleasure, my oldest sister brought me more Letrasets—copies of Zulu, Carnival, and Prehistoric Monsters Battle—leaving them at the nurses' station the next morning.

IN A CHILDREN'S HOSPITAL, there is a lull the week after Labour Day, when canoe lessons are done, when sport camps have finished, when highways have emptied of summer vacationers. So the other bed in my room was unfilled, the hallway outside my room quiet. I was not sure where the purple-faced boy went at night, and, because in a few days' time I was to be released from traction, fitted with plaster casts, and discharged from hospital—and we still had fourteen pages of *Papillon* to finalize—I asked Nurse Oickle, who had taken an interest in my partnership with the purple-faced boy, if he might be moved to my room. But the purple-faced boy never left the fifth floor, she told me, and needed to be kept under observation at night, and a shift to the second floor was out of the question. So I asked if my stay in hospital might be extended. But this, too, was impossible because the appointment for my casts with the orthopedic surgeon was booked for Friday morning. In this moment, the face of Patty Oickle from Herring Cove was faintly plump, solicitous, but baffled that I wanted to stay longer in hospital when there were, as she put it, "only three more jeezly days of summer left." So I asked, if the purple-faced boy couldn't be moved to my room, could I be moved to his? She wasn't sure but promised she'd ask.

The next morning the purple-faced boy was not present in the fifth-floor play area. He was somewhere having tests—he was in line for an operation to repair a congenital heart defect—and there was some concern whether his system could stand such a procedure. On my own, I worked on *Papillon*, but nervously, and only completed one image, a Triceratops whose horn-prong I almost mangled, very nearly twisting it in the final transfer. I had one last day in hospital and thirteen more pages to complete so I asked again if I could visit the purple-faced boy, wherever he was, and finally Nurse Oickle relented. I never learned if she got higher approval or simply snuck me in on her own. The Perpetually Smiling Porter wheeled me after hours to the elevators and we ascended to the fifth floor, moving beyond the play area and through a room of odd incubators where, inside, were cocooned, pinkish, wrinkled creatures—newborn infants—I saw, some smaller than newborns, and some with open chests, for this was the neonatal ward. I was mystified that hidden on the fifth floor was an entire subset of other patients, preemies kept alive in ICU isolation. And, in the doorway to his room, in his hospital bed, was the purple-faced boy.

He surveyed the scene, reviewing his fellow-patients with steady interest. His colour was not good—his cheeks seemed desiccated, the consistency of tissue paper, the result, perhaps, of some augmented medication—and his thoughts, as ever, seemed far away. How many kids had he seen come and go? What *did* he know? From six o'clock we worked till ten, working until my eyes were dry, my fingers cramped and trembling. "Wanna leave the rest till tomorrow?" I asked, shaking out my hand. "The last two pages?" At that moment an exhausted-looking anesthetist arrived, confused to see me with the purple-faced boy. She told me I would have to return to the second floor, that a night nurse would arrive shortly to take me back to my room. I absorbed the sights around me, the pills and ointments at his bedside, the varied prescriptions on his rolling lunch table, the books piled in the windowsill. And all the books he read—where did they dwell? Where did they go in his imagination—where did their meanings reside? I stared at the purple-faced boy, this boy whose name I would never know, contemplating his care and diligence, the shift and flicker of his eyes. He was oblivious to the distractions of the other room—the beep-beep of the electrocardiograms, the chorus of haphazard breathing—and working on the Letraset with a single-pointedness of concentration I was only now beginning to fully appreciate. I was conscious of my staring at him, as he must've been conscious of my staring at him, as he must've grown used to all sorts of people staring at him, but the example of his intent was deeply meaningful to me and, as I was wheeled out of the room, I reached in kinship to my colleague, touching at the crab claw that held the double-pencil.

AT THE END OF THE SUMMER, I was freed from traction, encased in hip-to-toe Petrie casts, and given a wheelchair. After two months in hospital, I was free to scissor off my hospital identification bracelet and return to my family's life. My parents were busy divorcing that month, no one in my family was able to meet me, and I was told a taxi would be coming. I had no trousers that could fit over my plaster casts and so there I was, in pullover and Y-front underwear, waiting in a wheelchair at the front doors of the children's hospital. I was so bewildered to be outdoors amid seagulls and flying beetles and smells of cut-lawns and thoughts of going home that I hadn't really registered the unorthodoxy of my appearance. It was only when the taxi arrived, and the driver—who lifted me from my wheelchair and stowed me in the back seat—kept repeating that it was nothing to be embarrassed about, being in your underwear, no, it was exactly like being in a bathing suit, exactly like it, sure, just like being in a bathing suit, that I felt ashamed. For I sensed his humiliation for me, a blinking kid in underpants, unable to walk, waiting alone at the hospital, clutching a pencil case of curiosities. The driver was packing the collapsed wheelchair into the trunk when someone knocked on the back window. On this morning, the face of Patty Oickle was drawn, anguished. She opened the car door and gave me the copy of *Papillon,* saying I should keep it. I was never told of the purple-faced boy's death, exactly, but I guessed it, I felt it, and from her face I knew it.

Years afterward, my older sister would talk of him, recalling in contemplative moments the person she'd seen for a few minutes one Monday morning. "He was probably better off not being alive," she said. "A boy like that—he's better off." Life seemed random to me that summer, death more so, I was only a kid, seven years old, but my sense of fairness was disturbed. Something seemed off in the universe. But I had been given the gift of a book. Coming home that afternoon, lifted back into my house, I opened the final pages of *Papillon*. On the next-to-last page, in the top corner, was the blended image of two Super Action Transfers, a lion with the head-and-wings of an eagle—a gryphon. It was a work of keen talent and I was impressed by the rightness of the proportions, the invisible seam between creatures, the gleam of assurance in the eagle's eyes. The last page was blank and I would wonder for years why it was left this way, deciding at last that it was simply a sign of things to come.

The Pigeon Lady

WHEN SHE WAS A LITTLE KID, my youngest sister had a habit of running away. It wasn't the I-hate-you-guys-and-I'm-escaping-forever sort of running away. It was more the what's-inside-this-hollow-tree-probably-a-tunnel-to-an-enchanted-kingdom sort of running away. "Wandering off," my mother called it. "Katie, she can't help it. If you don't watch her, she ends up on somebody's rooftop, waving at clouds, talking to sparrows." The last of six children, Katie felt she was sometimes forgotten or ignored or presumed negligible, so she and Faith, the next-to-youngest, looked for their own kinds of connections in the world. They were a little more than a year apart, my mother dressed them in matching outfits, and they were pretty inseparable—stockpiling Barbies in a velvet Crown Royal bag, trading Paul Lynde impersonations, dueting on the piano—but where Faith was social, outgoing, literal, Katie was notional, dreamy, intuitive and when Faith began going to school in the afternoons, four-year-old Katie was left on her own.

NEASON AND BOBA were her first Imaginary Friends—flying horses who lived in her sock drawer. Rupert Pocket slept in a night-light. Vuvy and Noo-Noo she set places for at Sunday dinner. Scroop and Melnick, the Doy-Doy Monster, all manner of night-tripping elf and faery otherkin glimmered in her imagination, but to Neason and Boba she always returned. The soft sound of their names, the inflection of phonemes, had on Katie a hypnotic effect and she sifted such sounds into her own idiolect. You would hear her out in the backyard, singing to herself, babbling their names over and over. Inside, she diverted herself by staring at boa constrictors in the World Book Encyclopedia, doodling her name in colouring books, watching miscellaneous television. This last practice had its hazards because some story points, like Dumbo and the clowns, or anything to do with Bambi's mother, could destroy her for days. "Katie," said my father, "doesn't have a lot of insulation from creatures in distress." This sequence culminates in the I-Blame-the-Babysitter incident when a newbie sitter did not know to prevent Katie from watching a movie on television called *Ring of Bright Water*. Returning home from dress rehearsal one Thursday night, my mother found her youngest child howling, grieving, miserable in onesies pajamas. Grabbing a legal pad, and gargling with Amosan—my mother was a stubborn champion of offstage vocal rest—she scribbled the words, "I Blame the Babysitter" and this line would pass into family vernacular as our version of The Butler Did It. So if you were to drop and break a bottle of ketchup or forget to clean the litter box, you might stare vaguely out a window and murmur, "I blame the babysitter."

Katie did not really appreciate the catchphrase, so shaken was she by her encounter with the movie, and months later you would find her sitting at the bottom of the backstairs, tears spilling down her face, clenching a Fisher-Price Little

People with such force her elbow shook, as she contemplated a world for river otters that allowed for such a ditch-digging labourer and such a shovel.

IT WAS A RAINY TUESDAY AFTERNOON—around 1972, I think—when Katie was four-and-a-half and I was nine that I found her colouring in the basement television room. Katie cultivated a certain disorder in her dress, displaying, say, one of our mother's clip-on earrings on a shirt collar or an elastic ponytail holder around her wrist. These ponytails holders—Faith and Katie called them hair bobbles—were ornamented with two plastic balls, the balls coming in red, blue, clear, and yellow. In recent weeks, for some reason, Katie permitted only the blue type on her person and all others were flung in fury across the room. Today she wore bell-bottom slacks and a fuchsia blouse with a white Peter Pan collar—a collar buttoned up to the top—and she lay on her stomach surrounded by markers and paper. Now it could be a trial colouring with Katie because she didn't really care to match the cap to the marker—she tended to mix by feel—so a pink cap did not guarantee a pink marker and green markers might be capless for days. She was, however, very invested in her work. Head bent fast to the floor, she'd filled several pages with her squiggles, dutifully scrawling over and over the same six-pointed star. She was using an implement new to me—a Mr. Sketch Scented Marker—a stout device with a chisel-tip. It smelled richly of blueberry and I asked where she got it.

"I got it—" said Katie. "From this boy in play-group that I know's sister. She has a whole set. We traded. But guess what?"

"What?"

"This one time in play-group?" Sitting quickly upright, Katie pulled the ponytail holder from her hair and started spinning it on a finger. "A spider tried to get me."

"What kind of spider?"

"Dandy Long Legs. I saw it and then—and *then?*" Katie blew some hair from her eyelash. "Then I didn't."

I watched her draw another six-pointed star. "Why do you keep drawing that?"

"I don't know what these *are*. I don't know what these spinky things are. My hand keeps drawing it but what if isn't something?"

I was reaching for a red marker when Katie shoved at my hand.

"No!" she said. "You don't know how to touch it."

I explained I was a pretty good drawer.

"No!" Katie guarded the paper with both hands. "You'll do it backwards. You'll crackle it."

I looked again at what she was drawing. The six-pointed glyph I recognized from comic books. I would know it later as an asterisk—and once my uncle had explained its mechanism to me—but I'd forgotten what it did. It had something to do with swear words, I thought, and I told Katie it was a letter in a swear word.

"Swear word?" Katie sneered. "No way. Because there's big ones and little ones so why they are on the same page? And move over."

"Who said there's big ones and little ones?"

"Boba."

"How would Boba know anything?"

"How would *you* know anything?" Katie stared at me, impatient. "And move over, I said."

I stood up, deciding to go and get a comic book, from my uncle's collection in the room next door, to make my case. Limping back with a stack of *X-Men*, I returned to see the outside basement door wide open, a shuddering branch of a honeysuckle tree, and Katie dropping over the backyard fence.

ARE THERE TWO CHILDHOODS? I think there's a Generalized Childhood shared with anyone who's been a kid. Events like First Nosebleed, First Remembered Dream, First Diaper Blowout are probably pretty similar no matter what century you're born. But there is also Specific Childhood which is unique to you and the circumstances of your space-time. I think Katie was still in the generalized first, because my *God* she was a random kid, chasing the memory of a firefly, the smell of a thunderstorm, two dimes in a rain puddle—she was like a pilgrim running after a religion still to be discovered—but I'd moved into the specified second and wondered at the whys and wherefores of the world. In fact, as Katie flees a neighbour's backyard, her fuchsia blouse flashing past spring dandelions, let me relate a few specifics. Discerning readers may be wondering why *I* was home this Tuesday afternoon and limping around with comic books. Once I'd been a wild child. Like Stephen Leacock's hero, I'd run madly off in all directions. But for the last three years I'd been suffering from the after-effects of Legg-Calvé-Perthes and, although I'd been cut out of my hip-to-toe casts, my legs had emerged pale and frail and dismal. I was supposed to adapt and recover using crutches but a kid at school named Biederman got big laughs when he stole one of my crutches, stripped off its foam underarm pad, and waggled it provocatively in front of his zipper. To avoid such gags, I left my crutches home. I hopped. I shuffled. I frowned at my classmates. There was concern about my lack-of-progress so I was sent to weekly physio where I struggled to improve my rotational flexion and my attitude toward my rehabilitation. Lousy at both, I started skipping appointments and sneaking home. I was sulky, I was glum. I think, like Katie, I was trying to find where my thoughts belonged—in what world, through which house or person—because often, no matter how many specific thoughts I had, it was rare they counted as much as everyone else's.

THE HOUSE KATIE was standing in front of was the Haunted Mansion. That's what she called it. Everyone else knew it as the Pigeon Lady's house. It was a dilapidated Second Empire place, once royal blue, now faded grey, and set back from the sidewalk by a circular driveway. The property was dark and noisome. Dozens of pigeons gathered here, roosted here, flapped and waddled here. Neighbourhood groups often moved to expel the flock, citing civic ordinances and health concerns, and these initiatives would work for a while, but a few birds were always present. This old house, with its slumping roofs, peeling shingles, with its rotting, sodden steps and rose bushes tangled wild through a ruined gazebo—and all of it splodgy with pigeon droppings—seemed to represent everything that was deranged and broken in the adult world and when passing by, even in the company of my older sisters, I crossed the street to avoid its creepy, decrepit energy.

But Katie, I saw, was standing on its very front steps, gazing curious at a pigeon on a sagging eaves-trough. This was an intricate creature who with scarlet eyes was blinking Katie into abstraction. Katie, even on a good day, was prone to little absence seizures. "Churrs" my sister Carolyn called them—she and I had variations on these chills-and-shivers too—and I can explain them by saying they were a complex of response that mixed a sense of sound-and-colour with an internal emotional moment which anticipated a time in the future when you'd be remembering this selfsame multi-part experience. I didn't like them because they seemed a very imperfect form of premonition. I don't know what Katie thought of them—she gave herself over to seventeen other ways of thinking anyway—which might have been why she saw fit to carelessly push open the front door and advance into the darkness of the Pigeon Lady's house.

FOR SOME SECONDS, maybe a full panicking minute, I stared at the house. When Katie did not rematerialize, I hopped up the steps, rang the doorbell, and waited. Looking through the open door, I saw the windows were covered with taped-up garbage bags, the glow of daylight falling off into shadow, gloom, darkness. I called Katie's name and waited for my eyes to adjust to the dimness. Something seemed off in the house, as if I had walked into the after-echoes of an argument. My sense was not of fear but of weird—of *wyrd*, really—and obscure adult sorrow. Inside were a few sounds, a groaning radiator, a creaking door, the muffled bump of upstairs movement, I wasn't sure. I'd never seen the Pigeon Lady. Rumour was she was an old woman slowly going crazy, someone who hated kids, and I was pressing on a push-button light-switch—and imagining children being pulled by their ankles and stuffed head-first into hampers—when Katie appeared, squinting from the sudden brightness and clutching a can of Orange Crush.

"Katie, what're you *do*ing?"

"It's Boba." Katie blinked her eyes, concerned. "He ran away."

"Where'd you get that pop?"

"The people here—" She twitched with a shrug. "They give you Orange Crush."

"What people—the Pigeon Lady?"

"Pidgy what?" Katie giggled. "No. But the lady here? She could fly once. But she kept bumping into telephone poles."

"That's not even—Look, if we go right now, I'll get you Pixy Stix."

She drank from the pop. "I want Fun Dip."

"Same thing."

"It's called Fun Dip. With Lik-a-Stix."

"Okay. Fun Dip. Deal?"

Placing the empty can on the floor, Katie slipped her bangs behind her ears. "If we find Boba or leave him a note then okay."

"And then we're leaving. Then we're leaving. Deal?"

"*Okay,*" said Katie. "Deal."

She ran up the grand staircase two steps at a time.

Pulling myself up the bannister, I saw the place was huge—an old, old residence of curving stairwells and winding hallways and parlors with furniture shrouded in bedsheets. At the top of the stairs, Katie stood beside a marble-topped table, investigating a single opened drawer. Inside were two silver matchbox holders, a floral pin-frog, and a View-Master, a plastic gadget that, when held to the light, was used to view colour slides on a removable cardboard reel.

"*Whoa,*" said Katie, grabbing the View-Master and bringing it to her eyes. "Binonculars!"

"Katie, you're being a spaz. Put that back."

"I just—" She spun away from me, obstinate, not wanting to be touched. "I just want to see something."

"That's some other kid's toy. And there's not even a thing in it."

"No—because—I'll put you an example." She directed the View-Master toward a door at the end of the hall. "This is the way to Castle Wackbirds." Moving carelessly again, as if her mission somehow depended on carelessness, she clattered down the hall and up a second staircase.

After a very impatient moment, a very try-me-one-more-time-and-you'll-see-what-happens moment, I bumped the drawer shut and followed her into the attic. The third floor was fusty with the smell of clothes left too long in unaired rooms.

Hanging from ceiling racks was a swarm of suits and coats, all on wooden coat-hangers, all sheathed in dry-cleaner plastic. I found Katie in a corner squinting into the empty View-Master, the device crooked on her face.

"Katie, we're going right this minute—"

"I saw someone in the window!"

"Who—Boba?"

"No. A ghost."

"What kind of ghost?"

"A *real* ghost." She clicked the View-Master lever. "Boba told me when he lived here in a dream."

"That's not even—Katie, we have to go. Leave a note. That's the deal."

"But my blue marker!"

"Katie—" I stared at the splintery floor, familiar with this feeling of frustration, rising within me, for another kid's attachment to their own specialness. "We had a deal. And you're being a frigging little brat and I'm not even kidding—"

"If I forgot my marker, how I can write a note?"

I shook my head, furious, and in a spill of anger I told Katie she was a little liar and I didn't believe her little lies or made-up stories about Boba or ghosts and I didn't care if she told Mom and Dad because she wasn't going to get any Fun Dip or Lik-a-Stix or *anything* and turning in the attic I ran slap into a withered figure, its face distorted through the hanging plastic, its fingers scraping at my face and closing around my head, and with a swoon of failure I knew I'd been captured by the creature of the house for finally I'd been fixed and trapped by the Pigeon Lady.

EMLYN ELIZABETH MAIR WAS OLD, older even than the century. She was born in Halifax in 1894—exactly when I'm not sure—I never discovered her real birthday. Our visit coincided with the birthday of her older brother, Edwin Mair, although he hadn't celebrated a birthday in more than fifty years, having died in 1917. The morning of his death, Edwin and Emlyn were visiting one of their father's ships, the tern schooner *Revenant Prince,* which was loading hard pine on the south side of Pier Six. Recently engaged to a young man named Jollimore, Emlyn had dragooned her older brother into accompanying her to a meeting with the tern's captain, who was soon to sail for Perth Amboy, and who was expected to return with fabric and dress materials from New York for Emlyn's wedding. This was a few minutes before nine on the first Thursday in December, the weather bright and clear, in the sea-salt air a tang of coal smoke and frost-melt. On the other side of the harbour, about eleven boat-lengths away, an incoming French steamer was just then colliding with a Norwegian vessel, the grinding impact provoking a fire that would detonate the munitions in the hold of the steamer, resulting in the largest accident the world had ever known. In the moment of the Great Halifax Explosion, Emlyn Mair was moving first down the gangway of the *Revenant Prince,* holding the hand of her brother behind her. Both were flung into the air by the force of the blast, the pressure wave sending Emlyn pinwheeling into the sky past broken trees and spinning seagulls. She was found three miles away, hanging from the telegraph wires at the bottom of Barrington Street, blind in one eye, covered in soot, naked except for her boots. Following behind her, Edwin Mair was likewise sent flying—and dispatched to kingdom come. Thousands perished in the disaster, corpses were splattered all over the city, a final body located in the Halifax Exhibition Grounds as late as summer 1919, but Edwin's body was never found. All that survived of Edwin Mair was a finger, his own wedding ring still on it, discovered in his sister's fist when she awoke that afternoon in the temporary hospital at The Waegwoltic Club. Emlyn would have chunks of shrapnel, shards and slivers of glass, purply imbedded in the back of her neck and shoulders for the rest of her life. But she would live. For whatever reason, through whatever Grace or Fate or Fury, her life would extend beyond the morning of December 6, 1917. Ever since that day, because she had lived and her brother had not, because it had been her idea to visit the ship, and because she blamed herself for his death, Emlyn Mair would take Edwin's birthday as hers, celebrating his life and receding from her own. For she would break off her engagement to the young man named Jollimore and move indoors for the rest of her life. The day Katie and I met her, she was seventy-six years old, a spinster perched and teetering in the high numbers of her old age, one of the city's elderly curiosities, the Pigeon Lady, shell-shocked, extraneous, an infinite dowager in a bobbed wig and a crumbling house twelve times too big.

"NO ONE'S BEEN up there in years," said Emlyn at the dining room table. "Haven't opened those rooms in years. Wings are closed off. Since before the war. Takes too much heat. But pass along the mint jelly, would you? That's the chap. Are you sure you won't have a lobster? No?" She made a kooky giggle and smiled as if she felt her personal charm was proving only deeply and irresistibly winning. She wore a wig of bobbed brown hair and often, when turning this way or that, the wig over-shifted, a curling lock spinning off her forehead and over her eye—but since this was her sightless eye I don't think she noticed. The retina of her good eye was damaged, too, but functional, and she took pains to protect it—she could only fitfully regulate the size of its pupil—which is why she wore sunglasses indoors and kept the house darkened in perpetual twilight. Her nose was neatly aquiline—it would not have looked out of place on a Sitwell—and she wore a long pearl necklace loosely coiled around her neck like a flapper. Her dress was straight and loose, the colour of pale champagne, with spiraling bead work, a shawl collar, and tapered sleeve-cuffs. Her most marked characteristic was the curve of her left shoulder. Her scapula, broken in the explosion, had not properly mended, her left shoulder twisted sinister because of it, and this gave to her figure a crooked aspect, a slant extending even to the middle finger of her left hand which was warping now toward a glass of sherry on the dinner table. As her fingers closed around its stem, a wristwatch, which must have fit her once, popped from her dress-sleeve and drooped from the bones of her wrist like a bangle. "Please start, won't you?" She brought the sherry to her lips and gurgled back a swallow. "Mint jelly?" She handed me the silver sauceboat. I dolloped out some mint jelly, thinking it was Jell-O, and passed it on to Katie who sat with the View-Master at the other end of the table, somewhat perplexed by the enormous plate of food in front of her—pork tenderloin and scalloped potatoes, jellied madrilène and Brussels sprouts, radicchio coleslaw and pearl onions, as well as a wedge of blue cheese.

"Well now—" Emlyn jiggled her glass. There were only three of us at the table. A fourth place-setting had been prepared and, though no dinner had been served, there was a full glass of sherry. Emlyn clinked this glass with her own and turned to me. "To absent friends and present hearts. Cheers!" She clinked my water glass then turned toward Katie—who got up on her chair, leaned over the table's flickering candles, and touched a new can of Orange Crush to Emlyn's sherry glass.

"Cheers!" repeated Katie, swigging from the pop. She placed the can beside the View-Master. And promptly belched.

"Ha!" Emlyn cackled—a single blurt of laughter—and lowered her sunglasses to gaze at Katie. "She's a crackerjack find, that one."

"Excuse me," said Katie, her lips quivering with a half-smile. Picking up an oyster fork, she jabbed at her Brussels sprouts. "This smells weird."

I was explaining my sister could be a picky eater when Emlyn raised a hand to silence the table. Chewing on a resilient piece of pork, she asked, "Did you hear the telephone?" She listened. "Someone keeps dialing this number. They ring it over and over. Why on earth?" Emlyn stared fixedly into the hallway, as if daring her enemies to emerge from its darkness. "Strangest thing." She finished her sherry, picked up a fork, and contemplated the rest of her dinner. "This spot of cheese doesn't agree with me." She pushed a piece of blue cheese around her plate. "I don't care for it, do you?" Emlyn called across the table to Katie. "Don't eat the cheese. You'll get the glotch!"

"The glotch?" Katie glanced up from trying to balance her oyster fork on top of the View-Master.

"Doesn't do to get the glotch. And my God, is that the telephone?" Emlyn struck the table with the bottom of her fork. "Can you believe it?" She rose from the table, plucked a bottle of sherry from the mahogany credenza, and returned to her chair. "I wish to God they'd stop, don't you?" She tittered at the absurdity, trying to seem vivacious, like an actress stage-laughing in a play. "Who *are* these people?"

She refilled her glass. The sherry was making her tipsy and as Emlyn Mair became drunk, I felt her strange contradictions, the alcoholic movement between memory and spontaneity, between subjects past and objects visible.

"What do you suppose this is?" She reached across the table and seized the View-Master. "Flimflam men coming to the door to sell one gimcrack thing or another. Now the Frigidaire I like. That's very useful." She dropped the View-Master to the table. "But I don't go in for all these new fandangle things. Belongs to the boy of the house, I suppose."

I'd been leaning to one side to put Emlyn in line with the bullseye mirror on the far wall—I was not convinced she wasn't supernatural and was confirming she produced a reflection—but at this mention of a boy in the house I nearly toppled from my chair.

Turning to see what I'd been looking at, Emlyn decided it was the silver framed photographs on the credenza. "Ah—" She put a hand on the closest photograph, a family portrait of a severe-looking couple presiding over an array of smock-dressed girls and sailor-suited boys. I identified Emlyn as the youngest, about four years old, her hair in ribbons and pin-curls, and holding in her hands a fluffy kitten. "My father," said Emlyn, picking up the photograph. "He was a great man. Had the first motorcar in the city. Sent ships all over the world. Made the Deepwater Pier." She passed me the photograph. "But he didn't care for the Canadas. Wanted no part of the confederacy. At the Charlottetown Conference, why Poppa took a rifle and shot it up and down Richmond Street!"

Katie slipped off her chair and came to look at the photograph.

"And my brothers," said Emlyn, musing. "They were brilliant. Merlin came first at Dalhousie. Walked away with every prize. And Howland, he was premier. My sister Ferelith, a great beauty." Reaching for the glass of sherry at the empty place-setting, Emlyn's fingers closed instead around a candle in the candelabra, knocking over the candle and sending a frightened Katie bolting under the table. The candle flamed a few moments before an indifferent Emlyn spilled some sherry on it. "But Edwin," she said, staring at the smoldering wick. "My brother Edwin, Edwin was different. Edwin was a different sort." Within her coiled pearls on a silver necklace was a gold wedding band. She touched at this and said, "*Such* a sweet fellow. And very kind. And so sweet for being kind. Do you know?"

I nodded, keen to agree, but I felt, from the way she was frowning at me, and the way she was blinking away the moisture from her eyes, there was a danger I might not understand this the way she wished. Her thoughts seemed to be circling after some contrary detail. Emlyn Mair was someone who wished to settle down with an understanding she'd properly worked out the meaning to something, a meaning she could then place in an appropriate pigeon-hole of her mind. But some detail wasn't allowing her to settle down, some detail was flapping loose and delinquent, and her eyes flickered with disturbance.

"There was a portrait of the boy from the other yesterday." She twisted to look at the credenza. "Where did—Good Christ." She went silent. "If it isn't the *tele*phone again! They've gone too far this time. Why, I'll sue. I'll sue this city. If there's one—"

"Are you looking for this?" Katie sprang up from under the table with a school photograph.

"Ha!" Emlyn snatched it. "I *told* you. Didn't I tell you?" She pointed at Katie as if to demonstrate what true genius looked like. "Keep your eye on this one. She's got a quality, this one here. I like the cut of her jib."

Leaning out of my chair, I saw the photograph showed a beaming little blond boy in a white shirt and striped tie. "Hey," I said, recognizing him. "That's that kid—"

"You know my nephew, do you?"

"Cyrus Mair." I studied the photograph. I'd met this kid. I'd *known* this kid. We had together one of the funnier afternoons of my life. And I'd forgotten him? I suppose Halifax was like that. Kids came and went. They were sent to school. They moved away. They disappeared into hospitals. But I felt ashamed that Cyrus Mair, a kid whose acquaintance promised events fantastical, I'd completely failed to remember.

"Now there's a boy!" said Emlyn. "He'll bring us back from the brink. You'll see. Put this family back on the map." She smiled, a fleeting spasm in her face, and helped herself to more sherry.

I looked again at the photograph—it suddenly seemed very important to me—and inspected it for clues. Penned on the back was his name, *Cyrus Francis Mair* in slanted cursive handwriting, and penciled beside his surname was an asterisk—that glyph again—which seemed to signal a run of related text, beginning with a smaller asterisk, along the bottom. Here printed in pencil in a child's hand was the strange-looking phrase *Cheltenham Prep Michaelmas* but I was mostly struck by the recurrence of an asterisk and I was turning to include Katie in these spinky-related developments when I felt someone's fingers firmly gripping my elbow.

"All right, Mr. Flimflam," said Emlyn Mair, jingling with her other hand a small silver bell. She stared at me, her wig askew. "Would you like to really see something?"

I REMEMBER NEXT the vast backyard—though I might be conflating visits—but I recall the wild weeds and brambles and rose bushes and certainly I remember, beneath the timber rafters of the garage, a flat-bottomed dory and old croquet box and—at the very back of the property—a Nova Scotian flag snapping at the top of a white-painted flagpole, colours flashing in the sun. I remember a gleeful Katie delving into a pit of discarded Christmas trees—decomposing, brown-needled, tinsel-ridden—and Emlyn jingling again her silver bell and the pigeons from the rooftops descending, dropping like shadows from the eaves and gables and chimney-tops. She lifted a dinner plate heaped with scalloped potatoes and slices of Parkerhouse rolls and slung these leftovers like slop into the dirt of the yard. Birds were loose in the air, flapping and trapped beneath each other, I remember a fright of squawks as two collided in front of Katie's face. Few scenes in my early childhood could be said to be phantasmagorical—like I said, I didn't get out much—but I'd like to submit to the judges *Emlyn Mair Among the Pigeons* for, when remembering this commotion, it seems a moment out of Nightmare, the flutter of wingbeats, the scatter and scramble of pecking birds. Emlyn watched these dramatics, amused. The more agitated the birds became, the more she enjoyed herself, making single snorts of laughter and waving erratically in the air, as if conducting some invisible symphony. "Have to be careful," she said to Katie. "Can't be too careful. One thing or another gets fouled up and you have the devil's own time putting it right. But you see a sign. You see a sign. When it arrives, you'll know." She watched as two pigeons struck at the same slice of potato. "The grey one there. Look how sick he is!" This was a king pigeon, full of strut and bumble and favouring its right leg. "He's had a turn. Won't last long. Hopeless. Hasn't got the stuff." Emlyn visored a hand over her sunglasses. "But look at that one. With the fickle spot. He's a little fighter. Look at him go!" Something had changed in her relations with us, she was playful and defiant, and whatever detail she'd been searching for, she'd found it now. "Life takes a lot of twists. The world's a harum-scarum place. But when one reaches a turning point, it's best to know which way to go. I really think so, don't you?" Turning to me, she made a charming smile—a smile radiantly certain—and I realized she was sharing this with us not as an adult with two random kids but as an individual with two likeminded spirits, and I realized, further, that, in some way, in some Emlyn Mair way, she *cared* about us.

WHY WOULD SOMEONE spend their entire life remembering a dead brother? Was it crazy? Was it noble? Over the years, my mother would field a number of drunken phone calls from Emlyn Mair—for whom my father would do some legal work—and considered her crazy. "When I think of all the times that woman called your father drunk and complaining about her bill. This strange, strange old woman, she's had this horrible life and withdrawn from the world, but at the same time you don't want her to end badly, you know? You're sort of sympathetic."

It was understandable, my father said, that the woman might be thought a little eccentric but he didn't think her quite crazy.

"A little eccentric?" said my mother. "The woman's an absolute fruitcake. She hasn't come out of the house, Stewart, she hasn't seen the light of *day*, for God's sake, in fifty-five years. You call that eccentric? Puh. Who knows with that family? They don't need a reason that makes sense to anybody else. And to think a child's living there with all those jeezly fucking birds. I suppose she's drunk half the time anyway so what does she care? Honest to God, Emlyn Mair, that family, they've got a lot of junk in the attic. A lot of ghosts."

The woman was grievous strange, you had a sense her contradictions obsessed her, but there seemed to me a bravery to Emlyn Mair. She was pursuing in her mind an entirely different set of specifics and persisting in her imagination was a vision of her family as a sort of dynasty, as tycoons in some grand capital. I would be fascinated by the Titus Mairs, this once-splendid family, and fascinated with Emlyn

Mair, a figure who seemed to have emerged out of an early daguerreotype. And I mention all this because, to put these scenes on my storyline, the Mairs would become *my* enchanted kingdom—I would dream my life in their vicinity—and my general admiration for their exploits, my mooning over their failures, and my marveling at their perpetuities, would pervade my youth and childhood. For this afternoon marked the day I began to understand that what you choose to believe in—a set of flying horses, a long-dead brother, the mysteries of a family—can determine what you yourself become.

SIX O'CLOCK ON TOWER ROAD and within the clouds the sun brightens, sending watercolours through the rainy sky—deep reds opalescing to scarlet and pinkish blues to sudden violet. Waiting for me in the wind of the sidewalk, Katie holds a third Orange Crush. She takes a sip and asks, "Is that cat still alive?"

"Which cat?"

"In the picture."

"Probably not. That's before wars and everything when pictures were in black-and-white."

"So I wasn't even *born* yet?"

"Me neither."

Katie takes another sip, her teeth stained faintly orange. "And who was the other table-place for?"

"Her brother? I don't know."

"But is he dead?"

"I guess so."

"And the kid in the school picture, you know him?"

"Once I did. He came to Bonnie's birthday party."

"That lady," says Katie, flicking some hair off her forehead. "She made a deal. With the ghost."

"Who said that—Boba?"

"No." Katie puckers her lower lip, fretful. "Boba's gone."

"Where'd he go?"

"Well," she says, taking my hand. "He got the glotch!" She is in the middle of a fluid peal of giggles—and pulling me down the sidewalk—when she squeezes my fingers. "Aubrey!" She stoops to grab something in a puddle. "An Easter egg?" Her voice rises to a playful shriek. "And it's *alive!*" Making a dimply smile, she holds in her hand a pigeon egg, pale blue, about the width of a quarter. "Can I keep this? Because this is so—this is so—this is so *beautiful*."

"Yeah, probably."

"*Yes*!" Katie runs triumphant down the sidewalk, the pigeon egg held to her heart. As I watch my sister dash away, in the air between us glides a dandelion seed head, fluffy in all directions. I touch at this drifting spore, watching it soften against my finger, and it seems to me a three-dimensional asterisk. But whether it's a footnote to a moment that's gone before—or if it indicates a run of meaning still to come—I don't know, but I do understand, finally, shivering, and watching it float above my head, that there is magic in the world, if only I might let myself see it.

Crisis on Earth-X

I WAS FOUR YEARS OLD when Uncle Lorne came to live with us. He was my mother's younger brother by twenty-two winters, a mistake of uncertain paternity according to my sisters, and he joined our household when his own was in freefall. "Nanny and Dompa are drunk all the time is why," explained my sister Bonnie. "That's why he's like that." Nanny and Dompa, living in Montreal, were moving into some marital hurly-burly during this time, so it was decided, mostly by my father, that twelve-year-old Uncle Lorne would benefit from the relatively steadier environment of our house in Halifax. I was eager to have such company for in my house I was surrounded by women—my significant mother as well as two sisters above and two below.

Uncle Lorne was a singular and decidedly non-feminine addition to our house. He arrived with hobbies fully formed, with habits and rules and secret disciplines. He made models of Iroquois helicopters, completed abstract jigsaw puzzles, and, in an amazing display of homemade engineering, constructed a lunar docking station for our Major Matt Mason action figures from the parts of a rotary phone, a discarded bicycle tube, and a Fram oil filter. He showed me how to draw propellers and Gatling guns and Batman's cowl—an image I am still known to improvise on unopened letters from Revenue Canada. Uncle Lorne owned more than a thousand comic books which he kept in boxes under his bed. Each purchase was thoughtfully registered by title and number and condition on blue graph paper inside a mauve Duo-Tang folder. Though he followed many comics, he was closing in on complete runs of *The Justice League of America* and *The Brave and the Bold*, back issues of which he acquired from a mail-order concern in Passaic, New Jersey. This endeavour, among others, was funded by delivering *The Mail-Star*, the city's afternoon broadsheet. Uncle Lorne had a route of one hundred and sixty-three newspapers, an ambitious amalgam of three existing smaller routes, and on Wednesdays—when the paper swelled with advertising flyers from Sobeys and the IGA ("Two-for-one 1-2-3 Jell-O!" "Try new Beef Noodle Hamburger Helper!")—I was pressed into service as sidekick and all-purpose lackey. The dropped-off newspapers came in bales held together by blue twine. In winter, they were fearsome cuboid chunks of frozen newsprint. But the day I'm remembering is not winter. The day I'm remembering is one day away from true summer, a Wednesday in late June, one of the longest of the year. I am now ten, Uncle Lorne eighteen, and the city is strangely warm, daylight endless, a dragonfly soft-lifting on an ocean breeze. We are far afield. From the Wellington Street drop-off we have ranged to The Nova Scotian Hotel, back through the Dalhousie University campus, and are now tramping westerly on Jubilee Road. We are covering another boy's paper route—Chris Cody, one of Uncle Lorne's intimates—and this adds fifty-two papers to our travels. But even four hours into our overland explorations, I don't mind. This afternoon alone I've been shown a live seal in the Life Sciences aquatic tank at the university. I've been taught a new climbing technique called "chimneying." And here at the bottom of Jubilee Road I see the street literally sinks beneath the sea, the Northwest Arm flooding up the slope of a concrete boat ramp, the setting sun a thousand times refracted in its waves. Though I can hear my uncle calling for me above, I take a moment to imagine Aquaman underwater beyond this boat ramp, spinning away from the shallows to some murky sub-stratum of the North Atlantic, perhaps rising buoyant through sun-filtered depths, bursting to the surface to rendezvous with the Batboat, the two superheroes racing toward a far horizon. A few weeks before, I read a *Justice League* two-parter about a supervillain zombie called Solomon Grundy, a story that featured in a heroic role the grown-up Robin of Earth-Two, and in my mind I decide to place this fully formed Robin in the Batboat. I admire his blended costume, his motorcycle, and how he has assumed the mantle of crime-fighting when the Batman of his world began to dodder—because, to be honest, recently I've been wondering if events might force me in a similar direction. Solomon Grundy required a team-up between the Justice League of Earth-One and the Justice Society of Earth-Two, and the series has become my favourite team-up story ever. I keenly anticipate the next interworld issues, numbers 107 and 108, copies of which have been ordered from New Jersey for both Uncle Lorne and me. My copies will be considered paid in full if I do eight more Wednesdays on the paper route.

Uncle Lorne calls for me again and this time I straggle up Jubilee Road where he is smoking a cigarette. He allows himself one cigarette after the papers have been delivered. He puts out the cigarette on an old and furrowed telephone pole, leaving the filter inside a vertical crack, and exhales, his chin bobbing in time to some percussion heard in his head. Uncle Lorne has many internal rhythms whose patterns will remain somewhat mysterious to me, just as he seems someone whose personality may remain fundamentally unknowable. “Kink-man,” he says, using a family nickname. “Ready to race?” A NOTE OF PERSONAL HISTORY: as many of you will remember, the last few years for me have been spent on crutches, in a wheelchair, or fretfully limping, and it’s only now, at the age of ten, that I am recovering motion and strength in my left hip. Naturally this conflicts with my desire to be the World’s Greatest Athlete because my limp and shortened left leg lend my walk a crooked, hop-along quality—an extraneous feature, I like to imagine, that disappears in the madness of an open sprint. Although I still find it tiring to sustain longer efforts, Uncle Lorne has devised a system whereby the distance run is increased each Wednesday by twenty sidewalk squares. We started close, South Street and Tower Road in March, and are now advanced to Robie and Jubilee. I am given a head start of fifty resting heartbeats—Uncle Lorne holding two fingers to his throat to count his pulses—then he will charge after me.

Taking off my shirt and tying the sleeves around my waist, as I’ve seen some older boys do on the Dalhousie campus, I say I’m ready. Uncle Lorne inspects the winter pallor of my stomach. “Whew,” he says. “*Fish belly!* Fish belly on the old grub.” He speaks as if this is a joke already established between us. “Fish Belly Grub. Grub-a-dub-dub. Race with the Grub.” It is one of his recreations to explore the associations of words—which he sometimes pronounces in confusing and menacing variations. But I take his meaning as only teasing, tighten my laces, and crash off, propelling myself down the sidewalk beside the Camp Hill cemetery. I take the corner on

South Street at top speed, losing my balance and dispersing my wild centripetal motion by straying into the street itself. As I speed past the Killam Hospital, I hear a commotion somewhere behind me—a rush of sound that is my uncle closing the gap between us. Slinging myself around a stop sign for extra momentum, I meet Tower Road with out-of-control, berserker ferocity. I know, like the grown-up Robin of Earth-Two, that there are do-or-die moments when you simply *have* to prove yourself. Seeing our house, and sensing a win for the first time, I flash a giddy look behind me—only to allow Uncle Lorne, on the other side, to spring up the steps of the front porch and, as he always does, touch the door latch, signaling the end of our contest and his victory. I protest if only I *hadn't* looked over my shoulder, losing precious split-seconds, this time I could've won, would've won, *should've* won. Uncle Lorne bobs his head again, noncommittal, and mentions that he thinks I ran my best race so far. He pulls open our front door and pauses in the evening air. I am just noticing a viral spread of pimples on his chin when he says, quietly, "Run your own race, Grub. Run your own race." With that semi-cryptic koan, he vanishes inside to his basement bedroom, and I limp happily into the kitchen.

This is a time before microwaves, when the warm up of a dinner is achieved through the sorcery of a double-boiler—which means leaving a plate of dinner (in this case, pork chop, mashed potatoes, and carrots sliced with a serrated cutter) on a pot of simmering water. There are two plates tonight, and I see it as a sign of my rapidly advancing maturity that I've been so singled out. As I touch the dinner plate with the tip of a quilted oven mitt, a song begins on the kitchen clock-radio that my mother uses to check her approaching rehearsal times. I don't really know what radio songs are, that playlists turn over, or that the song you hear one summer might vanish the next.

But "Band on the Run" is around that year, in the way a new neighbourhood kid might be, or in the way you might notice a surplus of ladybugs on a bathroom window one afternoon. I've heard the song before but it perplexes me because the opening is filled with so many different progressions, each sounding like a different song, I often confuse it with other offerings on the radio. But as I identify it for a first time, my continued contact with the warmed plate touches off a number of attendant details in and out of the kitchen. The windows are beginning to lose their evening light. The floaty purple fragrance of lilac blossoms is unmistakable in the backyard. The kitchen cupboards, painted turquoise, show signs of blue where the turquoise paint has been chipped—and so my response to the song seems turquoise-blue with an after-sense of lilac and when a crescendo of horns fades to allow for the strumming of an acoustic guitar, alternating the chords of C and F Major 7, the song seems finally to become itself. In a moment of autistic dreaminess, I stand unmoving at the stove, fixed between these two chords, and it's only when the singer sings about rain exploding with a mighty crash am I released from my abstraction—and a multitude of synesthetic meaning explodes for me, moments at once emotional, sensory, and intuitive, and as they shimmer and gather and burst again I realize it's the happiest I've been without knowing particularly why I'm happy and this song seems to be a part of it, and not just accompanying it, but activating it, coordinating the mood and circumstance and manifold instant. "Band on the Run" on June 20, 1974, is a strangely overwhelming solace for me and will be ever after linked with the events of that summer, and the possibilities of that year, and though many of the proceedings turn out horribly, I am still grateful to the song for what it engenders in my imagination—for it conveys a sense of precarious possibilities gorgeously arranged and met and fulfilled.

UNCLE LORNE'S DOOR was closed when I went into the basement—an obsolete coal room done over as his bedroom—so I continued into the rec room, a recently dry-walled creation beside the furnace room and home to rainbow-coloured wall-to-wall carpet, a folded-up ping-pong table, Nanny and Dompa's deteriorating wicker cottage furniture, and a Sony Trinitron television on a rickety stand. I turned on the TV and stood spinning the channel selector, alert to the probable appearance of *The Six Million Dollar Man*. As I noticed a familiar and above-average episode of *Bewitched*, the story where Cousin Serena forces a song on Tommy Boyce and Bobby Hart, I became aware of some indications I was not the first to set foot in the room. On the carpet, beside a wicker armchair, was an unopened can of Fresca, a bag of Fritos Brand corn chips, and an SX-70 Polaroid camera, a recent birthday present to my oldest sister Carolyn. Not that it was Carolyn who would leave such a gift unattended in the basement. It was, of course, Bonnie, my older, contiguous sister and long-standing nemesis within the family. With the arrival in the house of this gadget, Bonnie had taken to photographing assorted personalities off the television screen at extremely inopportune moments. Where these photographs were idiotically hoarded I wasn't sure—but lately a number of blurry, underexposed Polaroids of Björn Borg, The Partridge Family, and Tony DeFranco had been found behind the radiator in the upstairs bathroom. I have successfully kept my sisters' details out of these narratives but a few words might be appropriate here. Bonnie, two years my senior, was principally in a lifelong, unwinnable competition with Carolyn, the first-born, who was and has been the perfect child—perfect manners, perfect marks, perfect hair—and always thoughtful, responsible, and over-achieving. Bonnie, when she was alive, was domineering, tactical, and ultra-impulsive—a girl never slowed by an unexpressed thought. She stood now in the doorway, holding a CorningWare bowl full of homemade popcorn, her head tilted to one side, and looking at me with the smile that Tolerance Gives to the Misguided. "Uh, what do you think you're doing?"

"Watching 'The Six Million Dollar Man.'"

"Uh, no, you're not. Because did you say 'reserve?' Were you sitting down and did you say 'reserve?'" Bonnie quickly touched her tailbone to the wall, repeated this code word, and straightened up again. "Because if you weren't and you didn't then we're watching what we want to watch. Plus I was here first and you're out-voted so tough titty."

My two younger sisters now materialized in the area behind Bonnie. They were clad in worn and matching flannelette nighties and each held in their hands a cereal bowl of popcorn—the effect was rather like two novice members of the junior choir advancing with opened hymnaries.

"What're you guys watching?" I asked, stalling, not prepared to walk away from the television.

Bonnie explained they'd been planning all week to watch a movie called *The Parent Trap*. I had not heard of this plan. I was offended by this plan. And I refused to believe I'd been consulted about this plan. What was this movie even about?

Uncle Lorne came out of his room to investigate the crowd in the newly boisterous rec room. "What is *what* movie about?" he asked.

"'The Parent Trap.'"

Uncle Lorne looked to the ceiling, as if to properly assemble his thoughts. "It's about these kids." He glanced at Bonnie for verification. "Twin sisters, right? And one night they're waiting for their parents to come home and then—Kink, do you know what gelignite bullets are?"

I said I didn't.

"Plastic explosives used primarily in automatic weapons—"

"That's *not* the movie, Uncle Lorne," said Bonnie, with bold impatience. She was pointing at her stash of junk food, ready to launch into a further defence of her viewing rights, when from upstairs we heard our parents come in the front door, their shoe-steps resounding over our heads. All of us, through acquired habit, wordlessly decoded the noises above for signals of disposition, humour, inclination.

"Mom's drunk, you guys," said Katie, with casual nonchalance, nibbling a single piece of popcorn. "Bet you any money."

Our mother, as it would turn out, was not yet drunk. She and our father had been at a party celebrating the opening of *A Midsummer Night's Dream*, the gathering held across the street in the rented rooms of some new friends, Mr. and Mrs. Abbott—although my sister Bonnie maintained these two were not formally married. When first informed on this point, I wondered if Mr. and Mrs. Abbott were perhaps a travelling gypsy duo who assumed diverse identities and defrauded townspeople out of their children. But the Abbotts, it turned out, were not gypsies or conmen but something else altogether as exotic—they were draft-dodgers, expatriate Americans from Wheeling, West Virginia, who had driven to Nova Scotia on a Honda 450 motorcycle in the summer of 1968. They lived first in an unheated commune in the Annapolis Valley, on the other side of West Paradise, and came to Halifax when their two daughters reached school age. These two daughters, September and Autumn Dawn, were fourteen months apart in age and bizarrely identical to me. Both wore tie-dye shirts and homemade pants with no pockets. Both had blonde hair down to their waists. Their hair was sometimes held back in pinched thickets by yarn string-ties but September, and especially Autumn Dawn, did not care for these yarn string-ties and often the girls ran around with hair loose and unfastened so encountering them in a neighbourhood game of hide-and-seek was like coming face to face with a feral child who had been lost for some months in the black mountain hills of Dakota.

The Abbott household had a somewhat lax philosophy toward personal upkeep and one or the other girl was always scratching a stye out of an eyelash or separating a scab from a kneecap. Since arriving in Halifax, Mr. Abbott had secured a position as the stage carpenter for Neptune Theatre. Mrs. Abbott had some undefined connection with a new organization called the Ecology Action Centre. She was also a folk artist of some commitment. She worked mostly in macramé, collage, and silkscreen. Because my father had done some pro bono legal work for the Abbotts regarding their immigration, our family had been the recipient of two silkscreened prints—and, as we kids trooped up the stairs from the basement, I saw my father was now in possession of a third, a sort of lacquered silhouette of three ponies in a salt marsh.

"Jesus, Mackie," he said to my mother, shaking his head. "Where are we going to *put* this goddamn thing?"

My mother, who this evening was wearing a lime-and-purple print dress—what Carolyn called the Jo Anne Worley dress—pulled open the refrigerator and reached for a bottle of Blue Nun before saying, "Your father made us leave the party early. Like anything's new."

My father put the silkscreen print on the kitchen table and made a slight tip of his head, his eyebrows contracting in bemused concentration. It was a familiar gesture which meant he was wondering whether he should imply his real reaction—which was, in this case, that he considered the party overrun with dubious people and dubious practices—or simply forgo any response at all.

"Because," continued my mother. "This one couple was passing around a marijuana cigarette. As soon as your father saw that, we were out of there."

"Well," said my father. "How's that going to look? It happens to be against the law."

"Loosen up. Their friends were very nice. When in Rome—"

"Okay, Titania. That's plenty, thank you. Time to get these kiddles to bed." He pointed at my youngest sister. "You? Bed. Now. And I mean it, Ditsy."

My mother grabbed a plastic juice glass from the dishwasher and poured herself four fingers of white wine. "They're anti-war, you know, these people. Flower children. They think anything's possible. The wife's a women's libber. Vivien. But very sweet. Him? I'm not so sure. Wes is the saintly type. Wants to do good. Like build a barn for mentally retarded kids in New Brunswick." She tossed back half the wine. "Sure. Why not? But what are they going to do with a *barn*—shear sheep? Honest to God. Be careful of these so-called saints, children. Believe me, people who act like saints—a lot of so-called saints are trouble. Living in a dream world. Telling people what they don't want to hear in the first place. And the more Wes is doing good for some retarded kid, the more he's neglecting his own family, you watch."

My parents' conversation continued over the next few hours, sometimes softly in almost inaudible murmurs, other times erupting into strident tones of drunken hostility. By this time, I was lying in my bed, sleepless, restless with every wrongful twist of my bed sheets, staring at my ceiling. The streetlights outdoors created a familiar overglow in my room and I stared as tiny dots of winking dimness generated patterns on my paint-cracked ceiling, patterns I often collected into recognizable images—the man with the nose, the happy cow, the mud-splattered ogre—the last of which I was having trouble looking at more than once. As I heard my parents make their way up the front stairs, I closed my eyes and prayed to God they wouldn't get divorced again.

"Stewart, would you mind not being such a—"

"Mumsy? I don't want to hear another word of this."

"—prig. They're just trying to do good in the world. *Their* life isn't only about making money."

"Sure, sure, Mumsy. Relax. Relax, kid."

"I hate it when you get like this."

"Here we go. Here it is. It's all coming now. I'll take the rest of that wine, thank you very much."

"You want to lose your hand? Just tell me something. Why don't you try something new for once in your life—like in the last twenty years? That's the problem between me and you. You don't care two shits about the environment. And I do."

"The environment? How in the *hell* are we talking about the environment?"

There were a few thudding and bumping noises—which I guessed to be my mother's foot slipping off a step and her subsequent stumble into the creaking banister. "Well," she said. "I hope *I* never ridicule what is wise and good. That's a quote. You can look it up."

"Yes, Mackie. Beautiful performance. Exit stage left with a bear."

"It's exit *pursued* by a bear. Get it right, for Christ's sake. For once in your crumb-bum life, would you get something right?"

This exchange was followed by the closing of their bedroom door, a brief lull, a night shriek, and the smashing of a bottle. My parents began as actors—they met in college in a play—so we kids were used to these theatrics. But tonight seemed a return to the drear uncertainty of three years ago and as I tried again to fall asleep I began to wonder if what I wanted for myself was really relevant at all.

UNCLE LORNE WAS AN ARCHIVIST, a tinkerer, a published poet. The year he came to live with us, he was seized upon by the middle school English teacher, Mr. Jones, who chose three of his poems for the literary section of the school yearbook. Two were about Imperial Rome ("Roma Aeterna") and a third, and for me most vivid, was titled "Wild Dogs." It moved with the pace of a Blake lyric and started with the line, "Perturbed eyes and carious teeth." What was this word—perturbed? Or carious? Or gelignite? In what furnace were such words? Where had he gleaned such lore and stuff? The poems were signed "Lorne Anthony Wheeler," one of the few times I saw my uncle's full name in print. When he was in Montreal, living in Notre-Dame-de-Grâce, Dompa had given him a rubber stamp with his full name and address on it (a very Dompa gift), and this blue, inky imprimatur appeared on the cover of many of my uncle's earliest collected comics—before he realized making such a mark might devalue the artifact. Uncle Lorne left Montreal just before Expo 67 and, though he seldom talked about it, I could feel, from how he once pinned to his corkboard postcards of the geodesic dome and the Habitat 67 housing complex (communiqués from Benoit Charbonneau and Thompson Oldring—precious friends I'd never meet), that Nova Scotia must have seemed for him a far and distant outpost of empire, and Halifax, vis-à-vis Montréal, a city much reduced in circumstance. I decided it was to cosmopolitan Montreal that he owed his strange intelligence.

My uncle and his abilities I mostly regarded with reverent awe, although I knew he was somewhat eccentric, as if his clockwork required further assembly. Because while Uncle Lorne was made up of a lot of quick parts, not all of them worked, and some were changing colours, and still others awaited their final function. His vocabularies, his silences, his keen intrigues and esoteric associations were all clues, as I sensed them, to the inverted kingdom of his imagination.

"My brother's mind certainly works weird," my mother would say. "No, Lorne's brilliant, he is, but he's not always exactly *here*, you know. In the real world." I sometimes wondered if I would ever understand him. And I wanted to. I wanted the fellowship and solidarity and stability such an understanding would supply. My sisters had no idea how Uncle Lorne thought and they'd mostly stopped trying. "You know," said Carolyn when the gelignite comment reached her desk. "That's just Uncle Lorne humour." Bonnie agreed. She tended to speak about Uncle Lorne in a respectful but detectably marginalizing manner and sneaking into her tone lately was the implication that Uncle Lorne was increasingly out-of-touch and peculiar—as if, for her, he was already beyond the point of no return. At the end of June, Bonnie said to me, "You know the Abbotts are atheists, right?"

"So?"

"So Faith asked Uncle Lorne what atheists were and you know what he said? That atheists were families that drown their own pets. Is that supposed to be funny? Like a Chris Cody joke?"

"Faith knows what atheists are."

"But what if he tells Katie that? She's young and she'll believe him." There was no attempt at a tolerant smile here. Bonnie was offended by Uncle Lorne's deliberate subversion of a religious matter and she would attribute this wayward attitude to the growing influence of Chris Cody, the other paper boy. Christopher Cody was a giggly, bushy-haired teenager who would arrive at our backdoor ostensibly to watch *Kung Fu* with Uncle Lorne. Later, he might be found shambling around our furnace room in tinted aviator glasses, eating Munchos Chips, and listening on headphones to Grand Funk Railroad or Cream or Santana—albums whose psychedelic cover art used to frighten and confuse me as a small child. To my uncle, Chris was Commander Cody, a name always spoken in a hoarse, back-of-the-throat style, as if Uncle Lorne's voice were suddenly parched with fatigue or thirst. This voice was used in all manner of Chris Cody settings, often with deliberately sinister implication, and sometimes even in non-Chris-Cody situations, when a bored Uncle Lorne might seek to surprise you by creeping into the rec room to loudly whisper into your ear, "Boris the Spider!" which was the name by which this diversion came to be known—as Uncle Lorne's Boris the Spider trick.

I was wary of Commander Cody. On a winter Wednesday at the newspaper drop-off, he once chased me into a snow bank and put snow down my back. In May, I was kicked out of the rec room so he and Uncle Lorne could watch a Clint Eastwood movie. And lately, now that both had grown greebly moustaches, Chris Cody had taken to commandeering my uncle on missions into the musty Halifax downtown—to the Hollis Street Tavern, the Ladies Beverage Room, and something called the Fabulous Lobster Trap. On Dominion Day Sunday, stepping out our backdoor to walk to St. Matthew's United Church, my younger sisters and I happened upon Chris Cody's recent vomit, some of which had fallen through the porch slats, but most of which was still intact, congealed in a kind of fractal dispersion pattern, swirls and streaks emanating from a wet epicentre not far from an unfortunately situated Malibu Skipper doll. Chris Cody was found in his clothes in our basement bathtub, Uncle Lorne in the wicker armchair, and our family's station wagon on a sidewalk on Barrington Street, the passenger's side of the vehicle wrapped around a utility pole. My father, not known for his severity, grounded Uncle Lorne for the rest of the summer and grimly recommended he seek out a better class of companion than Christopher Cody, who had been driving the car.

"Commander Cody has crash-landed," my uncle said afterwards in his Boris the Spider voice. "He will be flying with his Lost Planet Airmen no more. He has been marooned on the Red Planet. Commander Cody, over and out."

My sister Bonnie was blunt in her relief. "Thank God—that guy was such a gook."

"A *gook*?" Uncle Lorne said, in his normal voice. "Bitsy, do you even know what a gook is?"

Bonnie used the term as she and Carolyn always did—to mean an awkward or unseemly person. "Chris Cody's a gook," said Bonnie, flatly.

"No, Bitsy," said my uncle, with some impatience. "A gook's a Viet Cong. As in Victor Charlie. As in they *were* blown up with gelignite. Why don't you get that straight?"

THAT WEDNESDAY there was no race home after the paper route. Uncle Lorne's mood precluded it. He chain-smoked all the way back to Tower Road, preoccupied and changed. In the last few years, I'd noticed divagations. For most of my youth, Uncle Lorne was the lilting fall of the Byrds' high harmony line in "Mr. Tambourine Man." He was the kid staring with steady excitement at the movie poster for *The Endless Summer*. He was that brief half-second when he dipped his face forward before clearing his bangs from his eyes with a flick of the head. But now—now he was no longer the sort of candid, open-air kid you might approach on your first day in the Scout Troop or the Soccer Skills camp. He was no longer a kid. In one moment he was my colleague and pal, ironing the creases out of a *Teen Titans* comic or giving me the stick of bubble-gum from his baseball cards, and the next he was bringing home a fluorescent black light to place above a felt poster, or watching a Bruce Lee movie marathon, his dark bangs so swoopy and shaggy they barely allowed for a sightline. By July of that year Uncle Lorne had become a longhaired freaky person, a hippie in a hemp poncho and bell-bottoms fraying beneath the soft heels of his suede Adidas sneakers. He was reedy, gangly, finishing a surge of growth that put him well over six feet, taller by far than Dompa or my father. He was still proudly himself, equal to any context, unsurprised by developments great and small, but he was losing interest. Just as I was beginning to really read and appreciate and care for *The Justice League of America*, Uncle Lorne couldn't care less. For a while his curiosity was stayed by the Marvell Comics universe, especially the metaphysics and Kirby dots of *The Silver Surfer*, a loner adrift in the cosmos, as well as the Kirby titles started at DC, *The New Gods* and *Mister Miracle*, but his previous absorption was no longer evident. It was an effort for him to dream the superheroes, when before they'd sort of dreamed him. His thoughts entered their mythology only when my presence reminded him. "This place, Kink," he said to me on that walk home, dropping a last cigarette on the sidewalk and scuffing it out with his sneaker. "This burg—" He sighed as if unable to delay a judgment that had become screamingly obvious. "It's like living in the Bottle City of Kandor. It's so cut off, it's bogus. It's beyond bogus. It's so bogus, it's rogus. It's an embarrassment of rogusness. And everywhere fossified. Fwa!"

Arriving at our house, we saw my mother had left a note taped to the door, "Dinner at the Abbotts! Love Mom." There'd been considerable interplay between the two households since the solstice. My sisters Faith and Katie were turning seven and five that summer and September and Autumn Dawn were turning six and four—and so best-friendships were made fast and fixed. It worked for my mother not only because she was in *Midsummer* every evening but because she was rehearsing a new play during the afternoon, something called *Godspell,* so she was at the theatre day by day by day, from eleven in the morning to eleven at night. When he wasn't in New Brunswick volunteering at a summer camp, Mr. Abbott was building sets for *Godspell,* so Mrs. Abbott became the go-to parent for both families, a responsibility she met with deliberate composure. Of the two, it was Mrs. Abbott who seemed to me saintly. Vivien Abbott was the calm of a Peter, Paul and Mary song. She was slimness and silence and ovals. She wore her hair long and unstyled and parted in the middle, shaping her face in the oval of a cameo brooch. Soft on her nose were the side-lying ovals of her granny glasses. From her neck, a pendant swayed in elliptical arcs as she stirred a vegan stew made from backyard zucchini. Beside her, leaning against the kitchen wall, were two twin-arched gothic windows rescued from a falling-apart farmhouse, and, as she looked at us kids with calm, impassive eyes, supplying us with a very patient, open-ended expectancy, it was as if, in all her self-effacing ovals, *she* were somehow transparent—as if she were merely a frame through which to view the world. She was, on the contrary, at least to us kids, highly palpable for she conveyed in an instant her respect for the aims underlying a child's inarticulacy, mystification, and helplessness. Vivien Abbott was one of those vigilant, soft-talking mothers who never had to raise her voice because children, sensing her intrinsic decency, never wanted to disappoint her. She went about braless in paint-flecked peasant smocks and overalls, sometimes the side-swell of a breast plumping into open sunlight. But Mrs. Abbott, and the Abbott family in general, acted as if nakedness wasn't anything to particularly panic about—a principle rather new to our street. For some reason she had a reputation as a free-thinker and radical—censures I tried not to hold in mind as I was worried they would lead to restrictions on our visits. Earlier in the summer she let September-and-Autumn-Dawn and Faith-and-Katie paint the kitchen furniture any way they wanted—I was sitting on a chair splashed with many colours—and I decided these kinds of experiments explained her reputation for licentiousness.

The Abbott's house, while not actually under construction, was primitively open concept. An interior wall had been partially demolished, plaster-and-planking standing by for the insertion of those gothic windows, and the place had the air generally of a workshop or folk art atelier. There was no real distinction, say, between Kitchen and Bedroom, where Autumn Dawn had forgotten three dinner bowls on a bedside table, or Painting Studio and Bathroom, where four silk-screened canvases were furled and stored in the plunger stand beside the toilet. Delivering the evening meal to Mr. Abbott in his garage workroom, it was not a shocker to pass a salamander's terrarium given pride-of-place in the middle of the dining room table, or to find the back steps littered with yarn-and-stick God's Eyes, or the backyard walkway strewn with books, where, for example, *Harry the Dirty Dog*, a long overdue library book, competed for space with two hardcover copies of *Zen and the Art of Motorcycle Maintenance*, an apt combination, as the day would have it. For Mr. Abbott, wispy in a denim shirt, wide-wale corduroy trousers, and Wallabee shoes, was working on cleaning and reassembling the Honda Black Bomber he and Mrs. Abbott had ridden to Canada six years before. Now, even to me, this looked like a never-ending side project, with all those parts and pieces lying on the floor, sacred relics of their fourteen-hundred-mile pilgrimage across the Allegheny and Appalachian mountains. But, as a single moth sputtered against the swaying light bulb that hung overhead, shadows forming and reforming under Mr. Abbott's eyebrows, I remember shivering with an augury of different days to come as Uncle Lorne, placing the bowl of zucchini stew on a plywood worktable, asked in an unusually clear and respectful voice if Mr. Abbott might like some help repairing the motorcycle.

GODSPELL IN OUR town was an event, a portent, an advent of the Sixties a few years after the decade had passed. Stages in Halifax were mostly determined by Noël Coward and George Bernard Shaw and, as my mother called them, "those jeezly Agatha Christie adaptations." My mother's loathing was a by-product of her rising animosity for Dawson Redstone, the artistic director of Neptune Theatre, a cunning Yorkshire man from whom she got, or sometimes didn't get, parts in plays. But these pommy, cobwebby dramatic choices faded into the shadows beside the bright lights of *Hair* and *Jesus Christ Superstar* and *Godspell*. My mother was forbidden to audition for *Hair*. Regardless of the purity of the work's vision, my father thought it professionally questionable to pursue a situation whereby a client might hire a lawyer in the morning only to see that same lawyer's wife "flouncing naked downstage" later that night. A deepening feud with Dawson Redstone precluded involvement in *Superstar*. But *Godspell*, the Broadway soundtrack for which was rarely off our living room turntable, set off my mother's sense of possibility and vocation. Now in the newsreels of my mind, my father often appears in black and white. There he is in skinny suit and tie, holding a swaddled Carolyn for her christening photo. Or there he is in a formal grey-toned studio portrait to mark his appointment to Queen's Counsel. Or there he is in a white-bordered snapshot where he seems to be giving the toast to the bride in the dining room at the Waegwoltic Club. But the images of the 1970s were suddenly free of borders and crowded instead with perky instamatic colours, just as the designs of the day were crowded with starbursts and poppies and flowers. My father's concession to this freedom was to grow—for a few months—frizzly sideburns and to acquire, while on vacation in Antigua, an absurdly-speckled batik sports jacket that he was permitted to wear in continental North America exactly once. But my mother's response was manifold. My mother came of age in the 1950s when Doris Day was the very model of the modern wife-and-mother. When a social situation required my mother to be on her best behavior, she went first to her Doris Day routine. She twinkled with good humour, good will, and good grace—with what a young woman thought was pleasantly expected of her in Polite Society. There was a pressure of unsaid opinion, yes, most often released in the steam of an awkward pause or an abrupt turn in topic. This implied what was thought but was never directly stated, so, moving on, no one need feel embarrassed. My sister, Faith, thinking later on this distillation process, would say, "You could never say anything bad with those ladies but the truth would always come out in a kind of backhanded compliment—making everyone feel weird and uncomfortable anyway." Now my mother, after managing five pregnancies and six children, more than once blew a gasket. "Motherhood sucks," was her postpartum remark when bringing home a final baby from the Grace Maternity. But her policy in public—in her mind—was always on the safe side of convention. She was a 1950s mom stranded in the 1970s. But meeting Vivien Abbott (and to a lesser extent another woman, Madge Wicker, who lies outside the purview of this current history) changed my mother, adjusted her understanding, and moved her to consider new schemes altogether. Why should she have hors d'oeuvres and dinner prepared every night at six o'clock—hurrying home to float olives and sliced radishes in a cut-glass water dish? Why should she be the one to ferry the kids to gymnastics and piano and soccer? There was an informal Sunday drop-in session at the Abbotts and, with *Godspell* up and running, my mother began attending what Gregor Burr, a colleague of my father, described as "some leftist, radical women's lib bullshit." How much value my mother saw in Vivien Abbott's steadfast logic and fair-mindedness I don't know, but these meetings appealed to something not yet fully formed in her character and my mother, who for various reasons was always looking for the other half of her personality anyway, began not only to question the assumptions and conditions of her life but to cast around for a means to transform them.

ALL OF THIS BELONGED, of course, to the doings of the adult world, a parallel universe a ten-year-old boy did his best to disregard. I kept to my crafts and sullen arts, mostly on the lookout for mutant zombies, radioactive spiders, and the remains of the space rocket that had brought me here to Earth. Charging recklessly down the basement stairs, I touched only the steps that didn't creak. This meant leaping the bottom three stairs and immediately somersaulting—purely as a means to dissipate the tremendous shock of impact. This feat accomplished, I swung my hand into the darkness of the rec room, not wanting to be ambushed by supervillains, found the wall-switch and flicked on the overhead light. Satisfied I was alone, I turned the television on and, in a show of private athleticism, jumped backward into the wicker armchair. There settled, I began to consider my future with the cast of the PBS series *Zoom*. They were not the Justice League, true, but there was a costume of a sort (blue-and-maroon striped shirt, bare feet) and one did have to bring to the side one's own signature power, witness Bernadette's arm-swinging thaumaturgy. My musings were interrupted by my sister Bonnie. She walked between me and the glowing television, flicking the pull-tab of an unopened can of Fresca.

"What are you doing?" I asked. "I said 'reserve.' And I'm sitting down."

"You can't watch TV right now. You have to water the ficus."

"What ficus?"

"If you don't water the ficus, it will die. And you're supposed to fill the humidifiers. Mom said."

"She's not home."

"She will be. She's coming home for the family meeting."

I said I didn't know about any family meeting, but even if I did, there was no knowing for certain I would be there.

"Oh you'll be there," said Bonnie. "Everyone has to be there."

Continuing my own line of reasoning, I explained that people might be surprised by what I could do. If, for example, I decided I wished to become a professional decathlete and compete in the Montreal Olympics, then how did anyone know for sure I wouldn't *win* the Montreal Olympics? Obviously they didn't. I was unpredictable.

"Yeah, like you'll go to the Olympics," said Bonnie. "You can hardly run. You'll probably never be able to run like a normal person. And you're supposed to get a hip replacement when you're thirty-five. That's what the doctor told Mom. The orthopedic surgeon. So you probably won't win anything."

This interpretation did not exactly square with my own plans for myself and, in a gesture of correction, I slapped at the can of Fresca in Bonnie's hand, sending it flying toward the wall where it collided with a metal bracket on the exposed underside of the folded-up ping-pong table. The can was now spinning on the carpet, a thin mist of Fresca spraying from a dented perforation in its centre.

Bonnie watched it for a moment, unmoved, then addressed me with matter-of-fact sangfroid. "You're paying for that."

I said I was not.

"You're getting me a new one. You're replacing it."

I said if I wanted, I could *run* to the store and replace it. I just didn't happen to want to run to the store at the moment.

"You couldn't run to the store."

I said of *course* I could run to the store—and back—and faster than she could ever dream of running to any store anywhere in all the worlds of the universe.

Bonnie gazed at me, unconvinced. "You want to make a bet?"

THE PROPOSED RACE is to The Little General, a grocery store and ice cream dispensary whose storefront is decorated with a bootleg Cap'n Crunch figure. It is on Spring Garden Road, not an insurmountable distance for me, though going there and back almost doubles my recent Wednesday runs. Bonnie takes off like a shot. I choose a steadier pace, knowing that these "rabbits," as Uncle Lorne calls them, tend to peter out after their adrenalin subsides. But Bonnie does not peter out. She vanishes up Tower Road until her shirt is a speck of red wavering into invisibility. By the time I arrive at the store counter, Bonnie has come and gone, a localized ache is persistent in my every other step, and I am unable to keep from limping. Trying to stay focused on the race, I draw on my reserves of berserker rage. It lasts two blocks before a searing pain escapes from my hip, as if my pelvis is beginning to crack. On South Street, I stop running and swear at the sky, horrified by my inadequacy, crazed to be living on a planet where such injustice is allowed to occur. In a sulk, I do not finish the race, I wander aimlessly, and a half-hour later I am walking up the back steps with a pint of chocolate milk and a *G.I. Combat* comic. The backdoor, strangely, is ajar, the hallway empty. On the kitchen table, double strangely, a mug of coffee is still steaming and so is the meatloaf and rice on the seven served plates. I call out for my mother, my sisters, my uncle, my shouts wending their way from righteous confusion to plaintive unease to all-out horror as I hurry upstairs to the vacant second floor. In the bathroom, I turn off a hot water tap. There is not a soul in the house and only now do I recall previous evenings when we have been directed to the Abbotts for dinner. But ten minutes banging on their front and back doors rouses no light or movement. I am in the third stage of panic, my worried brain flashing with abduction scenarios, when our station wagon coasts up the street, everyone in it but me—the family meeting. Uncle Lorne, uncoiling himself from the back seat and stepping to the curb, is wildly overtaken by my youngest sister, Katie, in such a rush her yellow flip-flop is left on the grass behind her. "Oh, Aubrey!" she says, ecstatic. She hugs me around my waist, her head sideways at my elbow. "We're moving. We're getting a new house! It's *so* big. And everyone gets their own room. Even me!"

WE WOULD BE LEAVING the only home I'd known. The new house, on Dunvegan Drive, was not far from the Jubilee Road boat launch where Uncle Lorne and I strayed that June afternoon. It was a split-level modern place with brown wall-to-wall carpeting, white-painted rail banisters, all-new plastic windows. And it was big—the finished basement had five rooms of its own. There, us kids were given a rec room big enough for the TV, the now fully-opened ping-pong table, and the old living room stereo, an all-in-one Clairtone console. Carolyn had come home with the *Band on the Run* album and one evening I was listening to its title track, mesmerized by the spinning green apple of the centre label, headphones fully on my ears, when the ceiling lights flashed on and off—a phenomenon quickly connected to Bonnie's presence in the doorway behind me. "What are you *doing*?" I asked, talking over the music in my ears and indicating by my tone that I was moments away from all-out rage.

With tired officiousness, Bonnie informed me that I had to come upstairs for another family meeting.

"*Another* family meeting?" I took off the headphones. "What's it for?"

Bonnie left the rec room. "Didn't you hear? Mom's leaving Dad again."

"Who said that?"

Bonnie started up the stairs. "Because she wants to start her life over. She's leaving. You really didn't know, did you?"

I sat beside Faith and Katie in the barely-furnished living room, all of us on chairs pulled from the dining room. My youngest sisters' legs were not long enough to reach the floor, and their flip-flops swung hysterically back and forth as they tried to keep from crying, though their cheeks were wet with tears. The meeting was notable for their efforts to choke away their sobs, my parents chain-smoking menthol cigarettes, and the serious monologue that issued from my father as he informed the family that he and our mother would be separating in the next few days, explaining she would be moving to New York for an unspecified period of time. I stared at the systems of cigarette smoke as they rose and dissolved in the corners of the ceiling. Apart from numb surges of sympathy for my father, I wasn't sure what to feel, but I remember thinking it was repulsively inappropriate that Uncle Lorne was not present. He'd lived with us for eight years, as long as Faith had been alive, and, yes, he'd misbehaved but he'd been grounded for it, and to decide not to include him in such a family meeting seemed irresponsible and insensitive and just *wrong*. At that moment, as if ready for his entrance, Uncle

Lorne pulled open the side door. All of us in the living room went silent and for a few moments we listened to Uncle Lorne move about the new house. There was the sound of two brief nasal sniffs and the noise of him sorting through the most recently rerouted mail, before he went still, having heard Faith and Katie's sniveling.

My father called out, "Lorne, would you come in here a minute?"

Uncle Lorne stepped into our proceedings, shared a glance with my mother, and then, as if acknowledging a pre-existing understanding, simply shook his head and turned around and glided back out the side door.

I ran to him and found him on Jubilee Road smoking a cigarette in front of a telephone pole, his chin bobbing in time to some imaginary music. In his other hand, he held a packaged envelope from Passaic, New Jersey. "Whose race you running now, Grub?" he asked, smiling, contemplating me with amused affection. He carefully slid the comic books out of the package, showing me the team-up issue of the Justice League and Justice Society. "Crisis on Earth-X, Grub," he said, reading the issue's title and presenting me with my copy. The story was about a mix of superheroes sent through a dimensional transporter to an alternate world where the Nazis, having won that earth's Second World War, controlled everybody with a mind control ray. It was a bit much for me to absorb all at once and I asked to look at the other comics. Spying the distinctive checker-top of Silver Age DC comics, I realized with an excited jump that his new acquisitions finished a run of *Justice League* and that my uncle, Lorne Anthony Wheeler, was now in possession of a perfect, unbroken consecutive sequence of the *Justice League of America* from November 1960 to the present moment. There were rumours of two cousins in Dartmouth who had amassed a whole run, and a brother-and-sister team in Cape Breton who had all but the first three issues, but those were achievements shared by two people. Uncle Lorne had done it on his own, as he shifted from city to city to city, as he moved from his own family to ours. A collection started when he was seven years old, with a purchase at a Lawtons Drug Store in Truro, was now inviolably complete as of August 26, 1974. I asked about his plans—to complete another title? To put his *Justice Leagues* in a vault? "Negatory, Grubster," said Uncle Lorne, pushing his still-lit cigarette into a wrinkled crack in the telephone pole. He moved his gaze to look across the Northwest Arm, contemplating the far horizon, before speaking to me in a weary, exhausted voice, suggestive of his Boris the Spider diversion, but more as if he really *were* exhausted. "I don't think so. Time to exit the Batcave. Time to adios before the planet explodes. Time to get the hell out of Dodge."

"WHAT HAPPENED that summer?" my sister Faith would ask me many years later. "When Mom and Dad separated, that really shook me up. We were like the perfect frigging family. Mom and Dad's friends were shocked. Weren't you? I remember Mom saying she felt Dad was just checking things off. 'Get a law degree? Check. Get a job? Check. Get married and have kids? Check.' But without stopping to think what it would mean to her. I'm not sure that justifies running off with what's-his-nuts who played Jesus in 'Godspell.' That lunatic in the Winnebago. But do you know I have not seen Uncle Lorne since the day of the family meeting? Since that summer? He didn't come to Carolyn's wedding, did he? My God, do you blame him? Why would he? What a sin, the poor thing. It falls apart with Nanny and Dompa and he gets fobbed off on us. It falls apart with Mom and Dad and what's he going to do? Live with Aunt *Kate*? The poor bastard." Faith's choice of words was not consciously literal, and however treasonous it might have been to suggest in childhood, later evidence would point to such a conclusion, that someone beside Dompa was Uncle Lorne's father. What were Uncle Lorne's secret origins? I never knew. Even my father, keeper of a hundred of the city's secrets, may not have known. Uncle Lorne makes a cameo appearance in a Super-8 movie of Katie's fourth birthday. In that footage, he runs up to the birthday cake to smile prankishly at the camera, showing both sets of teeth, squinting from the incandescent camera light, before lightly kissing Katie and retreating off-screen. He must have been seventeen at the time and you could see how his features had elongated—eyes slanting, eyebrows darkening on the ridge above his nose—charismatically vampiric. He always had the dash and darkness of a nocturnal superhero like Deadman or Nightwing or Dr. Fate. It was only when this birthday film was transferred to video twenty years later that I saw with adult eyes, when he withdrew into the shadows, just how shy, how Asperger's-y, how *nervous* seventeen-year-old Uncle Lorne really was.

WHAT HAPPENED to my parents' marriage was happening everywhere. Divorce, a legal dissolution rather rare the generation before, rushed toward its 1970s statistical zenith. Many families were dissolving—there were crises on infinite earths—but this did not exactly reassure me. After reporting to a bearded child psychiatrist who asked rather over-placidly which parent I wanted to live with—and me not being able to answer—I lapsed into a surly, uncomprehending funk. Everything seemed in disarray and, as we began the exercise of unpacking in the new house on Dunvegan, I was noticing omissions. There was a yellow water pistol that had not made the move, a number of *Laugh-In* stickers, and, most ridiculously, Uncle Lorne's entire comic book collection. "We moved everything," Bonnie told me. "Carolyn said the old house is finished. There's nothing left but garbage."

"It's *not* garbage—"

"If it was in a box, Aubrey, it got moved. Did you check the basement? Why do you even care? They're just Mom's brother's old comics."

I began to explain the reasons why this collection was significant but, for whatever reason, my ideas came out all at once—emotional, jumbled, and, in anticipation of Bonnie's disapproval, abruptly defensive.

She regarded me with a mix of puzzlement and disdain. "I feel sorry for you," she said. "You're just like him—weird. You're going to be just like him—weird and alone with no friends and pathetic, loser."

Quite immediately I formed an interior resolution that my sister would have to be considered absolutely irrelevant if I wanted to preserve any of my own ideas about my life—and, in response to her last statement, I simply made for the side door and pushed it open.

"Where do you think you're going?" she asked. "You can't be like this if you live with us!"

I did not answer and, stepping outside, swung the door shut so it cracked the door's peek-through window. From inside the house, Bonnie asked again where I was going and, already sprinting away, I screamed I was going to the store to get her a Fresca—to get everyone in the world a fucking Fresca—*that's* where I was going. But I ran without knowing where I was going. I was passing by the Camp Hill cemetery before I realized, as some maple seeds helicoptered into my eyes, that the late summer evening had darkened into night. For some minutes my mind had been empty of self-awareness and turning the corner on Summer Street I eased into a single-pointed, euphoric state where I was, finally and simply and transcendently, running my own race. I arrived at our Tower Road house as the last hints of colour vanished from the sky. I went to the backdoor, where Chris Cody often banged to be let in, and turned my key in the old Otis lock. I stood a few moments in the back porch, my clothes damp with sweat, listening for cues to other occupants. Curiously, recalling the Mary Celeste moment of two months before, a plate of dinner had been left on a double-boiler but, as I could quickly see, the water had boiled dry and the meal was crusted and cracked and sticking to the plate. I turned off the burner and opened the unplugged refrigerator—four tins of Pepsi, a shriveled carrot, a jar of Dijon mustard.

I took a Pepsi, closed the refrigerator, and walked to the front hall. There was a trace of Mr. Clean in the air—a faint and bitter smell that made the few straggly details all the more hopeless and remote. The rooms were bare but here and there were a few abandoned expressions of our family. A plastic container of Kaopectate, a chalky medicine Carolyn swigged during exams, stood like a forgotten sentry on the front stairs. The fallen leaves of the departed ficus plant, whitened, dried, dead, trampled into the shag carpeting of the living room. At the end of the hallway, a mimeograph from Katie's kindergarten forgotten on the floor. I picked it up and saw it was a spelling test that had been folded into a paper fortune teller. Katie had made some effort to decorate it using a blue Flair marker. But all the verve of the home, all the dreams and desires, all the hopes and fears of all the years, of course all of these were gone. The Tower Road house was now some anonymous structure—hardwood floors, stained carpets, mottled walls where late Mrs. Abbott's silkscreens had hung. Turning from the living room, I opened the basement door and went down the stairs two at a time, calling for

Uncle Lorne. In the centre of his room, the fluorescent black light tube was stuffed in a metal garbage can along with a pillow, a broken model of a gun-boat, and his mauve Duo-Tang folder. I took a moment to open and drink my Pepsi, the taste from the tin mixing with the disturbed dust in the air of the basement. Then I dropped the tin into the garbage can and pulled out the Duo-Tang. Across from each entry, in Uncle Lorne's expert and miniature handwriting, was a dollar value for every comic book. At the bottom of each page was a tally and, flipping to the end, a grand total for the entire collection, the circled sum of thirty-four hundred dollars. He would not use any of the thirty-four hundred dollars for the motorcycle—the Abbotts, free-minded Americans, would give him that as a gift—and he spent very little as he motorcycled along the Trans-Canada, sleeping in camp-sites, staying with the Oldrings in Vermont, a cousin in Calgary. The purple of the Duo-Tang and the blue marker on Katie's paper fortune teller I found very calming, in the way that the colour combination of lilac and blue can calm you when your family is falling apart and you have no control over your future, and the colours recalled to me my experience of "Band on the Run" and so the song returned unbidden inside me, complete, continuous, the soundtrack to a few more moments of my summer, and in the upstairs hallway I found a bare mattress, diagonal on an empty floor, and fell on it, face down, my hands under my hips, and lay there, exhausted, sweat evaporating from my forehead, soon falling asleep, knowing I was absolutely alone for the first time in my life.

Fudge

ONE AFTERNOON WHEN I WAS NINE, I played a soccer game at Westmount School. This was the northernmost fringe of my known world, in a disorienting subdivision by the Halifax Shopping Centre. It was the last Sunday of the summer, the Sunday of Labour Day weekend, and we lost 3–2 in penalty kicks. I flubbed my shot and missed the net entirely. I was under family orders to bicycle home immediately following the game, before it got dark, but I was gloomy with defeat and I didn't like my bike. It was a girl's bike, a hand-me-down from my older sister—a blue CCM Rambler refurbished with a white banana seat. To me it looked like a clown's prop with the banana seat, no crossbar, and low handlebars.

I was embarrassed by it and waited till my soccer team left. I hadn't even locked it, half-hoping it would be stolen by a bored kid wanting a joyride or a junky contraption to push off the cliff of the railway cut. But my bike was still there after the game, on its side, and, as I picked it up and pushed it toward the school, clomping the mud off my cleats on the pavement, I noticed a group of kids congregated around the school courtyard. Some kids lingered in the corners. Others skittered on the roof. A boy with red hair stood in the centre with a not-fully-inflated soccer ball. But all attention was on another kid, maybe thirteen or fourteen, but older looking because he was fat and had a moustache. This kid trudged into the courtyard, dragging a Koho hockey stick.

At first I thought I was watching a low-energy street fight or the aftermath of a street fight. The big kid with the hockey stick was pummelling people. The kid with the soccer ball was next. The kids on the roof had escaped. But it was just a game of stickball or a North End variant of stickball, sort of soccer baseball with a hockey stick. The kids in the corners were standing at improvised bases, the kids on the roof were outfielders, the kid with the soccer ball was the pitcher. And the fat kid was the batter. He wore a blue parka with a fur-lined hood, Kodiak boots, and brown corduroy pants. And, in the way that fat kids always seemed to wear pants too big for them, these brown cords drooped beneath his belly and hips. But unlike most fat kids, he didn't yank them up to hide the waistband of his underwear. He just let his pants droop, even though this would have constricted his batting motion.

He took aim on a pitch, swung viciously, and missed. From the rooftop came hoots and jeers. The soccer ball bounced back to the red-haired kid. Another pitch and the fat kid let it go by. There was some controversy whether this was a strike, whether the ball had caught the lower corner of a painted square on the brick wall behind him. But the fat kid shook his head and glared at the pitcher. Then he shoved some hair off his face and tightened his grip on the hockey stick. A kid on the roof said "Fudge" and this word got chanted over and over, in tones of irony and fear, and I realized with a shiver of alertness that the fat kid with the hockey stick was Howard Fudge—*the* Howard Fudge. The name was a distant legend to me, like Beowulf or Dirty Ernie or Billy the Kid, and before this afternoon I wasn't sure if Howard Fudge actually existed or if he was just some mythological creature my uncle invented to torment me. But here he was, Howard Fudge, the toughest kid in the North End, a kid who told teachers to fuck off, who pissed in the gas tanks of cop cars in the police station parking lot, who crashed a Toyota Celica into the Hyland movie theatre when he was *twelve*, Howard Fudge, a fearless kid liable to do anything to anybody—here he was at Westmount School playing stickball with a bunch of little kids on the last Sunday of the summer. Something in my look or posture must have advertised my new knowledge because I felt Howard Fudge's attention on me at this point, noticing me for a first time, and I thought to preoccupy myself with some detail of my soccer uniform, as if I might be troubled by the top of my shin guard. When I looked up, the last pitch was in the air and I saw Howard Fudge smack it into the sky, sending the soccer ball above us all, over the heads even of the kids on the roof. As those kids scrambled to retrieve it, Howard Fudge looked at me and lobbed the hockey stick in my direction. It clattered into the front spokes of my bicycle. I stared at it, my heart turning to panic, then I ignored Howard Fudge, got on my girl's blue bike and pedaled off, head down, legs pumping.

Safely away from Westmount School, I was puzzled by a few particulars. Why was such a big kid playing with little kids? Was he bored? Were his real friends somewhere else? What would I have done if Howard Fudge wanted to fight me? And were those Westmount kids Bad Kids? I thought further of Bad Kids. The boy who said the F-word outside my bedroom window when I was four, and the teenagers who smashed my mother's flower planters in the middle of the night, and the kids in the Halifax Forum parking lot who smoked cigarettes and threw rocks at people they didn't know. What happened to these kids that made them think their behaviour was appropriate? Why did they do the things they did? But as the summer day dimmed and twilight began and as I rattled into the leafy streets of the South End, those questions fell away and I was left with the one idea I would remember to report to my sisters and uncle. Howard Fudge was real and I had seen him. I had seen that he was capricious and odd and bullying but, like kids everywhere, filled with his own kinds of folly and truth and instincts and humour.

THREE YEARS LATER and my parents have separated again. My father resides in the new Dunvegan house with my two older sisters. When she returns to Halifax, my mother moves into a place on Larch Street with my two younger sisters. I am the middle kid and shuttle between households, living mostly with my father, excepting furloughs when, sleeping bag in hand, I troop over to my mom's new flat. It's an improvised existence and I am unsure how to adapt to the rearranged reality of shared custody. I know I'm supposed to pretend everything will be fine, but my known world has been distorted—certainly my notions of my known world have been distorted. Though I walk the same streets I've always walked, past houses where inside my friends are indifferently watching *Happy Days*, for me it's as if a few land mines have detonated beneath the city somewhere. The landscape seems altered and desolate. I am often alone in my new room, tracing a *Kamandi* comic or scanning the TV listings for comedy movies. I find the unsupervised freedom distantly oppressive and, as I wait for a new normal to emerge, I reassure myself that my life is only somewhat suspended and that moments of fulfillment and euphoria are still possible.

It is with the candle of this idea gleaming in my imagination that you find me now, in Grade 8, at work in the kitchen of my father's house. The night is Halloween and I still imagine that Halloween can transform and transport me—which is why I have spent four hours devising my most complicated costume ever. Underneath, I wear white. Over this base, I wrap toilet paper, paper towels, adhesive tape, tensor bandages. From my sisters, I borrow a purple lip pencil and darken my eyes. From my mother, I take Stein's stage blood and squirt it into my sockets and nostrils. I thread authentic plaster cast bandages around my eyes and head. In the hall mirror, I am pleased with the effect and stepping out the door at six o'clock, I am sure I am among the most fully-achieved Mummy costumes in the district.

At six-thirty, when a storm spills the remains of a gale on our coastal city, I am less sure. Within ninety seconds, instead of being costumed as a fearsome mummified ghoul, I am essentially walking around in long underwear, a sopping white turtleneck, and covered in decomposing toilet paper—with now lumpy, now heavy bits of plaster stuck to my head and hair. There is still good candy to be got, I know, but I am not sure whether I will be among those who collect it. Cowering at a bus shelter on Inglis Street, I watch the storm blow rain sideways, batter treetops, snap phone wires, before mysteriously lapsing to drizzle and fog. In another minute, the clouds clear, the air grows moist and mild, the sky lightly violet. The city now has a freshly diluvial quality—sidewalks wet with fallen leaves, intersections a slurp of mulch and broken branches—as if flood waters have newly receded and it wouldn't be absurd to see a dolphin stranded in the top branches of a spruce tree there.

I leave the safety of the shelter and decide to cut through the backfields of Gorsebrook and Saint Francis junior high schools. From there it is only twenty minutes to my mother's flat where I am due this night. In an almost buoyant mood,

I crest the last and steepest hill to behold in the field below a skirmish of unknown kids. They are older, with cigarettes, and I worry immediately that these are the Halloween kids who egg houses and smash pumpkins and steal UNICEF boxes. They are North End kids—I recognize one from a remote Scout troop—free-ranging far from their normal territory. To see them on Gorsebrook Hill is like seeing a wolf pack on a golf course. I think about returning the way I came and simply getting myself home on the sidewalks but I want to see what's going on. Two boys throw rolls of toilet paper at each other. Another tries to write his name with lighter fluid in the baseball infield. For some minutes, I watch a kid in a red down-filled jacket on a ten-speed bike. Racing down the slope of the teacher's parking lot, he jumps the ten-speed off the lip of the pavement and tries to forward flip himself, still on the ten-speed, onto the grass of the baseball diamond. He fails each of three times I watch him—the bike splattering on the ground, a pedal coming loose, spokes popping—but with his spirits undaunted. If anything, he seems excited by disaster. The boy is fearless, reckless, and, I would later learn, drunk out of his mind on pure ethyl alcohol stolen from the children's hospital. I am passing scared to see such kids, and I keep close to the wire-linked fence that runs down one side of the hill, my head lowered, my strategy to be a solitary fly-by-night stranger. Halfway down, in the furthest outfield of the baseball diamond, I see candy scattered in the soaked grass: a Charms Blow Pop, a two-piece pack of Chiclets, a tiny green Aero bar. I am reaching for the Aero bar when Howard Fudge stumbles out of the high bushes near the fence. He clutches a twenty-six ouncer of rum and brings it to his mouth to drink. As he chugs almost half the bottle I see he's wearing essentially the same costume—blue parka, faded T-shirt, brown cords, Kodiak boots. The only concession to the holiday is a pirate's eye patch, flipped up on his forehead, and what looks to be regulation handcuffs dangling from his belt buckle. In his free hand he drags a grimy and tattered black garbage bag—the source, I realize, of the scattered candy. "A little of the Captain Morgan tonight," says Fudge, wiping his mouth with the sleeve of his parka. "Whoa, fuck. That's going through me. Probably have to puke again." He grabs my pillowcase of candy. "What do you got for me? What do you got? I don't like these. I like these." Fudge ruptures a bag of Hickory Sticks and feeds his mouth with sticky fingers. "Hey, kid. You want some gum? Bubble Yum?" He turns to scream at the baseball diamond. "Johnny! Get over here!" He looks again at me. "What's your name?"

"McKee."

He gropes in his garbage bag and produces an unopened pint of vodka. "Okay, McKee." He passes me the bottle. It feels heavy in my hand. "Here's a mickey of Smirnoff I ain't drinking tonight. Trick or treat. Smell my feet. Think you can drink that mickey?"

"McKee."

"Uh-huh."

"Why do you have handcuffs?"

"Don't ask questions you don't want to know the answers to."

"But where'd you get them?"

Fudge sniffs. "I rolled a cop."

A kid comes over—it's the red-haired kid who's been trying to flip the ten-speed into the baseball diamond. A plastic Halloween mask hangs around his neck.

"Johnny, this is Mickey," says Fudge. "And Mickey, this here's Johnny Red." With a swing of his chin, Fudge indicates the parking lot. "Trish still here?"

Johnny Red shrugs.

"How far'd you get?" asks Fudge.

"Farther than you," says Johnny Red. "I fingered her."

"The fuck you did." Fudge drinks some rum and looks at Johnny, suspicious. "You don't even know what fingering is! Does he, Mickey? Tell him, Mickey."

I begin to explain that to finger someone is to touch them or caress them but Fudge doesn't let me finish because he has started laughing, a high-pitched giggle that could just as easily come from a six-year-old.

"That's not what fingering means, Mickey," he says. "Fingering is when you stick your finger in the girl's twat." He giggles again. "Johnny, you better take care of Mickey here. Make sure he gets home all right. But keep your hands to yourself." Fudge chugs the rest of the rum and biffs the empty bottle at the fence. It bounces off the wires and disappears in a tangle of weeds. As Fudge stumbles down the hill, Johnny takes my pillowcase of candy. He is considering a bag of ketchup chips when I offer him the vodka.

"Hey, thanks," says Johnny Red, finding nothing unusual in my offer. And as he twists off the sealed cap, I realize I've seen Johnny Red a few times before. He was the pitcher in the stickball game at Westmount School. And last year I'd seen him speed down the sideline and score a left-footed goal in the Under-14 soccer championship—which was when I learned he was also a skateboarder, track star, and provincially-ranked kickboxer. With his wavy red hair, sun-lit blue eyes, and chipped front tooth, Johnny Red is a locally famous pretty boy, the kind of kid who only has to lean against a tree and girls discover him. Teenybopper girls, my younger sisters among them, will ring his family's doorbell simply to get him to come to the door. "You know Johnny Red?" I'll be asked later. "You seriously *know* him?" His real name is Jonathan

Boutilier, that last word a once-elegant Acadian surname, four-syllable music like *bibliothèque—Bou-til-i-er*—but over the generations the name has been bluntly Anglicized to rhyme with root beer.

Johnny has two gulps of the vodka and returns it to me. "Thanks, Mickey," he says, his eyes going wide. "Hey, you want to get hit by a car?"

I ask what that means.

"Well, it's fucking amazing," says Johnny, exhilarated. "Fudge gets these old beater cars and comes after us, right? Tries to hit us when we're running? Last night the bumper caught me right here and—" He points to his thigh. "Boom! Just a little bump but I went fucking flying! I been hit by a car must be the last three weeks in a row. You got to try it. It's pretty jackass but it's a fucking rush, I'll say that."

Someone yells for Johnny. The kid who has been trying to spell his name with lighter fluid has succeeded in setting a garbage can on fire. Seeing this, Johnny runs to join him, not a care in the world. I am left with most of my candy and a half-pint of vodka. I have smelled beer, which is marshy and foul, and tasted red wine, which is tannic and adult, but vodka's cold colourlessness puzzles me. What do I do with a half-pint of vodka? I drop it in the grass. Take a step. Go back. Open it. And, with the flicker of a distant fire in my peripheral vision, I down five fingers of vodka on Halloween night in wet long underwear on Gorsebrook Hill. I am twelve years old. Immediately, I feel a furious medicine loose in my system. I'm hot, cold, sloppy, tight. The growing sense of contamination frightens me and the next thirty minutes are a half-colour dream sequence of fast-approaching curbs, unstable crosswalks, a chestnut in street water vanishing down a gutter grate, and finally I arrive home, stone drunk, my pillowcase of candy quite empty except for, what I will discover later, almost hidden in the mix of chip crumbs and peanut shells, a single hardened piece of chocolate.

MY FRIENDS HAD NAMES like Timmy and Tommy and Ranald. Fudge had friends with names like Johnny Red and Sneaky and Frenchy Burger. There were also Surging Herman, String Bean, Sully, Big Fish, Beasley, Bubbles, Fuzz-Head, Chug-a-Lug, and someone called Blomgren. He called me Mickey. Nicknaming was an easy invention for Fudge and these names indicated the kind of cartoon fraternity he lived in, or wanted to live in, and I list them in such detail because I copied them down as I heard them. In these pubescent years, I carried with me an extra copy of *Watership Down*—I'd received three copies at Christmas—and in its blank flyleaves I scribbled lists and jokes and doodles of werewolves. Fudge's nicknames belonged to people from an alternate Halifax, a Halifax outside the scheme of the city as I knew it. This was a place of rogue adolescents who wandered university campuses for fun and profit, rink rats who scrambled around the stands of the Halifax Forum, hoodlums who hung out all day in the Scotia Square food court. These places in turn seemed linked to the mythology of an older, grey-misted Halifax—that there was, say, a secret undersea tunnel between the Old Town Clock and Georges Island. Or if you wore green on Thursdays it meant you were gay and going to Citadel Hill to be gay with other gay people. Or that there were twenty-six Volvos on the bottom of Bedford Basin. This was all some years ago now, back in a Halifax of stubby bottles of Ten Penny and foil-lined bags of Scotties potato chips, when slush on a store's foundation might melt away to reveal a cloth election sticker for Robert Stanfield. The city seemed then a more pluralist place, home to twisting streets, hopscotch kids, clapboard houses—a folk expression of the Maritime demotic. The houses are still there, of course, painted mimosa now with teal trim, front façades appointed with brass carriage lamps and decorative flower boxes. But I liked those selfsame wooden Victorian houses precisely because of the missing shingles and peeling paint and sagging porch stairs—when a side door might lead to a draft dodger from Virginia needing a gram of hash. Or grad students wanting acid for a house party. Or a women's macramé group refilling an order of pot. Delivering drugs was a new kind of paper route for me, it brought me into landings I could never have imagined, and Fudge was the ferryman into these underworld ports of call. He steered me into a Halifax I didn't know was there.

As those nicknames attest, Fudge was keen on fellowship and enjoyed his role as King of the Bad Kids, but I wondered if the rumours were true, and surely they were, that he was directed by an impulsive and violent temper. In the beginning, I certainly believed he was unstable and dangerous and I behaved as if sooner or later he was going to punch me in the head—there was always a looming sense that Fudge was going to punch you in the head. I don't know how he himself understood it. I think he liked his reputation of unpredictability. No one on the street could guess what he was going to do or how he was going to do it. Fudge had his own feral way of seeing things, his own Fudge-logic, Fudge-skepticism, Fudge-fairness. Once on Wellington Street he stared sadistically, or what I took to be sadistically, at a cat that had been run over by a motorcycle. It was crushed, belly ripped open, a squooge of intestines seeping through the lining of its stomach. Fudge scuffed it with his boot, then picked it up with a newspaper and flipped it into the trash—a gesture I've always remembered for its grace and harsh necessity. It was sometimes tricky to divine what Fudge noticed and what he didn't so it was with uneasy pride that I learned he liked my mother, who was now living three doors away from Fudge's mother on Larch Street. "You're old lady's a hoot, Mickey. She's a real spark-plug." Both women were newly-single and living in rented flats, which explains why I met Howard Fudge a third time, after Westmount School and after Halloween, when visits to our mothers coincided.

I was in the backyard trying to coax my sister's runaway kitten out from under a patio when Howard Fudge, now a burly sixteen-year-old, slogged through the alders behind the back fence. "Hey Mick," he said casually, as if we'd seen each other only moments before. He told me he'd been waiting an hour for Johnny Red at the Horsefield, an area of woods and baseball diamonds near the Coburg Road railway cut. "Fucking Johnny," said Fudge. "Always late. *Always*."

I asked where they were going.

Fudge jerked his head to one side. "We're supposed to buy this ounce and Johnny's nowhere to be found. So now what am I supposed to do? Jesus." He leaned over the back fence, reflective. "Hey Mickey," he said, looking up at me. "You got any money?"

WHAT DOES A TWELVE-YEAR-OLD KNOW? I'm taking tennis lessons? Oh, that makes sense. Probably I will win Wimbledon. I've been given my sister's guitar? Sure. Because music is my destiny. I'm going in on an ounce of Panama Red? I have no *idea* what that means. But I can normalize it because a kid can normalize anything. A year before, I inherited my uncle's afternoon newspaper route and I've been saving to buy a rare Batman comic but these savings I choose to give to Howard Fudge. Later that day, Fudge buys the ounce from someone called Blomgren and I am given my share, a baggie filled with thirty-seven joints. That Friday, we meet at a Sadie

Hawkins dance at the Convent of the Sacred Heart, a private girl's school on Spring Garden Road. When I arrive, Fudge and Johnny have sold out their stash. On the sidewalk outside the gates, I am swarmed by unknown kids. Grade 9 girls in Black Watch kilts are thrilled to see me. Everyone calls me Mickey. "Finally, Mickey gets here." "Thought you weren't going to show, Mick." "Mickey comes through in the clutch!" I sell each joint for two dollars and watch my vinyl wallet swell with other people's money. I gross seventy-two dollars on a thirty dollar investment and in that moment, counting all those wrinkled bills, I feel my identity morphing from Comic Book Nerd to Mysterious Stoner Outcast.

MY MOTHER WAS DATING. My father was sunk in work. My four sisters, as always, were obsessed with their friends and feuds. But the rest of the city glimmered curious with teenagers and it was with these possibly like-minded kin that I began to cast my fate. I saw an opportunity to lose myself in a world outside my own precincts and guessed that my association with Fudge would deliver me into new circumstances and new vocabularies of being. "You want to smoke a spliffy? Spark up a hoolie? Whoa. This shit's strong. You sure that's homegrown? Fuck, I am *baked*. Want this roach?" These years marked a time, too, when I understood it wasn't desirable to do well in school. School-smart was a liability. It was better to smoke dope and drink Bacardi and suck the butane out of a Bic lighter so you could spew it on a lighted match—*fwoosh*—blowing flames like a carnie. In the space of ten months I would forget all about The Justice League and polynomials and *The Tempest* and fill my days with whip-its and bong hits and Sudafed, Pink Floyd and Purple Jesus and Blue Microdot, dazzled to move through such candy-coloured rainbows.

SCENE. FRIDAY EVENING IN FALL. Fudge and I dawdle on the railway tracks beneath the South Street railway bridge. It is dusk and getting cold in the way a December day gets cold—bleak orange sun, wind chilling our noses, stiffening our fingers. Fudge is in his blue parka, hands in his pockets. I shiver in a Lopi sweater and Davy Crockett jacket. Johnny, in his red down-filled jacket, is just now billy-goating down the jagged slate of the railway cut.

"Finally!" says Fudge. "Here comes the little faggot." He throws a grape Bubble Yum at Johnny. "You say you're going to be somewhere, you *be* there, buddy. If not, you call the guy to tell him you're going to be late. That's common knowledge, Johnny. Common fucking knowledge."

"Better late than never," says Johnny, walking on one of the rails.

"What?" says Fudge, his reply more like *whuh* to indicate his rising frustration. "Grow the fuck up, Johnny. Be normal for once."

"Only human."

"Then be a normal human for once." Fudge carefully lights a joint and passes it to Johnny. "See? I handed it to you like a normal person because I'm going to be a normal person when I grow up. What're you going to be when you grow up, Johnny?"

Johnny thinks about that. "A stunt driver. Or a cop."

"Oh, Johnny," says Fudge. "You'll probably go to car wash school. Or be a hairdresser in Toronto, won't he, Mickey?"

"No," says Johnny, stubborn. "I want to be something." He sucks on the joint. "Like a stunt driver. Or the chief of a prison."

"A *warden*, Johnny. It's called a warden."

"Hey," says Johnny. "I just seen this movie at Trish's about torture and shit in other countries."

"Is *that* where you were?"

Johnny presses his lips together, holding the smoke in his lungs. "But, oh man," he says, exhaling. "The shit they were doing in these chambers."

"Who's in it?"

"It was all unknowns. Anyway, they took you downstairs to these torture chambers with this spike? Of all places, you don't want to get tortured there."

"What kind of spike?"

"Hey," says Johnny, sucking on the joint and peering into the sunset. "You know the name of Elvis's plane?"

Fudge looks at him, baffled. "Elvis's *plane*?"

"Echo Poppa. You know all that Air Force language? Like your name would be, um, Hotel, Oscar—"

"Oscar?" Fudge giggles. He is fond of Johnny but the official party line is that Fudge is only moments away from losing all patience and punching Johnny's head in. "Johnny, that's enough. Put down the joint. Walk away from the joint. You're too high to talk to."

These are the aimless conversations of numberless nights and many of our get-togethers go absolutely nowhere. Most afternoons we smoke dope in Johnny's basement, fanatically listening to Genesis or Supertramp or Jethro Tull. Or we loiter outside a school dance. Or get chased off the St. Mary's University campus by the commissionaires. Then we walk home in the wetting drizzle, waiting always for some commotion to deliver us from our random teenage lives. Moods change—in the mercuriality of adolescence, relations flash from fear to boredom to laughter in a moment—but so little seems to *happen*. Drama, havoc, event, that's what we crave. Which is why I recall, in hallucinogenic detail, the rest of this October night. For it marks the first time I do real drugs, a great and visionary episode in my young life.

Under a darkening sky, we make our way along the railway cut to Point Pleasant Park, two hundred acres of wild at the city's southern tip, where a high school is presenting a student council sponsored event, a bonfire on the beach. I've heard of these affairs but I'm not prepared for the madding crowd of kids, the fires and drunkenness. Bushwhacking through trees, we meet in some hiding place known only to Fudge two girls sitting cross-legged on the forest floor, smoking and trading back and forth a jar of moose piss—a liquor brewed by blending steals from parents' cabinets. The first girl is Trish Blundell, Johnny's default girlfriend, and the second is Deb Smear. Now Deb Smear is stingingly cute—a Grade 8 girl in jean jacket and jeans, a red rose delicately embroidered on each rear pocket—and probably the most flagrantly sexualized person I've seen up to that time. Certainly I have never seen anyone wear jeans as tight as she does, and I study her when she isn't looking at me. Which is most of the time.

Deb Smear is the queen of a phylum I am to meet later in multitudes, teenage girls in eye shadow and lip gloss, feathered hair lightened by a bottle of drugstore Sun-In, often drunk, sweet, from places like Fairview or Spryfield or East Chezzetcook. Deb Smear is from even farther, a settlement called Shad Bay, and the place-name frightens me for it evokes a No Man's Land of beer empties, abandoned Dairy Queens, and grounded fishing boats. And yet from these rural routes springs someone like Deb Smear, a creature who radiates powers of instantaneous self-assurance and allure. I wonder about these girls—they are mysterious and complicated in ways I can't divine. Gorgeous in dangly earrings. Sharing a bottle of Southern Comfort. Talking, drinking, flirting. Making out with someone. Crying over someone else. Wiping dribble off their chin. Pulling up their jeans. Stumbling, mumbling, plastered. Passing out, mouths open, stomachs pumped.

"Took you long enough," says Deb Smear, standing up. She looks at me, skeptical. "Who's that?"

"This is Mickey," says Fudge, with little enthusiasm. "He's all right. It's his first bonfire. And Mickey, this is Titless."

"Don't *call* me that!" Deb Smear swats Fudge with an open hand. "You don't call your girlfriend that, you fucking asshole."

"I mean," says Fudge, making a put-upon smirk. "This is Little Debbie."

"You don't call me that either! Johnny never calls Trish names like that. Have some respect for once in your life." Fudge says nothing. Deb Smear fishes in her rear pocket and brings out a pack of Players Lights. "So this is your first bonfire, hey, Mickey?" She picks out a cigarette. "Your first hootenanny?" Before she lights the cigarette, she looks to Trish with a sneer of curled lip, perhaps the beginning of a wicked smile or simply a blasé expression of boredom, I can't tell. It is a masterpiece of ambiguity and I notice how Deb Smear speaks out of the side of her mouth, her lips quivering with small movements, as if she's full of secrets, as if there are things she knows I'll never guess.

I ask if the hootenanny means there'll be banjos.

Deb Smear finds my question hysterically funny and from her mouth comes an absurdist guffaw. She bends over, laughing, and twists her head to look at Fudge. "Your friend's pretty funny, Fudge-stone."

Fudge makes a this-is-what-I-have-to-put-up-with look and produces a Ziploc baggie. Inside are dark little shapes, like pieces of cereal. "Ever done shrooms before, Mickey?"

"I want one!"

"Calm down, Deb," says Fudge. "I'm trying to explain something here." He wraps a mushroom in an empty Bubble

Yum wrapper and gives it to me. "You take one and chew it and wherever you're trying to get to, fifteen minutes later, you're there."

I put it in my pocket.

"Now me," says Deb Smear. She takes a mushroom, pops it in her mouth, and spins to me. "Maybe there's banjos, Mickey, we don't know. But you can bet your ass there'll be something. Fucking right there'll be something. You're in for a ride now, buddy-boy. Because there's always a party with me and Trish on the go. Never a dull moment when we're around. We're action. We make action happen. We're it."

And so the five of us, along with hundreds of others, traipse down to the sea, swarming toward a convergence of desire and event, wanting the moment to rush in and deliver us into our futures. It is a bonfire for a city high school, the night before a football game, and I imagine the student council at one time intended a pep rally and weenie roast around one of the fire grates on the beach. At ten o'clock when we arrive there are four hundred kids and three fires, two of them blazing wild. I am selling my mushroom to a boy I know from Sunday school when I see Fudge heave a very solid-looking picnic table over the beach rocks and up-end it into the nearest bonfire. It soon belongs to the biggest fire I have so far witnessed, crackling fierce, sending billowing sparks fifty feet into the night. And where's Johnny Red? There's Johnny Red, falling out of a pine tree. I watch him drop fifteen feet, carom off a thick branch near the bottom, and bounce into the flames of the smallest fire before rolling into the sneakers of a Grade 11 girl. He is springing up, eager to climb another, when the first police vehicle bumps along the shore road toward the fires. "Paddy wagon!" comes the cry. "Paddy wagon!" I look for the kid from Sunday school but he's vanished. The whole congregation is vanishing because if the cops catch you with drugs or alcohol, you will spend the rest of the night in the Drunk Tank, a call made to your parents in the morning.

Quickly I eat the mushroom and race after Johnny. For twenty minutes I run through the woods like a commando in a war, struggling to keep up, dry branches slashing at my cheek, my boot-bottoms slipping on pine needles. Ahead of me, Johnny takes to hiding behind trees, then jumping out to tackle me, screaming, joking, happy. We arrive back on the railway tracks to find Fudge, Deb Smear, and a kid with a wineskin named Veeper. He passes the wineskin to me and I squeeze a mix of gin and Kool-Aid into my mouth, tripping from the mushroom. I smell trees and thorns and the reek of freezing dirt. Collapsing to the ground, I pick at the frosted dew on the railway—a sensation that starts in my mouth a taste of rust and stones and sullen earth. I imagine thousands of dead Halifax people sliding wet in Halifax graves, soil mucky with earwigs, glow-worms. Full in my nose I breathe the smack of creosote, a trace of withered autumn leaves, listening to the tones of Johnny's voice as he's interrupted by the prehistoric clittering of a flying beetle. Opening my eyes, I watch this beetle's flight through thistle tops and over the exposed gravel of the railway and imagine it rising to the black klim of sky where phantom crows chase higher air. All my ideas spin and spread into the sky, leaving me to wonder at this newfound religion and whether a single imagination might unite the universe. This is the last thought I register for I'll black out and puke hopelessly later that night in the back seat of Fudge's Ford Pinto as he drives me home. He carries me senseless to my father's house where my oldest sister takes me in. There deposited, I awake the next morning sick and feeble, staring at my bedroom ceiling, not sure where I've been, what has happened, if I will ever feel normal again.

FUDGE DIDN'T MIND ME puking in his car. In fact he never referred to it. Afterwards he would only remember how entertaining I was. "You should've seen Mickey the night he did mushrooms the first time. Fuck, that was comical. He gets there like, 'What's a dog? It's this thing that runs around for everybody.' You remember that, Mickey? Fuck, you were tripping. You're like, 'I understand trees for the first time. We used to be fish!' What a mind. Unbelievable. You wouldn't know it was the same person." He turned to me, smiling. "Oh, Mickey. You're a strange little guy. I couldn't figure you out for the longest time. Then I realized you're just shy. But you're all right. You're a pretty good head."

Howard Fudge liked me. I was part of his crew. He took me on his rounds. Fudge had freestanding memberships in a number of Halifax dives and flats and flophouses, most frequent among them a neglected dwelling on Willow Street, back when the neighbourhood was sketchy with broken glass and front-yard scrap. The backdoor on this house was corroded, tilting, wedged open with a red plastic Pop Shoppe crate. The door led into a back porch and kitchen and main floor where there was a cosmic abundance of pot, the green fank of smoked dope everywhere in that Willow Street house. In the bathroom, joints forgotten beside toothbrushes. In the shag carpet, dozens of dropped roaches. In the kitchen sink, knife-tips blackened from hash use. Over that winter, I would encounter in this house any number of hippies and Black guys and Celtic-looking riffraff, all men in their twenties and thirties and scary and cool and dangerous.

But that first afternoon, there is only one other person, someone called Blomgren. He has tangled blond hair and a blond beard—a General Custer look-a-like in a striped engineer's cap and Bruins jersey. He is friendly and jokey and acts as if he has a number of attractive options on the go. "Here comes the Fudge," he says when he sees us. In socked feet, Blomgren walks across the shag carpet and grabs a Pizza Delight box off the floor. He offers us cold pepperoni slices and beer. Fudge tries to contribute to the pizza but Blomgren holds up a hand, as if the idea is ridiculous. "Forget it, Fudgey. Save your quarters for the jukebox." Blomgren spins to face Johnny. "But what about you, boy? Let's see the colour of your money." Johnny doesn't move, unsure what to do. Blomgren smiles. "I'm just messing with you, son. What's his name, Fudge? This good-looking kid here."

"That's Johnny. And the little one's Mickey."

"Hey, boys. Welcome, welcome. Let's get to it." Blomgren pulls out a plastic bag stuffed with loose weed. He shakes the seeds out above the opened pizza box and asks, "What'll it be today?"

"Is Sneaky here?" asks Fudge, sitting on the arm of a lopsided sofa.

"Fuck knows where Sneaky's at," says Blomgren. "But I can take care of you gentlemen today. How much you want?" I can tell Blomgren is amused to be talking to us and it's my feeling that to sell half a pound of pot to Howard Fudge and his sidekicks is not the biggest order of business in Blomgren's day.

Now Vance Blomgren is a serious criminal, a small-time crook, and full-time fuck-up. Adopted son of Milly Rees, a madam who runs girls out of the Regal Taxi line, and cousin to Deacon Vickery, one of the bigger drug wholesalers east of Montreal, Vance Blomgren drives a Buick Century convertible and operates an after-hours bootlegging service out of the Willow Street house, it's listed in the Yellow Pages under *Bottle Delivery*, and I have never met anyone so carelessly charming and corrupt and insulting. The guy traffics in a number of automatic phrases—"Out of the way, Stagehand," "First day with the new legs?" "You trying to Jew me around?"—phrases often skeezy with racist implication, although he does share the Willow Street house with a Black guy named Sneaky Tynes.

"That Sneaky's something else," Blomgren tells me one day as we watch Sneaky drift out the front door and down the sidewalk. "Just look at him go. He's like the definition of the word nigger."

HE SAID IT, I DIDN'T. I repeat it here because it leads to material I have so far avoided reclaiming—just how racist and backward and penny-dreadful many of the neighbourhoods of Halifax could be in these years. For in my childhood, grown men and women still used all-purpose phrases like Chinaman or Coloured Fella or Indian Giver. But these were mild compared to the grimy folk legends Vance Blomgren repeated. Whether anyone ever did go "brooming coons" on Creighton and Maynard I don't know, but that fable and that fucked-up phrase haunted the minds of thousands of kids over six generations. The folklore was, at some time in the city's past, white people drove up and down streets in the North End and, off the back of a truck, smacked Black people with a broom. Or whitewashed them with a mop. For fun. Creighton and Maynard. The streets were mentioned so often in my youth, by Vance Blomgren, Howard Fudge, Deacon Vickery, and others, that I thought it was some squalid inner city junction, but, as I would later learn, the streets run parallel and never touch. Except in my mind they did. Creighton and Maynard for me was an intersection of fear and loathing, deficiency and loss. When older kids told you this brooming coons story, and I was seven when I first heard it, I was thrilled to be included in such illicit materials, even if I sensed it was, over the long view, sort of mutually degrading. But not everyone is interested in the long view. In Halifax, the tidal repetition of received attitudes is everywhere, in all waters, and it would be a number of years before I understood the South End could prove as much a ghetto as the North.

IN MY PRESENCE, Vance Blomgren tells seventeen racist jokes which I dutifully copy into the endpapers of *Watership Down*. It is in the midst of this somewhat covert activity that Fudge finds me one day, sitting at the kitchen table in the Willow Street house. "Cocoon?" he says, reading over my shoulder. "Wetsuits? Hockey pucks? What are these? Fucking *racist* jokes? What the fuck? Oh, Mickey, man. Come on." He pulls the book from my hands and rips out the offending pages.

I protest it's my favourite book and the jokes aren't mine but Blomgren's.

"Blomgren?" asks Fudge. "Blomgren told you these?"

I nod, half-lying, and ask to have the pages back.

Fudge tosses the torn pages at me, but keeps the book a vague moment. "Blomgren's got a fucked-up sense of humour. He can be pretty funny, for a skinny cocksucker, but be careful. Because he can't be trusted worth shit. And if you ever do a deal in this house, go through Sneaky. You and Johnny remember that."

Sneaky Tynes, to give him his due, is a stern-looking mixed race dude with freckles and a disorganized afro. He seems to occupy a strange half-life in lumber yards and massage parlours. He has a reputation as a playboy. "It's Sneaky to the street," he says to me, pretending to check over his shoulder. "But Quincy to the ladies." His moods are quixotic and changeable. He messes with white kids, hassling them toward a confrontation, only to collapse into laughter, shoulders weak, a hand covering his face. Many years later, Quincy Tynes will re-enter my biography at a crucial juncture, saving my life in another city, but when I am thirteen I am mostly terrified of him. He is beyond my experience.

"This your favourite book?" asks Fudge, starting to look through its pages.

Feeling oddly contrite, I tell him he can keep it if he wants.

"You want to *give* me your favourite book?" asks Fudge, picking idly at the fur-lining of his parka hood. But I can tell it means something to him that I've offered this gift. He is touched that I've included him in something private to me. "Mickey gave me this book," he'll say later. "It's about talking rabbits. I thought, Talking rabbits? What the fuck? But it's pretty good. They wanted to find the girl rabbits, I can relate." Afterwards, on other days, I will notice Fudge looking at me, as if he expects me to start a story or remember a detail, as if I am someone who might take the lead when he isn't interested in leading. I am embarrassed by this connection and by the connection Fudge wants it to be. I am young and find his favouritism troubling. I don't understand it, think it vaguely unnatural, and his intentions for a closer friendship I resist because it means I have to recognize his attentiveness, his kindness, his loneliness. If I'd known more about the world, I might have realized Howard Fudge was a little in love with me. But I didn't. I wanted our friendship to be only ridiculous and provisional, just as I wanted this whole period of my life to be ridiculous and provisional. I didn't want it to matter. I didn't want any of this to matter. In the end, I knew Howard Fudge was limited, that I was brighter, that there were and would be a number of social situations where I would be welcome and he would not. He was seen as slovenly and rough and gauche, a fatso drug-dealer in Kodiak boots. I tried to ignore these half-thoughts, hoping Fudge wouldn't pick up on them, but he was a deep-sensing Maritimer, with many more feelings than he had ways to verbalize, and over time he probably intuited and registered the shifts in our relations. Not that, to be clear, I could possibly have articulated any of these feelings back when I was thirteen, but I did know I was obscurely relieved when Fudge was arrested for punching a bouncer at The Seahorse Tavern that New Year's Eve. In the early hours of the new year, Fudge was brought home drunk-and-disorderly by two uniformed cops and Ralph Fudge was made to understand that his son, soon to be age of majority, was becoming known in the city as a problem. The next week, Fudge was dispatched to King's-Edgehill in Windsor, Nova Scotia, a boarding school in those days considered a country club for delinquent rich kids, and I was left alone with Johnny Red.

LEFT ALONE WITH JOHNNY RED, I was not a good head. Left alone with Johnny Red, I was a bad egg. I shoplifted at Woolco. I dropped bottles off the top of Fenwick Towers. I wandered with him all over—Dutch Village Road, Mulgrave Park, Jelly Bean Square. I was in awe of Johnny Red, this gorgeous, doomed kid. He was in more than a few ways what I wanted to be. One winter day, Deb Smear and I watched him gouge a Kiss logo into the paint of the Angus L. Macdonald Bridge. "People get ideas about you, man," said Johnny, coldly finishing the last letter. "The older you get, the more they get ideas about you. And you can't stop it. You can't control it. So what do you do when other people say what's normal? Fuck them up, that's what!" His face softened into a dimply smile, to show us he was kidding. "Forget I said that. I was just peeking into someone else's dream they was dreaming." He shambled off toward the Halifax side of the bridge, red hair flying in the wind. He'd acquired a hobble over the winter, from crashing a Ski-Doo off a skateboard ramp, and walked with a left-leaning shuffle. He could still move with agility but it seemed something was trickling out of his life and abilities, and I wondered if he would ever be the perfect athlete he once was.

"Okay," said Deb Smear, coming up beside me and whispering in my ear. "Johnny's a guy who I have no idea who he is in person, right? He's like the spaciest guy on the face of the earth. But, let's face it, he does call Trish and he did give her a Christmas present." She showed me a thin necklace around her throat. "It's just a little silver jobbie he stole from Fairweather. But at least he gave his girlfriend something. Fudge is like the flip opposite of that. He doesn't care. He doesn't! He didn't even call me on my birthday." She sucked on the necklace, her face blotchy with winter paleness, and took out a flattened pack of Players Light. She pried it open to see a loose cigarette next to a skinny-looking joint. "Is that it? Hey Mickey, what happened to all the pot?"

SCENE. ATTIC OF THE WILLOW STREET HOUSE. Johnny and I sit with Vance Blomgren among loose flaps of fibreglass insulation, mildewed *Playboy* magazines, and an empty bottle of Golden Glow Cider, watching him roll joints. Fudge is still away at boarding school. He's instructed us to deal only with Sneaky Tynes but Johnny is troubled by Sneaky and uncomfortable in his company. His instinct is to buy from Blomgren. So I sit beside a smelly, hungover Vance Blomgren—a first encounter with adult-strength body odour, which to me is a combination of cumin and rank puddle water. "Good news and bad news," Blomgren says, blond bangs falling in his eyes. "Good news is Thai Stick only comes around once a year and I got an ounce for you. Bad news is Deacon creamed us off the top." Johnny is reaching to examine one of the joints when Blomgren slaps his hand away. "You got suicidal tendencies, son? You'll get your ninety joints, don't worry. I'm trying to look out for you. That's why I'm rolling them extra thin." But

Johnny complains the thinness of the joints will make it look as if we're trying to rip people off. "Jesus Christ," says Blomgren. "I try and do the younger generation a favour and you turn around and pull this shit on me? What's that about? Here then." He drops a hundred perfectly rolled joints on the floor. "Happy Fucking St. Patrick's Day."

THE THURSDAY OF MARCH BREAK, Fudge returns to find us at a house party in Clayton Park blazed out of our minds. "Mickey, you're fucking out of it, aren't you? You drop acid again? Look at you. You are fucking *pinned,* buddy. So what are you, some drug-fiend stoner since I'm gone? Listen to me. I'm trying to tell you something. If you do drugs, you switch around. You don't do the same drug over and over. That's how you become a fucking addict. Where's Johnny?"

We find Johnny in the basement, sitting on a freezer, drunkenly kissing a girl in a pink ski jacket. "Johnny, I got orders out front. You holding?" Johnny passes Fudge a baggie of joints. "These are measly little joints," says Fudge. "Who fucking rolled these?"

"Blomgren."

"Blomgren? Why'd *he* fucking roll them? How much you buy?"

"Ounce. But Deacon Vickery ripped him off. That's why it's not a real ounce."

Fudge glares at us, suspicious. "But you *paid* for an ounce?" He doesn't wait for an answer. "Blomgren ripped you off, Johnny, you fucking tool. He jacked the rest of that ounce and rolled them small so you wouldn't feel left out. Didn't I tell you not to trust the guy?"

"It's only ninety bucks. Who cares?"

Fudge cared. This transgression worked away at his sense of fairness and mission. He began to talk about it as if Blomgren had cheated him personally. "Whenever somebody unnecessarily fucks with me for no reason," he'd say, slowly shaking his head. "I can't help but want to punch the fucker's head in." Fudge spoke of getting even with Blomgren, getting back at that peckerhead once and for all. Now this *was* a different order of business from Fudge slugging a kid in a schoolyard, which Johnny and I'd often witnessed. This was going after Vance Blomgren, a twenty-two-year-old man, cousin to Deacon Vickery, someone with biker friends, someone who knew the guy who knifed the guy in the bathroom of the Misty Moon on Gottingen Street. How was this going to work?

SCENE. A SNOW-STORMY AFTERNOON on the last day of March Break and one of the last days of my random adolescence. Drifts of fresh snow, pant bottoms thickening with ice, cars skidding into curbs. Fudge sees Blomgren's Buick Century parked at the Kentucky Fried Chicken on Quinpool Road. Inside the trunk we imagine bags of pot, cases of beer, quarts of liquor. In that stubborn teenage way, we try and jimmy open the trunk lock with our own keys. Johnny is prying off the chrome Buick emblem when I realize it's not a convertible and not Blomgren's car. At that point, the car owner comes running out of the KFC and we're chased away down Quinpool Road. We buy grape shoestring licorice at the Candy Bowl. We bumper-hitch in the snow down to the Armdale Rotary and walk up to frozen Chocolate Lake, nominally looking for the house Johnny grew up in. We are the only people on the ice.

Now the day is waning grey, dimming sun behind indifferent clouds, and Fudge is cold and wants to go. We see Johnny standing over a hole he's made in the ice. With bare fingers he takes a slab of slate from the shore and drops it in the hole, trying to make it bigger. Why? I'm not sure. It's a Sunday on March Break and the activity seems like the appropriate way to end the afternoon. For a while we join him, carrying heavier and heavier pieces of slate and shale, watching them bubble down into the watery dark. Johnny looks above him as a bunch of sparrows scatter into the sky. "You know the Inuit?" asks Johnny, staring after the birds.

Fudge stands at the hole in the ice. "The *Inuit*, Johnny?"

"The Eskimos. They only got a language in 1971."

"Like a written language?" asks Fudge. "Like a symbolic—what do you mean? Like they didn't have symbols?"

"No, no. They had symbols but they didn't mean the same to everybody."

"Johnny, what the fuck are you talking about?"

"Because the symbols meant different things to different people. The Russian ones are working on the same thing right now."

"The Russian Inuit?" Fudge glances at me, more annoyed than amused, then back at Johnny. "Jesus loves you, Johnny," he says. "But everyone else thinks you're an asshole. What are you trying to fucking say?"

Johnny is about to reply when he notices the first drops of blood in the snow. His hand, he sees, is dripping with blood. He holds it to his chest, protectively, as if it is a baby bird. "You guys," he says. "I think I cut my finger off." The sharp edge of a slate chunk has caught between the knuckles of his ring finger, shearing it off clean. Fudge examines Johnny's martyred hand, the whitened stump, the seep of blood, then goes down on one knee. He feels around the ice surface, searching for Johnny's finger. So do I. Later, in my mind's cinema, I see it plummeting in the water, the camera following it certain fathoms in the lake, a smear of colour spiralling into darkness. But we never do find it.

Fudge gives up first. He starts trudging towards the shore where some kids have gathered to stare at us, wondering who we are, and what we're doing on the ice yelling at each other. For want of anything better to do, I rear back and fling a rock in their direction. It smacks the tree above their heads, emptying a branch of snow.

Johnny remains at the hole in the ice, screaming for us to keep searching.

"We're not going to find your fucking finger, Johnny," shouts Fudge. "Face it."

"Sure," says Johnny, staring into the hole. "Be like that. Be like that, Fudge. Except one day you're going to fucking *die*, man. And no one's going to care either."

"That's if we grow up, Johnny," says Fudge, stepping off the ice of Chocolate Lake. "That's if we grow up."

HOWARD FUDGE would grow up, and marry, and become a father. Which surprised me since I imagined him a bachelor adult, bombing around backroads on a snowmobile or ATV, joining sweaty buddies at the Legion Hall in an April thaw, his hair gone white, his face steaming. After high school, I would hear of Howard Fudge but never see him again. He would do a semester at Acadia University and get an assistant manager's job at the Radio Shack in New Minas. The map of Highway 101 is dotted with motor vehicle fatalities, especially on the curves between Windsor and Wolfville, and it was twelve miles east of Wolfville where the manager of the New Minas Radio Shack went off the road and lost his life. At the funeral, a half-drunk Howard Fudge met the widow, a petite woman with a Dorothy Hamill haircut named Etta MacKinnon. Fudge would quit drinking and drugs, marry Etta MacKinnon, and move to Antigonish to open a car dealership called Colonial Mazda. He and Etta would have three sons, one of whom was born with cerebral palsy. Googling him last summer, I saw Howard K. Fudge was the chairman of the pipe organ restoration committee for St. Andrew's Church. And Johnny Red? I used to wonder what would happen to Johnny Red. Back from university one Christmas, I saw him in the basement of the Halifax Shopping Centre, clerking in the kitchen appliance section of Eaton's. He pretended not to see me and I pretended not to see him. Jonathan Boutilier's life would obscure with mishap and addiction. He would follow a future of sexual assault, forcible confinement, robbery, theft, and a three-year turn in the Dorchester Penitentiary in New Brunswick.

SOME WEEKS AFTER Johnny lost his finger on Chocolate Lake, Beasley and Bubbles were playing euchre in the ping-pong room at the Waegwoltic Club when Johnny wandered in and mentioned he'd just fucked Deb Smear on the railroad tracks below the Horsefield, news that would influence a number of local conversations. That summer was memorable for multiple reasons: Elvis died, Voyager launched, and two former friends got set to fight. The venue was the Halifax Commons, in the scrub grass between the tennis courts and baseball diamond. Sixty of us showed up. Comparing body sizes, it seemed absurd that Fudge, a hulking porker of a bully, would ever lose to Johnny Red. But Johnny was the quickest kid I'd ever seen, a champion kickboxer in his weight class, and capable of roundhouse kicks that would drop a pony. He was also crazy. Within seconds of the fight starting, some cruel spirit was released in Johnny and he rushed at Fudge, jumping above him and stunning him with a downward-flying elbow to the temple. A mess of punches was exchanged. Then Johnny landed a spinning back kick below Fudge's ear, sending Fudge sideways, staggering him. Fudge was off balance, as if he wasn't sure where he was, or as if he thought the ground beneath him was shifting, when Johnny's right cross thumped him full on the mouth. Johnny rushed forward, starting a round kick aimed at Fudge's chin. This time Fudge was able to dodge and grab Johnny's boot. He pulled Johnny one way, bounced him to the ground, and fell on him. And once Fudge had you in the dirt, no matter how many blows you landed, no matter how fast you squirmed, no matter even if you had a six-inch spike in your fist and tried to gash his face with it, as Johnny was about to try, once Fudge got you down he used his body weight to crush you to the earth so he could straddle your chest. Johnny bucked and thrashed, scraping Fudge's chin with the spike, but Fudge sat on Johnny's sternum, got his knees on Johnny's arms, and punched Johnny's head in. Three times I saw Fudge use this move in a fight and three times the other kid was beaten to a bloody mess. I watched now with fascinated horror as blood from Johnny's nose and mouth soaked into his Levi's shirt, the snap buttons torn open to his bellybutton. "You're a fucking bug," said Fudge. "You know that, Johnny? You're a fucking bug." I thought it would end there, when it was clear Johnny was losing ability and focus, when spinal fluid began leaking from his nose, but Fudge dragged a still-twitching Johnny into the baseball diamond and handcuffed one of his ankles to the fence behind home plate. He was about to kick his face in when some teacher ran over, babbling about calling the police, and we all dispersed, sickened, thrilled, exhausted.

A few days later I met a subdued Johnny at the King of Donair, his face shiny with bruises, his skull fractured in two places. "It was worth it," he said, meaning what happened with Deb Smear. Not that he pursued the attachment. In fact, I doubt Johnny ever saw her again. Deb Smear, who had bruises all over her back from fucking Johnny in the railway cut, who would have two abortions and a miscarriage by the time she was seventeen, who walked me giggling to my first bonfire—she went to live with her grandmother in Minto, New Brunswick. After that, I didn't know anyone who saw her again. Following the fight, Johnny enrolled in the Halifax Vocational School, Fudge returned to King's-Edgehill, and I filtered into a public high school. There I will meet sarcastic older kids who, in their knowledge and range of behaviour, will seem like citizens of an entirely different city. What of my dealings with Fudge? These years were unregulated, improvised, full of faults and wrong turns, just as my friendships were. I had no great plan but I sensed one night, while talking to some kids lined up to see a movie called *Quadrophenia*, that I wouldn't be seeing Howard Fudge anymore. I was looking for a new way to be in the world.

ANOTHER GAME, NOT SOCCER or stickball, but football in the rain at the Wanderers Grounds near Citadel Hill. The field spattered with fallen leaves, the oil paints of autumn. It is Grade 11, a day before Halloween, and I am with Cyrus Mair behind the bleachers, beside the bubbled enclosure of the Junior Bengal Lancers riding stables. We are stoned and dressed as Mods in second-hand suits and desert boots, another costume. I have not seen Fudge for over a year and buy my weed from the kid who sits next to me in my Modern World Problems class. In an inside pocket of my suit I have a family-sized Smarties box crammed with sixty-seven joints and rolled-up bills. I am giving Cyrus a joint for his walk home when Sneaky Tynes and Howard Fudge appear out of the rain. Sneaky asks if I have any drugs. Fudge glances at me once and doesn't look at me again, preferring to stare into the mud. I am fumbling with the joints in my Smarties box, asking Sneaky how many he wants, when Sneaky simply grabs the box from my hand. He picks out four joints and goes ominously still, his lower lip nudged forward in thought. Then he abruptly turns and walks away with all my joints and all my money.

"Hey, wait!" I say, in a voice that starts gruff but finishes in a squeal of girlish panic. Sneaky reconsiders, gives me the four joints as a peacekeeping gesture, but keeps the other sixty-three and my cash, dropping the empty Smarties box in the mud. In a return to childhood, and childhood's feelings of powerlessness, I begin to cry, my tears mixing with trickles of rain, my feet soggy in my desert boots.

"Fudge," I say, getting some control over my voice. "Come *on*, man. Fuck."

Fudge stops. I have a memory of him in this moment, an indelible image of him in his blue parka, standing with his back to me, resolute, gruesome, but not without some weird fucking majesty. Then he spins around and comes back and punches me in the head. I feel my lower jaw separate from the rest of my face. Touching my cheek with two fingers, I yell his name a second time. But Howard Fudge doesn't turn around. He walks off with Sneaky Tynes in the drizzling rain. In his way he is trying to tell me something.

Wheelers

MY MOTHER'S MAIDEN NAME IS WHEELER—in her early roles she's credited as Mary-Margaret Wheeler—and the Wheeler family ethos, as my father would tell you, from time to time possessed everyone in our household. For my father and I lived in a house of girls and women. Imagine a back hall of scuffed figure skates, rubber boots, ballet slippers, mismatched high heels, a broken flip-flop. Picture a second floor where dance routines are rehearsed at all hours of the morning, doors are perversely slammed, sweaters are illicitly borrowed only to be returned "completely reeking of fucking cigarettes." My four sisters competed for clothes, friends, time in the bathroom, nights with the car. They competed to be heard. There were skirmishes, schemes, hormonal swings, unburdening emotionality. Nights could be loud. When I was young, I tried to make connections between all factions—I let them give me manicures, I let them put my hair in braids—only to later explode in survivalist anger. MY SISTERS TALKING: "Remember when you ripped off your Tarzan pajamas? What a psycho!" "Mom's right. You need therapy." "You know when you mooned me and Faith? We saw your balls and they looked shrimpy. In your *face*! And fuck off because I actually *don't* talk about other people." How to respond? The unstable spin of feminine non-logic can overwhelm a single guy and, after the age of twelve, I vowed to never again take anyone's side or get sucked into any argument. My mother presided over these histrionics from afar and seldom intervened. When indifference was futile, she could commit to the scene with the full force of her personality and in these moments the female members of my family seemed united in a singleness of lunacy. It was rampant in the house and halls and provoked in me a confusion of sympathy so absolute I had no idea where their contradictions ended and my own instabilities began. So, with such *Sturm und Tollheit* looming overhead, I can tell you most of what follows occurred some thirty years ago on a slushy late December afternoon when my mother began the proceedings sound asleep in a full bathtub in the house on Dunvegan. For the second time in an hour, Katie, my youngest sister, called to my mother that she was wanted on the telephone. But this information did not really infiltrate my mother's dreaming brain. She lay in the bathwater, her head at an awkward angle, her mouth a smidge above the water's surface. Katie, on the other side of the door, stood listening for some kind of response or movement, but, hearing none, returned to the staircase. It was only when Katie's footfalls faded from the doorway that my mother stirred, eyelashes fluttering, elbow twitching, finally awakening. "Who's there?" She pushed herself into a sitting position, a pink mesh sponge slipping from her shoulder. In another second the swirl of her dreams would dissipate and her full identity return to her, bringing with it all the concerns, perplexities, and divinations that free-float on any given day. "Ditsy?" She stood up, bathwater rinsing from her, and reached for an orange beach towel draped over a nearby radiator. She sniffed the towel, feeling where it was damp from earlier use, and quickly swabbed her shoulders, arms, legs. She called a second time and stepped out of the tub, careful to avoid the debris on the fringed bathmat at her feet, debris she seemed surprised to see. Which was: a three-pack of miniature Henkel Trocken champagne, a red Lego brick, and a water-warped paperback copy of *Anne's House of Dreams*. The first item had been liberated earlier that afternoon from a reunion luncheon for Dalhousie University's School of Nursing, Class of 1955. It was a degree my mother abandoned to go into acting but she'd been convinced to crash the reunion by two of her classmates. The Lego piece belonged to my mother's first and, at the moment, only grandson. The book had been hers since childhood. Frowning a half-moment, she picked up the Lego piece and paperback, brought them to the sink, and placed them on a built-in tiled shelf. Why this frown? The whirligig of my mother's likes and dislikes, and where it might spin on a given day, was something few could figure or predict and what was obsessing her on this winter afternoon was anyone's guess. It could be the reminder of being a grandmother at fifty, or the memory of a ringing telephone, or Neptune Theatre's current season, or some theatricals still to be played. Whichever—with sudden compulsion, as if she felt the present scene needed fresh energy—she turned away from the sink and reached into the tub to pull out its rubber plug. She took a plaid bathrobe, not her own, from a two-pronged hook on the back of the bathroom door and, pushing her arms through its sleeves, walked out the door into the hallway. Fading behind her in the bathroom was a sense of fragrant vapours—the down-draining water redolent of Pear's Transparent Soap, lavender bath oil, and the everyday assorted effluence of an adult woman's metabolism. "Hello?" she said, tightening the bathrobe's belt. "Where are you? Ditsy?"

My four sisters—Carolyn, Bonnie, Faith, and Katie—went by the family nicknames of Itsy, Bitsy, Titsy, and Ditsy, although my father often changed that third appellation to Mitsy, especially in formal correspondence. My mother did not always care for formality—nor did she stand on ceremony. "Ditsy," she called down. "Who was on the phone?"

"Nan."

"She probably wants to know when she's getting picked up. Not that I haven't told her three times."

"No. She said she's not coming. And the real estate lady called for Dad."

"Not coming? She complains and complains she's not invited then when she *is* invited she's not coming?"

"She said she's sick."

"Sick?"

My maternal grandmother, Evelyn Anne Wheeler, known to us as Nan, was spending her first winter in Nova Scotia in some time. She and my grandfather, known to us as Dompa, had wintered in Sarasota but with my grandfather dying of congestive heart failure three years before, and my grandmother suffering a small cerebral hemorrhage at the Trimingham's perfume counter in Bermuda—after which she'd been on a more or less constant stroke watch—my mother decided it best to move her back to Halifax and into Saint Vincent's Guest House.

"With Nan," said my mother. "It's always a little more complicated. She likes to play head games, you know. And she likes to be in control."

"She was using her Big Whisper Voice."

"And after getting me to give up my hair appointment for her?" My mother came down the stairs, her hand sliding along the bannister. Framed on the walls around her were posters for productions of *Deathtrap, Chapter Two,* and other plays she'd acted in. "Imagine," she said. "Thinking you can get a hair appointment the week before Christmas. But you know Nan. It's all about her hair. She's on the phone, it's about her hair. She's opening a bottle of wine, it's about her hair. She's down at Emergency, it's about her hair." At the front door, my mother stooped to gather the day's mail. "Maybe it's better she's not coming. I mean Nan's a wonderful woman. No, she is. Until that third drink. Third drink and she's peeing on the floor."

Standing up, my mother stared through a glass panel in the front door and considered the house under construction across the street. It was vertically composed, made with red cedar and solar panels, and very unfinished. Not only was it out of style with the street's other houses, but its incompleteness—the lot disordered with backhoe tracks, cinderblocks, and two-by-fours—gave the place a raw, defective quality. "That mess of a house," said my mother, with fresh awareness of nuisance. "It just looks like shit. Bringing property values down, my God."

There was, I should say, a *For Sale* sign on our house. For four years there'd been a *For Sale* sign on our house. Some eons earlier, my parents had divorced, only to reunify. But complications—familial and financial—persisted. The material takeaways were an enormous short-term debt and my mother's wish to move to a smaller, cheaper house. But, to avoid further tribulation, she wasn't going to buy until she sold. "I wake up in the middle of the night," she said, sorting through the mail. "And I have visions of that 'For Sale' sign blowing in the wind for the next twenty years. By then the roof's fallen in, the windows broken. No one's buying houses right now. No one." Turning from the front door, she said, "Did Carolyn show up with the salmon? Ditsy, where are you?"

MY SISTER KATIE lay watching television in the living room, her head somewhat acutely propped up by a baseboard, her feet in striped toe socks. Katie was fourteen, but a very young fourteen, and, unlike my sister Faith, who at fifteen was drinking and dating her way through multiple social circles, Katie dwelled in a protracted teenybopperdom. She was slim, quick, "coltish," as the heroines were described in the YA books she daily demolished, and for the last months she'd been trying out a series of obsessions. Her latest fascination began with my mother's appearance in a revival of *The Gingerbread Lady*, continued through repeated viewings of *The Sunshine Boys*, and recently resulted in her commitment to a dialect I'll call Generic New York Wisecrack. Which is why, when my mother took a step into the living room, Katie, without shifting her gaze from the television, simply said, "Hey, Ma. Dinner's when?"

"Guests are invited for seven. Kids can eat any time. Did Itsy bring the salmon?"

"She went to the cat clinic."

"Cat clinic?"

"Cat clinic. Bird clinic. Who am I—Marcus Welby?"

"Ditsy? Enough." My mother crossed to the television and was about to switch it off when she recognized someone onscreen. "Is that Walter Matthau? Christ, he's looking old. Katherine McKee—" My mother faced Katie. "Look at me. Where'd she put it? The kitchen or the basement fridge?"

"I'm fourteen years old! I should know where the fish is?"

"The salmon, Ditsy."

"Fish, salmon. You're going to nitpick?" Katie rolled on to her stomach. "Adults get salmon. Kids get what?"

"Shepherd's Pie."

Katie nodded, judiciously. "Is the shepherd fresh?"

"Ditsy—" My mother shook her head. "I forbid you to watch any more Neil Simon. You're cut off. Did she drop it off or not?"

"*Yes*. Kitchen fridge."

My mother flipped the mail on a hall radiator and returned to the stairs. "I'm going to get dressed. If Nan calls again, Ditsy, let me know."

Getting up to press rewind, Katie shrugged. "The thing about salmon," she said to herself. "It's not funny. Pickerel? Pickerel is funny. Kippers is funny. But salmon?"

NOT FOUR SECONDS LATER, the front door swung open and my father entered the house carrying a box of Perrier. Plastic bags containing bottles of wine were hanging from his wrists and a red Twizzler licorice dangled from his mouth. Without taking off his shoes, he carried his purchases to the kitchen and eased them onto the kitchen table. "Bitsy, Ditsy?" he said. "Which one are you? Could one of you crap-artist kids help with the groceries?"

Katie came to the doorsill and looked in. "Out of left field he comes running with the craziest questions."

"Christ," said my father, tripping over an empty milk carton. "Could we have one day in this kitchen when there *isn't* an open garbage bag on the floor?" He glanced at Katie. "Peanut? Go find your mother. She's got a dozen people coming over for dinner."

"Find her yourself. She's upstairs."

My mother, now wearing a full slip over tea-stained sweatpants, appeared at the stair top and gazed down at my father with—what would be called in the stage directions—an amused air of distant suspicion.

"There she is," said my father with an open smile. "Look at you, twisting your hair, you get more and more beautiful every day. How about some kisses?"

"Did you remember the Campari?"

"Campari? Who drinks Campari?"

"*I* don't drink it, genius. But your esteemed colleague, Roz Weinfeld, newly appointed to the bench, drinks it and she's the reason we're having this dinner. Remember? It was the one thing I asked you to get."

My father considered this with narrowing eyes, the Twizzler dangling from his lips. "All right, Little Miss Mums." He shifted the licorice to the other side of his mouth, like a backroom bookie rearranging a cigar. "Make a list and we'll get Baby-boy to get it. Because, God knows, whatever Mumsy needs, Mumsy gets."

"It's whatever *Lola* wants, Lola gets."

The line in question was from the musical *Damn Yankees* and, for my parents, another installment in a never-ending game of name-that-quote. Both had strutted and fretted some time upon the stage and had within their imaginations a number of dramatic parts. So the evening might see variations on Elyot and Amanda, Nathan and Adelaide, George and Martha. My parents moved within a series of personas but to what extent they were using these personas, and to what extent the personas were using them, was not always easy to establish.

"Some days I hate that goddamn law firm," mused my mother. "Do you ever wonder what it's done to us?"

"As fun as that sounds, Mumsy, wondering what might've been, do you mind terribly if we stick to the here and now? You might want to get dressed."

"Oh, McKee. You've lost the plot. You've lost the plot, kid."

"Sure, sure," said my father. "You contain multitudes, Mums. Now would you mind containing dinner?" He smiled again. "And I better get some kisses around here or there's going to be real trouble."

Just then, Katie bumped open the front door and traipsed in with four bags of groceries. As she moved past my father, he grabbed at her shirttail. "When I met her, Ditsy. She was nothing. She had half a degree and two dirty jokes."

"Dad! Don't stretch my shirt! And that lady called you back."

"Just second, Peanut. I'm trying to tell you something about your horrible mother."

My mother arrived at the bottom of the stairs and, pushing shut the front door, said to him, "Quit terrorizing the children, would you, darling?" Ambling into the kitchen, she whispered over her shoulder, "And fuck the firm."

"Did you hear what you said?" He was staring at her as if her remark were perhaps the absolute zenith of her derangement. "You're a *terrible* person."

"Honestly, Stewart. Why do you talk? Why do you even open your mouth? Some lawyer." She opened the refrigerator and searched for the rumoured salmon. "You want to tell me where you've been the last hour? The Halifax Club?"

"For your information, I was taking discovery on a case."

"Which case?"

"Well," said my father. "I'm not at liberty to discuss it."

"Stewart—" My mother whirled around to look at him. "Tell me it's not Gregor Burr."

My father adjusted his tie. "I said I can't discuss it."

"Gregor Burr?" She sighed. "What a jerk. I personally can't stand him. What kind of guy who, when he's elected Member of Parliament, starts messing around with teenagers? He's a goddamn sleaze. And such a tendentious son of a bitch. He could be a role model for the youth of this province and instead he's assaulting high school girls in the stairwell of the Lord Nelson Hotel. Why can't he go to a prostitute like a normal person?"

"Do you *hear* what you're saying?"

"Don't give me that rise-above-it bullshit. Why are you always defending the bad guy?"

"That's yet to be determined, my dear."

"That's not what I heard."

"And what did you hear, Mary-Margaret Wheeler, pray tell?"

"Well, asshole, what I heard was a different story. Like the city hasn't heard a different story."

"That's enough of this talk, thank you."

"Oh, I'm not allowed to say anything?"

"No, you can say whatever you like. You can print it in the paper if you like. But if the people you describe take your remarks to be defamatory you may be forced to prove what you allege in a court of law."

My mother tilted her head, unimpressed.

"This isn't all my doing, Mums. It's just we have something here called the rule of law—"

"I'm familiar with the fucking *rule* of law, Stewart. I'm also familiar with this man's history. He stuck his tongue down Caitlyn Jessup's throat. Marge McLean, he pinned her up against a car in the Sobeys parking lot. Marge McLean! I mean how drunk do you have to *be*? And Bev Noonan, he muckled on to her at the bar convention, lifting up her dress at the coat check. And God knows how many more there are."

"Those are not the sort of stories you want to repeat."

"Why? Because they happen to be *true*? And from what I've heard about this teenager, he finally went too far. It's tantamount to raping her."

"Mackie—"

"Well, what would you call it? The teenager said penetration and the RCMP identified the semen on her skirt as his." My mother looked at my father, severe. "Did he admit it?"

"I can't repeat what's said in-camera. You know that."

"Ian Pulsifer tells Connie—"

"How would *you* know that?"

"She told me!"

"Exactly. Look, I can't discuss the facts of a case with you. Or what a client says in discovery. You know I can't. And that's final."

These arguments, sound as they may have been, did not have a wholly persuasive effect on my mother. "Listen," she said. "I applaud Tiggy for standing by him but come on, Stewart. Everybody knows what this man's like. Every single person in the Conservative Party knows what he's like and they're all letting him get away with it. That's what makes me so sick. It's like with an alcoholic. They're enablers. If someone doesn't say, 'No, this isn't right.' Then who's to stop him? *He* obviously can't stop himself. But they won't say anything because everything's going so well up in Ottawa right now. Yeah, well, stick around." My mother saturated her next word with contempt. "*Men*. Puh. There ought to be a revolution."

"I feel it's underway."

My mother glanced at my father before looking up toward what, in a theatre, would be the first row of the balcony. "When the hurly-burly's done," she said. "We'll look back and wonder what we've done on this Earth. And what will we say? That's the sixty-four thousand dollar question, Stewart. What'll we say then?"

Before my father could answer, the doorbell rang.

DODIE RUMBOLDT was a sweet, dithery woman who dropped by our house for the flimsiest of reasons. She worried about everything and lived in a tizzy of worsening possibilities. My mother was loyal to her because they'd grown up next door to each other in Truro. "Dodie Rumboldt has wanted to be my best friend for forty-six years," she said, on her way to the door, seeing who it was. DODIE: A SELECTED ORAL HISTORY: "She was always big, you know? I mean *big*. I never knew her when she didn't look like a tent coming toward you. And her wardrobe went purple for a while. She was one of those ladies in purple. Like you don't know how much weight she's gained because you're distracted by all the purple? Let me tell you something. You're not fooling the cheap seats. Then she got a boyfriend. Did wonders for her. She lost over a *hundred* and fifty pounds. Jogging with weights. Eating right. Looked great. But now? She's gone too far. Can't stop. Some thin. Scared skinny. She's going to give herself a nervous breakdown. Well, her mother's had terrible Alzheimer's. Her mother's in Saint Vincent's on the third floor just out of it. Not much fun having a mother whose memory's gone. But Dodie and her father have been bricks. Visiting every day. Every day one of them's gone to see her."

The doorbell rang again. Composing her face into a smile, and with a very convincing demonstration of calm, my mother opened the door.

"It's Dad," said Dodie, putting a hand to her throat. "First it was his heart. Now it's his hip. He fell doing the snowblower. They have him at the hospital and I think they're going to keep him overnight. You just never know if this one's—"

"Oh, Dodie," said my mother. "It's his hip? I'm sure he'll be fine. He's had a replacement before, hasn't he?"

Dodie nodded. "I could just *feel* something was going to happen this month. All month I could feel it. My mind's just been *racing*. I mean I know life's what happens when you're doing something else but this?" She pressed her lips together. "I've been down at the hospital all afternoon. I just left."

"Was he awake when you left? Were you able to talk to him?"

Dodie was nodding again when she spied Katie in the dining room. Katie had her hands full of silverware and was setting fourteen places for dinner. "Oh?" said Dodie. "Mackie, you have company coming. I should go."

"Don't be silly. Wouldn't dream of it. You stay for supper."

"But I'm not dressed for it."

"We'll find you something. You come talk to me. Ever peel a potato?"

"Well," said Dodie, with a surprised giggle, as if this might be the third funniest thing she's heard in her life. "I might've peeled one or two."

AND SO THE EVENING, for some minutes, advanced without further ruckus, my youngest sister setting the table, my father shaving in the upstairs bathroom, and me rising from the basement, while my mother sat Dodie down with a glass of white wine at the kitchen table. Which is where Dodie learned of my mother's plans to poach a salmon in the dishwasher. "I have *never* heard of anything like that," said Dodie, watching my mother drizzle two large fillets with white wine, lemon juice, and butter. "In *tin* foil? On a wash cycle? Mackie, honestly, I've never."

My mother, holding in buttery hands a bottle of Chardonnay, was pouring herself a glass of wine when the telephone jingled. She glanced into the dining room and with a look indicated that Katie should answer it. Katie walked into the kitchen and shyly picked up the receiver. "Hello?" After a moment, she covered the mouthpiece to say, "It's the real estate lady again." She held out the receiver to my mother who was wiping her hands with a blue J-Cloth. Which is when my father entered and with a nimble two-step filched the receiver from Katie's fingers.

"What are you doing?" My mother turned to Dodie. "What is he doing?"

"Sh, Mumsy," said my father. "Go have an olive."

"An *olive*? Give me that phone."

My father turned his back to the room, effectively blocking all access to the telephone.

Deciding on another course of action, my mother grabbed her glass of wine and was on her way to the hall extension when my father, after several curt, somewhat inaudible, but mostly professional-sounding, instructions, replaced the receiver.

With glaring eyes my mother re-appeared. "What did she say? What did you tell her?"

"There's an offer."

"The couple from Boston?"

My father nodded.

"I knew it."

"They made an offer this morning and—"

"What is it?"

"It expires tonight at six o'clock."

My mother glanced at the clock on the stovetop. It showed two minutes to six. "How much?"

"Well, I suggested—"

"I don't care what *you* suggested! I want to know what the offer is."

"Three seventy-two."

"Take it."

"I said we'd only consider bids over three eighty."

"You did not. You did not—" She studied him. "Stewart, are you out of your mind? This house, need I remind you, has been on the market for four fucking *years*! We get one offer in four years and you think you're John Kenneth Galbraith? Call her back this instant. No—just—*move*. I'll call her."

"You will do nothing of the sort," said my father, disconnecting the telephone.

From somewhere inside my mother burst a howl—a melismatic mixture of crying and laughter—and with a vicious spin of her wrist she flung her wineglass at the window. After it smashed against the windowsill, she stared at my father, livid. "Why would you do that without talking to me? When you know I've been out of my mind with worry. *Why* would you do that?"

"Mumsy, you're behaving badly." My father felt his neck, above his shirt collar, for shards of broken glass, then extended his hand toward Dodie, who was still sitting at the kitchen table, her eyes wide with panic. "Dodie, I'm sorry to say, your friend's gone berserk."

"Stewart," said my mother. "I have met some jackasses in my life—"

"Beautiful, you love me. You wouldn't change a thing."

"I've got news for you—" In the back hall, my mother grabbed a ski jacket and guided her feet into two rubber boots. "If I had to live my life over again, I'd do it alone."

"Performance to follow. Applause, applause. Fanfare, trumpets, exeunt omnes."

"No. Just mine." She raised her voice. "Aubrey! Get your coat—"

"Mackie?"

"Because I'm leaving. I've had it. I'm through. My nerves can't take it."

"Sure, sure, Mums."

"Stewart—" My mother's voice weakened with a note of frailty. "Why would you *do* that? Without talking to me? Why?"

My father reached for her hand. But she shuddered away from him, fiercely blinking her eyes, and marched into the hallway. "Don't *touch* me!"

Silent on the stairs, Katie and I watched our mother zip up the ski jacket, yank open the front door, and charge outside into the sleet and snow.

TO ME SHE WAS INCOMPREHENSIBLE—a possible narcissist, a perpetual actress, a charmer, a drinker, a fury. "Your mother's larger than life, kid," my father would say. "She's something else, a singular sensation, and one of the great unsolved mysteries of maritime history." My mother was twenty when she quit Nursing and went into the theatre and, very arguably, her life from that point became one long, unfinished performance. She started as an ingénue of shaky self-esteem. Feelings of nervousness and shy defiance were useful for some roles—Miss Julie, Juliet, Ophelia—but further vitalities were needed. A FEW DIGRESSIONS: my mother holds the record for most appearances in productions at Neptune Theatre and ringing the walls of the administrative office on the second floor is a succession of her head shots. Not only do these form a year-by-year photographic biography of my mother, but they also showcase a sort of folk history of commercial photography and period hair styles. Around the time of her Medium Wavy Shag, she and my father divorced. During the years of their estrangement, many were the conversations among my sisters regarding how my parents' nights were spent, wondering who got together with whom and for how long. "*All* Dad's friends have crushes on Mom, you dink. Don't you want to know who she was with?" I knew my mother cultivated friendships with Art College types, sculptors in hand-knit cardigans, potters with love beads and mandolins, and dwelled for a time in a Volkswagen van with a man named Elkin Duckworth. This was a New Brunswick actor, effeminately gay, the lead in a celebrated local production of *Godspell*, and afterwards known to us as Jesus of Moncton. Their relationship, my mother maintained, was a love affair in all ways but sexual. She and Elkin took a cabaret to BAM, Strasberg on Fifteenth Street, and acid on Halloween, before he transmigrated to Laurel Canyon and she returned to take custody of my two younger sisters. From America, she arrived super-charged. She'd been radicalized. My mother lived less than three months in New York but, for the rest of her life, auditioning for roles in Halifax's two-and-a-half professional stages, she rather carried herself as if she were only three steps away from walking onstage at the Lyceum Theatre in midtown Manhattan. The expectations of the Halifax audience were irrelevant now. In her time away, she'd gained access to a more primordial emotional life. She'd learned to "go there," to trade and traffic in her emotions, emotions all the more potent if she actually believed in them. And believe in them she did. There was conflict in her acting now, vulnerability alternating with impatient superiority, and the friction between the two sparked real electricity. She was celebrated. She was profiled. She acquired groupies. There was a dental hygienist—known to us as Stalker Don Walker—who did not miss an opening night in twenty-three years. (During my teeth cleanings, he had the somewhat exasperating habit of asking about my mother's shows when his soap-scented fingers were far inside my mouth.) Donald's companion was the Dartmouth actor Brandon Merrihew, known to us as Uncle Brandy. Onstage he was Jimmy to my mother's Evy, Sir Toby to her Maria, and offstage he was her pal and drinksy confidante. Brandy was enamored of, and border-line obsessed with, my mother, and his holiday compliments were so effusive as to veer into a dementia of overflattery. His remarks after my mother's turn in *Streetcar*: "There she is! Nothing really astounds me but you, Mary-Margaret, *you* astound me. You confound me. You wear the crown for me. When I saw you on stage, I said to Donald, 'There *is* magic in the world. That Mackie McKee has done it again.' No one can touch you, can they? Not then. Not now. Not ever. Really, Mackie. Hail to thee, blithe spirit." Emotive disturbance and evidentiary emotionality—these were her new vitalities but such Method did not belong to my father's process. Societal and practical exigencies played their parts in my father's flight from playhouse to courtroom but he contained multitudes all his own. He would learn it was not really in his professional interests to be emotionally open or emotionally uncontained. The practice of law, which was to be his calling and prevailing vocation, demanded he think first, strategize second, emote never. It actually took me *years* to figure out I was raised within these two mighty monarchies and, digressions done, now might be the time to check in with the subject that was me.

There in the moving car, beside my mother, very much in the passenger seat, sits the lurking figure that is Me at Nineteen. This Aubrey McKee seems a faraway incarnation, a gorky kid beset with contradiction and compulsion and greatly incomplete. A growth spurt has sent me near six feet but left me awkward, pimply—I am known to my sisters as Treetop and Pizza Face—and my signature has not stabilized in years, the capital K of my surname lurching wildly ahead of the final two letters. As earlier explained, it is my tactic, in these *Walpurgisnächten,* to keep calm and follow the example of my oldest sister. For Carolyn is the sane sibling in a crisis, supremely self-controlled and largely aloof from family politics. So, as my mother fulminates, I suppress All Feeling and mutely stare at a softcover actor's copy of *Hedda Gabler,* published by Dramatists Play Services, which has been left in the slush of the plastic floor liner.

"Why is he doing this?" My mother punches the steering wheel. "A month ago he was willing to drop the price to three fifty but *now* he wants to play tough guy? I would've offered three seventy-nine to let them know we're willing to budge. No one knows. No one knows what I have to put up with. Do up your seatbelt, please." She checks the rear-view mirror and swings up Jubilee Road. "Your father acts like everything's fine. This unfounded optimism he has, thinking everything's going to work out. Well, unless you take steps to make *sure* things work out, I want to tell you, they don't. Do up your seatbelt, Aubrey."

I grab carelessly at the seatbelt but the retractor pulls it from my fingers, the metal latch smacking against the window. My mother does not appear to notice and seems disposed only to stare out the windshield. The evening has become for her a primal assertion of self and despite her questions, I do not think there is a part for me in her one-person show. I do up the seatbelt and peer out the window. Fog is everywhere in the city, the falling snow has changed to wetting sleet, and my window reflection is smeared with moisture.

"We owe three hundred thousand dollars! I was always taught to live within your means. Your father spends it as soon as he gets it." Speeding into the intersection with Oxford Street, she turns sharply left, our tires slipping sideways on the paint of the wet crosswalk. "I'm fifty years old. I'm too old to be in debt. I say drop the price and rent a place. I don't care where we live. But your father wants the right address. Maybe he needs it to have the confidence to win cases but—Jesus—who's this asshole?" My mother squints into the rear-view mirror where the reflection of high beams from an upcoming vehicle has begun to blind her. "For the love of Pete." She pulls over to allow this vehicle, an ambulance, to pass. After it has gone by, its rotating light flashing on my mother's cheek, she checks over her shoulder and swerves back into the laneway.

I am still studying my reflection in the rainy window, the Christmas lights of St. Thomas Aquinas shimmering outside, when somewhere in my memory shimmers a scene from four years before, when my family is split and I am wandering smashed on Kempt Road and I see my father inside a brightly lit Harvey's restaurant. He is alone at a booth, his table covered with case briefs, legal pads, an orange cheeseburger wrapper. As I teeter outside, a stranger exits the front doors and with this airstream the wrapper breezes off the table but my father does not notice, so absorbed is he in his preparations. He has this day ninety-two files in various stages of discovery, development, and trial, and he seems so solitary, eating by himself at ten o'clock on Friday night, when once we'd eaten together as a family, and I consider the ideals he once pursued—a life where his wife wasn't running off, where his family life was secure, where he could manage everything through diligence and force of will—and I think to wave hello to him, impulsively, absurdly excessively, in a way we sometimes had, but as the doors reclose and within their glass my scruffy reflection appears, I am too ashamed to say hello and have him see me fall-down-drunk—and all of this is getting close to the crux of my feelings of what-the-fuck powerlessness regarding my father and mother and sisters and me and so, returning to the scene-in-progress, and sidebarring for a moment my instinct to smash a fist through the windshield, I twist in the car to ask where, exactly, we are going.

My mother sighs, sensing a change in my manner, and asks, "Do you have the list your father gave you?"

I say I left it at the house.

"Well—" She rubs at her forehead. "Can you remember what's on it? The Campari, Gouda, the what-was-it?" She glances at me, irritated. "I don't have time for one of your moods, Aubrey. If you're going to be like this, I can stop the car and you can get out. In fact, here, I'll do it myself." She spins the steering wheel, beginning a very unstable U-turn—which sends me into the armrest of the door—the car coming to a skidding stop on the other side of the street. She gets out, steps over a rain-melting snowbank, and slides toward a payphone beside the Oxford Theatre. As she inserts a quarter and dials, I become aware that her get-up—ski jacket, full slip, sweatpants, rubber boots—is not quite suitable for public walkabout. I am thinking again of Evy from *The Gingerbread Lady* and her last-chance struggle with, what she calls, this "human being business," when my mother hangs up the phone, her face grim with new information. "It's Nan." She stands very still, the falling sleet fluorescent in the lights of the theatre marquee. "Saint Vincent's called to ask if we picked her up." She makes a fluttery sigh. "No one knows where she is."

MY MOTHER LIVED THE FIRST YEARS of her life in an orphanage. My grandmother had become pregnant before she and my grandfather were married and the stigma of being an unwed mother, in those days, was such that she chose to give her firstborn away. "It's not as if she was a pregnant teenager," my mother recalled later. "She was twenty-*four*, for Christ's sake. But Nan grew up in the Depression. In that era, respectability was the most important thing. Respectability, security, appearances." After my grandmother's figure recovered, after she'd married properly into wedlock, and after she'd given birth to a legitimate daughter, my grandfather prevailed upon her to repossess the first and so my mother, at thirty-seven months, rotated back into the Wheeler ménage. "Dompa loved Nan. But so did everybody else. So did half the city. And in those days, you didn't get divorced. What you did was argue. And drink. Their marriage was like a lot from those years, I guess. And during the war, that was a party every night. Up at the Officer's Club." My grandmother drank. Liquor was a magic fundamental to her spirits. Dipsomania was everywhere in the years of my childhood, someone or another was always sloshing toward the end of the line, and you learned from an early age not to take it personally. At family dinners, you'd see her sneak away from the table, totter into a hallway, only to later rejoin the room, talkative, flirtsome, hilarious. She was then at ease with herself and her various energies expressed themselves in sweetness and light and contagious unpredictability. She let you operate the electronic ice-crusher for her Crème de Menthes. She sent you a cheque on Labour Day. She grabbed your hand to sing high harmony on "Happy Birthday." But over the years there was a gradual faltering and aspects of her behaviour—the monomania, the suggestion of paranoid self-involvement, a drift toward delusion—seemed to darken every scene and family occasion. My father, whose preference was to speak well of everyone, conceded his mother-in-law had become "a bit of a loose puck."

"After Dompa died," my mother explained. "Things took a turn." My grandmother became quite close with a widower in Tampa but, when he couldn't commit, she focused her attentions—briefly—on a tennis instructor, after which she made a move to Bermuda. "You should've seen her in Bermuda! Now Nan's a good-looking woman—big bosom, long legs—but there are age-appropriate clothes, you know? Your father and I arrive in Bermuda and here's Nan tricked out like a Vegas showgirl. Seventy-three years old in hot pants and a lace-up tube top with matching headband?" My grandmother's bachelorette adventures resulted in some confusion and real infirmity so she'd been relocated, not without protest, to Halifax. "Here's the thing with Nan. All she wants is a man. She doesn't care what kind. She just wants someone to make her feel special. Well, her parents spoiled her. Her husband spoiled her. Her boyfriends spoiled her. But when there's no one left to spoil her, what's she going to do then?"

WHEN WE ARRIVED AT SAINT VINCENT'S, the ambulance that had passed us was flashing in the parking lot, a paramedic loading through its backdoors someone strapped to a wheeling stretcher. "Good God," said my mother, as the ambulance rolled on to Windsor Street, its siren sounding. "Who do you suppose it is?" My mother walked across the yellow-painted lines of the parking lot, her face set in a pensive frown, as if there were two or three plot twists still to be endured. Inside, we moved past the reception desk into the lobby and there, at the far end of the hall, as if only a few beats behind cue, my grandmother appeared, frail and quivery and checking behind her, as if persecution might arise from some new quarter. Summoning her strength, she began to walk very evenly, with chin held high and a frozen smile—the expression of a visiting head-of-state—and she stared at a point in the hallway ahead of a heavyset elderly woman in a Lindsay tartan dress. Though I vaguely recalled this second resident as a family acquaintance, I saw that, for the moment, my grandmother was choosing not to favour her with recognition.

My mother, sensing something very unfinished about this interaction, but reassured to see my grandmother among the quick, was about to greet both women when my grandmother—spotting my mother—stumbled for her and grabbed her hand, as if on the verge of complete collapse.

"Oh Mackie," she said, her voice shaking. "There's been the most horrible accident." She took a stagey sort of breath. "It's Dolly Hollibone. We were coming out of the service and this little boy came roaring around the corner—some people here don't care *who* their children knock into—well this boy banged right into Dolly and her glasses went flying and she fell and—*crack*—she's broken her wrist. The ambulance just came and took her away."

My mother, while listening closely, was also noting my grandmother's slightly overdone appearance. Her bouffant curls and blonde highlights had been newly maintained and she was wearing hoop earrings, burgundy lipstick, a low-cut burgundy dress, and matching slingback heels. "You look awfully nice, Mum. What service was it? I see you got your hair done."

"This? Same thing I always do." My grandmother sniffed. "It just breaks your heart. Here she was, all set to go to her granddaughter's concert, and Dolly ends up being taken to the hospital!"

My mother nodded and asked, "Was that Elsy Horne in the tartan dress?"

"Life's full of surprises, I suppose," said my grandmother, her face twitching with worry. "But my God, that could have happened to *anybody*."

As my grandmother talked, we'd travelled—without particularly deciding to—down the hall toward the elevators. Stepping into the nearest car, my grandmother resumed her earlier, imperial manner, and I saw she was performing in her imagination an entirely different drama from many of Saint Vincent's other residents, one of whom, in an inside-out turtleneck sweater, shuffled toward us looking fully bewildered.

"He lives in the Twilight Zone, that one." My grandmother pushed the close-door button. "Sometimes you can get a straight answer out of him. Other times? Jabberwock." She shook off a shiver. "And homely? Imagine having to kiss that every night."

Taped inside the elevator was a variety of colour photocopies. These announced Jazzercise sessions, Christmas carolling, prayer groups. I was reading a bulletin about a memorial service when my grandmother said, "That's what Dolly dragged me to this afternoon. I didn't mind going to funerals when they only happened once in a while. But this place?" She made a pained smile, as if there were further details to be divulged. "And do you know what hymn they chose? Mackie, you won't believe what hymn they chose. 'They whipped and they stripped and they hung me high and they left me there on a cross to die.'" She smirked at us, as if her own dismay had just been wonderfully validated. "I mean it's the tackiest, most God-awful hymn you can imagine. For a *funeral?*"

MY GRANDMOTHER sat at her dressing table reapplying her mascara, the table surface busy with poinsettias, an eyelash curler, a slim rouge brush, a silver hand-mirror, a square-bottomed decanter of bourbon, two cut-glass tumblers, an unopened box of Thank You notes, and, in a pine frame, a photograph of my grandfather, the print so dislodged most of the image was lost within its matting. A smell of floral perfume pervaded the environment, seeming drenched into everything from the padded coat hangers in the closet to the embroidered linen doilies on the dressing table to the white lace collar of my grandmother's burgundy dress. A television, in another resident's room, was loudly tuned at the moment to a Christmas special where a tenor was quavering through "O Holy Night."

"I used to know the name of that song," said my grandmother. "Is that Andy Williams?"

My mother, after a brief frown—for my grandmother's failure to remember a favourite Christmas carol was another of the day's mysteries—sat on the bed and, following a moment of private deliberation, gaily leaned into the room. "So, my dear, how are things in Glocca Morra?"

"Well," said my grandmother. "Seventy-four isn't sixty-four, I want to tell you. I've got three more years and then my looks are really going to go." She reached for the decanter of bourbon and, with a slight palsy in her right hand, poured herself a drink. "Now normally I wouldn't take a drop of hard liquor—"

"No," said my mother. "Just a forty-ouncer."

"But my nerves today are shot. Put everyone in such a state, what happened to Dolly." She raised the glass, a bit erratically, spilling a dewdrop on her wrist. "Cheers, my dears."

For the last few minutes, my grandmother had affected a mood of playful detachment but, as she smiled and over-sniffed some moisture in a clogged nostril, the rest of the room began to sense the mood's essential falsity. My mother was about to say something, probably to inquire after Saint Vincent's reasons for thinking my grandmother missing, when footsteps approached in the hallway.

My grandmother turned and directed a radiant smile toward the doorway. When this visitor, an elderly lady in bifocals, hobbled past, it was clear this was not whom my grandmother was expecting and she reacted with a series of micro-expressions—a spasm of annoyance, a flinch of pain, and finally a slow-building pout, as if she were concerned a conspiracy was being somewhere set up against her.

"Who's that?" asked my mother.

"Joyce," my grandmother replied, firmly, clutching her glass of bourbon. "Her daughter, Mary-Lou, she sings with St. Martin's-in-the-Fields. She won a Bafty—She won a Bafter—She won an award. Her mother's a Morrow. Well—" My grandmother inclined her head. "Was. All the old families are gone. The Mairs, the Morrows. They hardly exist anymore. Oh, people used to care about each other. But it's all segmented now."

"Who are you kidding? You never cared about anybody. You couldn't wait to get away."

"Well," said my grandmother, bitter. "I still can't." She stared at her jewelled wristwatch as if she feared it might be broken. "I've got to get out of this place. I've *got* to."

"And go where? Back to Florida?"

"How am I going to do that? I have no money."

"What about Dompa's pension?"

"Ha! I drank that away."

"Well," said my mother, reaching for something on the floor. "As long as it didn't go to waste." She picked up a fold of toilet paper. It was vivid with a smear of lipstick where someone had blotted their lips. "You're looking pretty good, Mum, for someone who's supposed to be sick—"

"I called to say I wasn't coming."

"So why get your hair done?"

"For the—the service."

"Mmm-hmm. This is the real world. The one I have to live in. Hoop earrings and high heels? For a funeral? Something's going on."

Nan's attention was drawn again to the doorway where a looming shadow preceded the appearance of the woman in the Lindsay tartan dress. For some minutes, this woman had been lurking like Hamlet's ghost—a rather portly, slow-moving Hamlet's ghost—but she now looked in and fixed my grandmother with a distasteful, vindictive stare.

"She's always got something up her skirt, that one," whispered my grandmother, going to the door. "Making a big to-do. I'd just as soon trip her."

A few murmurs passed between the two women before my grandmother carelessly swung the door shut.

"That *was* Elsy Horne," said my mother. "Dodie's godmother. What'd she want?"

"I have no idea." My grandmother flipped her hair. "The Catholics, they're always ganging up on people. Thinking their way is the best because it's the oldest. Well, let me tell you, I was in Rome once and I'm so glad I'm *not* Catholic. All that blood."

"What'd you say to her? Because you said something."

"I don't know," said my grandmother, reaching for the decanter of bourbon. "Go screw yourself and your dispensation from the Pope." She refilled her glass. "Oh, she gives me the pip, that Elsy Horne."

My mother was frowning. It was the day's starkest frown, a sort of intricacy of thoughtfulness, but in another moment all frowns would vanish as the pieces of the play for her came together. "Oh, Mum." She stared at my grandmother with real helplessness. "You did not. Tell me you didn't. Tell me you're not carrying on with Dodie's *father*."

Moisture came unbidden to my grandmother's eyes. Another fit of expressions began to form in her face but none really seemed to take. It was all somehow terrible to see.

"*That's* who you were expecting? But he didn't come today, did he?" My mother rose off the bed. "Mother. Look at me. His wife's *upstairs*. She's right upstairs. What in the name of God were you thinking?"

My grandmother was staring at us, but staring without any recognition. Attempting to speak, her mouth began to form words but no sounds were coming out and instead she made a simpering, crooked smile. Pushing on the dressing table, she suddenly started out of her chair, went over on a high heel, and toppled to the floor. She lay where she'd fallen, shivering.

My mother knelt beside her and felt for a pulse. At this touch, my grandmother screamed, as if she'd been stabbed with a letter-opener, and clutched at the foot of the dressing table. There was real madness in her eyes, a sort of feral cunning that showed no idea but resistance.

"Aubrey—" My mother stood up. "I'm going to tell the duty-nurse to call a doctor. Stay with Nan. And—" She looked at my grandmother's wristwatch. "It's six-forty. Remember that time." She opened the door and fled in rubber boots down the hall.

My grandmother's face was pale beneath smears of rouge, her eyes gleaming with tears, her lower lip dribbling a gossamer line of phlegm. I was aware of a smell of raw urine—there was a dampening in her burgundy dress—and when I got down beside her she made me understand she wished to be taken to the bathroom. We rose to a hunchbacked, standing position and I guided her to the bathroom, her hand feebly shooting for and grabbing the diagonal safety bar on the wall beside the toilet. After a few side-to-side leveraging movements, I was able to remove from the crumples of her dress and pantyhose her incontinence pad, the absorbent lining for which was thoroughly soaked through. She pulled up her dress, established herself on the toilet, and waved me out of the room. I closed the bathroom door and went to the hallway, wiping my hands on my jeans. I scanned the hall. Seeing no one, and mindful of my mother's direction to stay put, I went back and opened the bathroom door, startled to see my grandmother sitting naked on the floor beside the toilet, a moist bit of feces mysteriously balanced in the groove of her collarbone. The burgundy dress, pantyhose, foam-cupped brassiere, and high heels were discarded on the tile floor. She sat stricken with fright, vulnerability, and—what was worse—an absolute confusion as to where she was and what was happening. Which was when my mother returned. Flicking the dirt from my grandmother's shoulder, she said, "Let's get you to the bed, Mum." I helped heave my grandmother off the floor. A flush of sweat had risen all over her, making her skin slippery, and I dug my fingers tightly into the wattles of her underarm to make sure she didn't slide away from us. We staggered across the room and bumpily lowered her to the bed.

Scarcely conscious, making no effort to conceal her nakedness, my grandmother sprawled on the bedspread, a hoop earring bending under her cheek.

"Aubrey," said my mother, watching her. "Go see what's taking so long."

My sprinting steps in the hall overlapped with a second shriek from my grandmother and, swiveling around, I saw, framed in the proscenium of the doorway, both women lying on the bed, my mother looking alertly into my grandmother's eyes. "You be strong, Mum. Doctor's coming any minute. You squeeze my hand. Just like that. That's it. You hold on now. I'm right here."

Karin

IN MY LATER TEENAGE YEARS, I belonged with helpless ardour to an outfit called The Common Room. We were an autonomous arts collective, a semiotics research team, a coed gang of adventurers. We were Nova Scotian, mostly Halifax-born, and we had plans, projects, crushes, crusades. We rowed the waters of the province in second-hand suits. We formed punk bands. We wrote letters, songs, treatments for books. We established a joint bank account that is still, as far as I know, collecting interest on its remaining fifty-seven dollars. Our ongoing and evolving relations were sort of fucky and devoted and inexplicable. There is a preface in Thurber where he suggests that, for a certain type of figure, "the confused flow of his relationships with six or eight persons and two or three buildings is of greater importance than what goes on in the nation or in the universe." For me those six or eight persons were my colleagues and associates in The Common Room and the flow of our relations *was* my nation and universe. Who were they? We were Tom Waller, Gail and Brigid Benninger, Babba Zuber, Cyrus Mair, myself, and Karin Friday. Did it all arise because of Karin? She had the tape, she was the voice. She was the girl and the adventure. Babba Zuber, full of endogenous goodwill and long one of the city's most acute noticers—and I will quote her extensively, deferring to many of her analyses, as we go forward because more than any of us Babba has been a class secretary who's kept track of our brave new world, that has such people in it—Babba once explained her take on Karin like so: "To tell the truth, at first I sort of dismissed her as a rah-rah, go-to-Queen's, daddy's-little-girl girl. You know, the preppy athletic girl who's used to male companionship and male interest and who kind of ends up with gorgeous children and a distant husband and a drinking problem. But why would that girl like Cyrus Mair?" As she always did, Babba paused for my reaction and normally she regarded me with a slightly cringing expression, her amber eyes skeptical behind black-framed glasses, listening in the way she listened to any of us, as if she were more than slightly worried some new catastrophe might overwhelm one of us—if we were superheroes Babba was Ultra Cautious Girl—but in this moment, faced with the severity of the historical circumstance and both of us having come out the other side of it, she gazed back at me only very directly, as if listening without preconception, without bias, as if setting an example for listeners everywhere. "I just think," she said, "that Karin was trying to create a family in us, the family she didn't have, really, and of course that got all fucked up by the end but people forget how spontaneous and charming she was when we first met her. She was one of those people you feel you've been waiting your whole life to meet. She had a way of becoming this gorgeous person for everybody maybe without even knowing it herself. She could make another person mean *everything*. Wasn't it that way for you?" I can't recall my reaction to Babba that day, I wasn't sure then as I'm not sure now—I can confuse my sharps and naturals—and, try as I might, I've never been sure what to make of Karin Catherine Friday.

BUT IN THE years before her flux of circumstance, long before the advent of Karin Friday, I was just another kid with vertical hold control issues. And when my parents split a second time I became something of a motherless child. Over these schism years, I lived with my father and two older sisters in the house on Dunvegan. In the interests of getting me off the streets and socially adjusted, I was enrolled in a number of pithy pursuits—Scouts Canada, Pee-Wee football, speech therapy, highland dancing, and, abandoned after twelve weeks, weekly guitar lessons where a bearded, hungover hippie in a leather fringe vest frowned his way through the chords of "More Than a Feeling" and "Dust in the Wind." It was because of a Wilson Pro Staff tennis racquet left behind by my uncle—and the televised dramatics of Jimmy, Björn, and John—that I became interested in the idea of tennis. To tennis I applied myself with the sort of early-morning fervour normally only associated in Halifax with junior hockey. In summer, I packed two lunches and stayed at the courts, playing anyone and everyone. In winter, I dressed in ski-jacket and gloves and kicked away the frozen puddles so I could use the school parking lot and highest wall as a private backboard facility. I was coordinated, I had aptitude, I had desire, and before long I was one of those wiener kids in a bandana who takes huge cuts at any ball that comes up short. In tournaments I became known as a roaring boy, someone who might hit a hot streak and demolish any opponent or, just as likely and just as often, explode with unforced errors and emotional torment. I wanted to win, or, if this makes sense, I wanted desperately to not-lose. Losing did terrible things to my equilibrium and sense of self. At thirteen I was ranked in both

Fourteen-and-Under and Sixteen-and-Under and saw my name in the newspaper for a first time. I played the regionals, provincials, captained a Junior Davis Cup team. By fourteen there were only a few kids my age who were legitimate rivals. There was a band of brothers named Burr who lurked in the bigger tournaments, a Cape Breton cruncher named Shane McBain, and a kid from Dartmouth with whippy strokes named Monaj Ponambulam. Arriving on the South Shore for the summer's first tournament, I checked out the matches-in-progress and my possible opponents. On the farthest court, Shane was playing some skimpy-looking kid, a sniffly blond boy so little he looked like a kid from Twelve-and-Under. The kid wore a long-sleeved red turtleneck shirt, cricket trousers, and plimsoll sneakers—the kind you'd see on an elderly widow as she tottered amid rhododendrons. He was playing with a heavy-looking Dunlop Maxply and, in the thick fog of the Lunenburg morning, the way the sleeve of his turtleneck drooped past his fingers and along the grip, the racquet seemed a sort of prosthetic wooden extension of the turtleneck itself. We played no-ad scoring in these junior days, an expedient, get-it-over-with scenario, and I was astonished to see, after a flubbed half-volley at Deuce, this blond kid violently thrash at his right calf three times in some controlled, personalized fury. On the next changeover, he produced from his racquet bag a Pippin apple. He ate this very methodically, with a fullness of concentration more appropriate to a seminary student, closing his eyes in don't-distract-me meditation. Now Shane McBain was a crash-and-burn bruiser who played a game of pounding serve and volley. But this skimpy-looking kid began getting everything back, playing a game of absurd defensive retrieval—he was maybe the greatest ball chaser I'd ever seen. In the course of one rally, I saw him dig out a dying drop shot at the net, chase down a monster forehand two hits later to just barely float back a flimsy lob, and then, on the resulting overhead, run and *climb up* the chain-link fencing at the back of the court—a manoeuver I'd not seen before and wasn't sure was entirely legal—and then, hanging off a corner-post, fluke a knuckleball backhand past Shane McBain, who was standing at the net very much dumbfounded, very much what-the-fuck-just-happened, very much who-*is*-this-kid. The momentum turned on that point and on the next changeover the skimpy-looking kid draped a scarf around his neck and played the last three games wrapped up like a consumptive, quivering, sneezing, and coughing up bits of sputum as he willed himself through a fever and to the end of the contest. He won that match and later that tournament, playing the final in hearing protection headphones, the kind you'd see on an aircraft worker, and this skimpy-looking kid was, I realized, a child seen by me some years before. This kid, of course, was Cyrus Mair.

WE SALLIED THROUGH the summers, Cyrus Mair and I, playing tournaments all over the province, billeted with strangers, sleeping on church floors, hitching rides with event organizers. We played on carpet courts improvised inside curling rinks, asphalt courts cracked with spring swelling, weedy clay courts with doubles alleys four feet from a community hall. Our opponents in these boonies showed up on dirt-bikes, competed in mirror sunglasses, trucker caps, sleeveless football jerseys, and with frying pan grips smacked serves off hideously low ball tosses, beasted forehands off their back foot, and went for running smashes from the baseline. These kids were dinkers and slicers, hackers and moonballers, often with only one real offensive weapon—a big serve or a slugging two-handed backhand—and mostly unable to keep a rally going beyond six hits. Cyrus and I travelled through our teen years as the Big Two in our cohort, opponents and doubles partners, both of us deciding as juniors to enter the Men's Singles draw at the Nova Scotia Open. This was the biggest deal in the province, a multi-category tournament held every August on ten courts at Halifax's Waegwoltic Club, and on the middle Thursday of the tournament, on an extended weather-delay, I was sitting on a park bench with a teenage Cyrus Mair, watching the grey Har-Tru courts darken with drizzle, troubled by his seeming indifference to me. A moment before, I'd asked a question to which he'd remained formidably impassive. With an orange garbage bag arranged around his head as a rain cover, he sat cross-legged reading a book—*my* book actually—cocooned in his orange garbage bag and impermeable mid-puberty weirdness. He was smart—I knew by now he'd skipped two grades—but Cyrus Mair was a weird kid. He was a tennis junkie, a constant reader and, compared to most fifteen-year-olds, decidedly strange. The bright little boy I'd met as a kid had become a quirky, aloof kind of teenager. I'd witnessed such transformations before, from chatty child to pensive adolescent, most notably with my Uncle Lorne, and I wondered if, like my Uncle Lorne, Cyrus was choosing to hoard his thoughts now only to punk them out later. Although we were advancing in years, Cyrus was still very much a stripling. In the summers we played tennis, he was slim and elfin and preoccupied—often sideways to the room—as if he were mainly engaged in some personalized form of solitaire. At his most haploid, when he was wearing his hearing protection headphones or soaking his wrists in ice water before a match or, as he was now, shivering and reading in the drizzle under an orange garbage bag, the kid seemed bizarrely unfinished and self-involved. There was a sort of invisible force field around him—he shimmered with an aura of touch-me-not—and right away you sensed he was the sort of person who did not like to be disturbed. I can tell you he was modest about toileting generally, he ran the tap, and squeamish specifically about strangers and their goopy emulsions. He was mostly content to be overlooked and left to his books, even if, in this instance, it was *my* book. What was my book?

There is a mythology of jokes when one is younger that seems to thicken and saturate between the ages of eight and thirteen, perhaps the peak years for Joke Receptivity. I must have absorbed hundreds of them, and during that time I'd had a compulsion to record and categorize all the jokes I'd ever heard—Change A Light Bulb Jokes, Snail Jokes, Elephant Jokes, Dead Baby Jokes, Newfie Jokes, Silly Sally Jokes, Dirty Ernie Jokes, Dumb Blonde Jokes, Helen Keller Jokes, Knock Knock Jokes, Mommy Mommy Jokes, Guy Goes To The Doctor Jokes, Why Did The Whatever Cross The Road Jokes, Book Titles By This Funny Name Jokes, Dirty Limericks, Shaggy Dog Stories, My Car Broke Down Can I Stay With You For The Night Tall Tales, Guy Walks Into A Bar One-Liners, Funny Handshake Gags, Scary Your Husband's Hanging In The Tree Swish-Swish Friend-Of-A-Friend Urban Myths, Snappy Comebacks and Put-Downs, and a few Unclassifiable Items besides. All of these I studiously inscribed into the endpapers of my hardcover copy of *Watership Down*, many of my entries spilling into the internal pages proper. Intrigued to learn of such an artifact, Cyrus had asked to see it for a casual examination, I thought, but he was now some minutes into a diligent reading of what seemed to be the book's actual text. When I realized he was reading beyond my own annotations, I asked what the hell he was doing. But, as described, Cyrus had entered a sort of fugue state and I saw from his rapt dweebiness that he would not reply. I was trying not to care, really, what he thought of the book because I'd learned, from previous you-should-read-this-book and have-you-heard-this-song instances, that Cyrus was almost impossible to impress and very resistant to foreign enthusiasms. In fact, beyond a freak interest in Kid Flash and the keyboard solo of "Follow You, Follow Me," I'd never successfully inspired Cyrus Mair's curiosity in anything. I didn't know what the guy was thinking or wanted or wished for. Who did?

Just at that point, Cyrus looked up, rainwater dripping from a central, overhead crease in the orange garbage bag. He scanned the purple thunderclouds with closed lips, uneasy, as if searching for an opening he couldn't identify. Then he better arranged the orange garbage bag around his head and opened a package of Cherry Nibs. With most candy, Cyrus was very generous. He gave away whole fingers of Kit Kats, freely distributed Fruit Stripe Gum, but with Cherry Nibs he had a fastidious, no-sharesy policy. So we both knew, from long-established practice, he would be consuming every last one. Cyrus had a sort of occult contrariness—even in his stillness he seemed to imply what we could and couldn't do—and so I turned my attention elsewhere.

At my feet was a rusting can of Wilson tennis balls as well as my tennis racquets in their green racquet covers. The covers sheltered a variety of particulars—tricolour wristbands, a coverless issue of *Mad* magazine, a baggie of three joints, a digital watch with a Velcro strap—and I busied myself with putting on and firmly tightening my digital watch, not wanting Cyrus to offer me any Nibs, not caring what he thought of the book, not wanting any interaction at all. But there was something about the soft licorice candy and the mustiness of the weather that drew the fragrance from the Cherry Nibs, making the misty air keenly redolent of cherry flavouring—leaving traces in my hair and on my skin—and generally evoking the foreboding aura before a migraine. All afternoon, some mental congestion had been growing within me because of the low-pressure system, the constant drizzle, Cyrus's geeky autism, as well as the rising influence of a pop ballad, "If You Leave Me Now," which I was hearing for the sixth time in my life as it played on the Samsung radio in the opened window of the pro shop and sign-up booth. I'd never really had anyone leave me, not anyone my own age anyway, but this song seemed to speak to some poignant part of me and I guessed that this was probably exactly how I *would* feel if someone were to leave me. I'd never told anyone what I thought of this song, nor how uncanny my connection with it was—on this sixth listen the song was, if anything, even more pronounced in its emotional power—and for the life of me I couldn't understand, in fact I sort of *resented*, how this song knew something about my secret heart that I myself hadn't yet guessed. As the acoustic guitar solo wormed deeper into my vulnerable brain, I got up from the bench and left Cyrus Mair and his Cherry Nibs and wandered the grounds of the Waegwoltic Club as obscurely saddened and perplexed as only a fifteen-year-old boy can be.

I had not walked more than sixty paces toward the open sea when I saw a girl on the lower courts practising her serve in the rain. She was alone, maybe fifteen or sixteen years old. There was a sense of precise movement and vibrant colour—yellow-and-white Slazenger tennis dress, pleated blonde hair held back on either side by symmetrically-placed and matching white barrettes. When one of her serves hit the net tape and bounced back into the air, she let the ball drop into the court, skipped up to it, and blasted a two-handed backhand with a sudden wrist-twist of top-spin and a rotating motion of her upper body. It was a moment of supreme integrity embodied in athleticism—a sort of convergent moment of instinct and decisiveness and girlhood—and this moment was Karin Catherine Friday, a kid visiting from Oakville, Ontario, and staying that summer in Halifax with her grandmother. But I didn't know any of this then. All I knew—as I watched her ball jangle off the fence in front of me, still full of spin, jinking this way and that—was there was a mysterious rightness about everything she did. On the near side of the court now, she glanced at me, snapping her fingers and thumb together in a quick sort of greeting. It was a gesture of real friendliness, actually, as if seeing me was the one meeting she was hoping for—as if she were happy, finally, to encounter someone who saw the world as she did.

"Hey there," she said. "Are you with the tournament?"

I said I was in the tournament but not exactly with it.

"Oh," she said. "You're not exactly with it?" She bent toward an opened Adidas bag. Within the bag was a surfeit of effects—I had an impression quickly of Trident gum, Bonne Bell Lip Smacker, a People magazine, a Slazenger warmup jacket—but my gaze went first to a space-age device that seemed from the future, a small stereo cassette player I would later understand to be a Sony Walkman. There was also the matter, beside the Adidas bag, of three immaculate-looking Chris Evert Autograph tennis racquets still in factory plastic as well as the three shoe-tags on her yellow Tretorn sneakers. I'd played every club for five hundred miles and didn't recognize any of the tags. All of these details meant she was out-of-province and probably rich or sponsored by Wilson—which would mean she was very talented and possibly nationally-ranked.

She stuffed the racquets in her bag and stepped out of the fenced-in courts, clanging the door shut behind her. "Do you know someone named Kelly Gallagher?" she asked, slinging the bag over her shoulder. "She's my third round. But I'm supposed to play three different matches today if you can believe it. Singles, doubles, mixed. Plus there's some lobster barbecue. It's enough to make you barf up some puke." She touched at the white barrettes to confirm they were still in place. "And here it is raining on the longest day of the year. The vernal equinox or endoplasmic reticulum or whatever it is. Do you know what it is, Mr. Tudball? I always get those mixed up." Though she was looking up and down the vacant courts, there was a strong sense she was quite peripherally aware of me. "I actually like that no one's here. It's like nothing's ever going to happen. Of course the sun could come out and this place could fill up with billions of people. With Kelly Gallagher and all her whatnots. Who knows? Who knows what awaits? Perhaps there are French fries." She respectfully extended her hand. "I'm Karin, by the way."

"Hello, Karin By The Way," I said—and perhaps a word or two should be jammed in here about Aubrey at Fifteen. At fifteen, I was your standard-issue Pothead Tennis Bum: hair untidy and sunbaked, shirt untucked, Stan Smith sneakers very scuffed. In my younger years, as man and boy, I had in motion so many murky ideas, of varying purposes, that I wasn't really equal to explaining what I felt or thought and tended to withdraw instead into drugs and playacting and sarcasm—I had some idea these procedures would be taken to be interesting. I hadn't really settled on a coherent social identity and around new people, especially girls, I was sometimes conscious of my below-average height and a recurring white pimple that lurked problematically within one of my nostrils. Of course I was also at the age when I was becoming very responsive to tennis dresses and I wondered at the mysterious hiddenness within such clothing and how, for example, without too much ado, a tennis ball might magically materialize from under the skirt. But in the main, especially on days of oppressive congestion, I tended to ignore girls and other people—they were occupied with a world of details beyond me—and I acted as if I was so into tennis I didn't really care about anything else.

"Want a fry?" Karin bent into the canteen window and paid for her order on tiptoe, the back hem of her tennis dress rising up sharply. "I suppose I could give you a French fry and then you could like me." Taking the cardboard dish of fries, she soaked them all with ketchup.

"I like people whether they feed me or not."

"You do?" She squinted at me as if she were completely disgusted. "Who *are* you?"

I told her my name

"No," said Karin, shaking her head, as if in response to an absurd fabrication. "I think it's Tudball." She picked out a French fry. "But here's a French fry, Tudball. Does it have gookies on it? Whoopsy. Let me wipe it off. It's actually wilting. But it's good enough for the likes of you." She passed me the French fry and took a step forward, experimentally smelling my shoulder. "Aubrey Tudball!" She drew back. "You smell like a wet dog. You smell like a ten-year-old sleeping bag. You smell like a champignon. Why is that? Are you a champignon?"

I said it might be my new cologne.

"No, I think it's because you're a newt. And you like to smell newty." Returning her attention to her purchase, she was startled to see in midair a foreign body, something slim and green and larval, in front of her face, suspended on a free-blowing silken thread. "Ew! What the flip? Get this paramecium off my flipping fries." She stabbed at it with a French fry. When, for whatever reason, the larva swung directly into her face, Karin dropped the fry in fright and made a sudden giggle. Now Karin Catherine Friday was a daring girl with a variety of communicable laughs, especially this high-pitched giggle, which began with an involuntary sniff of voiced breath—sounding more in her nose than her mouth—and which signaled unexpected delight. It was very contagious, this half-giggle of hers, and for months afterwards, when I was far into my winter term of high school, I would hear my own version of Karin Friday's careless giggle issuing from my nose in the middle, say, of a math unit on cotangents.

WHEN THE THUNDERSTORM BROKE, an electrical squall exploding above us, Karin went dashing toward the clubhouse. I found her in one of the rooms of the restaurant, her Adidas bag dropped to the floor, both of us sopping wet, shoulders hunched forward so the rainwater would drip off our chins rather than down our backs. "That storm—" said Karin. "That storm hit me right in the couscous."

"The where?"

"Aubrey Tudball." Karin touched again at her barrettes. "What are you doing? Are you soaking wet? Are you still a champignon?"

I *was* soaking wet, my nose cold, my skin goose-bumped. Making a move for the hallway, I said I was going downstairs to get some paper towels. "You okay with that?"

She frowned. "Did you just say I looked fat?"

"No, Wiggins. Paper towels."

"No, you said I should lose ten pounds and had a fat ass."

"Oh, wait. That's it exactly. No, I'm going to the bathroom—"

"Boys are gross."

"To get some paper towels."

On my way back with a stack of paper towels, I was checking my reflection in the glass of a framed photograph of past presidents of the Waegwoltic Club, relieved to see my nose was generally blemish-free, when I heard the crash of a window breaking. Returning to the room, I saw Karin standing in front of a ruined window, a sparkle of broken glass on the hardwood floor, the splintered end of a stout tree branch lodged in the fractured window frame. As I joined her in looking at the wreckage, lightning flashed in the sky and a second surge of rain splashed against the windows. The power winked off, giving a sort of apocalyptic quality to our situation—darkness in the afternoon, lightning tinting the room blue—and, instinctively, we both backed away from the window, our bare elbows touching, slippery with rain. I glanced at Karin to see her tennis dress splattered with moisture, a glisten of watery ketchup on her upper lip, her eyelashes moistened into star-points. She looked at me with open eyes, leaned toward me, and kissed me on the mouth. I remember how eager were her soft, open-mouthed kisses, the murmurs she made as I kissed near her throat, the pattern of peeling sunburn on her exposed shoulder. After some moments, Karin moved to take a step back but my hair, straggly and rain-damp, caught in one of her barrettes so it was a few seconds before we disengaged from each other, our temples colliding as we separated, the barrette springing loose and falling to the floor.

I picked it up. "Your barrette, Madame."

"Oh. Thank you, kind sir. What would I do without my barrette?" She neatly inserted it in her hair, dried her arms and legs with paper towel, and in the next moment she was grabbing my wrist and spinning my arm to read my digital watch. "What time is it? Oh, God, Tudball. The time has come, the walrus said. I've really got to run. My mixed is at four."

"In a lightning storm?"

"No, Ding-a-ling. Didn't you hear? They're making us play in a flipping school gym. Classy, I know." She plucked her bag off the floor. "Any advice?"

"You're playing mixed? Go after the girl."

"Go after the girl? What if she goes after you?" Flinging her bag over her shoulder, she touched again at both barrettes, a trifle coquettishly—a first gesture that betrayed any sign of nervousness or self-consciousness.

Taking the last, unused paper towel, I wiped from her cheek the smear of ketchup that had been preoccupying me the last few minutes and which had spread, in a sort of diluted, post-smooch curlicue, toward her left ear. "There," I said. "I just sort of wanted to do that."

"See you next time, Mr. Tudball," said Karin, staring at me. "Probably I won't see you again for billions of months."

"Probably not till after your hog roast."

"What do you have—a bionic memory or something? It *is* a hog roast. With lobsters." She snapped her fingers and thumb together. "Au revoir, Monsieur," she said, jouncing out the door of the clubhouse.

I didn't follow her outside but I listened as she skipped up the ramp toward the tennis courts. I was trying to figure out what had just happened. There were two or three uncertainties to our relations I couldn't figure out. This girl, this figure from faraway, from the future, really, for she seemed to have arrived from some new continuum of girliness, she had such a swift knowledge of the moment yet she was often pretending to be confused by what was going on. This would become a trademark diversion of Karin Friday, I'd notice, how she affected to mishear or misunderstand what you were saying, faking a ditzy ignorance, only to further pretend she was taking offense at what she thought you were implying. It reminded me of a little kid singing a nursery rhyme and pretending she *wasn't* getting the lyrics wrong. I found her flirtiness touching—and her riffs on the characters from *The Carol Burnett Show* seemed sweet and I was flattered she'd kissed me—but she was maybe a bit genuinely crazy, at odds with six or seven uncertainties, some real, some maybe not so real, and there may have been something within her that was completely loopy and irregular. It was a small node with bits of orange and violet in it—the size, say, of a swallow in a storm—but it was there. I did feel there was something lovely and abiding about the person she could become, though. My own understanding of her fell off somewhere—I didn't know where or why—I just knew I wanted to astonish her.

PLAYING TENNIS, I HAD PROBLEMS. I had problems with my volleys, I had problems in my head. I tended to win everything but the last match where I would flame out in the final, trying to hit my way out of trouble, going for big shots that weren't there, berserkly energetic in a losing effort, the bigger drama on court becoming my relationship with my own failure. The various disturbances growing within me that week at the Nova Scotia Open would result in me getting thrown out of the tournament. On a scorching afternoon, on a day when I was alternately cracking forehands crosscourt and shanking backhands into the fence, I would smash my best racquet and use a number of swear words in a fit of I Hate Tennis frustration, this during a match against Bunker Burr, an eighteen-year-old hotshot with a kick serve, losing by disqualification in the third set after I had three match points in the second set tiebreaker. Bunker had gleam in his eye and jump in his step. He advanced through his half of the draw in form and in the zone, defeating me in the quarters, destroying the junior tennis coach in the semis, and meeting Cyrus Mair in the Sunday final. Cyrus would lose this match in a flurry of mistakes—this from a kid who could go *days* without an unforced error—and in fact he'd never win another tournament or play tennis seriously again. But I don't know if it mattered to him. That afternoon he ran off the court, sweaty, glowing, a forelock of hair tapered to a point. "I met that girl," he said.

"What girl?"

"The one everyone's talking about."

"Who? Karin?"

"She's just like us."

"Who is—Karin?"

"Yeah," said Cyrus. "I think she's a genius of life."

KARIN CATHERINE FRIDAY was cute, carelessly cute, effortlessly cute, and in certain slants of light she was deliriously cute. She was one of those young women, like Kelly Gallagher or Megan Beckwith, who get known in the way instantly cute girls get known beyond the borders of their school and neighbourhood simply for being freshly gorgeous. In the seaside city of Halifax, where the Scots-Irish and African-Acadian and Nordic-German gene pools mingle and stream, where in some waters beauty spreads through the female population like a virus, Karin would become a regular contender for Prettiest Girl on Spring Garden Road. She embodied a quintessence of *girl* with all that word's connotations of agility, rapture, and caprice. She was high spirits and high cheekbones, snow-blossom skin blooming into rosiness, her chin left-leaning to allow for the sweeping fall of abundant blonde bangs. In the junior and senior highs of the day, certain girls were celebrated because of their perceived resemblance to cultural ideographs and cinematic reference points. *Zum Beispiel*—Suzanne Snyder was considered stunning because, with her flared mouth, smoky eye shadow, and lacy peasant blouses, she was the closest we had to a Spanish Dancer. Similarly, the full-figured Kelly Gallagher—she of auburn curls and an alcoholic father—was our candidate for Freckly Celtic Druidess. Brigid Benninger was a Neurotic Snow White, Robyn Izzard a Nubian Princess, Megan Beckwith a Hillybilly Amazon. But Karin Friday was polymorphic. She floated. She shifted. She was a number of people all at once, shimmering between Tennis Nymph, Mayfair Flapper, and Hitchcock Heroine. She carried a number of symbolic identities—it was as if she could be anything you wanted her to be, almost as if she had no real control over her own nature or allure. In many moments, especially as a flip tweenster, before she achieved notoriety, I sensed she was embarrassed by her prettiness and generally acted as if she'd been given some prize she didn't ask for and for which she didn't particularly want any responsibility. She didn't flaunt her looks. She acted as if she hadn't earned the privilege. Her silliness, her playacting, her impulse to make jokes about herself, these were all maneuvers of social distraction. She did not wish to be regarded as an object of beauty. She preferred to behave as a goofball extrovert so you forgot how she looked. But I was one of those for whom Karin's fluid liveliness—the nose-wrinkling at the absurdity of a strange person, the lip-sneering at the salacious behaviour of a drunk friend, the puckered lips at the cuteness of a manic toddler, motions and attitudes she animated with a multiplicity of intonation and inflection and split-second eye-movement and which were as natural to her as breathing—lit up as something of a revelation and would establish a pattern of flirty female behaviour that I would seek out again and again, moth to the flame.

Now the leading ladies of the town, whom my mother assessed with a pageant devotee's obsessive-compulsion, were a source of much conversation in our house. My sisters, ever sensitive to the import of womenfolk, and communing with other females in some non-verbal, pheromones-and-territoriality way—in what was really some highly feminized version of quorum sensing—my sisters appreciated Karin for her beauty and observed her as they could, quietly waiting to see if she revealed herself to be a friend, bitch, dimwit, or rival. My mother's reaction was typically swift. "Oh she's a nice-looking girl. She is. That kid's got a lot of options. Maybe too many. Because my God, Aubrey, that child flirts with *everybody*."

SCENE. A FRIDAY IN OCTOBER. Karin and I walk up Oxford Street after playing tennis. We have become hitting partners, practice chums. My tracksuit is dark, hers light blue, and inside our jackets our shoulders are warm, not yet clammy. Karin is teasing me about what she has decided is my enormous crush on Kelly Gallagher—someone who walks on court with a quasi-intentional teeter-totter of her bottom, someone Karin has beaten three matches in a row, but someone whom Karin has decided should be elevated to a position of generic enviableness. "Oh, Kelly," she says. "That Kelly, you're obsessed with her. Just admit it for once."

"With who?"

"'With who.' You know who."

"Who—Kelly Gallagher?"

"Yes," she says with mock-annoyance. "Kelly Gallagher. I'm talking about Kelly *Gallagher*." Karin repeats the name over and over and it will become a recreation of hers to pretend to hear this name for the first time, the sounds of the name celebrated as phonemes to be repeated in phlegmy, guttural fashion, perhaps building, when giddy or drunk, to falsetto ridiculousness (Gully-*Gully*-Ga! Gully-*Gully*-Ga!). Karin is wonderfully absorbed in such intrigues, her quivers and giggles seem to bring her to the brink of some exquisite chaos—a chaos which, very possibly, she might be willing to share with you—but I notice how her laughter subsides as we approach the lineup at the Oxford Theatre.

Tonight's movie is some unknown phenomenon called *Quadrophenia* and I notice the kids in the lineup are starkly different from the motley schleps in my high school common room, the kids with whom I skip class, smoke dope, and play penny-a-point Hearts. The kids in the lineup are from various high schools and among their crowd is Jeremy Horvath, eccentric in a black mohair sweater, creased trousers, Beatle boots. I have respect for Jeremy Horvath and his friends and all their junk and foibles, but up to this time I've felt that their cool kid exclusivity, their semi-precious interests in Minimoogs and Fortran and polyhedral dice, does not exactly coincide with my own scheme of things. There is something about his vigilant alertness, a sort of nothing-is-lost-on-me watchfulness, which makes me want to continue walking past him to the end of the line. There we encounter Brigid and Gail Benninger. Brigid is sleek with black hair. She is considered to be unimpeachably gorgeous, if somewhat aloof. To me, she seems indolently self-absorbed and perpetually spacey. It is the younger sister who has always compelled my attention. Gail Benninger is known as a sort of constantly furious teenager, as one of the wilder girls in the city, and someone at the mercy of an impulsive and profane temperament. A year before, I was not surprised to hear from my younger sisters that Gail was sternly grounded for not only wanting to go as the Pope to a Halloween dance at her school, the Convent of the Sacred Heart, but for sneaking out and attending this dance costumed only in a green garbage bag, *and* for getting caught later that night egging the statue of Jesus Christ on the school's front lawn—all of which acts of performance art resulted in a month of lock-down. I remember an afternoon, some weeks following these incidents, when I saw her crossing Henry Street with silver duct tape over her mouth, a symbolic gesture for I knew not what.

Now in person Gail has an energy of unworried independence. It is a vibe which can veer, I will understand later, depending on her blood sugar levels, toward random contentiousness and even outright antagonism, but there is something about her boldness and absurdly thick hair and radical oddness that makes her tremendously noticeable.

Tonight she has taken her school's regulation uniform—baby blue blouse, Black Watch kilt, navy blue leotards, Mary Jane shoes—and essentially destroyed it only to reconstruct it with safety pins and inserted zippers. The torn fabrics are bound and pinned tightly to her sturdy-looking physique, the shoes shined to a perverse sheen. She is fourteen years old. I have mostly stayed within the toss-and-tumble of druggy jock life but this movie event, charged with music and fashion—for many of the other girls are dressed in go-go boots and miniskirts—makes me wonder at the rising relevance of the city's alternative crowd. Who are they? What do they want? Where will they go? I am considering how best to take my leave when Karin simply steps toward Gail to say, "I love your shoes!"

VARIOUS COMMON ROOMERS arrive like postcards out of the past when I conjure our history, our scenes, our shows—figures appear in many forms and solid states. At some appropriately advanced juncture, I will refer the curious to such interludes as "Cyrus Mair in his Rooms," "The Glower of Jeremy Horvath," and, always a favourite, "Lying in Bed with Gail on Her Period," but this early to-do in front of the Oxford Theatre has real precedence in my mind and, as I recall it now, I realize it is linked to a cluster of associations—impressions, scene sequences, and half-thoughts—that I feel for Gail and me, for Karin and the impending Cyrus, and indeed for all of Halifax. It's the moment, really, when I first thought to properly understand the place—or when I first felt I might someday *try* to understand the place—and I date this chance meeting at the Oxford Theatre as the beginnings of our gang and conspiracy. My memory of the exact order of events is spotty. The movie is sold out. Jeremy Horvath and his crew get in. Gail and Brigid do not. "We suck," says Gail. "Because everything we do sucks. Just like this night sucks."

I mention the night is not over and at the Dominion supermarket on Quinpool Road I wander the aisles to buy provisions—three cans of Reddi-Whip, a package of Sudafed pills, Russet apples. We tramp down to the Horsefield, a local stretch of greenery, home to a Little League baseball diamond, a playground, and various meadows, the four of us popping two pills each and huffing the gas from the dessert topping. With the wind through the October leaves, the blue smell of Brigid's cigarettes, something seems open-ended in the night and soon we sit red-eyed under a tree on the other side of the outfield. I watch Gail consume a Russet apple in its entirety—fruit, seeds, core—soon twirling in her fingers nothing but the stem. Conscious of my attention, Gail returns my gaze, without self-consciousness or restraint, and takes from me the box of Sudafed. She reads its medical information. After a passing stare into my eyes, she returns it. "Get a lot of colds, do you?" she asks, defiant. I am deep into a description of the benefits of pseudoephedrine when she holds up a hand to shush me. "Oh, what do you know?" she says. "You look exactly like Robby Benson." This is an American teen idol of the day and I do not think I look much like Robby Benson and readers should know that, at various intervals, Gail has said I look *exactly like* Jim Morrison, Sir Wilfrid Laurier, and the young Debra Winger. I feel I should add, in a spirit of full disclosure, that during a sleazy period of my adolescence, the Jim Morrison resemblance I did very little to suppress. Thinking of these moments with Gail, and thinking generally of Gail, and watching the plastic grocery bag flutter in the wind above our heads, I am reorganizing my understanding of her, deciding she isn't just universally angry, that there are vectors to her defiance and, though I still find her peculiar, I am deciding I am impressed by a girl who has such tough opinions and who stands up for herself, even if it may bring her trouble later on. And with Gail it surely would.

Karin's Walkman is produced. The blue-and-silver contraption provokes curiosity and each of us takes a turn listening to the cassette inside. This is a homemade mix-tape—a TDK D60 sent to Karin by an ex-boyfriend in Toronto—and the rush of music adds a sudden soundtrack to our evening. Gail is the first to listen. Smoldering within her is an antipathy for anything mainstream, blowdried, or Top 40 but this unknown ex-boyfriend has put some thought into the making of this mix-tape, starting loud and lively then skewing slow and ambient, cross-fading songs we've never known. These songs will become touchstones of my sonic youth: "Janie Jones," "Submission," "God Save the Queen," "Kiss Me Deadly," "One Hundred Punks," "52 Girls," "Rock Lobster," "I Wanna Be Sedated," "Sheena is a Punk Rocker," "Blitzkrieg Bop," "Jocko Homo," "The Robots," and finishing with "Energy Fools the Magician," "Nostalgia," "Ever Fallen in Love," and "Why Can't I Touch It?" Gail is fascinated by the progression of music just as I am fascinated by the symbol she has drawn in black marker on her thigh through a hole in her navy blue leotards, a capital "A" with a circle swirled around it. She hands the Walkman to me as Karin asks, "You guys come here a lot?" I study Brigid and Gail, private school kids with nothing to do, sitting under a tree on a Friday night, stoned on whip-its and Sudafed by the woods of the railway cut. "Yeah," says Gail. "We come here every Friday night—" She turns from Karin to gaze at me. "To see what Robbie Benson does."

"And what is this place?" asks Karin. "What's it called?"

"This place?" I put the headphones on my ears and press play. "This is The Common Room."

KARIN'S REACTION: "I had the best time at the movie we didn't see, Tudball. It was the highlight of the season. That Brigid girl? Stunning. But—oh my God—Gail? I *love* her. Gail Gail Bo Bail, Banana Fanna Mo Mail—I love her! I do. Probably I will love her forever. She's such a perfect little boober. And so volumptious! At first I thought she was sort of—you know?" Karin thumped her chest with a fist. "Relentless. *Relentless*. You know? But really she's brave, I think. She's so brave. I love how strong she is. I love her aggressiveness. I wish I was like her. I'm sure she thinks I'm a ditzy doodle. I'm sure she thinks I'm a dippy jockette. So we should get a cake—an adventure cake—and travel to some island in the sea. I'm up for anything, Hot Pants. We're right beside the ocean, for flip's sake. We must go places! Know anybody with a boat?" Karin was born in Oakville, Ontario, though her mother was originally from Nova Scotia and, the summer we met, her mother was newly divorcing and making up her mind to move back east, choosing to settle in an area outside Halifax called Fleming Park. There she and Karin lived in modest means, in a wooden bungalow off Purcell's Cove Road, within view of the Dingle and the deep-blue sea. Karin's relations with her absentee father were strained, distant, moneyed. I would never meet her father. Michael Friday was an executive with Air Canada in Toronto. He travelled the world and sent his only child the spoils of foreign lands—a Walkman from Kyoto, a Vespa from Milan. "He's a little unpredictable," said Karin. "I mean, he's good at finding something he can be mad at you about. But then later? He feels guilty and buys you stuff. Tennis lessons was his idea. Piano was his idea. Appleby was his idea. Everything was his idea. But my mom moving here? Probably a good thing." When she came to town, Karin was enrolled at the Halifax Ladies College where she had the distinction of being the only sixteen-year-old in the city to pilot a scooter to school. This was a time of proliferating acquaintance, the persons met were many and plentiful, and any new kid, any boy or girl, might be conscripted to your own rebel alliance. There were six public high schools, each a thousand kids strong, and dances and rock shows and football games commingled these nation states. Impounded in an all-girls private school, Karin thrilled to hear of such outings and chose to set up The Common Room as a small company of adventurers. Learning of a sleepover on McNabs Island by my high school's Outdoors Club, Karin was determined to organize our own excursion. She recruited Brigid and Gail, with them assembled coolers of foodstuffs and wineskins of plonk, and asked me again for a boat. I knew of very few boats that could be got for free but I did remember a flat-bottom dory in the Mair house garage and, knowing my former doubles partner might be home for half-term holiday, I telephoned an inquiry. Cyrus would like to come along to supervise, he said, as one of the oarlocks was loose, he added, and, though I was wary of his nervousness, I agreed—we needed another guy anyway—and soon was helping to secure the dory to the roof of his family's purple Mercedes-Benz, wondering how his force field of touch-me-not might spin into our venture.

SO WE SAIL AWAY for a night and a day, a modern day Famous Five, our craft stowed with camping supplies, mildewed life jackets, a Sara Lee chocolate cake, each of us taking a turn rowing or munching from a bag of Cheezies, Karin trading her Walkman for Gail's paperback of *Jaws* and reading aloud the dirty parts, though scared of sharks all the same, watching the waves with a hand over her face. Approaching the island shore in darkness, we do not find the other campers and are too late to set up tents—ground sheets and Mylar sleeping bags scrunched on the pebbly beach, a fire in the drizzle and smores with Graham Crackers, M&Ms, and *guimauves* as Karin calls them, a word which passes into our shared vernacular. Words and phrases with Karin tend to assume new meanings, the sequence of her thought progressing in a free-for-all jumble without the regulations of logic or intelligibility. She uses words to suggest fondness for a person or situation and palpable in her inventions is much affection and goodwill. I am flattered she lets herself speak so freely, lapsing into a Little Kid persona in front of us all, though at one time, of course, I did wonder if such intimacies were meant for me. But Karin is the kind of person who enjoys herself no matter where she is. She simply feels at home in the world and considers every man-jack who comes into view as the playmate who might perfectly even up teams. But this outing to McNabs is exhausting for me—I am obsessively studying everyone's reaction while pretending not to be—watching where Brigid steers her attention, when Gail's eyes flicker with interest, who receives Karin's most delighted smiles. We talk and drink and disperse. I don't sleep much, afraid I'll miss something, and rise before dawn to look alone at the green-dark sea, wondering at the ocean-going container ship just now departing the harbour. I am thinking of relations and the idea of young women, remembering how once I'd heard an older kid shout "Jennifer!" across the street at a Grade 12 girl, the name sounding like a prayer or desperate plea, and these early morning notions, and the winking lights of the container ship, and all the qualities of the isle, begin to overwhelm me with their immensity and the glimmerings of so many other ways to be.

Further along the beach, Karin wriggles out from under the upturned dory where the girls have been sleeping. She ambles over, her blonde hair stringy from sleeping outdoors. "Hey there, Tudball." She sits on a beach stone with the bag of Cheezies. "What's happening?"

"Thinking of the sea. Shanties, bilge. That sort of thing."

Lowering her voice, as if she is sharing something confidential, she says, "Can I ask you a question—"

"Flotsam. Yardarm—"

"If it's not too personal."

"Boom vang. Wait—why isn't it personal?"

"You know your friend Cyrus?"

"A little bit."

"I think he likes me."

"Why not? You're kind of cute and he's a demented person."

"I know! He's like this complete freak of nature who's always—"

"Who is—Cyrus?"

"—talking because he has to learn everything for himself and tell you about it."

"Tell me about it." Off to my right, the sky begins to pastel with colour and in morning dimness I see the shape and contour of Karin's cheek.

"But sometimes," says Karin. "Sometimes his ideas are sort of like teleportals into another universe where everything—boop-de-doop—transmogrifies into some flipping boondoggle."

"Totally."

"Yeah," says Karin. "It makes me cry a little. I don't know why." She checks the fingernail of her middle finger. It's bruised and empurpled. Rowing the night before, she crushed it between oar and thwart. "My fingernail can't decide to fall off. And it stinks something terrible. Like the inside of someone's gym sneaker."

"Probably it got transmogrified."

"And, fuck, it's cold. Feel my hands. Isn't it supposed to be summer?"

"Not in October, Wiggins."

"Plus everything's covered in cheese dust! Probably we should tidy up before we get attacked. God knows what's roaming around out here."

"In case of attack, it's best to be tidy." I reach for the Cheezies. "Then what? Every man for himself?"

"Oh?" says Karin. "I like every man for himself." The sun flares above the treetops and Karin on the beach examines the day's first shadows. "Even if I'm just some floofy girl."

When talking at close quarters, Karin has a habit of staring clean over your shoulder, as if she's noticing a stranger who is just now walking toward her—for various reasons she is judicious about prolonging eye contact—but as she glances at me here, in the first morning light, I feel the verve of her direct gaze. Karin's eyes to all of us are a shifting wonder, delighted, ironic, and perplexed as they may be, but it is the colour that dazes you. Her eyes are green—absurdly green, mallard duck green—it's a green that has a way of fading to grey as her thoughts move on but in the first moments of effervescence her eyes flash with fresh emerald amusement. That autumn, and in the seasons to follow, and if you follow Babba's line on this, it often feels as if Karin is investing each of us with a talent, an intelligence, a cleverness we may not actually have, but we seem to have, when Karin confers it upon us, staring with her very green eyes into our own. Many years later, when I date someone who will become a movie star, I will be acutely reminded of the smile-with-your-eyes sparkle of Karin Friday. It is a somewhat dazzling smirk, conscious of many angles, and absolutely aware, I think, of its own phenomenal appeal.

THE MORNING SUN gleams a few minutes before disappearing in fog, then drizzle, then rain. At noon, having searched the island, to find it empty, and sensing worse weather to come, we begin to pack the dory. "Cyrus Mair," says Karin. "Are you there? Are you coming?"

Back at the sodden fire pit, Cyrus sits unmoving in the rain. He's been listening for some minutes to the cassette in the Walkman, his hands held tight to the headphones.

"Cyrus?"

"Just second," he says. "Stop talking."

"Stop talking?" Gail in rubber boots is pushing out the loaded dory. "Why—so we can hear ourselves get soaked?"

Cyrus has gone very still so he might listen to "Blitzkrieg Bop" by The Ramones. Finally he glances up to say, "We could do this."

"Do what?" says Karin. "Make tapes or get soaked?"

"Make songs."

Karin looks at me, perplexed, then to Cyrus, whereupon she is provoked to ask, in a tone both charmed and frazzled, "How can we possibly do *that*?"

THE NEXT MONTAGE, IN MY MIND, explodes with the rackety audacity that starts up a Clash song. It's the moment when some crumb-bum kid in a basement finally solves the opening chords of "Clash City Rockers" and plays them over and over, fast and fuzzy, astonished to generate in her basement the same charge of energy she has so far experienced only from the recording itself. As her strummed chords propel us forward, heedless of wrong notes or screeches of feedback, I will hurry over times, turning the happenings of many months into a few paragraphs. There we are, looting the Mair family library for its overflow volumes, driving them downtown, and hawking them at the used bookstores on Hollis and Barrington streets, with the proceeds purchasing a scrappy old Telecaster at Herb's Music on Gottingen. There we are again, in cross-dissolving one-shots, phoning to arrange weekend rehearsals, picking out chord progressions from vinyl records, learning bass lines, gamely loading our second-hand gear into car trunks on snowy streets, setting up at someone's house party, bouncing off the drum kit, knocking a floor lamp into a living-room wall, sweaty with encores.

A case could be made that Karin's mix-tape, which was copied and recopied and passed from hand to hand like a sacred relic, was the ur-artifact of the Halifax punk scene—that some rough magic migrated from inside those songs to inside ourselves. And in certain drunken moods I have attributed the city's entire alternative-rock renaissance to that single cassette tape. But the truth was that kids everywhere in Halifax-Dartmouth were swapping tapes, forming bands, and putting on shows. Rising in the city generally was a reaction against the soft schmaltz of Boston and Kansas and Chicago. Across the sea, London was calling—and we lived for their gods and voices. Punk galoots soon sprang down our sidewalks in safety pins and chopped green hair. Poppets lolled in fishnet stockings, spiked bracelets, black-eyeliner. Skinhead yobs spouted Crass and Kafka.

Who would you have met—and how would they have looked—if you were walking these weeks on Grafton Street? There were two brothers, Torben and Orville Fludd, who *were* English punks, transplanted from Bethnal Green, and famed in Halifax as the real deal. The brothers Fludd were in perpetual sibling skirmish—they slam-danced with their hands in their pockets—and formed a thrash-punk band called Scum. They were slight and feisty, obstinate about dark vinegar on their fish and chips, and spoke in working-bloke slang: "The Silver Hornets, they're bloody brill, yeah?" "There you go again, talking shite and banging on about the Hornets. Basically playin' wif your generals is what fat is, you fucking plonker." "No, mate, they're pure dead brilliant so whyn't you fuck off?" There was Beamish Mingo, a hulking guy I'd known in Boy Scouts, balding at seventeen, who made himself over into a skinhead, cleanly attired in a singlet, suspenders, black jeans, and gleaming Doc Martens. He performed as Eins Zwei Drei! and would later move to Winnipeg to follow a career in art history. There were New Wavers—Jimmy Lavender Boots, Gina Sleath, Angela Silver, Helen Hopday—and a slew of hardcore punkers like Mosey and Posey and a kid with a Mohawk who called himself Gash Ragged.

We played these first years at Woden's Nog, one of the few places downtown that booked non-union music. It was a second-floor coffee shop, a bohemian embassy of sorts, managed by Astrid Whynot, ex-girlfriend of Theo Jones. She was a noted balladeer and lighting designer who taught part-time at the Halifax Folklore Centre. In those early years, Woden's Nog fit into an expanding calculus within the city. I remember the Rebecca Cohn Auditorium showing *Amarcord* in their Sunday night film series. Down the street, on the third floor of the Student Union Building, was the Dalhousie fantasy role-playing society, home to stanky war gamers happy to clear up the difference between a trance state and astral projection. At Wormwood's Dog and Monkey Cinema, you might be disturbed by *Eraserhead* or *Kagemusha*. Deep downtown was the Nova Scotia College of Art and Design, where Yankee profs practised conceptual frottage and the student body hosted droning noise-rock bands from Toronto. And soon to open was Backstreet Amusements, a hole-in-the-wall arcade of video games, alterna-misfits, and all-purpose punk mojo. Red Herring Cooperative Books, the Khyber building, the Seahorse Tavern, the college radio station CKDU—all of these contributed to a counterculture musically presided over by the bands from those years: the Flipperbabies, the Clap, the Swankers, Scum, Headless Inchball Blue, 12XU, Straight New Blister, Murder and the Cats, and, of course, the Silver Hornets, who were fronted by singer-songwriter Jeremy Horvath. With Liz, his art college girlfriend, Jeremy moved in beauty like the night, sharply solemn with his Fred Perry shirts, punk-pop riffs, a Rickenbacker Capri.

We in the Common Room were aware of these older kids, we were learning the sets of the city, but no one really knew us or who we were. We were at once within and without the scene. In the space of a winter we came together, a set unto ourselves. Recruited into our ranks were Babba Zuber, because she had a van, and Tom Waller, because of his electro-technical meticulousness. We thought we could do anything—we had fantasy conclusions for our projects—we thrilled ourselves with our hope. The Common Room became a place in our collective head and we were all learning how to get there. We had something more in common: we didn't care if we were misunderstood. As adolescents, each of us was contending with a jumble of conflicting personal conceptions, but the Common Room liberated us from these conflicts—or at least freed us from having to *worry* about conflicts—because within it we were simply contagiously happy to learn what one another were thinking. And as interests became apparent, our jumbles were given direction. We became sarcastic and assured and worked up vocabularies and amusements all our own. We understood certain kinds of experiences in the same way, and we were willing to consider other kinds of experiences in new ways, even ways that hadn't yet finished developing. We filtered details out of the world—details from movies and songs and books we liked—and mixed them into forms of meaning beyond the assumptions of our classmates or parents or teachers. It was all a newness, I recall how fresh everything seemed—how the world seemed to assemble itself for our exploration—and a fragile-but-growing sense of possibility. Essentially, we sought forms and structures by which we might understand the world and articulate ourselves, and one of these forms and structures, I was sensing, was this very group of friends itself.

So let me say why the Common Room meant so much to *me*. My early years had been shaky. By the time I was in kindergarten I was aware my family had fault lines that would result in my mother splitting from my father. I was able to deal with this because I could jump higher and run faster than a lot of kids. Then I could no longer jump and run and I was put into casts and crutches for two years. Mobile again at eight, at ten I would lose my uncle—my closest ally in the house—and my parents would separate again. My family divided into two households: Mom-Faith-and-Katie versus Dad-Carolyn-Bonnie-and-Me. I would then be grateful for the kinetics of tennis, but would come to realize, like Karin before me, that many of my competitors had little life outside tennis, and that some—even the high achievers—were considered gorky and socially dubious. During middle adolescence, I was coping by doing massive amounts of drugs and disconnecting from my family, from school, from all regularly scheduled programming. Why? My notions of myself, and my own possibilities had always been very different from those my family, my friends, and most of Halifax had for me. This identity dissonance disappeared, of course, as it did for most teenagers, when drunk or stoned, but I was conscious that continuing with such procedures invited predicament. I really do think it was only through my friendships in the Common Room that I was successfully reintroduced into mixed society. These fabulists seemed like the only people who might possibly understand me. My friends were giving me a new identity—or they were giving me a new way, in fact multiple ways, to think of my identity, and my inside hunch was that such coevals would help me better become myself. Cyrus once remarked on the irony that, no matter how we might carry the world around in our heads, the world would never carry us around in *its* head. But I knew my colleagues and comrades in the Common Room would in their thoughts carry me, like Saint Christopher carrying travellers across a river. My God—to have a circle of friends within which my fledgling thoughts might find expression, discover their balance, and take wing was a tremendous deliverance for me. Cyrus and Karin, Gail and Brigid, Babba and Tom—they were highly cherishable items in my world. I gave my heart to them because they gave the possibilities of my life back to me.

CYRUS WAS THE VOICE that said we could do it. All it required was our deciding to do it. It didn't matter that it went well. What mattered was that it went at all. We turned to music to see what we could make of it without really knowing what that would be. The second-floor ballroom in the old Mair house became our head office, our home base and rehearsal space. There we played till our fingers blistered from our Fender strings. Afternoons disappeared into evenings, evenings into midnights, for no one left rehearsal till a song was written. Like Karin, like me, like all of us, Cyrus Mair had diverse versions of himself. He had different modes and humours, the pitch and rhythm and weirdness of which sometimes eluded me—manic and jokey one day, distant and sulky the next, truant another—but the guy, as in everything, was committed. He had some kind of vision, you felt that, and he kept in motion a number of obsessions. Karin became addicted to his hijinks and quizzically fascinated by Cyrus Mair. She called him Charlie Flippit and Cyprus Mail and made up nonsense rhymes about him. "Cyrus Mair is who knows where, and if you dare to breathe the air, don't be scared to breathe it bare, once upon a Cyrus Mair." To these she added little familiar pokes and prods of his person, and Cyrus, who up to this point in public life generally behaved as if he were trapped in a stalled elevator with a stranger, who had around him that nervous force-field safeguarding his personal space, Cyrus behaved as if this touchy-feely contact had always belonged to his day-to-day. Something about Karin opened up possibilities of engagement in him, in me, in all of us. It was a feeling of special destiny she gave us—or maybe we extended such sovereignty to her so that she might give it back to us. Over the next few years, more than a few problematics would emerge regarding this girl Friday, but in this first winter her flair and talent seemed always at the centre of things. For Cyrus, Karin was the thrillingest girl of the open era, a phenomenon beyond the range of his experience, and I think he swooned privately at each sight of her. He continued to speak of her as a genius of life and from this judgment I don't think he ever wavered. While I thought her intuitive sense of people genuine, and was often amazed by how swiftly and wordlessly she understood a moment, I did not think it genius. If at all she had a gift, it was a knack for making a man feel most alive in her company. Whether it was tennis or penny-a-point Hearts, I was never really sure what kind of game Karin Friday was playing. But for Cyrus Mair, she was all the game in the world and I knew now what he'd wished for—of course he'd wished for Karin Friday.

SCENE. A SUNDAY IN DECEMBER, the Mair House on Tower Road. Somewhere on the first floor, Emlyn Mair, resolutely hard-of-hearing, scrutinizes both her investment statement and various university applications for Cyrus, plotting his advancement. Cyrus, Karin, and I can be located in the second floor ballroom. To relieve the feeling of darkened confinement, the ballroom windows have been stripped of their garbage bag coverings and the room glows with snow-reflected sunlight, ceiling cobwebs twinned with their own shadows. The shrouded furniture has been cleared to the corners. On the threadbare Oriental carpet is an assortment of musical equipment: three mike stands with damaged-but-working Shure microphones, a Fender bass, three Peavey amps, a miscellaneous drum kit bandaged together with duct tape, a Sony boom box, a reel-to-reel tape recorder, several cassette tapes, and a children's turntable with built-in speakers. The general effect is rather like a derelict historical house hosting the remains of a pawn shop's going-out-of-business sale.

Cyrus sits with a Telecaster in a decaying wingback chair. Near his shoes on the carpet is a speckled oak leaf, a flattened kernel of movie-theater popcorn, a plastic tortoiseshell pick, an unopened pack of chandelier light bulbs, a busted EHX Big Muff pedal, a ruptured chestnut, two tiny blots of pigeon crap, an X-acto knife, filaments of blond hair, and a half-empty pint bottle of Mount Gay rum. He is silent, listening. Karin sits at an elderly grand piano, also listening, as I drop the needle again on *Love Bites* by the Buzzcocks, the three of us trying to work out the guitar solo to "Nostalgia." Karin manages the first few notes on the piano keys then slumps in frustration at the solo's rapid cadenza. We are stubborn about performing only originals at our first real show, but cover songs for later shows and for encores, we've agreed, are permissible. If, that is, we can teach ourselves the chords and notes, and a few solos, “Baby Baby,” “Promises Promises,” “Nostalgia,” are proving resistant to our ambitions. “What solo do you want to do instead?” asks Cyrus, after an hour of attempts, and I know Karin will say what she always says, and what she does say: “‘I Wanna Be Sedated.’ *Is* there another solo?”

Although she has natural talent as a pianist and vocalist, Karin is shaky on guitar and the Ramones solo just mentioned is probably the only solo she knows how to play. It is, very probably, even if you have never held a guitar, the only solo *you* know how to play, because the solo for “I Wanna Be Sedated” is pretty much just one single note double picked as the rhythm section slams through the changes. That song closes out the first side of Karin’s mix-tape, a copy of which I have in the tape deck of my family’s car outside, and I volunteer to retrieve it for the key reference. Out on Tower Road it has begun to snow, a light dusting that thickens into flurries. From the second-floor windows I begin to hear the ringing one-note solo of “I Wanna Be Sedated,” as played by Karin and Cyrus, and looking up at the darkened house through the snowflakes softly falling, within the single-lighted room I can see them madly pogoing up and down, their bodies jolting in and out of frame, the moment gorgeous and surreal, like an advent calendar window opened to reveal a shining scene, a signature postcard moment from The Common Room in December of our first year together.

THE COMMON ROOM PRESENTS FOUR BANDS FOR FIVE BUCKS. This is the announcement we poster all over the city—that we tape in elevators on the Dalhousie campus, tack on the bulletin boards of the six high schools, and staple into the plywood walls around construction sites everywhere. It is a first concert, a first not-in-a-basement-but-a-real-club gig, and we are sort of terrified, sort of whatever-let’s-do-it. The bands this night are Scum, the Swankers, the Submissives, and us, the Changelings—Cyrus, Karin, Gail, and me. Held on a frozen night, two days after Valentine's, the show begins with very few in the audience. I remember Torben and Orville in Scum, the sloppy art-punk openers, fighting over their single microphone, gobbing on each other, foreheads bumping, petty gods of misrule, during their encore the room finally filling up with the all-ages crowd, kids pre-drunk, front-loaded and tipsy, confused by the Fludd brothers who, for their finale, hacksaw a feedbacking Stratocaster in two. More appreciated are the Swankers and their raw covers of "Substitute," "Strange Town," and "Something Else." Next are the Submissives, a ghostly trio of damaged sisters from Kline Street, gothy and glossolalic, their three-part harmonies sweetly setting up the crash of our arrival.

We come on last, the monitors broken and torn from the earlier bands, stage lights blinding, the place low-dangled with cables and cords, the room now chockablock with folks—Gina Sleath, Bunker Burr and his little brother Boyden, Ricken Philips, my sisters Faith and Katie and their friend September Abbott, and at the back of the room Jeremy Horvath in a smart suit, slinking, intent. We don't care, we've shorn our hair, all of us in black, me in zippers and chains, Karin in a catsuit with silver spiked hair, green eyes kohl-rimmed—a Tomboy Punkette. Gail on the drums is remote and intense, her silence belied by a constant jagged energy, keeping time with wicked impulse, as if this is what she has been seeking all along. Cyrus himself a demented choirboy, vicious and vulnerable, nothing short of spastic, surprising everyone with what is released in him, slam-dancing on and off the stage as if the concussiveness of each shoulder bump will bust him out of some cocoon, his eyes madly gleeful. I'm on vocals for the first of our songs and I swear furiously, uttering every foul word in my young mind, feeling soundly right in my temper and tantrums, in this profane invention, for there isn't anyone there to kick me off the stage or out of the match. For *we* are the match. Our songs zip by faster than imagined. No sooner am I jumpy about the bass runs in "Sudafed" than I am charging into and out of them and we rush into what is next on the set list, "Head Tripper," "Clanger," "Ace Face," "Head Case," "Broken Steven," "Fandroid," "Dead End Ends," and then we are gasping, damp, looking around for an encore, knowing we've arrived at our final song, "Changeling Girl."

The song in its first iteration is built around a descending progression from E to E-flat to C-sharp minor and back to E-flat, all played as barre chords sweat-sliding down the fretboard. Cyrus's notion is to make two songs into one, fitting this first progression inside the chorus of "Dead End Ends," which, once transposed in key, proceeds from E to E-flat to C-sharp minor to B major. "Changeling Girl" starts fast, establishes its hook, then the chorus slows and falls apart, depriving the audience of its bedlam energy, as if the song has faltered to some random ending. Then with stray notes still sustaining, Gail kicks the drum and I down-stroke the bass, the two of us locking into groove, and the vocals resume, Cyrus screaming into a microphone and playing the transposed chords of the previous song, the B string now open as a dominant drone, the sections combining so Karin can sing the chorus of "Dead End Ends," floating her vocals over "Changeling Girl," all the while our tempo rising, Karin finally ripping into the only guitar solo she knows, twangling the open E string, the combined effect jangly and eerie and perfect to me. It is an idea of perfection at the same time it *is* a perfection, a pandemonium, the stage busy with feedback and distortion, the crowd pogoing, and I can feel the wooden floor sagging and springing, flimmer and thud, kids bouncing into the air, what is happening in the room a kind of metamorphosis—it is a glorious moment, berserk and unbounded, one of the great events of my young life, and there is Karin in centre-stage communion with the crowd, her guitar still ringing, her voice leading the audience in singalong, and finally it's done and I am wandering off the stage, wet with sweat, the windows streaming with condensation and Karin bumps through the ecstatic noise and crowd to stare at me, glaring at me almost, as if I might be responsible for the crowd, the music, everything. "McKee!" she screams into my temple. "Who did this?" "We did?" "We *did*, though," says Karin, hugging me close, our chests pressed together, her arms tight around me and between her shoulder blades I can feel her heart beating, Karin kissing not my face but my neck a little below my ear. "We *did* this!" And as I look to Karin, her smile to see, eyelashes wet-pointed, I feel we really have done it, we've conjured a concert out of nothing, produced a night, and I realize, all the notes and chords from this sequence fading, that Karin Friday is magic and everyone in that room is in love with her.

WE WERE FAMOUS IN THE CITY, we were Halifamous, we were the punk band with the gorgeous lead singer, and kids from all over—suburban preps, heavy metal sluggards, bluegrass hippies—came to see our shows. What thrilled me about a Changelings gig was the *realization* of the event, the arrant circumstance, the doing of the thing. In the crash and splendor of our shows, we transcended the grubby circumstances of Grafton Street, creating moments which at once matched and expressed a restless-in-all-directions punk wonderment. There was a Kraftwerk lyric from Karin's mixtape, "We are the robots," but in the world of Halifax, *we* were the robots. We were the clash and jam and damned, we were the Generation X—those were our stiff little fingers on the vibrators and sex pistols, that was Karin wearing the x-ray spex. For Karin Friday was a magical name in the city now. She was the girl dancing on the first English Beat record, the comic book sweetheart of a Roy Lichtenstein print. She was that girl you remembered forever and many were the nights you might linger solitary in a car to listen to the end of a radio song because it reminded you of her. She seemed a shooting star who streaked across the sky, fixed in no one's orbit, and aspirants several and assorted were drawn into her gravities. She was eighteen, no longer a tweenster kid but a maturing adult female and probably fully aware of herself as gorgeous. Karin was luminous, she owned any stage she joined, if she wanted, and wild was she to hold, though she seemed tame. "And so it begins," said my older sister. "The Karin Friday Invitational." And Babba Zuber: "If you look like Karin, you can pretty much go out with whoever you want." This being Halifax, there were differences of opinion. Mosey and Posey and the hardcore followers of Scum would have allowed that Karin was a dreamy vocalist but I'm sure they dismissed her as some dilettante tennis girl playing at anarchy. Howard Fudge, a hulking endomorph drug-dealer and my one-time mentor, famously did not care for Karin Friday. "That scooter girl," he said to Gail and me on the afternoon I bought a last dime bag from him. "The chick with the eyes? She's a little heartbreaker, no question. But she's just too much." Gail asked what he meant—too much what? "Too much bullshit." "Bullshit comes in many forms, my friend," said Gail, quick to defend a pal and confidante. But Howard Fudge, whose Fudge-headedness over time often proved relevant, may have construed something for I have not really detailed those instances when Karin *was* too much, when she seemed to force her giggles, when her girliness became presentational and semi-annoying, when phone calls to her were never returned or never referenced, when her impromptu talk-backs to the movie screen felt disingenuous. Of course there were some young women, those who moved in different circles, who risked harsher interpretations.

"I hate that perfect girl Karin," Kelly Gallagher confided one night. "She would never be my friend. Even for a second. You can just tell." For some dissidents, the impulses that motivated Karin Friday's magic and charm were not so far away from vagary or some strategic thoughtlessness. Later that afternoon, after the purchase of the dime bag, I made some mention of these discrepancies to Gail, musing on Karin's shape-shifting unpredictability, her flights and quirks, and made the mistake of using Karin's nicknames for me and Gail. Walking along Summer Street, Gail abruptly stopped and chose to stare at the sidewalk. Every few months Gail had begun delivering once-and-for-all sidewalk pronouncements. These rulings were often introduced by a quick shake of her head, as if to first clear her eyes of delinquent hair, but Gail had been serving in the Naval Reserves for some weeks that summer, sporting a three-quarter-inch brush cut, and in this particular moment there were few curls to shake away. "All you guys are in love with Karin," she said, finally, conclusively. "You and Cyrus and Jeremy and everybody. You say you aren't. But you are. And you always will be." She marched on—she wore that day a frayed cameo choker, vintage dress, and military boots, boots she clomped with authority along the sidewalk. "And the name is Gail. Not Gorbals. Or Birdy. Or Boober. It's Gail. What are we—the island of misfit toys? No more baby talk! It's like you doing drugs all the time. When are you going to grow the fuck up?" I knew from last month's pronouncement that Gail had decided there was within The Common Room a troubling subtext of sexual repression—though, to be fair, a troubling subtext of sexual repression was Gail's assessment of any *number* of situations—and she thought our cutesy affinities an exercise in avoidance behaviour. "The Common Room is totally fucked up and incestuous," she said, speaking, as ever, as if the rest of us were failing to confront some crucial social truth. "There's some weird fucking telepathy between us, maybe, but I'm not sure I *like* it. Because it feels like some retarded exercise in group dating! And the Changelings? I don't know. Everything's always Cyrus, Cyrus, Cyrus. And I'll tell you something about that guy. He's never fucking satisfied. Cyrus Mair? He's never fucking satisfied with anything. He has to be this little manic-depressive type who goes off hibernating and having nervous breakdowns in his Never-Never Land, thinking everyone's going to feel sorry for him and all his precious ideas, but excuse me they just *aren't*. He's an enigma. Right. I get it. Whatever. He certainly works pretty fucking hard at it." Anyone who has been in a band will recognize these intervallic hissy fits and I knew, from previous exchanges, that it wouldn't matter what I said next—the mere mention of these names had made Gail fretful and reactionary—and, in these moods, Gail could not be argued out of her verdict or position. "And you?" she said. "You're obsessed with him. In fact, *your* compulsion-repulsion, thank you very much, is that you're in love with her and obsessed with him. So—here's an idea—why don't you figure out this shit, quit doing drugs, and *then* talk to me." Gail and I were phasing in and out of a rather undefined relationship at this time, in the same way Karin and Cyrus were phasing in and out of similar undefinables, and I will add, without whipping out too much detail, that Gail had disencumbered me of my virginity a few weeks before. Although that conjunction, very much an expedient, get-it-over-with affair, was organized by Gail in a spirit of gratuitous experimentation—she was purportedly mixed up with another boy she'd met at Camp Kadimah—I was beginning to understand that very little was gratuitous in modern life. Somebody or other ended up paying for it.

JEREMY HORVATH AND CYRUS MAIR were two of the latest in a long line of Halifax Smart Boys. The city was rampant and replenishing with prodigies, Brainiacs, wunderkinds. "There's a lot of bright kids in this town," said my mother. "Not all of them make it. Not all of them can handle being bright." I'm not sure if it's the isthmus mentality, or the presence of so many universities, but smarter and snootier young men you will not find for a thousand miles and I've often thought a fairly long essay might be in order to explain the subset of the smart-but-damaged Halifax guy. Horvath and Mair were two of the more fulfilled expressions but the traits and glistenings were manifest in many. I'm not talking about the amiable boy-next-door who rewires his phone to make a radio or constructs a practical two-man hovercraft out of balsa wood. That's Tom Waller. The Halifax Smart Boys, the talent of six high schools, were young men of finicky brains, highly imaginative, often socially complicated—and sometimes projecting this complication into others, especially attractive contemporaneous girls. These fellows were needy and judgmental, derisive and awkward, sarcastic and insecure—snobby, funny, rueful, aloof—and existed in a space-time gamely managed by *Monty Python*, *Star Trek*, Tolkien, Herbert, Gygax, Devo, *Gödel, Escher, Bach*. Gail called them the Cyrus Clones and roundly considered them too-clever-for-their-own-good, pretentious, obnoxious, emotionally stifled, in a word—dysfunctional—and they were to a man as follows: Brian Bremner, Ying Lu, Henry Fleming Dunham, Mik Prsala, Ewan Gruber, Zal Glazov, David Feagles, Ian DeGroot, and Jeremy Horvath. Out of this swarm, it was only the last three who jostled for true preeminence and Cyrus reliably referred to these last three, for reasons never made clear to me, as Mr. Hoobalee-Boobalee, The Fabled Ian DeGroot, and Jeremy Fucking Horvath. They were a little older and a little more realized than Cyrus Mair and me. David Feagles was absurdly dour in an Old Halifax High Anglican manner, ever puzzling out philosophies he perceived as reticulate. The first person to use in my presence the word Hegelian, David would pursue notions of post-modern modernity at the University of Sheffield. Son of Symphony Nova Scotia's concertmaster, Ian DeGroot was one of those slack-mouthed power dweebs, slave to some repetitive fidgeting pattern, who seems borderline autistic but who all along is picking algorithms out of the middle distance. Ian would win a Rhodes Scholarship, complete a post-doc in complex adaptive systems, and end up in Santa Clara, California. But Jeremy Horvath was the prince regent of these freaks and considered the smartest of the Smart Boys. He had a habit of frowning and the precise mind of a clever young fiend. He was withdrawn and watchful, intuitive and changeable—which may be why it is difficult to successfully pin into a display case a considered analysis of his character. There was something hinky about his eyes. They seemed double-lidded, sleep-deprived, his eyelashes pale and Teutonic-looking. "Creepily cerebral," was how Gail described him. "There's something weird about Jeremy. He's not really human. He's like this alien-human hybrid from the future. And he looks like the sort of guy who's been sitting on the same piece of cheese since he was twelve." Of Jeremy Horvath I was utterly emulous—I wanted to be as good as or better than him and his lot. But Jeremy Horvath was very good at being Jeremy Horvath. His teenage speaking voice implied a multi-speed intelligence, alert to ironies and switch-ups, and his smarts and moods, when taken with his musical success and other feats more assorted, made him a supremely accomplished eighteen-year-old. He captained Dartmouth High to the finals of *Reach for the Top*, a nationally televised quiz show. He was the only person I knew who was offered a full scholarship to Harvard. He pretty much invented a side-kinking on-beat style of dancing, as if he were being sort of rhythmically electrocuted, that would prove influential on male dancing in the city for years to come. He was the best rhythm guitar player for days and he was the first person I knew who recorded and released a vinyl record. That summer, the summer after John Lennon died, The Silver Hornets brought out on their own label a three-song EP called *Girl Trap*. Those three songs, "High Numbers," "Radio Dial," and "Girl Trap," were not exactly everywhere in the city, but in my brain they were ever-present and astonishing. This was one of the first indie recordings to come out of Halifax, later cited in anthologies for its haunting post-punk soundscapes, and Karin Friday, I noted, the Changelings' Karin Friday, *our* Karin Friday, was listed as guest vocalist on the last of the tracks.

SCENE. THIRD FLOOR ATTIC of the Mair House on an August afternoon. Cyrus sits at a table covered with papers, reading a hardcover book. He wears a rumpled second-hand suit under a blue cashmere coat. No matter where he is in the calendar year, Cyrus is partial to winter coats, even winter coats, like this one, he may not grow into for another few summers. I recognize it as one of those previously worn by his father and exhumed from the clothes racks that once hung in this very attic. The space functions now as Cyrus's bedroom, albeit a bedroom where five-sixths of the room is given over to bookshelves. They stand at right angles from the walls and form a sort of labyrinth. The remaining portion of the room contains a small bed, or berth, really, of the sort you'd see in a submarine, and it's wedged into a corner beneath the room's only window. A window resolutely shut. Outside the afternoon is anything but overcoat weather and inside, the way the heat is trapped within the almost airless attic—sunlight steeping through the dusty smears of the window—room temperature approaches something you might encounter in an incinerator. Cyrus does not appear to notice, however, and sits diligently reading, unaware of my presence, unaware of the flashing reflection from his watch crystal, and unaware of a single white moth that, like a dazzle of confetti, chases this reflection into the shadows of the far wall. One of Cyrus's shirt collars has twisted with the knot of his tie and the collar kinks at an odd angle toward the ceiling, but Cyrus, being Cyrus, simply continues reading. Why? As earlier explained, the projects of the Common Room are financed by selectively pilfering and selling off the house's surplus books—the doubles and triples and oversized volumes, anything spotted or mildewed, and all of the encyclopedia sets. Vast numbers of books from the house have found their way back into the world, dispersing into shops far and wee—Guzzie's Book Exchange, Asher's Antiquarian Bookmart, Schooner Books—and, in this way, after a quart bottle of Harvey's Bristol Cream has been delivered as a surtax to Aunt Emlyn, bulky uniform editions of Sir Walter Scott and Charles Dickens and multiple copies of *The Vicar of Wakefield* are transmuted into Peavey amplifiers, microphones, sound boards, pre-amps. Cyrus feels contrite if he's not read a book before its departure and, even though I've pushed him to retire this system of read-and-release, often he withdraws, as he's done these first weeks of August, into shut-in seclusion, sequestering himself to read through a stack of decrepit hardcovers. Deep in these ecclesiastical phases, he might read for days in a row, oblivious to food or weather, with wrinkled apples forgotten and teapots stone cold.

"That kid reads too much," said my mother. "How's he going to learn anything? He should get outdoors. Didn't he used to play tennis? That boy, with his strange mind and reading too much, why is he always stuck up in some garret?" I explained it's more of a turret. "Garret. Turret. Bell tower. Whatever you want to call it, get him *out* of it, Aubrey. He doesn't need all those books. No one does. He could read from now till doomsday and never finish a fifth of that crap. They'll be the death of somebody, I'm telling you." But for Cyrus, each book became, in the very act of picking it up, the centre of the known universe. He was always reading as if an idea from a book might change his life forever and so he's determined to steer his eyes through every line of text, even if, as my youngest sister once discovered, the volume in question was a *Li'l Jinx Giant Laugh-Out* which, borrowed from Katie one afternoon at an ice cream-splattered picnic table, Cyrus regarded as reverentially as a first translation of The Upanishads. So he continues reading, bent over, staring into the pages of the hardcover. But it's a glazed, unrecognizing kind of staring, as if he's waiting for the right word or gesture to snap him out of his abstraction.

I want to tell him about "Girl Trap" and Karin but I'm never sure with Cyrus how to phrase my references to Karin—I am not clued-in to their recent goings-on—and there is an odd silence after I blurt about Karin singing on the track. With a quietude that speaks of a dozen ideas newly calibrating, Cyrus makes a snuffle but stays silent, as if he does not wish his run of thoughts to be interrupted, and I become conscious of a familiar sensation in the room. Moving further into his percipience has given Cyrus Mair an identity but it has also isolated him within that identity. And in his psychic vicinity, your thoughts become weirdly reoriented. You feel as if your ideas are being induced into a coherence Cyrus is slowly and stubbornly trying to generate. Immersion in this magnetic field does strange things to people. It mostly attracts Karin, beguiles Babba and Tom Waller, but repels Gail. She is very suspicious of its influence—in the Changelings she and Cyrus have been sort of vying for psychological control—and his strangeness makes her spiteful. And me? I sense there are contradictions present beyond my seventeen-year-old mind, but as I stand there, heat prickles starting on the skin between my shoulder blades, I feel that knowing Cyrus Mair will make me smarter—knowing him will make *everyone* smarter—and I do my best to integrate his charge and influence.

"That's amazing," says Cyrus, speaking with a conviction he will be completely understood. "That's very amazing, actually. For Jeremy Fucking Horvath. And his silver hormones. But for us it's completely irrelevant."

"Irrelevant. Right. That's what I was thinking. Know what else is irrelevant? Your collar's messed up."

Putting aside his book, Cyrus stands and moves to the bookshelves. "'Moonfleet?'" he asks, taking down a Penguin paperback. "I don't think so. Who wants to read that again?" He tosses the book to the floor. "And 'Silas Marner?' Print's too small."

"You should fix it. Your collar, I mean. The one on your shirt."

"A Borges," says Cyrus, tapping another book. "That's a keeper. Do you know the Borges?"

"I don't know the Borges." My face drips with moisture. With my right thumbnail, I flick away the sweat from an eyebrow and say, "Could we maybe crank up the thermostat? Or could I get a scarf?"

Cyrus stops in front of a hardcover. It's the copy of *Watership Down* loaned to him in our junior tennis days. "Richard Adams?" he says. "Isn't this yours?"

I tell him he can keep it.

"But isn't this where you record all your jokes?"

Because of my various drug-dealing connections, Cyrus grants to me an immense and purposefully absurd amount of street credibility, deferring to my expertise as if I'm someone who's survived a series of stints as a professional street fighter in the Halifax Shipyards. "Cyrus, that was three *years* ago. You ever read it?"

Nodding, he lifts out the book. "Where did you get all those jokes anyway?"

"What do you mean? I invented every one of them."

"But where'd you hear them?"

"From a guy in Gdansk. Guy Lafleur. I don't know. Pliny the Elder."

Cyrus places the copy of *Watership Down* on his table. He seems unable to leave it alone, however, and fusses with it so its edges are in line with the table corner. And I realize the personal force-field I've sensed in previous years has returned and seems to permeate all his goods and chattels. *Watership Down*, a tea cup, the pile of papers, a bottle of Quink—these seem possessed by a strange life force all their own. I stand very still in the centre of the room, wetly perspiring, pinpoints of sweat trickling down my spine toward the waistband of my pants, trying not to disrupt the room's frittery hoodoo.

Cyrus takes the hardcover he was reading earlier and holds it above his head. "Do you know this book?"

"Is that the Borges? I don't know the Borges."

"No. The Mayhew."

He passes me the first volume of something called *London Labour and the London Poor*—a collection of interviews with vagrants, mudlarks, and low-lifes published by Henry Mayhew in 1851. I open it at random and alight on the following fragment about a street kid. I decide to read the lines aloud, in a cheesy working-class accent, in my best Torben Fludd:

"'Yes, he had heer'd of God who made the world. Couldn't exactly recollec' when he'd heerd on him, but he had, most sarten-ly. Didn't know when the world was made, or how any-body could do it... Didn't know what happened to people after death, only that they was buried... Had heer'd on another world; wouldn't mind if he was there hisself, if he could do better, for things was often queer here.'" I finish my performance and take a moment to appreciate the excerpt, and the larger idea of Henry Mayhew. "The kid's right." I return the book to Cyrus. "Things *is* often queer here."

Cyrus is quiet, eyes quickening with new concerns. He steadies his gaze by following on the wall the reflected shimmer of his watch crystal. Then he murmurs, "We could do that."

"Do what?"

"What Mayhew did. But for Halifax."

"Interview homeless people? But there's only two of them. String Bean and Crazy Maddy."

"No. Put Halifax in a book. Like your folklore of jokes. But every person. Every thought. What everybody knows. Or not what everybody knows. What *we* know."

"Everything *we* know? Sure. Here's an idea. You're insane. And that's impossible."

"Maybe. Or maybe it makes everything possible."

"You mean put Crazy Maddy in a book or our experience of Crazy Maddy?"

"Isn't it the same thing? Think about it."

"I am thinking. I don't get it."

"Right now Crazy Maddy is someone we all know. But no one in the future will know her. It's like the Borges. 'What will die with me when I die?'"

"I don't know the Borges. Just to be clear on that."

"But if we put into a book everything we know, every little thing—"

"She does is magic?"

"Then it *becomes* what other people think is possible. Even if they disagree."

"Still not getting it."

"Exactly. It doesn't have to make sense. Or be linear. It's just an installation of moments. And the existence of a thing."

"The existence of a thing?"

"The existence of a thing," says Cyrus. "Because without it there aren't any."

IT WAS CALLED "THE HALIFAX BOOK." Other titles considered were "The Halifax Common," "Haligonia," and "Hafilaxity" but what was easiest was "The Halifax Book." It was to be a living history of the settlement known diversely as Kjipuktuk, Chibouctou, Chebucto, Hali, The Fax, and H-Town, and it was to stand as a correcting intervention to all the bullshit, spam, and flarf that had come down to us about the place. For this was to be a record of *our* Halifax—not the place evoked by print media of oil rigs anchored off Georges Island, or postcards of lobster traps heaped under stormy skies, or brochures featuring gap-toothed fishermen with seagulls atop their Sou'westers. On certain days your hometown can seem like a cavalcade of suckiness and all of us in the Common Room were oftentimes worried for Halifax. I know Cyrus considered it a sort of tribal accident, hopelessly superstitious, heartbreakingly sectarian, and his general conception of Maritimers, that is to say those fellows in matching rugby shirts who tunelessly bellow "Barrett's Privateers" while wavering at the urinals in The Seahorse Tavern, was linked with his general distaste for anything careless or incompetent—all the muddy corruptions and general mismanagements of thought at play in a city. Of course Gail thought the place its own little hell. But it was Babba who came closest to my own view.

"Halifax is sort of frustrating and lovable," she said the night we devised a first table of contents. "It's sort of crummy and magnificent." It was Cyrus's inspired insight to embrace the crumminess—to realize that in your hometown crumminess and magnificence are inseparable—and to seize the given moment in the city's life as moral fact. In the remaining weeks of that summer, Halifax became our religion, we its apostles, and the imagined book our scripture, creed, and Song of Songs. We drew it up. We sketched it out. We collated blueprints, histories, a bibliography of trees. We were going to keep at it till we got everything down on paper, every Pee-Wee hockey team, every Stadacona tattoo, every word scrawled in once-wet cement. And of course the thing never happened. Why? It was, in possibility and conception, the most ambitious of our ventures, but it was only one of many summer projects of The Common Room. There was our sponsoring of fifteen-year-old Huey Zuber's guided tour of "Suicides of the South End," a planned Super-8 music video for "Changeling Girl," and comprehensive rating-and-reviews of the city's buskers. I *loved* "The Halifax Book," I daydreamed on its proofs and fascicles—it seemed something on the way to wonderful—and a plan to respond to the meanings of all those scheming and dreaming around us seemed the best of our pursuits. But the project was fated to be a perpetual work-in-progress and after a rush of disorganized optimism the thousand pages of "The Halifax Book" petered out in false starts, dead ends, and shared neglect.

THE END OF THAT SUMMER was full of change. We were fluctuating, life was varying, and The Common Room itself was closing. People were leaving town, travelling into the world, flying into places far flung and cities unfamiliar. We were dispersing, differentiating, disbanding. The Changelings would last only seventeen gigs, from winter Grade 11 through summer Grade 12, our last concert played at half-strength, without Karin or Gail, at a rainy talent night at the St. Mary's Boat Club. Music was turning over. In the flicker of a few years Sid Vicious was dead, Paul Weller had become a rhythm-and-blues artist, and Jeremy Horvath, after a few detours into addiction, was on his way to becoming a real estate lawyer in New Canaan, Connecticut. The brief punk vogue in the city was done. I remember running into Robby Horvath, Jeremy's little brother and the bassist for the Silver Hornets, as he wandered baked out of his mind from a Dalhousie orientation session, slit-eyed and giggling, listening to something called UB40 on a Sony Walkman, the device ubiquitous now, his wavy red hair done up in Rasta dreads and beads and elastics, his headphones leaking sounds of snare hits and saxophone. He was carelessly humming along to a sluggish lament about Tyler-is-guilty-the-white-judge-has-said-so and I felt a gross distortion of the zeitgeist. Mine was not nostalgia for an age yet to come, as the Buzzcocks lyric goes, it was truly for a moment that had so swiftly come and gone. Musical trends cycle fast, I know, as fast as it takes a kid to clatter through high school, but I remember a feeling of queasy betrayal and dislocation. Why should punk be so quickly dumped? And why should Grafton Street co-opt every move from Carnaby, making over our styles to fit the dubby rhythms of Reggae, the blitzings of the New Romantics, the blancmange of the Synthpoppers? Punk Rock seemed to speak to the raw contingencies of Halifax, in all its rip-roaring gritty who-gives-a-fuck wildness. And yet in its wake soon splashed a waterish New Wave, the bars and clubs flooding with do-it-yourself pop combos like Jumper, The Fade Aways, and The Thunderhouse Blues Band, this last act, created around the boy-next-door appeal of Boyden Burr, an immensely and, for some, incomprehensibly, popular bar band that would regularly headline The Middle Deck, The Shore Club, and the great Palace itself. These bands were cocky and talkative and looking to party, theirs was a music of cover tunes and happy hour, leggings and blazers, encores and last-call-to-the-bar—the good-time vibe a gateway to misbehaviour of all kinds and prejudices. It was in her paid guesting gigs with Thunderhouse that Karin Friday would become known in the province, hosting a three-night home stand over Chester Race Week, performing on morning radio, and showing up in the weekend arts sections of the newspapers. In Halifax, as elsewhere, beauty creates interest and so it went with Karin Friday. Catch-lines for these features, at least in my mind, would trend toward "Pretty Girl Travels Fast" or "Cutie Ditches Oddballs" for there was a sense developing commonly that new opportunities were opening for our lead singer. This later version of Karin would coincide with a time when the city's downtown, once a mix of boho eclecticism and stately establishment, would develop over the decades into a theme park for university kids—essentially a movable drinking game for twentysomethings—as it remains today.

A CLOSING SCENE: PUBLIC GARDENS, STREETS VARIOUS, AND, FINALLY, THE HORSEFIELD. It is the first Wednesday in September in the sun-bright hours before twilight and as near as I can determine we Common Roomers are dotted all over creation. Barbara Zuber walks along Hirtle's Beach with her cottage sweetheart, a divorced scallop fisherman, considering his proposal of marriage. After a second summer in the Naval Reserves, Gail Benninger shops in the McGill University Bookstore in Montréal, pulling from the shelves a copy of *Discipline and Punish* by Michel Foucault. Tom Waller journeys toward Jadwin Hall in Princeton, New Jersey, where he will begin to pursue, as he is still pursuing, the Higgs Boson. And Cyrus Mair is—who knows where? The last I remember him was after the final Changelings gig—Cyrus on Benzedrine in the rain, lost in fury, throwing amps and gear in the back of the van. And me—I have gone on to spend the afternoon with Rasta Robby Horvath in the Public Gardens, smoking spliffies, talking music, and I walk out of its iron gates quite zonked, the world ablaze with Day-Glo pixels, creating itself every few moments, and I glimpse Karin Friday as she emerges from a press of people along Spring Garden Road. Her hair is long and loose and sun-lightened, with front-wisps pure white, eyes green-glinting in the sun. She wears a sleeveless gingham blouse, cut-off jeans, barefoot in Birkenstocks. When first I met her, a few years before, she seemed to arrive out of the world's future. Here on the sidewalk she looks as if she has come out of the city's past, for she has swung from Tomboy Punkette to Hippie Chick Granola Supreme—I have an impression generally of feather earrings, braided friendship bracelets, fading toenail polish. Whichever—she is in the full summer of her beauty and, as she moves to her Vespa, one hand holding her full-face helmet, the other wiping back a rush of hair, she is sort of continuously memorable. I have no idea what I say in my opening remarks, nor how floaty and spaced out are my follow-ups, reconnecting with contingent reality only after some minutes when I am behind Karin on her scooter, in her spare helmet, and listening to her Walkman as we motor down South Park and Inglis streets, Karin waving here and there at honking cars, now turning along Beaufort to race along the pavement beside the ocean inlet and railway tracks, through sleepy streets and the scent of family gardens, cooling barbecues, a sweep of darkling lawn. Everything seems a piece with summertime abundance, green leafiness all round, the city wide open, as if there are still weeks of summer on either side of us. I am listening to the final song of her mix-tape, "Why Can't I Touch It?" by the Buzzcocks, electric guitars trading riffs amid the hiss and flutter of the old magnetic tape, and I take in a number of synesthetic associations—the scooter's side mirrors blinking with daylight, a pink smell of shrubs and roses, the blue shale and clover of the railway cut, the fragrance of a shadowing tree as we round the corner, a flutter of loose butterflies squishing briefly into our faces, and I feel the entire evening seep and sparkle around me in a kind of fantasia all along the dip and rise of Beaufort Avenue. I sit close behind my driver, my arms around her waist, both of us happy, pleased to be with the other, and I'm aware of clean cotton and perfect girlhood and the perfume of her shampoo. Living in a house of many sisters, I know the colours and keynotes to a superfluity of shampoos, everything from Johnson's Baby Shampoo and Wella Balsam through to Alberto-VO5, Lemon Up, and Gee Your Hair Smells Terrific. From Karin I sense the greenish smell of Clairol Herbal Essence and this coupled with her hippie chick makeover sets off thoughts of waterfalls and damsels, circlets of flowers and pagan meadows. I contemplate the lacy white bra she wears, the shoulder-straps for which are flagrantly visible against the fabric of her gingham blouse, and I remember days when we smoked dope and drank and one night we were making out on the stairs of her back porch, her mother out of town, and we'd flirted randomly, truly, drunkenly, her blouse open, Karin undoing the worn plastic button on the front-release of this selfsame bra, the swell of her breasts I kissed as she tried to calm her breathing when I was kneeling down, moving her skirt above her hips and kissing wetly between her thighs as she pushed herself closer, her hands in my hair and another midnight besides, on an island beyond

Babba's cottage, on the last of our group sleepovers, in the flaming light of a beach fire when Karin after swimming was changing from her wet bathing suit and I saw how her pubic hair had been trimmed, the shaved area provoking a few pinkish stubbles on the inmost line of her thigh and I wondered at such grownup grooming decisions, and wondered, too, what she was thinking to show such sights to me. For she was aware of it, I'm sure, we were aware of each other in most moments, and now stopping her scooter within the greenery of the Horsefield, removing her helmet, and fingering some hair from her eyelashes, Karin turns away from me, almost as if she is privy to my run-on ideas and uncertain of their consequence, closing her eyes to angle her face toward the warmth of the setting sun.

I close my eyes, too, letting the sun blaze the insides of my eyelids scarlet, and for a few moments I feel as if I am thinking back on this person from a time when I will no longer know her—sensing a time in the future when I would be recalling these very scenes.

"You ever been to France?"

Opening my eyes, I say, "I was just thinking that."

"If you've been to France?"

"If you were going to ask me about France." Pulling from my pocket the remains of the joint I smoked with Robby Horvath, I light it and offer it to Karin. "You?"

"I did," says Karin, squeezing the roach between finger and thumb. "I just asked you."

"I mean are you going to France?"

"It's a plan, obviously." She sucks on the roach, one eye squinting from the smoke. "As one does."

"So who were those guys you were waving to?"

"Oh," says Karin, exhaling a single plume of smoke. "Just some guys who think they know me. Happens a lot now."

"Totally. Guys are noticing me a lot now, too. But whatever. Not important."

She swings her lower jaw to one side, quizzical, regarding me as if I might be someone peculiar, then returns the roach to me. "There was a psychic at Babba's craft fair today."

"A real psychic?"

"She said I was a very new soul."

"Where were you before that?"

"Um, on another planet." Karin touches at a red blemish beneath her eye. I am perversely grateful to see this blemish, an incipient pimple, on the edge-point of her cheekbone. "Probably you were, too, Tudball."

"Probably. And Kelly Gallagher, what's she?"

"Oh," says Karin. "She's an old soul. She's a restless old soul, that Kelly." Karin shakes her head when I offer her a last toke. "So can I ask you a question? You know your friend Cyrus Mair?"

"He's so unfair, that Cyrus Mair. That psychotic scheming freak."

"That's the one. Have you seen him?"

"Not so much. I think he's in an attic somewhere, you know, biting the heads off pigeons. I called him a couple times."

"Yeah," says Karin. "That's a little iffy considering he hasn't answered his phone in three weeks. As one does." Karin tugs on the frayed hem of her cut-offs so that a loose and flapping front pocket is properly covered. Then she glances at me, her eyes revealing some concern. "Everything's a little drastic at the moment. Not that it hasn't happened before. There just seems to be a bunch of extenuating circumstances this time around."

"He's good at those."

"He doesn't really talk to you and then maybe you'll get a long, weird letter from him in a year explaining it all."

"He's a weird guy."

"Oh," says Karin. "*Everyone's* a weird guy. And I'm not sure how everything works, okay? I don't always have the right Super Decoder ring."

I am nodding, thinking what to say next, when I simply return her Walkman. "Your mix-tape, Madame."

"Thank you, kind sir." She reaches for it. "What would I do without my mix-tape?" Her hand closes around the Walkman, by chance her middle finger pressing the rewind button. There is a sound of high-speed whirring, a sharp click, and then the spools abruptly slow and stop. Karin opens the casing to see the worn-out tape twisted off the capstan shaft and coiled beneath the pinch roller. "It's busticated?" Karin picks at the damaged tape. "Crapsticks. It got eaten by the machine. I guess it was going to happen sooner or later. It's just—that was my favouritest thing." With a shrug, she closes the casing, a ribbon of exposed tape trickling in the wind, and drops the Walkman in the front basket of her scooter. Karin gazes at the cassette, abstracted. "I know this sounds silly. But all my life I've wanted big boobs."

"Who doesn't?"

"Oh, Aubrey, I don't know. Sometimes it's better when it's just me and Babba and Boober. Not that we're always having, you know, *life* conversations but I think I understand things better with girls."

"Boys are gross?"

"Oh, girls aren't so great either. I mean you can tell a lot about a girl by how she gets you out of the way to put on makeup at a mirror—" Karin wipes at her eye, boldly, pushing a finger deeply into its socket, then, as if she feels she can't sustain such boldness, she loops a tress of hair behind her ear. "And boys are their own thing. But you guys are different. Most guys are usually scared to commit to stuff. Because what if it doesn't work out? Then they look bad.

Then they think they suck. I know I do." Bending forward, she pulls again on the hem of her cut-offs. "Like the guy in Toronto who made that mix-tape. He talked about doing lots of stuff. But he never did any of it. You guys did."

"You did, too, Wiggins. You were there."

"That's not what I mean. Because you guys keep turning yourselves into so many projects and I'm always trying to be as good as you. But you're always so much better at everything. And I'm not. I mean I know you guys can be a little woo-woo but you're still out there trying all your spiffy balls and—I don't know—maybe I fucked up all my gizmos because I'm not always as together and with it as you guys think I am." She sighs. "Plus the whole love-sex-babies thing? I'm not really as up on that as I should be."

"Probably you have to figure it out tonight. Before it gets dark. What're you doing later?"

"Tonight?" With a backward toss of her head, Karin indicates the ocean behind her. "Some wingding with Boyden. His pals at the yacht squadron."

"Extenuating circumstances. Hog roasts. I see." I have noticed a butterfly, faintly flapping, on the Vespa's front fender. Squatting to examine it, I see it's full-grown, mustard-coloured, and likely from the swarm we motored through.

"Tudball," says Karin. "Tell me something. And I know this shouldn't be a big, giant mystery but—Aubrey—are you even listening?"

My outward attention is still on the butterfly—its thorax has been dented into an edge of the steel fender—but inwardly I am considering Karin and all her queries and variables, her unisex flirting, her sundry sense of humour, her responses to life, these really *have* been like revelations to me, the way her eyes gleam with girliness, seeking to share the moment with you—and all through this evening I have been grateful to feel the joy of her looks—but ultimately I am sort of glum and disappointed. What bothers me is that she is able to smile so easily—and they aren't dishonest smiles at all but they come so quickly, so reflexively, they seem a reaction to almost everything and I want, finally, to be on the other side of the smiles that *matter*. For I feel as if I am just one of several young men she keeps in motion around her, the rest of whom are all taller and more striking than I am. And to learn that she is going around with Boyden Burr and his crowd—the great fraternity of popped collars and backward baseball caps—more than dismays me. It seems a betrayal of genius. All the different guys who drift in and out of Karin's life, some in a platonic, recreational way, many not, the transience of the relations, the almost disposable quality of the social life, I find curious, beautiful, and appalling. And kneeling in the Horsefield with a jammed-up butterfly I realize that not only will I never sleep with Karin Friday, and of course this has been something I have thought about—a *lot*—but I feel I will never really know her again at all.

"When I was little," says Karin, watching me as I begin to softly blow on the butterfly. "I thought butterflies were flowers that escaped." With these words, the creature slips off the fender-edge. Alighting briefly on Karin's elbow, it rises above our heads and follows an erratic up-and-down flight pattern before gently floating off toward the sea and horizons unknown. "You have a big heart," says Karin, staring after the butterfly. "Aubrey McKee."

"Got to start somewhere." I rise to her. "Now what was it? What's your big, giant mystery?"

But Karin has shifted into daydreaming quiet, her face half in shadow, the sunset off her right shoulder, and though she is still vaguely smiling at me, her smile seems to have lost some force around its edges, as if her thoughts have moved on but her expression hasn't quite caught up yet. She takes a step forward and lays her forehead on my shoulder, resting it there a second or two, as if out of respect, or pretend respect, I'm not sure. "Not important," she says, taking the spare helmet from me and plopping it in the basket with the Walkman. "That was my moment and I lost it."

She pulls on her own helmet, swings her leg over the scooter, and spins the key in the ignition. For a half-second I see my own face—sunburned, scruffy—in the fleeting world of one of her side-mirrors. And for a last time I consider the charms of Karin Friday, an enchantment of spiffy gizmos, crumpled butterflies, crapsticks and budding zits, blonde wisps and bright green eyes, though I am reminded it's a green that sometimes fades to grey, as it fades now, and, not knowing what next to do, I push a swoop of hair off her eyebrow. "Funny little world we live in, Wiggins."

"Mmm-hmm," says Karin, closing her helmet's visor and soon to vanish in a slanting shaft of light. "Everybody does."

IT WAS MANY YEARS LATER, very much *ex post facto,* when I'd passed into other vernaculars, when my connection with these associates was mostly attenuated and the Common Room demolished, that I received an anonymous-looking package in the mail, forwarded to my new address, half a world away from Halifax, containing the letter at the end of this section. It was never a candidate for "The Halifax Book," in fact it dates from a few years after that endeavour, but I include it here because, in many respects of mood and fluency, it seems an essential document of our life and soft times. It was written in blue ballpoint pen on nine pages of a yellow legal pad, dashed off the summer of the writer's third year at Queen's University, and shown here for the first time.

August 8 or 7

OH BABBA

Hello Hello Hello so where to start I'm not too sure I should be finishing my essay for this Feminist Theory and Discourse course that Gail made me take it's really good and I should've done more work and started paying closer attention ages ago but now it's over and the essay was due in April and I'm completely exhausted and too tired to write it so it's easier to unplug the phone and write you instead how are you?

So here I am on a Sunday morning all hung over and tranquil and fragile and feeling really young and really old at the same time and in front of me I have this ridiculous special delivery letter from Cyrus you-know-who which I refuse to open have you heard from him? I guess he's off at the ends of the earth somewhere I keep thinking I see him all over campus but of course it isn't him Babba I don't know what you heard but basically we had the scene to end all scenes in Europe so our Wonderful Beautiful Relationship came to its Final Crashing Sobbing conclusion it was just too much I don't know what it was I'll tell you about it in a second after I throw up

So I just read Jacob Two-Two Meets the Hooded Fang for the millionth time and for breakfast I ate a dozen homemade chocolate chip cookies that Gail brought over last night before we went to Boyden's where tout le monde was mingling and talking and having opinions and didn't they know me from somewhere? Gail and yours truly drank our guts out and ran over to the wine store on the other side of Princess and met this gorgeous guy in Pervert Park and was it ever fun playing piggyback til I fell and cut my wrist and went to Emergency for the third time in two weeks and got the proverbial butterfly bandage

I am pretty healthy tho and my European zits have miraculously cleared up except I have to pee all the time and I'm more than slightly late (again) but to answer your question I can't really figure out what Cyrus and I did in Europe the weeks just ran together and passed we went everywhere Dubrovnick, Avignon, Paris, Roma Roma Vaffanculo, Classical Greece, the Lost City of Atlantis and some other place I don't remember After I got summarily abandoned I spent a week recuperating at my dad's flat in St John's Wood splurging on cashmere and his new girlfriend took me to Wapping Someplace and the British Museum and some old Law Hall just ridiculously crawling with stained glass windows and old leather books but I do love London I love sitting in those Tube stations with those Fruit & Nut bars and the smells of all the different aftershaves Mind the Gap

Now being with Gail I'm-going-to-sleep-with-as-many-men-as-I-want Benninger is a non-stop pajama party but my God Babba I got her to row this session and last week she went home with this Cuban waiter guy from Chez Piggy who looks like he's been high every day since grade eight and the next day when our bus was leaving for the Henley Gail still hadn't shown up so the whole bus drives up to his apartment and I have to ring the bell for her she runs out pulling on her sweater her face all red and blotchy trying to shoo away this sniffing dog and staring down everyone on the bus my Lordy-Loo we lost by the way we always lose we crashed into some boat from Trent

But last night at Boyden's I really don't know about Gail sometimes rinsing her hair in patchouli and wandering around campus in these black dykey army clothes talking about fuck-mates and Nicaragua but last night she was so funny embarrassing the men trying to give them erections by staring at their crotches saying dirty things but Gail is kind of scary too she talks about having sex on pool tables and somehow alot of the people she knows have some kind of STD or use drugs that require needles it makes me feel scared seeing her kind of screw up her life like this or is she I don't know

I tried to talk to Brigid about it she just got back from Toronto but she's not very receptive she didn't really enjoy herself at the party she's seeing this rich Rosedale guy named Avram and deferring her LSATs so they can do some Gadna kibbutz thing but I'm sure they'll both end up at Osgoode anyway because one of his grandmothers died and left him a stinkload of money that was bitchy oh well Brigid doesn't care too much for me anymore I guess I'm not Jewish enough though that never seems to bother Gail

Boyden's applying to law school too and invited me to Chester for the end of August his parents bought that place they were renting for the kids but I don't think I should go I mean it's nice having men pay attention to you but silly when you catch yourself wanting to go back to how things were before you slept with them so yes Mind the Gap

I didn't really understand how wierd things were with me and boys til I was back here eating a salad on the verandah yesterday before Gail came over I was thinking of the day I can remember it so vividly when me and you-know-who planned to elope except you never know if it's a joke with him we ended up in Salzburg at this hostel sharing a room with these German and English swim-team kids plus the four year old daughter of the English chaperon guy from Manchester who was the only one around because all the German chaperons were going at it hot and heavy in every other room you walked into complete with screamy German breathing

We spent most of the day in this stupid kiddy playground being silly the kids were playing teeter-totter and swapping dirty words very funny to hear Detlev repeat them with German precision of course Cyrus got along beautifully with them playing Piaget and hitting himself in the head with a soup pot God he can be funny sometimes Babba they loved us him and me but I couldn't help feeling we were competing for them

Because one minute Cyrus is wonderful kissing everybody and the next for no reason he's in one of his presto change-o mood swings and being a terrible bunghole telling me why I shouldn't like Pachelbel's Canon and I'm the most looks-conscious person and how he hates what my clothes stand for even though the day before he said there's no such thing as symbolism and why can't I get that through my proverbial head?

So that was the Day He Went Wierd and the next was the kids last night together and Erin the four year-old was sad because she lost her invisible doorbell and I was cheering her up while that smelly old horrid pseudo-psychologist type from Manchester who had great tufty eyebrows but kept terrifying everybody with stories about bullfights and children with no fingers he says to Erin who's normally very self-assured and kid-looking Daddy hates little girls who bother him when he's drinking his coffee Daddy hates little girls who bother him when he's drinking his coffee Daddy hates I was going crazy! I said I'd help her find her invisible doorbell and went to get Cyrus to see if he was wandering the stairs being poetic or swatting at a diaper rash that wasn't there or just being embarrassed he's alive and can't find his own invisible doorbell

But I couldn't find him and couldn't find him and I've been through this a million zillion times with Cyrus going flip it so fine whatever I left to do the Sound of Music tour and lo and behold who surprises me at the I Am Sixteen Going on Seventeen Gazebo but Cyrus crying and confessing his whole life story asking if I remember the summer we met and what happened on McNabs Island and when he asks me to marry him I don't say anything because how can I when he's being so fuck off ridiculous?

O God I'll tell you the rest of that meltdown later God good thing I've only slept six hours the last three nights and good thing my World Civilization prof isn't hitting on me in his office asking me to play squash and inviting me to his cottage and have I ever visited Old Fort Henry? I really don't know what happens to people everyone seems so normal in school yet the older people get the more they write special delivery letters or apply to law school and what will happen to us all? Oh the common room, the common room, I do remember, I can recall, Babba what do you think? I guess it's sublime til it changes into something else and mostly I try not to get upset and I know there really isn't a need to avoid standing in the wind next to these old limestone buildings wondering what the fuck is going to happen to me for the rest of my life because I still have wierd Cyrus thoughts and he shows up in six-part dreams where someone else turns into him but it was him all along there must be some kind of unconscious significance there but it will be sort of disgusting only being with normal people now since he's my favourite person and I just feel so horribly dangerously neurotically sensitive to what people say I think my problem is that I keep sympathizing with everything

Well sorry about not going to your wedding when I thought I was eloping on my own Barbara Wells it must be wierd to have a new name when it's wierd to have a name at all but you know you can always visit Old Fort Karin I know that sounds like I'm a cheese so maybe you can melt me on toast or add me to pasta but yes I'd love love love to visit you there I really miss Jacky and the Comeaus and I get so jealous when I think of you so close to the sea and the weeds because if I can't pick blackberries and live like the Inuit I'd like to be in a room with big windows in an empty old house by the sea & finish all the books I've ever started

Say hi to all the kids for me I often think of you there lots of love and wet fish as if you need it the fish I mean

grosses bises
KARIN

Gail in Winter

I AM THINKING NOW of a day in December when the sun has brilliantly manifested after five full days of snow. Storms have left drifts all over, and the snowfall, pure white on roofs and branches, has begun to melt under blue skies—icicles dripping, windows streaming, snowbanks moistening into perfect snowball snow. It is a few moments before noon and I am sliding along Hollis Street on the flat soles of loafers once brown and belonging to my uncle but now dyed black and belonging to me. For later I have a formal occasion to attend. I am on my way to a wedding, actually, a wedding of some far-reaching repercussion as it will turn out, even for me, for the day, though one of the shortest of the year, will prove to be one of the longest of my life, my last real day as a Halifax person, and the symbolic end to my youth and formative years.

But in these first bright minutes the city seems a thrilling, raw place, an eccentric saltwater city two centuries decaying on the North Atlantic, and possible around the next corner is a figure of Dickensian scheme and consequence. I pass through streetscapes where stone townhouses neighbour lofty office developments, a tattoo parlour abuts a low-rise union for longshoremen, and ironstone warehouses preside over grimy wooden piers. At the Noon Gun I'm rounding north on to South Street, a Twizzler licorice in my mouth. Besides my uncle's loafers, I wear a Fred Perry shirt with all the buttons done up, a vintage suit from a second-hand store, and a camelhair duffel coat inherited from a grandfather. I am chasing a Suggs-inspired ska revival look, some years after it is fashionable, sure, but I am a moody youth, somewhat haphazard, and full of hope for myself and my friends.

I am on a Samaritan trip to see a friend, as it happens, and I bring a care package of unsweetened cranberry juice, Kit Kat bar, and a paper bag of further Twizzlers. The friend is Gail Benninger and Gail in the last few years has been ejected from a few universities (Queen's, York) and is now on a leave of absence from McGill where she's zigzagged into graduate studies. Things there have not been good. Hit by a rock at a pro-choice rally, arrested for staging an occupation of a campus administration building, Gail in Montréal was hospitalized for severe depression two months into term and so she's returned to Halifax to recuperate, and not to her family's home on Robie Street, but in a borrowed place empty over the holidays, a bachelor apartment in a Victorian rooming house on South Street. It's a yellow-shingled, three-story edifice, elaborate with porches and dormer windows, and inside the front hall linger smells of oak wainscoting and foreign foods, as if someone might have stashed and forgotten somewhere a pastrami sandwich. The complicated odours of the hallway merge with my apprehensions about seeing Gail, flavouring my understanding of her situation, and I think of her faltering in her gloom and isolation. For I am aware that many of her friendships have fallen away and she is more or less estranged from her family.

"My father's a pervert," she said the last time I saw her. "He's a gross and manifest pervert." She has suspended all relations with him and her sister Brigid she seldom saw. How to explain this? Gail would lose both parents very young, her mother at eighteen, her father at twenty-six, five years after the day under discussion, but at twenty-one she was still suffering from the convoluted after-effects of her mother's early death. It was my conjecture—if I might be allowed some free-form psychoanalysis—that her mother died at a time when Gail was just beginning to construct an adult identity separate from her parents and her mother's abrupt death from cancer interrupted and jumbled this differentiation from family. Gail would refuse to grieve the passing of her mother and she'd refuse to feel sorry for her imperfect, widowed father, and this willful decision to put her own feelings of resentment first became for her points of pride and personal principle. Her grief and suffering instead took the form of anger—anger at her mother for dying, anger at her father for straying—but some of this anger from time to time went deeply and dolorously inside her. Her struggles with authority, her impatience with the status quo, her bouts of depression, her contentious imperatives of self, I feel all of these issued—to conclude my pop psychologizing—from such uneasy transmutations.

"With Gail," said my mother, "you always have to be careful of her feelings. Well, with everyone in that family. But Gail most of all. Oh she's great in lots of ways. She's quick. She's very quick. And she's sensual. But angry? That kid's got a lot of anger. That girl goes looking for fights and most of the time she finds them. But Aubrey, you dated her for years, let me ask you, does she *like* people?" My relationship with Gail has been a very undefined association, an unpredictable, who-knows-what's-going-on association, but always a no-boundaries, no-secrets, all-access sort of association and even after we split we've been close. Very few weeks go by without some kind of contact between us. Back in September I received two birthday messages from her—the first, happily drunk and slagging off her own delinquency about missing the date by three days, and the second, the next morning, hungover, fragile, embarrassed, apologizing for what she called her drunken obnoxiousness. This very out-of-character humility—with its hints of self-loathing—coordinates in my mind with a moment from junior high when I found in one of Gail's discarded school scribblers, written over and over on the back page in handwriting increasingly jagged, the phrase "I hate parties and I hate dancing and I hate me," and as I push on her crooked apartment door it's this memory more than anything that provokes my protective instinct toward her—as well as a fear that one day she might cease to be.

SHE WAS UNDER rumpled blankets, staring as if recently awakened, though I knew just as easily she could have been this way for hours. Twisted beside her was a flannelette sheet, white with two lavender stripes, and further within the blankets was a paraphernalia of supplies and effects: an empty Kleenex box, a container of Gaviscon tablets, assorted books and paperbacks, and a bottle of Buckley's Mixture cough syrup. The room itself, high-ceilinged and a hundred years old, was decorated in general issue grad student—a bookshelf constructed from cinder blocks and unpainted two-by-eights, a drafting table, a pantry of mismatched crockery, a laminate-topped kitchen table with three different chairs, and a boombox on the hardwood floor surrounded by a litter of cassette tapes and loose sections of the local newspaper.

"Hey there." I bumped the door closed. "How are you, freak?"

Either Gail did not hear me or she pretended she did not hear me. She lay where she was, her face drab and unremarkable.

Finally, there was a flicker from her eyelids and she turned from a sunlit window to regard me, but still with a sort of mongrel despair in her eyes, as if she were powerless to oppose any new turn in her destiny.

"Jesus, woman. What's going on?"

Gail so often glowed with some grievance or passion it was strange to see her so dispirited, as if something had been bleached or drained out of her. "How can I," she said, quickly wincing, "be this fucking sick?"

"She speaks!"

"I'm so bloody depressed. I feel like going out and getting plastered. Just—why, why, *why* am I in Halifax?"

"You really sick?"

"*Yes*, I'm really sick." Putting an elbow on the futon, she propped up her head with a hand. "My throat's so frigging scratchy I can hardly talk and my teeth are like little fucking razor blades. Not to mention my head's just one big mess of snot." Though her face was passive, and my presence had occasioned no real reaction from her, I think for Gail a sense of obscure problematics had begun floating in the room. "Why are you here?"

"What do you mean? I'm here about your ad in the Auto Trader."

"Is this some charity thing so you can feel better about yourself? I'm no charity case." A wedge of hair, damp from sleep, dislodged with these first movements and flapped over her eye. "What's it like out anyway?"

"Beautiful. You should get some daylight into you."

Frowning at this mention of the outdoors, Gail arranged the flannelette sheet and blankets over her head and addressed me from under the covers. "I'm never getting out of bed," she said. "I hate everybody. I hate everything out there. God, I hate this place. I haven't been outside since I got here. I just roll around in bed like some kind of hamster person." She made a small sigh. "Just so you know, I've been in the same underwear for three days."

"So the legends are true?"

Pushing down the covers, Gail made a confused face, as if someone had forgotten to inform her that her visitor might possibly be a dolt, and reached for one of the paperbacks on the bed. It was called *The Woman Warrior* and between its pages, as a bookmark, was a run of toilet paper. Gail brought this to her nose and blew into it with real effort, though one nasal passage stayed resolutely congested. "This is the worst part of being sick," she said, one nostril speckled with dried mucus. "Having a glucky nose. But I think I can almost breathe again."

"Within her bed she is crafty sick? Fie!"

"I'm what?" Gail glanced at me with great suspicion, as she often did, then glumly swung her face to one side. Dank from lying under so many bedcovers and because she hadn't showered for days, Gail was calmly pungent, the smell of her sleepy body recalling to me prior days and nights when we shared a bed, during the musky beginnings of her period, in the mammal warmth of bedsheets.

She made a sudden move to rise and then, standing upright, she leaned to grab at a cotton scrim that hung above the window. She slid the scrim along a wooden dowel, straining on tip-toe so she could distribute the fabric fully over the window glass. Gail wore an over-laundered grey T-shirt and green underwear with a white elastic waistband. As she jiggled the scrim over a splinter, sunlight streaked along her face, animating her chestnut brown eyes, and for a few moments she rested her face in sun-warmth. I'd forgotten how her profile fairly demanded to be reckoned with—the clear line of the jaw, her nose, perfectly classical except for a faint Sephardic snubbiness that matched the curve of her eyebrow, and I remembered further, from four summers past, the radiant Gail of the Naval Reserves, when in her off-hours she went about bralessly, brazenly with closely shorn hair, a thin ridge of starter-pimples on her suntanned forehead. At seventeen, Gail seemed unstoppable, a newly adult woman at ease with her form and possibilities and when she chose at the end of that summer to relieve me of my virginity in the basement sauna of her parents' house I felt mystified to be transported into the frailties and mysteries of the grownup world and it occurs to me, as I remember all this, that Gail's name isn't really Gail at all but Malka, which means Queen in Hebrew, she breathed this in my ear, as a reward, as a sort of emotional keepsake, the first time we had sex.

"So what are you doing here?" she asked. "How did you find me?"

"Want to tell me what's going on? Nobody's seen you."

"Ah," she said. "Don't worry about me. When the Cossacks come, I'll just crawl under a porch and die." She considered my outfit. "You seem very pleased with yourself. Poncing around in your little camelhair coat. Why are you in a suit? You look like a Mormon." Gail reached for a can of Diet Coke on the floor. She opened it, took a gulp, and slumped back against the headboard. The beverage was an ongoing and habitual aspect of her daily life even though a year before it had torn a small ulcer in her stomach. "Oh, Jesus," said Gail. "Of course. What poor woman are you stalking now?"

"Are you really not getting out of bed?"

She took the Diet Coke away from her mouth with a little upward flourish. "I told you, no."

"Ah, I see. How can you get out of bed if you've not solved the mysteries of Rapa Nui? Fie, I say!"

"No, I don't think you get to say that." Gail was staring at me. "What is happening in that pea-brain of yours, McKee?

You're such a frigging idiot, I can't believe I was ever attracted to you. Whatever you're doing, it's not going to work. And you still look like a Mormon." There suddenly erupted from Gail a very resonant burp, a burp she made no effort at all to suppress. "My God, I haven't had sex in so long. Do you know any half-decent men? I mean men who aren't complete tools who would want to slam me up against a wall? Wait." Gail slowly squinted at me. "Is it Buf-Puf? Is that who you're stalking?"

This was a somewhat pejorative reference to Elizabeth Puffett, a female acquaintance three years our junior who bore a striking resemblance to the model featured on an Icelandic sweater pattern in the display window of The Yarn Shop on Quinpool Road. As a general rule, Gail considered my interest in other women to be unadventurous, frivolous, Presbyterian—in a phrase Titsy Goysy—but I detected a note of real dismissal in her voice.

"I could never imagine you going out with *any*one," said Gail. "But there's no way a girl like Buf-Puf's going to like you. You're all over the place. You've got all these cockamamie plans. You're the lunatic of a thousand ideas. And Buffy Puffett is a very conservative Convent girl who just happens to be a knock out. You think she's going to want to go *roof*-climbing?" Gail swigged from the Diet Coke. "I don't know what you think about things but it's just wrong."

Choosing to busy myself with other activity, I stooped over the kitchen table and laid out the unsweetened cranberry juice, Kit Kat, and Twizzlers. But Gail was alert only to an embossed envelope that fell to the floor from the inside pocket of my suitjacket.

"What's that? What did you just throw down so officiously?"

"I didn't throw it down. It fell."

"What is it?"

"Wedding invitation."

"Oh? Is someone getting married today?"

I said she knew exactly who was getting married today and that at one time we had discussed going together.

"So who are you taking instead—one of your sisters?" Gail seemed to be inspecting the cuticle of her thumb. "You know how I feel about your sisters. Your sisters are a tribe. They want to impose their own rituals on everyone. Especially other women."

"Thanks for the tip."

"I just don't know about women who keep dying their hair blonde, that's all." There followed a medium-pitched commotion from within the bedcovers—sounding like a sluggish blend of slide trumpet and soprano bugle—after which Gail shrugged and said, "Whoops. That one kind of rose up the crack of my bum. Excuse me." A soft, legume-y smell, implying in its organic history the green mulch of wet cow yards, dissipated in the air of the room. "McKee," said Gail. "I asked you a question—what was it?"

"Give me a moment. I'm just trying to—Give me a moment, please."

"It's just nature," said Gail. "What was I saying?"

"You were talking about farts as I recall."

"You know, if you could just stop being an insane, maniacal freak for one second then maybe I could remember what I was saying because—Aubrey, are you even listening to me?"

"*Yes*, I'm listening."

"I swear you have the shortest attention span of anyone I know." A dangle of hair spilled over her eye. With a savage flick, Gail cleared it from her face. "Where was I? What was I talking about?"

"Hey—here's an idea—why don't we open a window?"

"Piss on you, McBean."

"I think we tried that." I walked over and raised the inside window—its sash cord tightening with an abrupt jigger—and studied the old-fashioned storm window beyond it. At the bottom of its frame was a hinged wooden slat that covered three circular air-holes. It was frosted shut. Outside, snowflakes spun out of the darkening sky.

"What are you doing?" asked Gail. "How did you get like this? Really? I want to know." Putting down the Diet Coke, she assumed a rather carefree, supine position on top of the bedcovers. "You're so scattered, I swear to God. You never know what you're doing. You're fumfering."

"Look, lady, I'm trying to *do* something here." I bumped the window slat with the heel of my hand. I bumped it again. After a third bump, the slat trembled and came free.

"You're such a fumferer." Gail wriggled on top of her bed, twisting her hips this way and that, bending one of her knees, and in the next moment held in a raised fist the green underwear. "You're a complete and utter tool. In fact, you probably suck." She pitched the underwear at my head and, as I turned from the opened window, it caught me spang on the temple, the underwear slipping a little before its elastic waistband caught on the top of my ear. Gazing into my eyes, Gail's scream was full of delight. "Smell my panties."

"Excuse me?"

"Smell my panties! There's a pop-up book in there. Ha! That was like one of your jokes. I've become infected with your brain."

I walked, as decorously as I could with underwear drooping over my eyes, to the kitchen table. "Hmm." I sat down. "So what were we talking about?"

There was a small eruption in Gail's nose as she laughed again—it was a brazen laugh, really, it took her into almost any mood—and it was not so much a reaction to my deadpan delivery as pleasure in her own achievement. She jumped off the bed and walked over to sternly review me, little smirks dimpling on either side of her mouth. Then she plucked the underwear off my head and peered into my hair. "You've had those cowlicks your whole life, haven't you?" Her jaw was set forward in a contemplative, cowlick-assessing under-bite. "You look like Fran Lebowitz. You look like a Mormon version of Fran Lebowitz. But exactly. It's freakish."

Gail in her grey T-shirt was standing very close to me and I was briefly mesmerized by the pattern of swirling black hair on her forearm, and becoming aware of her further intentions for me, when from the hallway came a few noises off—a tenant stumbling or a packet of flyers dropping to the floor—and Gail looked up, instantly on guard, reacting, as she sometimes did, as if each new mortal was a direct personal challenge.

I went to the door, still crooked in its doorjamb, pulled it open, and stepped back as a cat nosed her way inside. This was a full-sized mackerel tabby by the name of Tinker, belonging to the apartment's regular occupant, and Tinker tended to treat all other creatures with maximum indifference. She moved swiftly to the kitchen area where two bowls were set on the floor, one holding stale water, the other crusty with uneaten cat food. I was filling the first bowl with fresh water when I noticed Gail behind me picking up the wedding invitation. She pulled the card from the envelope and read its text aloud. "Mr. and Mrs. Gregor Burr request the honour of your—oh my fucking puke." Gail's eyebrows crinkled with complication. "And you want to *go* to this?" She continued to gaze at the invitation. "Jesus. The Burrs. They're a real *master*piece of a family. I'm sure everyone's really pumped for this wedding. Or really jazzed. Or really amped. Which is it?"

"I think it's stoked. I think everyone's really stoked."

"Please—" Gail dropped the invitation on the table and returned to her bed. "Someone just put a bullet in my brain. My God, I have to leave Halifax. I have to leave this fucking place. I can't bear the thought of watching Boyden Burr grow old." Boyden Burr, the day's groom, was a rather inescapable Haligonian, an athlete, a rich kid, a singer who founded the stunningly popular Thunderhouse Blues Band, and someone I've known since I was four years old. His father, a well-known lawyer and Member of Parliament for Halifax West, was often in the news and a favourite subject of the scandal magazines. My policy regarding the Burrs, for a variety of reasons, was strictly non-interventionist.

"And you?" said Gail. "What's going to happen to you? You couldn't leave this place. You'll be here your whole life. Chasing your grand conjunctions. I'm just not sure it's going to work."

"What's not going to work?"

"Because of Halifax disease. It's all about what you do. What street you live on. What vacations you take. And it never changes. It's like who you are in grade twelve is who you are forever."

"But I'm such a frigging idiot—"

"No, you're not. Don't be a moron. Just stop."

"Stop what?"

"Oh dear God." Gail bounced a fist into the bridge of her nose. "You're losing it. You've lost it. You've already lost it. What's going to happen to you? Really. It's just—I don't know." She looked at me, pensive. "I'm worried about you."

"About *me*?"

"You are naive, Aubrey McKee. Fuck, you're naive. I always forget. You still think you can be friends with everybody. And that's nice. But people are *horrible*. People are corrupt and self-ish twat-heads. And it's naive to think they aren't. How have you not learned this? Maybe it's because you're the middle-child peace-maker, I don't know. You want everyone to get along so you act like a clown and get trapped in your schtick—"

"Fart—"

"Like, why are you this *parody* of yourself? Why don't you ever take yourself seriously?" Gail sprang off the bed. "Can you be serious about your emotions for once instead of having a ten-mile-away ironic distance? Why do you avoid everything? Doesn't that seem like a fact worth investigating?" Holding unwavering eye contact, or rather *forcing* unwavering eye contact, Gail began to back away toward the bathroom door. "Maybe it's worth asking why that happens. Maybe it's time for you as a twenty-two-year-old man to grow up a little and take some responsibility for once in your life." With these formidable words, Gail turned from me and vanished into the bathroom, the door closing with a pronounced click as its latch settled into the strike plate.

THIS APARTMENT was rented to a person named Paxton, a friend of Gail, a woman with a low-slung posterior, a crew cut, and a PhD from Cornell. She moved from New York to Nova Scotia to become the ombudsperson for Dalhousie University. She was butchy, low-voiced, mordant, and queer. I didn't like her at first. I didn't like her later either. It would be some years before I was comfortable with the concatenation known as Paxton. She was born Shelley-Anne Cluett in upstate New York and for reasons mysterious decided at twenty-six to change her name. Her new designation was chosen when in a thrift shop she found the name embroidered into a sewn-in panel on a Maritime Flooring and Tile work-shirt. Paxton was no-nonsense, watchful, and self-contained. She was *The Moosewood Cookbook* and Joan Jett, the Michigan Womyn's Music Festival and La Cave Restaurant. I met her two summers earlier when she was marshalling Gail out of a club called Rumours along with a transgendered, mixed race friend named Shasta-Ly. That evening Paxton was wearing corduroy overalls, cut off and hand-hemmed at the knee, a Bundeswehr singlet, distressed Blundstone boots, a tightly-wrapped kerchief around her left wrist, and seventeen keys clipped into the hammer loop of the overalls. She had deep-set eyes, furry armpits, and a compelling aura of fecundity—but I thought, and still think, seventeen keys was a bit fucking much. She spoke obsessively and snappily about ex-girlfriends, women who seemed to do nothing but infuriate Paxton, though they all seemed to still figure very much in her life. Indeed, she was spending the Christmas holiday *with* an ex-girlfriend because the ex had yet to inform her parents she'd broken up so she and Paxton were in Orlando pretending to be a couple until January. Gail had spoken vaguely of difficult circumstances—abuse, addiction—in Paxton's childhood as Shelley-Anne that were supposed to explain away the levels of distrust Paxton propelled toward me and my sort but I did not really accept this explanation, perhaps because I sensed Paxton's influence would loom large in Gail's semi-distant future.

Left alone in the main room, I went by the bookshelf and glanced over a few books by authors I didn't know—Szymborska, Irigaray, Dworkin—then considered the materials on the drafting table. There was a neat array of purple paper clips, seven sharpened pencils in a Dundee Marmalade jar, and an opened Kodak envelope out of which spilled several white-bordered colour photographs. In these images, Paxton's hair was long and lustrous and she was pictured with a very fit-looking Korean man. He seemed like the sort of chap in third-year med school who runs triathlons and volunteers at the Kids Help Line. He and Paxton were bent over with exhaustion and laughter, both wearing medals around their necks, joyously hugging each other, smiling at the camera. After a moment I recognized him as John Yu, a kid from Sunday school, and, recalling his details, I realized he and Paxton must have competed and won something at the Head of the Charles Rowing Regatta. They both looked very happy and I was jealous of their success and jealous that Paxton, a new arrival, a Come From Away, was constructing an actualized adult life in Halifax. Most of the time I was haunted by what I hadn't achieved, frustrated by my inability to realize my best projects, and threatened by a looming sense of disorder. I made messes, sometimes glorious messes, but messes all the same and I knew in Halifax I was mostly understood as a drug dealer, punk rocker, and wayward oddity.

There is a line from Northrop Frye, a writer whom in the last few years I'd mentioned so often that Gail had taken to calling him Northrop Dum-Dum, where he suggests we're all in the situation of a dog in a library, surrounded by a world of meaning we don't even know is there, and I was beginning to feel like such a spaniel, someone who doesn't quite get it, and I thought for a few moments of the many things I'd done, or half-done, and poorly, and standing by myself in a sublet apartment on South Street, wearing a second-hand suit, and watching as a cat appeared from under the bed to smell along the base of my dyed loafers, I saw myself as sort of strange and sad and isolated in the bizarre personas I'd created for myself.

THE BATHROOM DOOR swung open and out stomped Gail, *tutta nuda*. She charged across the room, her bare feet slapping on the hardwood floor. There was an ungainly quality to her progress—Gail tended to walk, even in a sundress, like a saddle-sore bronc-rider—and as she arrived at the window her nose bumped through the cotton scrim and into the glass. Annoyed, she pushed the scrim to one side and simply stood there, without clothes, daring the world to judge her, daring the world to deconstruct its own assumptions of nakedness.

Faint dimples were apparent on her lower back, on either side of her tailbone, and, just perceptible, near the top of her ass, around a plum-coloured mole, was an eddy of fine white body hair. Spinning from the window, she squatted beside the boombox and glared at the cassette tape inside. "I think I'm going out."

"Where?"

"I don't know. Just out."

"Why?"

"Because we suck." With a quick scowl in the direction of the wedding invitation, Gail turned to me. "I find it, frankly, sort of fucking ludicrous that you're going to that wedding."

"Open bar—"

Gail was already shaking her head. "I just find it a bit bizarre that you're even considering going when that family is such a fucking nightmare."

"The bride happens to be one of your closest friends."

"And you don't think it's all a business decision?"

"Gail—"

"Spare me the niceties."

I was surprised by this flippancy—later I would learn of the twenty-two page letter Gail had written the bride explaining why she could not in good conscience be present at the service—but I guessed that Gail's misgivings were really more with the groom's side of the aisle. Gail's relations with the Burrs were somewhat complicated, true, but I think she'd been determined to characterize Mrs. Burr as a dingbat Stepford Wife ever since a twelve-year-old Gail with her mother encountered the Burrs at the intermission of *Equus* and Mrs. Burr declared Gail too young to see it. Gail normally had in mind three or four Halifax-related thesis topics and The

Adaptive Preference Formations of Tiggy Burr was a favourite subset of The Ongoing Pretend of the Halifax South End. For Gail, the South End was home to the tanned and bland, the prosperous and deeply square, and she had a great and open disdain for what she took to be the ignorance and solipsism of the moneyed families of our neighbourhoods. To her, the South End was a self-perpetuating family compact regulated by the requirements of social standing and social privilege—and enclosed within sanctimonious notions of community—so I asked if this was to be yet another diatribe on the limits of my people.

"It's all about who's in and who's out."

"That stuff doesn't matter."

"It does if you're out!" Gail stood in the centre of the room, pubic hair lushly untamed, rather as if she were a nude model for a life drawing class who had decided to abruptly commandeer the proceedings. "It's not all lobster suppers at the Saraguay Club. The Grammar School? The Waeg? You think the kids in Spryfield and Jelly Bean Square—"

"I haven't met all the kids in Jelly Bean Square."

"And you won't. You think they all had the same childhood you did? Because believe me, they didn't. There's a gargantuan fucking difference. Aubrey, you grew up in a very insulated pocket of privilege. And the Burrs—putting aside the fact that the father is a serial rapist who basically walks the streets of Halifax scot-free—what does this wedding *mean*, really? And who's going to be there? It's going to be Boyden and his brothers and all those fucking reggae stoner sailing guys—Jib Whitelaw, Digby Lynk, Jamie *Swim*—that fucking council of assholes." Gail stared at me, more than a little alarmed. "They're *morons*, Aubrey. You've known them your whole life. And who else'll be there? All the little trollops that trail after them—Jody Jasperson, Pippa Flynn, Jenna

Tibbets—*that's* who's going to be there?" Gail clutched her head with both hands. "And Boyden, I know he can be this sort of jocky nice guy but he's just so *awful*. He's like this monstropolous dinkweed. That guy can tell himself anything. What Boyden Burr tells himself and what really happens are two different things entirely. And I'll tell you one thing." Gail spoke with full certainty. "Boyden Burr is only interested in Boyden Burr and that's all he'll ever be interested in. He has no interest in anyone else."

"How do you know that? We don't know that."

"Oh you think he's going to change?"

"Maybe he doesn't know any better. Give the guy some latitude."

"Doesn't know any better?" Gail shook her head as if she found my opinions only dismayingly juvenile. "Give the guy some latitude? Who am I—fucking Gandhi? No, Aubrey, Boyden Burr *doesn't* know any better which is exactly why I would never give him *any* fucking latitude. Do you think he's giving latitude to the families in Jelly Bean Square? Of course he isn't. You think he's interested in alternatives?" Gail's expression implied the situation was shoddy—or worse than shoddy—disastrous. "Boyden Burr is a spoiled little brat and self-satisfied fuck-wad who is going to do just fine now that daddy's got him into law school. So he can take the summer off and sail around and play some gigs and smile at the babes while he's butchering 'Stir It Up' or 'Brown-Eyed Girl' or 'Sweet Jane' or whatever the fuck song he wants to destroy."

"Thanks. Amazing. Really going to open up a dialogue."

"Dialogue?" Gail's face deformed with grotesque indignation, as if someone had just thrown dirt on her. "There *is* no dialogue! There will never *be* a dialogue. Not with these people. Because I'll tell you what Boyden Burr wants in this life, Aubrey. He wants a wife as hot as mommy and a house as rich as daddy and a summer place where his kids can grow up to be rich little douche bags just like him and where everyone can go sailing just like him and hang around the same fucking friends he's known since grade one and be pretty and rich and white together."

"I don't know if you've had this talk with your parents, Gail, but *you're* white."

"It's like some bizarre version of false consciousness! The whole place is. I mean, fuck, Aubrey, you're either someone who thinks things are fine the way they are or someone who thinks things can be changed for the better. Like this might come as a shock to you, but there are people in the world who think maybe investment in South Africa *isn't* such a good idea. Or land mines *aren't* so wonderful. Or female circumcision *isn't* so amazing."

"No one's asking you to circumcise any—"

"One of the reasons I'm not going to this fucking wedding is because I wasn't *invited* to this fucking wedding. I don't get invited to weddings anymore. I don't get invited to parties anymore either but I don't particularly care because I don't really give a fuck. They don't want me there. I know I'm difficult. Who cares? But the real reason I'm not going to their wedding, Aubrey, is because every fucking *day* is their wedding." Gail pointed at the newspapers on the floor beside the bed. "You know, I read in the paper about this poor girl from Shannon Park whose parents basically let her *starve* to death—" Gail shook her head as if she didn't know how to possibly continue. "And then I think of Karin and Boyden's wedding and all the wedding presents they don't need and I get so fucking furious at their smug-little, fucking-little, entitled-little lives it makes me want to scream. And I think, 'Why are people going to this wedding when we could be fixing this fucked-up city?' That's what I think. *That's* what I think." Gail sniffed and wiped at her nose, for she was crying now, or trying not to. "Don't you wonder why nothing ever *changes* in this city? Why it's the same families over and over again? Jesus. This city's going to get left behind. This *province* is going to get left behind. And you want me to go sit with George and Judy Asshole and Tim and Tiggy Tidbit and make small-talk about Babba's bridesmaid dress and—where are you going? That bathroom's really stinky right now. I mean it. It's a total stink-farm. Aubrey?"

HER MOODS, HER MOODS—in my life I've felt so lost and given over before Gail's moods and it had been so long since I'd been present for this particular vector, with all its variance and deviation, that a getaway to the bathroom seemed for me the only way forward. Gail was admirable, fascinating, self-involved—and quarrelsome, exhausting, ridiculous—and she would always be like this. She couldn't help but be like this. She was fiercely and impossibly herself. Most of Halifax tended to think of her as someone with an unstable and persistent Oppositional Defiance Disorder—but she had a crazy dignity and prescience, I don't know where she got it but my God it was hers, she owned it, she fairly burned with it, though sometimes it was all just too much for me. Here she was in the next room, stark raving naked, ready for all enemies, foreign and domestic—and I knew Gail in this mood was not about to surrender anything—but my worry was Halifax could not sustain her. For I saw on some subjects Gail had progressed to a sort of fanatical hatred that made up with insistency what it lacked in rationality. My worry was that Gail, with all her struggles, would not be able to process her furious disappointments and would only rage, rage, rage against whatever or whomever happened to be in front of her...There would come a time, much later, long after the events of this day had concluded and long after their details had dissolved into folk history, when I would miss this version of Gail, the vulgar, lickety-split, farbrente Gail, for this version would not last the years, and the specifics that prompted these present hysterics would be mostly forgotten, even by her. But of course I didn't know that back then. Back then, as I say, I was still full of hope.

THE SONG GAIL WAS LISTENING TO when I returned to the room I didn't recognize. It was a Cockney voice singing about the year 1649 and Saint George's Hill and how a ragged band of somethings came to show the people's will. It was "The World Turned Upside Down" by Billy Bragg but at the moment it was just a song on a boombox within whose spell Gail was wholly absorbed. Our friendship-relationship-exship lived within a continuum of music, starting with our own punk band, proceeding through Madness and the Specials, then into a sea of synthpop. Bauhaus and Joy Division, Yazoo and New Order, these were discoveries we swapped back and forth in mix-tapes but this Cockney singer, and his solo-guitar style, I'd never heard. On the bed, Gail lay on her stomach, bobbing her head, and softly singing along with the song. She had a way of singing—and barging through misheard lyrics—that I found sort of endearing and maddening and dubious but at the moment I said nothing, so personal seemed her connection to the song, so private her communion with it, and when the singer-guitarist hit an open E major chord it seemed to mean *everything* to Gail, her solidarity with those who were working toward justice, her sympathy for anyone marginalized from standard concepts of society, her righteous resistance to all those who stood in her way. It was about how other people were obstacles and how, even if she were forced far inside herself, one day she would be proven right and one day, by God, one day she was going to charge through all obstructions with some kind of greatness and by then she'd be a different woman, a woman who wasn't affected by weddings or cover bands or Halifax, *that's* what the song meant to her. When it finished, Gail went still a moment, preoccupied, then pressed stop on the boombox and pushed herself off the bed. She went to a pile of clothes in the closet and pulled out a pair of army pants and a heavy turtleneck sweater. As she dressed, she spoke to me in a deliberate way, as if she had some design in mind or as if—and this was a feeling I'd had for some minutes—she wanted something to be at stake between us.

"Aubrey," she said. "Just tell me one thing. What the hell happened to Cyrus Mair?"

I chose to say nothing. As you can tell, Gail kept in motion a number of prospects as to who might play Principal Villain in the skirmishes of her life and the person just named was always in contention. She was suspicious of any interest in the guy and the idea that people might be running around, moony-eyed with romantic admiration for Cyrus Mair, and there were a few, was for Gail a very impinging happenstance. He was also, it bears mentioning, someone who'd been twice engaged to the day's bride-to-be.

"I'd love to see what happened to the little freak." Gail pulled the turtleneck over her head. "But it wouldn't surprise me if he's gone for good. Have you heard from him?"

Tinker had leapt up to the windowsill and was now watching a seagull float in the wind beyond South Street. Before making a response, I stared at these two, waiting for some shift in the diorama.

"So?" said Gail, after a few this-silence-has-gone-on-too-long moments. "I suppose you're going to tell me Cyrus Mair *isn't* weird?"

Still facing the window, I shrugged.

"Because he is fucking eerie. I will never understand your passion for that mutant. I mean, I'm sorry if I don't find him so fucking magical. Like, he misses people he hasn't even *met* yet? Right. That's not weird."

Tinker flinched as a spit of sleet appeared on the storm window. Opening my mouth, and forcing my voice into a cracking falsetto, I made a loud and cretinous meowing noise.

"Aubrey, what the fuck?"

Staring at the sleet-spotted window, and speaking in a normal tone, I said, "I kind of liked it back when I was saying Fie. Remember that? That was good times. Good times when I was saying Fie."

After a brief sneer, as if I were someone she didn't really care to know, Gail sat on the bed and opened a balled pair of work socks. "I cannot fathom the weirdness. I really can't. I mean I know you want him to be a great guy and not a nut job but let's face facts, shall we? Remember New Year's Eve two years ago?"

I said I remembered the story.

"Because *I* certainly fucking remember. One minute he's saying how wonderful it is we're together and the next he's in some fit of panic and jumping out a window? What the fuck is that? I mean what the fuck *is* that? Excuse me if I find that a little bit of a horror show. And what he does to the Zubers, breaking into their house to steal pictures of their *foster* children? Does that sound sane? Does that sound reasonable? Or does that sound like the behavior of a fucking psycho?" Gail wildly shook her head. "I think he's mentally ill. I really do. I think the guy's insane."

"I'm not sure he's insane. Just sort of non-sane."

"Remember when you used to hate the guy?"

"I didn't hate the guy."

"And now you fucking worship the ground he slithers on. Because he's got some psychosexual hold over you. So you two are up in his tree fort swapping guitar riffs in your little circle jerk of punk rock fuckery, I get it. Why don't you just fuck him and get it over with?"

"Why does this *matter* to you? Why are you being like this?"

"Why are you defending him?" screamed Gail. "Because he's so *sensitive*? Is that it? I don't think anyone's that sensitive. Because I don't think there's that much to be sensitive *about*. Do you? Seriously. Tell the truth, asshole."

"I'm an asshole. Boyden's an asshole. Cyrus is an asshole—" I glanced at her. "What the fuck? We can't *all* be assholes. Because, Gail, you say this about everybody! What're you going to do when you're by yourself?"

"Look around!" said Gail. "I *am* by myself. Have you not been listening to anything I've said?"

Gail continued to talk, her expressions clever with contempt and outrage, but I would stop listening. It was my turn to look blankly at something and I stared at the unsweetened cranberry juice, Kit Kat, and Twizzlers untouched on the kitchen table. How can I explain Gail whom I've known so closely? She has been near the centre of so much of my life and thinking and there has always been between us a feeling of connection and when we were going out of course I often asked myself if I was in love with her and, even if I understood I wasn't always in love with who she was, I knew I could be in love with the person she might become but I was understanding, finally, with a sense of stalemate and dead end, that she was becoming someone else, someone I didn't really know, and the thought came to me that life was stranger, deeper, and more complicated than I knew, than I wanted it to be, and I guessed the coming years would be riven with conflicts and disorders beyond my understanding.

THE FLURRIES THAT FLOATED in the air minutes before have thickened into a blowing blizzard, sucking light from the room and warmth from the hardwood floor. The room lights dim as the furnace surges somewhere below, baseboards creaking, radiators clanking. On the windowsill, Tinker twists her head as footsteps sound in the outside hallway. Someone is moving with swift purpose toward the door. I am able to exchange a look with Gail before a knocking begins and I open the door to see in the hallway a young man—slim, blond, wearing a blue cashmere coat and carrying a heavy-looking briefcase—disparate details that resolve themselves into the person known as Cyrus Mair. He is nervous, jumpy—his awareness flashing in all directions—and I ask what's going on.

"Everything," says Cyrus Mair, his eyes glittering.

The Return of Cyrus Mair

CYRUS MAIR, WHIZ KID, RECLUSE, AND WEIRDO—jittery, restless, tremulous, querulous, fucked-up, rousing, mercurial, self-sequestering—Cyrus Mair in all his quiddity had not been seen in Halifax for some years and although he's only just now put in an appearance I'd like to pause the streaming media a moment before joining him on South Street. Gail asked if I'd heard from the guy and the quick truth is I did get, *pace* Karin Friday, a long, weird letter from him. After the fleeting moment that was the Changelings, after the dissolution of The Common Room, and after his loss of the Rhodes scholarship to the Fabled Ian DeGroot, Cyrus Mair withdrew into his family's house where he sank in secret studies, reading volumes foreign, antique, and contemporary. "That boy," remarked my father, "studies like a little Jesuit." There followed a bursary from Cambridge where one imagined him within crowds of Sloanes and toffs and stooped-over dons, walking ancient cobblestones, and disappearing variously across courtyards at dusk. The letter in question was one of sundry written from Cambridge, we were freakish, high-volume correspondents in our young adult years, but it happens to be the only written communication from him to me extant. All his other dispatches would vanish in a canvas canoe pack in the Coppermine River along with a Mylar sleeping bag, three iffy tangerines, and a paperback copy of *Dune Messiah*. The letter—after which no one would hear from him the faintest peep—follows below in its entirety.

PETERHOUSE
CAMBRIDGE
CB2 1RD
6 January 1984

DARKLING HAROLD:
So here I am a drunken son of memory, exhausted near a midnight, in this room which smells terribly of overripe fruit and inefficient heating, but I've decided finally to take your advice and so, as I've been drunk all holiday anyway, here on a Twelfth Night is your scotch-sodden letter. This might come out all at once so read quickly.

I guess I haven't made contact in a while. Too much here. Too much going on. I've received stacks of wonderful gifts from you: photos, books, musical scores, demo recordings, cassette tapes, all these pieces of your life you've sent, and here I've been wasting too much to write back. I've more than once wanted to reply and it's not that I haven't been thinking of everyone it's just that I've been thinking of everyone.

I started to write a few things which I abandoned and never sent. I can't seem to write letters anymore. We all of us used to write so many letters. So many feelings then, in the long ago, not really fully formed nor understood, from people who, in a very real way, don't exist anymore. And somewhere, too, I suppose, are all the letters I've written. I used to live on those letters. I couldn't keep from writing them. Now I don't want to commit myself to words. Don't like the sight of my own handwriting. Reveals too much.

Gail and Bridgette just left on the train back to London. They arrived here the week after Christmas, stopping by on their way somewhere, Grenoble, I think. So I've been playing host the last six days. I took them to a dessert evening organized by Ravi from Gloucester and Hislop-Hyphen-Harris, ten of us sitting round a draughty room in Trinity passing bottles of pink wine leftwards to each other. Ravi from Gloucester got very drunk and excited, rubbing his hands, prodding Bridgette to ask if I were gay, and sniggering about Trevor-Roper and Mensa and roasting people in bronze bulls.

"Brideshead Retarded," as Bridgette described it. She was a big hit, incidentally. No one dared take on Gail and her loony, leftist blather but Bridgette captivated. Here they were expecting some farm girl from the Colonies, not Thoroughly Cosmopolitan Bridgette. She really is the most exceptional bitch, you know. But I like her now, once she feels she knows you. She loves to perform, as if she's only vaguely aware of her effect on people. I don't mind it so much anymore. I have a personae with her that has nothing to do with the way I act with anyone else. But she seems to like it, so.

Walking back in the drizzle, I got in an argument with Gail and a married couple from Indiana. Gail was ranting, in her exasperating semblance of logic, about the State of Britain when the married couple from Indiana made some facile comment about France not being German today because Napoleon sold Louisiana. I said Napoleon would have sold Quebec just as fast and it went from there to the Seven Years War, the Boer War, the Munroe and Truman doctrines, the Mountbatten Plan, all the way up to Reagan. I don't know why but I am always forced into the role of Stodgy Traditionalist with these people and I got very oracular and declamatory: Cyrus Reaching for the Sententious Phrase and Hating Himself For It. All of it left me feeling, surprise, surprise, ill at ease and vaguely bitter.

I'm afraid I still have trouble liking Gail. It's instinctive. She's very agitated about something that has nothing to do with me. I know it's been a big relief for her to decide she disapproves of me. And Aubrey, she talks about you *all* the time. I think she was wildly in love with you, wildly envious of you, and wildly resentful of all of it. There's some ugly, dominating urge at work which is near to a very renewable supply of anger and distrust.

Before they arrived, I'd been ending up in different libraries, Bodleian, British, and ghosted in and out of London doing research at the Public Records Office. Whole lives, epochs, buried in shelves and shelves of documents, this muddle of lost histories. Gail is right, of course: Britain's fucked, the class system, the universities, the institutions, fucked a long time ago. Britain is Johnny Fartpants and agro and hillsides blowing with Twix wrappers.

Strange insularity here. I've been back in Cambridge a while but still feel displaced. I'm left pretty much on my own and I haven't been getting much sleep. It seems to snow and rain continuously. It's cold all the time. I'm cold all the time. I've fallen into strange rhythms. Before Gail and Bridgette came I think I'd gone three days without speaking to anyone. Sometimes it's very hard, talking to people. But voices. For the thesis I have a few progressions I have a hunch might fit together. And this bright glimmer of another thing that belongs to something bigger. Mostly my work has felt like a series of conjectures in search of an argument but I am publishing an essay, an offshoot of the dissertation, in *The Historical Journal* which is a big deal for me. It's called "Context and System," context being what you're born into, system what we make of it, contexts essentially always beginning and systems always failing, and it draws on ideas from M.A.K. Halliday's work in open dynamic systems. Very worth reading, by the way.

I haven't figured out a good way to consolidate it yet, and it gets pretty notional and abstract, and not the sort of stuff you enjoy, but a core idea is that every moment can be said to occur twice: first as it happens and again as it is registered in a recognizable structure of experience; just as this sentence lives now as I write it and again as you read it. Complexities arise when elements derive meanings from each other while serving two systems simult—just sec! Someone at door!

It was Ravi from Gloucester apologizing with Slivovitz! Don't know if I go for all that soteriology stuff you were talking about on the cassette tape. Isn't every day a religious experience? And I'll support Wallace Stevens before the Sons of Judah or the Fathers of Rome. "The final belief is to believe in a fiction, which you know to be a fiction, there being nothing else." It's certainly easy to get in a rush about establishing connexion, especially between things you feel haven't been connected before, then everything is lucubration and you're into that late-night Il punto a cui tutti li tempi son presenti scenario. Except now? Starting to feel drunk!

I agree with your Karin-Common Room thesis by the way. For all the reasons you said. We were so *close,* all of us. Didn't you get the feeling if she loved one of us she loved all of us? I felt interchangeable. I was spending more time in her head than my own, referring, deferring everything to her. I was always catching meanings where there were none, others I knew I'd missed. What did you call it? Let me get the tape. Fuck. Just spilled Slivovitz all over this. Really drunk!

And, yes, I do remember the last time I saw her. It was the Prince's Inlet Race, some summer Saturday, the woodsmoke of vanished afternoons and all that Wordsworthian garbage. I was a little worse for wear, exhausted with travel, upset I'd missed you in Halifax, headaches from the sun and drinking, the whole afternoon was a haze of sunshine and drinking. She was among the Jeremies, as you say, the Bohunks and Boydens. "He's really nice, really," said Babba, trying to draw some sympathy from me amid the mayhem on board. (Babba's wonderful. She knows I'm alive and won't let me forget it.)

Karin and Boyden were circling the boats after the race. I'm not sure if she saw me first but I remember their motorboat idling in our wake as I crawled up from below. She called out hello and said my name, the syllables sounding so strangely on her lips. It was a moment, anyway. Embarrassing, awkward, full of reversing perceptions. I was too drunk to sort through it and am still. She said a few things lost to the wind. But I understood the tone: solicitous, sympathetic. The last I remember, they were turning back to Chester, Karin holding the windshield, Boyden in sunglasses beside her, flaxen hair blown about by the wind.

12 January
Snowing again. I see I still have this. I've lived a few days since then. Bad Days. Fever. Chills. Swollen Glands. I've been in bed most of the time. Being ill like this, this constant nausea of failure, crying for no reason, I feel I've betrayed myself. So while everyone here watches "Sons and Daughters" as their Pot Noodles simmer on hot plates I try to remember phone numbers I used to know when I was young in Halifax before I was sick. However. Don't know if I answered all your questions but I will send this to you and hope it reaches you, wherever you may be. I am sending to the Australian address, care of Mr. Van Der Hoof, as it's the last address I have. I'm not sure why you want to go to Australia. Why does everyone go to Australia? Is Australia really so essential? Australia. Really? Why, Australia, why? But best of luck on the worldwide travel plan. I guess there are moments when I feel I want to clear out myself, wander to the unimaginably far distance, into the dust and heat, wreck myself on an island, crash into a train, fall into the sea. Still. Soon it will be spring and everyone will be reborn.

CYRUS

Wallace Stevens was one of a sacerdotal three for Cyrus—the others being Simone Weil and I.A. Richards—and many were the afternoons spent debating the relative virtues of such a threesome. Before we return to the symphonic tone poem which is the end of my relations with the Mair family and my last, real Halifax day, I'd like to make known a last little factoid, somewhat spooky, somewhat salient. Many years after the events herein depicted, when I was no longer young, in fact when I was down-and-out after having been fired from an appalling television series, I wafted into a second-hand bookshop on Salt Spring Island. There, beneath two volumes of a Chinese-English dictionary, I exhumed a book called *Parts and Wholes: The Hayden Colloquium on Scientific Method and Concept*. This was a little-known, ultra-esoteric academic title from 1963, hardbound in a blue-and-orange dust jacket with light sunning on the spine and foxing on the endpapers but overall in Very Good condition except for those pages marked up by the previous owner. The book was, of course, one of those scattered into the world *ex libris* Mair and so pre-owned and selectively scribbled-in by my friend. Paging through one of its essays, "How Does a Poem Know When It Is Finished?" by I.A. Richards, I encountered a phrase—*A poem is an activity, seeking to become itself*—underlined in ink and connected by a swooping arrow to a jotting in the margin, "Absolutely what I was saying Tuesday to McKee! Also common life people cf. sw." The handwriting degenerated, a trifle loopily, into illegibility in the next few words, so I'm not sure what else was being glossed, nor what those initials denote, but that line about poetry I've thought about often. Because while I write about the guy with some diffidence it is my considered conclusion that for Cyrus Mair each *person* is an activity seeking to become itself and I feel he looked on in some wonder at the poem each of us might become.

MY FIRST THOUGHT, when I had a moment to properly look at him in the sunlight and snow of South Street, was that Cyrus Mair had gone back in time. It's true the tousled blond hair, so plentiful in youth, had sparsified in the manner of a Notting Hill investment banker, and he was unshaven, with a scant growth of beard, but his face was sunburned and clear, his eyes bird-quick, and he was so slim and looked so young he seemed to have become his own younger brother. The shirt he wore was standard white, the tie purple silk, the suit charcoal grey, and wrapped around his throat I recognized his woollen Peterhouse scarf—a gift from Babba on his acceptance to Cambridge's oldest college—a smooth-cornered, blue-and-white striped affair, very close in colour tones to the flag of Finland, and which, at six feet long, had a maddening habit of snagging in the bi-folding doors of a telephone booth or catching beneath someone's shoe on the stairs. The blue cashmere coat I'd known for years. It had belonged to Cyrus's late father and, as earlier described, Cyrus as a teenager had taken to wearing it in all seasons. It was too big for him then and too big now, one sleeve drooping so far past his wrist only his fingertips were visible. He was so attached to this garment that I wondered if he'd begun to fairly *live* out of it—for its pockets abounded irregularly with day-old sandwiches, toothbrushes, smudgy fountain pens, and other non-sequiturs—and really it wouldn't have surprised me if, from its innermost folds, were to flutter out a black-capped chickadee. In his right hand, he lugged a dilapidated and heavy-looking briefcase and, as he set it on the sidewalk, one of the snap-locks popped open. Cyrus frowned at this change in its fortunes and was making a move to fasten it when a great sneeze shivered through his shoulders. So I asked if he was all right.

"I'm just—" He sneezed again. "Trying to feel all this."

"Sure you're okay?"

Cyrus remained stock-still, blinking and squinting as if something were interfering with his vision. Opening his eyes very wide, he lifted a hand to his eyelashes and, with forefinger and thumb, pinched away a lengthy strand of light hair. He stared furiously at this a split-second, as if it were some unknown, semi-precious filament, then spun it between his fingers and let it fall to the sidewalk. As it vanished into the slush, I felt a drop of perspiration trickle out of my underarm and down the side of my ribs.

"I'm fine," said Cyrus. "Sometimes people—people sneeze sometimes when they walk into direct sunlight."

"So where've you been—Cambridge?"

"Sort of. Been travelling."

"Where?"

"In some distant deeps and skies."

"Was it Leipzig? I hear people go to Leipzig."

"I've heard of those people. What the fuck's with those people? The Germans have a name for those people."

"When do you go back?"

"Today. Later." He spun his fingers in a vague circle. "Soon."

"You're on your way to the airport? Where's your stuff?"

"Don't have a lot of stuff."

"Who needs stuff?"

"Other people have stuff. People from Leipzig have stuff."

"Briefcase," I said. "That's all a guy needs. You can give away your stuff, you can change your name in Tucson, but you *keep* your briefcase."

In front of the Hotel Nova Scotian, around the statue of Edward Cornwallis, were scads of seagulls, and not a few dozen but a few hundred. They were assembled all over the snowy park as if they'd chosen to have an impromptu Annual General Meeting on the nearest expanse of land. They were facing west, wings tucked in, and Cyrus was staring at them. "What the fuck's with these seagulls?"

"It's disgusting. Why aren't they in the ocean chasing kelp?"

"Damn right." Cyrus grabbed a swoop of snow and started packing it in his hands. "You know what I think about that?" He reared back and biffed the snowball into the flock. Six or seven gulls started into the air, gliding and wheeling in a loose figure eight, all but one returning to the ground. The airborne gull flapped awkwardly before floating higher in the sky, higher even than the uppermost floor of the Hotel Nova Scotian, all the while squawking and shrieking in a sharp repeating pattern. It sounded like the High F sequence from *The Magic Flute* was stuck on repeat. Cyrus stood watching this gull with some solemnity, then whirled around, seized his briefcase, and set off along the sidewalk's curbstone, swinging his briefcase like a yodeler with a milk bucket. Of course I'd seen him a hundred different ways, in a thousand moods and modes, and in our lives between us ten thousand moments had passed, but to have my friend materialize on South Street was more than unexpected—at the same time the unexpectedness was absolutely in keeping with his trick of singularity. So I stayed a moment where I was, open to the music of the afternoon, listening to the street-salt crack beneath his shoes, and watching the gull somersault out to sea in a sudden squall of wind.

CYRUS I FOUND on Barrington Street talking on a payphone. Rather he wasn't talking, he was listening, and after a moment he crashed the receiver into its cradle-hook. Staring fiercely at the push-buttons, he brought to his eyes a rip of paper and checked a scribbled number. Not finding his change in the coin return, he rummaged some dimes out of a pants pocket, jammed them into the slot, and dialed another number. He waited. He glanced at the window display of Phinney's Musical Instruments, a once-splendid, now drab-and-poky department store, then shifted his interest to a nearby plywood construction wall. It was busy with bulletins of all kinds, among them a silkscreened print for a NSCAD graduation show, a Rickenbacker For Sale flyer with tear-away phone numbers, an advertisement for an upcoming Thunderhouse

Blues Band reunion, and, just visible amid all the paper fragments and rusting staples, the remnants of an original Four Bands for Five Bucks poster from the Changelings' first gig. While he waited on his call, Cyrus skimmed these notices, shadows of rising heat shimmering behind him on the ironstone of the Phinney's building. I studied these vapours, trying to figure out where they were coming from. It was as if something were burning somewhere, or some substance was being liberated as a result of something burning—and lost in my memory was a word for such a process—but Cyrus slamming down the receiver had the effect of returning my attention to him.

"Who you calling?" I asked.

"Wrong number."

"Who you trying to call?"

Cyrus scratched under his chin. "My thesis adviser."

"Isn't it late in England?"

"I mean the vice-provost. There's been a problem. In the commissary."

"Everything okay?"

"Everything's fine. Everyone's normal. Except for these—" He waved his hand to indicate the rest of the street. "These fucking Scandinavians!" Happy with this improvisation, Cyrus pulled a silver flask from a coat pocket.

"These fucking what?"

"That's the name for those people. That's it right there." He twisted the top off the flask. "I mean where do they get off coming here with their plans for social change? They come here, devising their *alphabets*—" He chugged from the flask then offered it to me. "You can't walk a mile in this town, you can't buy a fucking cupcake, without some Scandinavian trying to feel you up or get at your ski pole."

I took the flask and drank. "We getting day drunk?"

"Try and catch up. Just try."

"How much have you had?"

"I might've drunk a bit. But hey, I can quit anytime I want." Cyrus grabbed the flask and regarded me. "You know there's a guy on a soap opera who looks exactly like you."

"Identical in every way."

"His name's Dr. Something."

"That's me. That's modelled on me."

"And where'd you get that suit?" He examined it. "That one of your father's? Nice colour. Nice suit. Why are you so hot-to-trot?"

"I'm supposed to be at some wedding later."

"Yeah? I'm really busy, too. I'm supposed to be meeting someone before the airport."

"Who's that?"

"Well—" Cyrus twirled his fingers in another circle. "I haven't worked out all the specifics." As he was screwing the top on the flask, it fell from his fingers to the sidewalk. He glared at it. "Fucking Scandinavians." He picked it up and screwed it down tight. "Jesus, Harold. If you think I'm going to stand here to be stripped naked and beaten to death by some fucking Scandinavian, you've got another thing coming."

"I'm not really thinking that."

"Just wait till you're drugged and fondled and left for dead in a bucket." Cyrus was having trouble getting the flask back in his coat pocket and made room by jerking out a paperback. "See how you like it. It'll be a little late to take it up with the vice-provost then, I'll tell you that."

"What's the book?"

"This?" He gave me the paperback. It was a tattered copy of *The Twelve Caesars* by someone named Suetonius. "Total fucking genius. History of the Roman Empire written by a guy at the time. It's not only dates and battles but how people burped and farted and how impressive their toupees were and just all the insanity of being human. Here." He took the book and flipped through it. "Where is it? Oh yeah. 'Parricides were sewn up in a sack with a dog, a cock, a snake, and a *monkey*, and thrown into the sea.'" Cyrus cackled, somewhat sinisterly, and found another page. "I love this, too. The Emperor Tiberius used to train little kids, minnows he called them, to swim between his legs and nibble at his dinger." Smirking, Cyrus shook his head. "But Tiberius did have some pretty admirable qualities. One day, when meat got a little scarce at the zoo, he was thinking how horrible it was for the animals. So he lined up some convicts and said, 'Everybody from the bald guy to the other one.' Meaning *kill* them and feed them to the animals. Because there were some pretty terrific panthers in the Coliseum that day." He pushed the book back into his pocket. "Tell that to your Scandinavian friends, why don't you? While you're off at the Norwegian Consulate guzzling all your aquavit." He jumped into Barrington Street, in search of more change, presumably, and picked his way through puddles of flooding slush, a straggling scarf end, wet with snow, already beginning to freeze.

THE AFTERNOON WAS VEERING COLD—a December day that began brilliantly sunny, dimmed with storminess, flashed again into sunlight, was with the turning of the tide becoming gloomy and freezing. The North Atlantic was very much in the air, replacing the city's mildness with rough winds that seemed to breeze in from icebergs eight hundred nautical miles away. I was shivering at the intersection of Argyle and Sackville streets, watching a very full moon float over the city of Dartmouth, when Cyrus appeared with his briefcase below. He darted up the sidewalk like a madman. He was smiling to himself and I guessed some plan was beginning to move forward in his imagination. What it was, of course, I didn't know.

"I got the right phone number!" He waved a slip of paper above his head. "Better get you that drink."

"I think there's going to be a snowstorm. You might want to get to the airport."

"One drink never hurt anybody."

"Not sure about that. Plus I have to go to some wedding."

"What? You're coming. We have to storm the battlements!"

"Which battlements?"

"And if you don't come, you're a quitter." He clapped me on the shoulder. "It could get grim. There could be catapults and stinking pitch—"

"I'm not sure that's for me."

"So you're saying no?"

"No—"

"Certainly sounds like no. Quitter. Quisling. Harold! Sometimes these things are about belief. And the prologues all have ended. We have to choose—"

"Wallace Stevens. Right. You told me that."

Cyrus looked perplexed. "No, I haven't."

"Yeah, you did."

"I don't think so."

"Yup."

"Impossible." Cyrus stared at me, mystified. "I've never told anyone that in my life!"

"Okay. But you did. Maybe in a letter."

"In a letter? You sure it was me?"

"I'm sure. Wait. It was a guy in a soap opera."

"There it is!" His eyes leaking with excitement, Cyrus pulled on the door-latch of the Seahorse Tavern. "Finally you're *you* again. How long did that fucking take? Learn to understand your secret self why don't you?"

"I'm not sure drinking will do that."

"Are you kidding?" He dropped down the stairs of the Seahorse. "Things are going to change forever."

THE SEAHORSE TAVERN was the oldest alehouse in the city and it was, in the years we knew it, a very tolerant and undefined underground parlour pub where, within its refectory tables and church pews, you might find articling clerks, divorcing teachers, squabbling art students, laid-off stevedores, off-the-clock drag queens, able seamen on shore leave, a women's rugby team—all of whom would be welcoming the idea of draft beer and intrigue and drunkening. In December, the Seahorse was that feeling of being in a crowded local with winter winds outside, your face flushed after three drinks, the gusts from the opened door like something you'd brave on a fishing trawler, and at Christmastime, during Boxing Day Week, the Seahorse was a perpetual get-together and homecoming. A sampling on this Friday included Finlay Chaisson and Peter Dooder, two of the crew from Canada's America's Cup Challenge, back from Perth and drunk off their asses; Lee and Lolly Barkhouse, waitresses from The Keg having a pint before their shifts; Mowbray Morris and Fid Jumbee, two staffers from *The Chronicle-Herald* across the street; Palmer Von Maltzahn, only twenty-three and the most attractive bailiff in five counties; Jim Pitblado, a junior tennis coach, known to some as Cuddles because of his penchant for bleaching his hair platinum and taking thirteen-year-olds to the movies; Peter Noseworthy and Bug Corkum, laissez-faire pot dealers; Ally Buckley and Pip Hartling, two young women from the folk band Pony DeVille who would go on to form Shriek Records; Dawson Redstone, artistic director of nearby Neptune Theatre, in close parley with lighting designer Astrid Whynot, soon to fatally overdose. All of these were present circumambiently as I found some space in a corner of the main room. Dropping my duffel coat into a vacant pew, I noticed there was, somewhat unaccountably, a Trivial Pursuit card face-down on Cyrus's briefcase. I picked it up as if it were *exactly* the item I was looking for. Clarence Darrow was one of the answers and seeing this name, and not being able to recall the other lawyer in the Scopes Monkey Trial, and watching Cyrus return from the bar with multiple glasses of draft, all of this had the cumulative effect of dissociating me from the moment. For the last few minutes, a mix of impressions, little fact-thoughts and half-thoughts, had been sliding in and out of my mind—that I was feeling obscurely depressed, that my sock was wet inside my shoe, that a song whose name I'd forgotten was sort of repeating in my mind—but, watching Cyrus put his purchases on the table, I had a sense that all the scattered details of the day might come together if only I could realize their proper pattern.

"So—" Cyrus passed me a glass of draft. "Here's to the rest of this thing."

I clinked the glass against his and sipped at the foam-top. "So how've you been, Maestro?"

"Little burnt out. Might have an ague. But I got my canticles."

"Where'd you say you were?"

"Getting a phone number."

"No. Why are you sunburned?"

"Just second." He rubbed the chill from his nose. "I have to apologize."

"For what?"

"See those people over there?" He nodded toward the bar. "One of them was talking and he said this guy's nose was too big for his face—"

"Which guy?"

"And for a second I thought he meant you."

"Which guy said that?"

"The thing is, I was sort of *glad* he said that—"

"I don't know those guys."

"But then I felt bad. So I wanted to apologize."

"Was the guy talking about me?"

"No! But I *thought* he was and I agreed with him in my brain and that's why I'm saying sorry."

"So who was he talking about?"

"I don't know—" Cyrus drank from his draft. "Some idiot with a big nose. Who fucking cares? The point is, *I* was out of line. Let's face it."

"Right." I wiped some beer-slop off the table. "You see Cuddles over there?"

"I did see him as a matter of fact. I thought, My God, I know that man. I *am* that man."

"Uh-huh. And Pete Dooder and the boys?"

Cyrus turned to Pete Dooder's table, attentive to Dooder's hair-flips and head-nods, the what-are-you-going-to-do smile easing into the isn't-that-hilarious laugh. Pete Dooder lived in a world of Gore-Tex and sport humping and in high school we'd loathed the sort of chump he represented. But I could tell, from the way Cyrus was watching him, that he didn't need to hate Pete Dooder anymore and, in fact, in what was a very signature switcheroo, Cyrus now felt very fondly toward him, as if he felt a better Dooder lived within the one we knew and took for granted.

"Dooder's good," said Cyrus. "He gets so excited for himself. Remember when he was goosing everyone at Cathy Charles's party? It's so perfectly Dooder. He's just a guy trying to make his hair go right." Cyrus leaned to one side and reached into a coat pocket. "Now where'd I put that fucking phone number?"

"Again with the vice-provost? I bet she has nice tits."

Cyrus brought out a clutter of effects and spilled it on the table. My speedy cataloguing of these goods was as follows—the silver flask, a durable-looking fountain pen, the Suetonius book, an expired boarding pass scribbled over with inky handwriting, a rip of paper similarly scribbled over, a Golden Pippin apple, a paper bag of postcards from the Fitzwilliam Museum Shop, two unused airline tickets, Ganong Double Thick Mints in a torn cellophane wrapper, several crumpled English pound notes, and a bottle of prescription pills.

"What're those?"

"What're what?" Cyrus quivered. "The pills?"

"Those for your ague?"

"Oh—" Cyrus tapped his temple. "I've been crazy. Did I tell you? Ever been crazy?"

"Maybe a little."

"You'll know when it happens. If it does, you just take these." He grabbed the bottle and showed it to me, the word *chlorpromazine* on its label. "These are de-crazy pills. You take them and you're not crazy anymore."

"You're de-crazy?"

"Exactly. De-crazy." A loose mint rolled toward the table-edge. Cyrus popped it in his mouth and resumed his investigations.

"What are they for—depression?"

"For being a proleptic weirdo."

"What's that?"

Snatching up the looked-for rip of paper, Cyrus confirmed a telephone number. "Well, it's when—" He penned the number on the back of his hand. "You're sort of trying to extrapolate every moment to its most plausible conclusion within an infinitude of possibility."

"Sure."

"Sounds easy enough, I know, but you'd be surprised. On account of—" He dabbed some sweat off his forehead with his coat sleeve. "Being crazy. It's like when you're tracking a bunch of observable data-values in three-dimensional space and looking for some kind of optimific configuration but the input variables are changing so fast in some fluctuating series of algorithms that the latticed topology of space-time starts to morph and twist and collapse on itself because Cartesian coordinates don't really apply anymore and all the outpoints are becoming sort of ridiculously self-intersecting and unworkable and transfinite." He sucked on the mint. "Sort of like that. But with human thoughts." Stuffing his belongings back into his pockets, he sprang up and reached for his draft. "The anxiety of that can really mess with you. Especially if, you know, you haven't worked out all the specifics." He downed his draft, plunked the glass on the table, and marched off to find another payphone, his coat, fastened by a single button at the neck, swaying this way and that.

IT WAS JUST GENERALLY HELD that Cyrus Mair was one of the smartest people any of us would meet. You could talk to anyone, med students plodding away to be neurosurgeons, math nerds doing post-docs in Zürich, or know-it-all drop-outs setting high scores on *Asteroids*, there was just a vividness to his presence, a manic playfulness, and a readiness for quick thinking that you felt, that you registered, that you remembered. As a kid, I was almost afraid of his capacity to be conscious because complicating the interaction was Cyrus being so smart and sort of operating on the assumption that all moments—past, present, future—are more-or-less equally present that he often responded to questions you may have asked in *any* of your conversations with him. Which put you in the odd position of hearing answers to questions you no longer remember. Or haven't thought of yet. His were the smarts that made a boy strange. Many who considered him a prodigy also thought him peculiar and there was a gaining minority who believed him trending toward outright psychopathy. I was never sure how far to credit such assessments because, as much as he was keeping Quirk and Possibility alive in Halifax, and he was, Cyrus Mair also answered to the city's need for Failed Promise and Unrealized Talent. Halifax slashes its tall poppies as routinely as Dunedin or Dundee and the idea that some kind of philosopher prince was living on Tower Road, in the attic bedroom of the Pigeon Lady's house, was not a proposition the vast majority of Halifax was willing to entertain. The truth is, his character implied contradictions that did not resolve easily into a coherent unity—a unity that might allow the observer to settle comfortably with a sense of definitive conclusion. It was, I think, the opposite. So, rather than deal with his enigma variations, many simply dodged the provocation and were done with it. Of course there were others, this being gossip-ridden Halifax, who did not. FAIRLY RANDOM REMARKS: "This the guy who disappears from his own birthday party? Who's always in a suit? Pretentious doesn't *begin* to describe the motherfucker." "I made out with him once at a party, didn't see him for a year, then he rings my doorbell with a bottle of Pernod and wants to talk for two hours about music theory? Yeah. That happened." "There's something special about that dude that's weird and amazing and maybe not there." "He's the other guy in your band, right? Foppy McFopperson with the suits and guitar? That little fucker gave me chill-bumps. I saw him throw himself into a mosh pit and get back on stage bleeding like nothing happened. You punkers, man, you crack me up." "To be honest I didn't know what the fuck was going on there. I thought maybe the guy was just gay." Babba Wells, née Zuber, was, as always, more reflective. "What do you *say* about a guy like that? So weird. So deeply weird. Such a weird human being. And I'm not going to pretend I understand him or anything because I know he thinks of things I don't but I do feel that he's sort of *not* like other people. He's very curious. About things. But, my God, Aubrey, don't you want to have back all the hours and days we discussed the weirdness of Cyrus Mair? Because everyone always talks about him and every time it's like I don't want this to turn into another Cyrus conversation because I always feel I'm the worst, most cynical person whenever I talk about him and it makes me feel embarrassed that he creeps into every conversation. I mean, Cyrus is really gifted and smart but it can be a problem when he's doing well and it can be a problem when he's not because everything's so fucking personal with him. And he's the kind of person who, once you get to know him, you sort of realize you don't get to know him, you know? You're only getting close to what he wants you to think. It's complicated. He's complicated. And with Karin, I don't think she'd ever met anyone like him. She really hadn't. And maybe they weren't the right match but I always liked the way they looked at each other. You certainly saw the sparks there. And with her, I think he was searching for something that made him feel—I don't know—I don't know what it was exactly. Do you?"

IN THE BACK ROOM of the Seahorse Tavern, beyond the pool tables, was the subject of such commentary, a young man in an old coat, asleep on the floor, sitting slumped beneath a payphone, the handset for which dangled an inch or two off his sunburnt ear. While I'd been concerned by his disappearance, we were all familiar with his sudden exits—he bailed, he bolted—and I wouldn't've been surprised if he were on his way to Singapore. But here he was silently sleeping. I've always been intrigued by silent sleepers, given that I've been described to my face as a "snoring fucking wildebeest," but, further, the way his mouth was closed there was a Mona Lisa quality to his expression, Cyrus looking almost seraphic, as if his telephone call had sent him into some new rapture. Close by was a young woman—hair cut in bangs, Western shirt, ripped jeans—style choices which on most would signify Backwoods Hillbilly but the sureness of gaze and point of view indicated a young person of substance. Longtime readers of this column will recognize September Abbott, daughter of Wes and Vivien, once a kid with a ukulele singing Joan Baez, lately a folkie in a band called Pony DeVille, and soon to relocate to Vancouver to become simply September, singer-songwriter superstar, internationally famous for her fabulist ballads and six-octave vocal range. But at the moment she was just another lay-person noticing a sleeping Cyrus Mair.

He lay against the wall, his legs bent and crossed at the knee, the elevated tip of his shoe bobbing slightly with the pulsing of his blood. September stood watching him some time, studying his sunburned face, his white-spotted eyelashes, and reading what was written on the back of his hand. Sensing my presence, she dipped her head to ask, "Isn't that the songwriter from the Changelings?" I said it was and so she looked at him again, maybe remembering gigs she'd seen, or speculating on songs unwritten inside him, or recalling some of the stranger stories in circulation, that he'd had some crack-up or break-down or freak-out. To get right to that: two years before, an unattached Cyrus Mair had fled his own surprise party only to be discovered in and evicted from the open-air seal tank at the Dalhousie Life Sciences Centre. From there he wandered plastered to the empty Zuber home on Geldert Street. Knowing the family kept a spare key in a tin of Quality Streets in a backyard sandbox, Cyrus used it to enter the house through the basement backdoor whereupon he helped himself to and finished off a bottle of Zirbenschnaps. Rising to the kitchen, he encountered Feldman, the Zuber family dog, a Labrador-Schnauzer mix, with whom he passed out in a quilted doggie bed in the back porch. Dr. Zuber found them sleeping there the next morning, Cyrus clutching a black-and-white photograph, a snapshot of a Foster Parents Plan child named Amadu, which had been magnetized to and liberated from the door of the brown Kenmore refrigerator. No charges were laid.

TWENTY MINUTES LATER and new arrivals were shaking off dustings of snow, the floor was wet with slush melt, and Cyrus Mair was awake again. He was chatting at the bar with a young woman. She was in the first blush of youth with violet swooshes of eyeshadow, big hair in a side ponytail, and wearing a sheer blouse which showed an ample bust within a demi-cup bra. Now Cyrus was pretty susceptible to feminine beauty, a fresh complexion could destroy his constructs of self at fifty paces, and although he might be distracted by any number of spirits, you always guessed his interest in Karin Friday would remain paramount. But as the young woman pulled on his sleeve and gushed to the end of a sensational, if apparently semi-humiliating story, I could see Cyrus was listening to her as if her opinion very much mattered to him, as if she were someone who obviously put a lot of thought into everything she said, and he was nodding as if he knew just how privileged he was to be in the company of such a bold and original thinker. This little display, I should say, was a pretty good example of Cyrus Mair in the Public Domain. In many civilian situations, he was self-effacing to the point of invisibility. He had a decided willingness to be ignored or thought irrelevant but of course he was, in his suits and smarts and sunburned cheekbones, fairly difficult to overlook. Which was why the young woman was gazing at Cyrus with equal parts interest, suspicion, and puzzled amusement, as if she guessed there were a few things she were not privy to, and why, as he bumped his way through the crowd with a new round of draft, she stared after him with To Be Continued frisson.

"That the vice-provost?" I took a draft. "So I was right."

"Different vice-provost."

"How do you know her, the push-up bra?"

"In a vision once I saw, the push-up bra, the see-through blouse."

"Seriously, where'd you meet her?" I glanced at her again. "Jesus, is that Mary Mingo?"

"She's got some pretty terrific ketchup stains on that see-through blouse. I'd like to dedicate the night to those stains and—" Cyrus inspected the elbow of his coat for dampness. "The fucker who just spilled wine on me."

"It *is* Mary Mingo. All grown up. What were you guys talking about?"

"Just um—" Cyrus sniffed. "Juice Newton. Turns out I'm not that familiar with her discography."

We watched Pete Dooder approach the bar and sidle up to Mary Mingo. She gave Cyrus a joking look, a sort of I-told-you-what-would-happen-if-you-left-me-alone look, then made a klutzy face, stuck out her tongue, and smiled into her vodka tonic.

"Looks like Mary likes you."

"We went on date once."

"She try to feel you up?"

Mid-swallow, Cyrus shook his head.

"She didn't like you?"

"Nah. She couldn't handle my hideous deformity." He giggled. "She didn't like my orthopedic shoe." Cyrus regarded the room, giddy. He was someone for whom every moment was a carrier of possibility and, in the course of a day, he picked up so many meanings, seen and unseen, you often didn't know what prompted his reactions. But he was finding a lot to like in the Seahorse Tavern. He smiled. He smirked. He drank from his draft. He looked at me with a zany shake of his head, as if to share with me his general bewilderment, and squeezed my arm. "Oh, it's nice."

"What's nice?"

"Stuff."

"This is your oh-there-*is*-poetry-in-the-world thing?"

"Not asking for much. Angels playing in falling leaves. Sunrise on Jupiter. The little things."

I nodded, as if I agreed, but secretly I was nervous. For in his eyes was a furtive sort of joy. It embarrassed me and made me wish I hadn't seen it. What he thought of the world, *how* he thought of the world, seemed sort of ridiculous—he was sort of ridiculous—but no sooner had I considered such worries *they* seemed sort of ridiculous and I was left with Cyrus plainly staring at me, amused, expectant, very much himself.

AT THIS POINT in the narrative, I think it relevant to check in with my changing feelings regarding the day's marriage ceremony. I found it odd that two of my friends would not be attending, though I understood their starkly different situations, but there was also rising within me a resistance to my own wholehearted involvement. I have not really detailed so far my Troubles with the Law. They were extensive, embarrassing, and occasioned a number of alcohol-related injuries of my person. I'd spent a few nights in the Drunk Tank and showing up sloshed to a wedding service at Saint Mary's Basilica, where my family was waiting for me, wasn't seeming like the best idea. It would be understood, in fact, as another episode in the long-running series *Fuck-Up McKee*, programming my father was not really keen on, in fact I'm sure he wanted it cancelled and completely off the air.

So my plan, newly forming, was to sneak in later in the service, somewhere around the Eucharistic Prayer, and mix thereafter into the reception. Which allowed for more Seahorse drinks. For I was drunk and happy, and happy to be drunk, and happy to be with Cyrus Mair. Being in his company had reminded me of an immense current of ludic behavior—voices, mimicry, absurdist bits of business—that we shared and riffed on and whose existence I'd kind of forgotten. It was comforting reconnecting with it, after the fractiousness with Gail, and sensing the value of such electricity and how it might charge the afternoon I asked him about himself and his thesis and where he'd been the last two years.

"I get it." He nodded. "I know people think I'm wandering the countryside, sharing my bread with Kurds and hobos, and wallowing in my own filth. I get it. I'm not dumb."

"At least you got filth."

"Well—" He poured half his draft into my empty glass. "Sometimes it's someone else's filth. But the thesis?" He started jiggling a knee. "England's a funny sort of place to write a thesis. English people, they've inherited a topos, I don't know if that word means anything to you but it's a standing set of expectations or traditional themes or set of tropes about something and what's been in place there is arguably kind of longstanding and fucked up and has to do with history and how they're instantiated and held in place by history but history's changing—"

"History's *changing*?"

"It's going to get a lot bigger."

"When's that happening?"

"In the future."

"Sure."

"History will be way bigger. Our sense of human history to the Early Holocene especially will be *way* bigger. And more interstitially complicated. It should've happened ages ago but whatever. I mean we're just talking timeline history, right?"

"What do you mean—timeline?"

"Stop thinking about linearity for a second and figure it out."

"Just pretend I'm dumb for a second and explain it to me."

"Well," said Cyrus. "People tend of think of time as a linear progression that reduces contingency to a sequence of unmediated specifics resulting in Consequence A or Consequence B. That's the traditional notion of a timeline. But if you want to talk about final beliefs, it *is* a bit of a fiction. Because history's just one way of looking at time." He blew the froth off another draft. "Everything's going to be manifold soon anyway because the forms by which we engage with stuff are changing. Even the metaphors we understand stuff by are changing. It's going to be McLuhan times a thousand. So the old systems are going to fall away, which is fine, they always do—"

"What do you mean by systems?"

"Well—I don't know—anything from Catholicism to Marxism to any of the current and available modes of historical thought all the way over to precipitation patterns in the Yucatan Peninsula. Because, if we're going to be honest about the pathless immensity of phenomenological reality and the infinite, overabundant, overwhelmingly irrelevant complexity of it all—that we're confronted with every single waking fucking nanosecond—then for sure, Jesus Christ, people need systems." Still jiggling a knee, he shifted a few empty glasses back and forth, as if they were markers in a game. "I mean you can live without systems and embrace all identities and admittedly there are fundamentalists who seriously do *do* that—and that works for as long as the identities perpetuate the fundamentalists—but with systems it often comes down to the same questions. Like it's a question how much disorder can be exported to the context *outside* the system from which the system can then derive and renew itself. That's key. That's also when things risk getting junked out and becoming sort of pretty fantastically complicated and disruptive and difficult. Then there's going to be a reactionary instinct to move from open mode to closed mode in order to get things done properly. Or what people perceive as properly. It's about getting the balance right. But I'm not sure I've got the balance right."

"Because you haven't worked out the specifics?"

"Because I don't give a fuck."

"You don't give a fuck?"

He shrugged. "Maybe it's better not to understand it."

"Why?"

"Because maybe understanding something in systems and words is always separate from its pure and persistent reality." He watched me finish my draft. "Maybe it's *not* persistent, though, without language. Because maybe everything can feel itself to be a thought anyway. I don't know. I don't know how this thing got started. And I'm not sure it does you any good if you think you *do* know. So maybe it's better not to understand it."

"Not to understand what?"

"Everything." Cyrus drank off his draft. "Maybe it's better to be *in* it than explain it." He was making that giddy smile again, his eyes bright. "That's why I came back."

OUTSIDE THE STORM WAS WORSE—a sense of high winds and unstable atmospherics, snowfall in plump white drifts, smells of tidewater and diesel fumes.

"Phlogiston," I said.

"Excuse me?"

"The word I was trying to remember. This theory of a substance given off by burning bodies. It's obsolete now."

"Phlogiston," said Cyrus. "Sure. Like Spontaneous Generation. And frogs in the mud. Except it's fire in the sky." He shuddered. "Jesus. This *is* a fucking snowstorm." He fastened all the buttons of his coat. "Winter is within us. And the sea is all around us. And so is Juice Newton." Staring into the street, he said, "Harold, you better get to your wedding."

"Not exactly my wedding. What about your phone calls? I understand if you have to ditch me."

"I'm not ditching anyone!" Turning to me, Cyrus spoke with some dismay. "Why does everybody keep *saying* that?"

"So no vice-provost?"

"One last call. To confirm. At my house."

"All comes down to one last call? And then what? Leipzig?" I reached for his briefcase and yanked on it, surprised by its heaviness. "Fuck, what do you got in here? Gold bullion?"

"What do I got?" Cyrus wrapped his scarf three times around his neck. "Beurre d'arachide." This was a phrase drawn from our tennis-identified idiom circa 1977. It was invoked whenever you drew one of the Burr brothers in the first round of a tournament and it was meant to imply generalized displeasure at the perversity of the universe. For a while, we repeated it so much and so often that my youngest sister co-opted the expression, using it as she shooed away a spider, say, or tried to close a sticky window, or even as she followed rebelliously one of the Burr family down a sidewalk, Katie hissing over and over in a whisper, "Beurre d'arachide! *Beurre* d'arachide."

"That's like—" I looked at Cyrus. "What's that guy's poem? He has some peanut butter and buries it in Oklahoma?"

"I placed a jar in Tennessee," said Cyrus, stepping into street-slush and waving at a Regal Taxi. "Try and keep up, bud."

"No," I said, watching him. "Peanut butter. Why you get stuff wrong all the time, I'll never know."

A busker, pervasive in Halifax, even in December, was singing and playing acoustic guitar on the sidewalk. Out in the middle of the street, in the middle of a snowstorm, in effect, was Pete Dooder, free of his companions and dancing by himself to the busker's song, a song whose title I was just able to identify, "It's My Life" by Talk Talk. Dooder revolved in the street, eyes closed, singing the chorus to himself. To me, it seemed a perfectly appropriate activity and the combination of the song and Dooder and my perception of the moment seemed wonderfully connected and I added this to the other I'll-remember-this-moments I'd been holding in my mind—a peach in the gutter outside Gail's boardinghouse, the Trivial Pursuit card in my pocket, Mary Mingo's look of disgust as she tasted someone else's drink, and two or three further details that seemed worth remembering but which, as I ran toward the taxi, vanished from my mind like fish into deeper water.

THE MAIR HOUSE at 1121 Tower Road is forever fixed in my imagination as a convergence of civilization, enchantment, and dereliction. To walk into the house was to travel back into the past, into a still-life of clotted cream, steamer trunks, a tarnishing silver tea service. Nothing seemed to change within it for a century. I loved its old-fangledness, its Haligonan mysteriousness, the Mairness of its everything.

Cyrus and I arrived to a long-ringing telephone and he went dashing into the dark, letting fall his briefcase, lunging for the receiver, and slapping at the light switch above the rolltop desk. With his call in progress, I stepped around the toppled briefcase and went to see about refreshments. In the gules and purpure of the pantry, odors schemed and mingled. I sniffed moldering shortbreads, mildewed linens, and something else, a strong greenish smell, like a liqueur spilled into a musty throw cushion. Amid the cordials and sours, I selected a quart of Beefeater Gin, a dusty can of Bitter Lemon, and two glass-bottomed pewter tankards. From these I fashioned two gin fizzes. I was drunker than I thought because, after cracking open ice cubes from a stainless-steel tray, the lever-action was so satisfying I immediately searched the freezer to crack another. Plopping four mammoth ice cubes into each pewter tankard, I walked double-fisted down the hallway.

The sounds of pigeons outside, unremarkable when we arrived, seemed to separate into distinct sounds—the flutter of wingbeats, a rheumy hyperventilation—a sense of many birds was imminent and the word infestation was occurring to me when, not for the first time that day, I heard Cyrus smash down a telephone receiver. Walking into the front hallway, I set one of the drinks beside him. But Cyrus did not appear to see it. He sat at the rolltop desk, staring at the black rotary telephone. He was faint, uneasy, weak with some internal quivering. And I asked if he was all right.

"I don't know," he said. "Why?"

"You seem shaky and messed up."

"It's a full moon. I'm sort of—I don't know—shaky and messed up."

"You don't look like yourself."

"Who do I look like?"

"I don't know. Some Scandinavian."

He looked up, glancing not at my eyes but at some spot below my shoulder, as if it were too much, just then, to encounter another person's energy. I'd never seen him like this, he'd never shown himself to be so fragile, and I wondered if this infirmity were somehow my doing.

"How was the phone call?" I asked. "Meeting someone before the airport?"

He shook his head. "Not happening. Probably the biggest not happening of not happenings. I thought I was going to meet someone. But now I'm not."

"Was it important?"

"I don't know." He massaged his eyes. "It was kind of a big deal. We were going to talk about the purity of hope, where the sky meets the sea and, you know, how our destinies are joined briefly in a dream."

"But now you're not? That sucks."

"Yeah, that sucks. That sucks so bad. It's of a suckosity so out of this world it's not to be believed." He slumped forward in the chair. "I travelled forty-three hours to be here."

"So what's the new plan?"

"No plan." He sighed. "Maybe stay here a spell."

"Storm some battlements?"

Staring unfocusedly at the telephone, Cyrus said nothing.

"Not everything's over." I drank from my gin fizz. "We can still go into the future."

"That's the rumour."

"What's that going to be like?"

"The future?" Cyrus sniffed. "It's going to be exactly like now. Except we won't be alive." He rested his forehead on top of the rotary telephone. He closed his eyes. He seemed to be breathing principally through his nose. Then Cyrus Mair was asleep again.

HE STAYED WHERE he was, resolutely still, for two or three minutes. When it became clear he would not be stirring, I tossed back my gin fizz, put the tankard on a wooden-topped radiator, and went to find my duffel coat. I glanced around. The ornate arched hallway, the Delft tiles around the fireplace, the greys and blacks of the pigeon droppings stained Jackson Pollock-like on the windows of the storm porch—

just the entire *house* seemed to me a rich and textured work of site-specific art. When she was a kid, my sister Faith described the Mair property as the "most spookiest haunted house ever," and during your first few visits, sure, you were regularly searching its shadows for Morlocks. At certain times in the solar year, evenings in high summer, this feeling of otherness might dissipate, but the idea of further presences, a person in the next room, another listener on the phone-line, a stranger on a rampart, generally persisted so I was not really startled when I saw a pigeon staring at me from the grand staircase. The creature seemed indifferent to my presence, slowly blinking, settled on the landing for all the world as if I were in *its* house. I was thinking how best to direct it out-of-doors when, striding up the stairs, I slipped on some pigeon waste, my loafer sliding backward and smacking hardwood. At the noise, the pigeon started into the air. I watched it flap into the freedom of the stairwell, its neck-feathers an iridescent green in the glow of the chandelier, before the lights of the house winked once, twice, and went out completely. Three seconds later, the lights clacked back on and I heard a voice, faltering but unmistakable, from a bedroom on the second floor. "Who's there?" asked Emlyn Mair. "Boy, is that you?"

EMLYN MAIR, the Pigeon Lady, Cyrus's aunt and benefactress, one of the city's longest-living eccentrics, Emlyn nowanights mostly lay abed in the master suite once occupied by her parents. When I think of her, and marvel at the Living History of her, it seems fantastic she'd lived through all the decades to this December evening. For this was someone who in her childhood had walked with Fathers of Confederation, spoken with men who'd fought in the Civil War, lunched with Prince George Saxe-Coburg. But for her the last Friday of the year was just another Friday, another evening of dusk and darkness and dessert sherry. I'd never really known anyone to drink alone in a house, day after day, but Emlyn Mair drank alone in her house, day after day, receiving her newsletters from the Imperial Order of the Daughters of the Empire, sorting through her papers, doddering toward inebriation. Her bedroom was wonderfully over-furnished with dust everywhere—dust on the tulipwood chiffonier, dust on the floor lamps and footstools, dust on a silver framed baby photograph fallen to the floor. Returning it to a flotilla of family photographs on a nearby bureau, I realized the turbaned baby pictured had once been Emlyn Mair. And here, some ninety years later, within the great canopy bed in the centre of the room, propped up by satin pillows, was the very same Emlyn Mair. She had always seemed old and ailing, but to see her now, cheeks smeared with scarlet blush, eyes milky with glaucoma, face emaciated within a brown curly wig, was to look on someone preposterously elderly.

"Who's there?" She cleared some phlegm from her lungs. "Flimflam? Happy Christmas. What will you have?" She flapped her hand at a bedside table cluttered with bottles of Harvey's Bristol Cream, boxes of After Eight chocolates, and water glasses so long evaporated of water they were grimy with dust. "Surely you'll have something. Pass me the pen there? Wait. I can manage." She took a ballpoint pen and stabbed at the cellophane of a new After Eights box. "Want a chocolate?" She offered the dented box to me. "Have as many as you like."

I pried out an After Eight and mentioned I'd seen a pigeon in the house.

"Which one?"

"Grey with a white wing."

"That's Maisy," said Emlyn. "She goes with Frank. She'll find her way out, I expect. Always has." She flicked a finger toward the bedside table. "Have some sherry? I think there's a bottle hereabout. Glass on the rug there."

On a floor rug, I found a grubby crystal goblet. I scrubbed it clean with a finger and poured us both some sherry as a gust blew through a gable top, straining the bedroom's windows and sending wind screaming down the shaft of a chimney.

"Snowing again, is it?" Emlyn sipped her sherry. "You feel a draft? Check to see the flue's closed, won't you? That's a good chap. And if the power goes out, best to light a candle now. On the dresser there."

I located a silver candelabra on the bureau and lit its three candles. Nearby was a cut-glass vase which seemed a source of flammable materials—cobwebs, dead wasps, desiccated roses—so I moved it to a footstool.

"My father," said Emlyn, observing me. "He planted those roses. The rose bushes in the side garden, they were planted by my parents after their marriage." She turned to gaze at a string of dust on the ceiling. "My brother, Howland, he wanted apples, like the Golden Pippin in the backyard, but I asked Poppa for roses. Oh, was Howland cross! That was Howland all over. Stubborn. Convince himself of anything." She made a tense smile, her eyes abstracted in candlelight. "Howland," she said. "When he was older, he got himself into a bit of a tangle. He was keen on this girl. A man gets an idea about a girl and he's never the same. And that's all it is. An idea. A piffle. But this girl, well, she got him into a very queer street, let's just say that. That we can say." She sighed. "What day is it?"

"Friday."

"No, I mean—" She listened to the blizzard outside. "What part of the year?"

"December."

"December? I suppose. I never learned. In this city? Who does? Not really. Doesn't depend on the husband a woman takes. Depends on the choices a woman makes. You see that and—" She yawned. "You're governed by no one."

She would speak in this way, as if revisiting some former conversation, and wanting to impart some precept or principle, but it wasn't clear she understood what she was saying. Or who she thought she was with. In fact, I was noticing how one of her eyelids was drooping, and wondering if she was in the midst of a stroke, when the lights of the house went out again.

Emlyn lurched upright, her wig left behind on a pillow. "Who's there?" She stared into the darkness of the hallway. "He's come back. He wants it back."

"Who does?"

"Edwin—" She turned to me. "Howland, find out what he wants."

I picked up the candelabra and stepped into the hallway, slightly scared in my drunkenness I would set fire to the wallpaper.

"Is no one there?"

I peered into the hallway. "Don't think." Apart from my own distorted reflection in a blackening mirror, I saw nothing.

"Really?" said Emlyn, falling back to the bed. Without her wig, her bald head looked strangely insectile. Putting down the candelabra, I moved to nudge her wig back on. When I drew close, she seized my hand and squeezed my fingers so tight my knuckles cracked. "What did you see?"

I said I'd seen nothing.

"God's hooks—" She relaxed her grip on my fingers. "I don't know what got into me. It was the strangest mix of my brother and someone I didn't know. How extraordinary. What a curious adventure."

"What is?"

"All of it." Sadly smiling, she raised her glass. "Top up?"

I refilled our drinks. Placing the Bristol Cream on the floor, my loafer, slick with pigeon waste, slid off the rug-edge to the floorboards below. In my doltish, hopping shuffle to regain my balance, I kicked the bottle over. It clanked to the floor and trundled somewhat elliptically under the bed. I went down on one knee and passed a hand below the bed-board but, feeling nothing, got flat on my stomach. A first glance revealed a flotsam of effects in a seabed of dust. Not only the Bristol Cream, but a white Slazenger tennis ball, a girl's ivory shoehorn, a four-dollar banknote from the Bank of Nova Scotia, and, on a thin silver necklace, a gold wedding band. For the majority of the city, the Mair house was a reliquary of worthless oddments, but these curios, suffused with so much memory—as I felt they were for the lady of the house—became charmed in my sight and seemed to sort themselves into the transcendent paraphernalia of the Emlyn Mair Expeditionary Force. I brought out the sherry and wedding band, puffed away their dust, and presented them to Emlyn.

"Where'd you find that?" she said, setting aside her glass. "Give it here, the ring."

As she grasped the wedding band, I took a moment to arrange her brown wig back on her head. Which I did, awkwardly. Not that it mattered to Emlyn. She was dedicated only to my discovery.

"How long have you had this?"

After a drink of sherry, I said it might've been there a month or two.

She nodded and arranged the necklace around her head, this gesture happening very slowly, and with great care, as if much depended on its proper administration. "And December, you said it was?"

I nodded.

"Of course it is." A tear slipped from her sightless eye. "It's always been. It's why he's come back. You see a sign."

A weeping Emlyn Mair was something new for me. We'd always been respectful of each other—I liked to think she had a genuine interest in me and my fate—and recalling her kindness I held her hand again and asked if she wanted me to get Cyrus.

"Just fine, dear. He's answered his call."

"Sorry?"

"A little lie-down. That's all." Her hand twisted in the necklace, a finger flitting through the wedding band. "Did I tell you?" said Emlyn, in a new tone of voice. "I go for surgery next week. On my eyes. Can't do it here. General anesthetic, you see. Can't be sure what will happen. After that, it's a mystery." She shared with me a splendid smile. "Close the door, would you? That's a dear. And take the candles. They make zigzaggy lights in my eyes."

Putting my sherry on a marble-topped table in the hall, I took the candelabra and softly closed the door behind me, leaving Emlyn to rest darkly in her room, amid her strings of dust and memory.

ALONG THE SECOND-FLOOR HALLWAY I noticed peeling wallpaper—a fleur-de-lis pattern in delphinium blue—hanging in tatters and tears and obscuring an array of family photographs framed along the wall. I held up the candelabra. I'd seen the photographs before, but I pretended, as I sometimes do, I was seeing them a first time. To judge from the cavalry moustaches in the older tintypes, a number of Mairs had been gazetted to the Gordon Highlanders or deployed in the Royal Canadian Dragoons. The womenfolk were seen variously slicing wedding cakes or presenting rose bouquets to queen consorts. The images generally evoked what the family was like at the turn of the previous century, in all its primp and pomp, and I wondered at the scenes that had sparkled here, the music that sounded within these windows, for some moments overwhelmed by the meanings of another family. A sense of memories within memories was never-ending and, as the Mairs gazed out at me, I felt as if they were somehow with me, or not with me, but watching me, appraising my looks, presuming on my possibilities. In fact, one of the portraits, a fierce chap in pince-nez and side-whiskers, seemed to be solemnly directing me down the hallway. I complied. But after six steps, my passage became obstructed by books. Thousands of books—musty, dusty, oversized, decaying. Moved from Cyrus's attic bedroom, they were now double-loaded within the bookshelves and stacked along the floor of the curving hallway. I saw penny dreadfuls and travel memoirs, disordered volumes of fiction, an immense atlas, a slim book of poems by Rupert Brooke, a Modern Library leatherette of *Daisy Miller*, and something called *Jack Harkaway's Boy Tinker Among the Turks*, a book whose title can still confuse me. I was about to return downstairs when I glimpsed, at the end of the hallway, a scattering of index cards, some face-up, some face-down. They'd been flung to the floor during an altercation earlier that day. I didn't know this at the time. And the greenish smell identified earlier *was* green—it was a spill of Clairol Herbal Essence shampoo within Cyrus's toppled briefcase—but I didn't know that either. There was much I didn't know. Setting the candelabra on top of *Trees of Nova Scotia*, I gathered a dozen index cards and sat myself on the floor. I took a measured sip of sherry and, in the spirit of a kid assessing a new pack of O-Pee-Chee hockey cards, sorted through my pickings. On each was a typed-up quotation. Some care had been taken to compose and justify the quotation in the middle of the index card. For more than a few minutes, when all outside was stormy dark, I read through the cards by candlelight, their matter following below:

WHITESIDE: Listen, you idiot, how long can you stay?
BANJO: Just long enough to take a bath. I'm on my way to Nova Scotia. Where's Maggie?
WHITESIDE: Nova Scotia? What are you going to Nova Scotia for?

— *The Man Who Came To Dinner* (1939)

De Sesambre passames une baye fort saine contenant sept à huit lieues.

— Samuel de Champlain (1607)

"Not to mention Hafilax, Nova Scotia."
"Not to mention?"
"Well, you know—"
"Yes, I know."

— The Mamas and the Papas (1966)

"I adore Canada," Miss Daingerfield said. "I think it's marvelous."

"Did you ever drink perfume?"

— *The Sound and the Fury* (1929)

It is humbly propos'd that the Inhabitants of his Majesty's Province of Nova Scotia shall be incorporated by Royal Charter of as like form with that granted by King William and Queen Mary, dated the 7th of October 1692, to the Inhabitants of the Province of the Massachusetts Bay.

— William Shirley (1748)

Sea breezes, in so far as they were good for the complexion, were regarded by us as a means and not an end, for at that time it was our idea to live in capital cities and go to the opera alight with diamonds—"Who is that lovely woman?"—and Nova Scotia was clearly not a suitable venue for such doings.

— *Love in a Cold Climate* (1949)

We caught fish every day since we came within fifty leagues of the coast, the harbour itself is full of fish of all kinds; all the officers agree the harbour is the finest they have ever seen.

— Edward Cornwallis (1749)

The place where you are, where you are building dwellings, where you are now building a fort, where you want, as it were, to enthrone yourself, this land of which you want to make yourself absolute master, this land belongs to me.

— Mi'kmaw Elder (1749)

Dill Harris could tell the biggest ones I ever heard. Among other things, he had been up in a mail plane seventeen times, he had been to Nova Scotia, he had seen an elephant, and his granddaddy was Brigadier General Joe Wheeler and left him his sword.

— *To Kill a Mockingbird* (1962)

Once installed in the local hotel, my father ordered drinks for the grown-ups, then took us to whatever amusement, usually meager in summer, the little provincial towns or Canadian cities afforded. I remember Halifax as a blankly dead and depressing place, where there was nothing to go to see except a show of performing horses.

— Edmund Wilson

Ce port est un que le meilleur que la Nature peut faire.

— Jacques-Francois de Brouillan (1702)

The town is built on the side of a hill, the highest point being commanded by a strong fortress, not yet quite finished... At length, having collected all our bags and all our passengers (including two or three choice spirits, who, having indulged too freely in oysters and champagne, were found lying insensible on their backs in unfrequented streets), the engines were again put in motion, and we stood off for Boston.

— Charles Dickens (1842)

As to the expedition proposed against Nova Scotia by the inhabitants of Machias, I cannot but applaud their spirit and zeal, but I apprehend such an enterprise to be inconsistent with the principle on which the Colonies have proceeded. That province has not acceded, it is true, to the measures of the Congress, but it has not commenced hostilities against them nor are any to be apprehended. To attack it therefore is a measure of conquest rather than defense, and may be attended with very dangerous consequences.

— George Washington (1775)

Then you flew your Lear jet up to Nova Scotia
To see the total eclipse of the sun.

— Carly Simon (1972)

Herewith I enter the lists as the champion of Nova Scotia.
— Charles Hallock (1873)

These quotations, I recalled, once formed a prefatory section of epigraphs in "The Halifax Book." There were many more index cards on the floor, thirty or so, but before collecting them I took some personal time. I was having a small but palpable feeling of calm. With the power off and the storm outside, the temperature inside the house had dropped but for me the evening was warmly coalescing, sifting into place, finally, maybe definitively, there was a stillness seeping into the house and into me and, in one of those weird intuitive calms that visits me at strange intervals and floods me with identity, I was absolutely aware of any number of agreeable details within the house's delicate psychometry, from the Bleu de Roi tableware in the pantry downstairs to the shrouded wingbacks in the second floor ballroom to the possible further adventures of Jack Harkaway. There was a contemplativeness and calm I would forever associate with this moment and, whenever I've needed my best thoughtfulness, I've travelled inwardly through time and mental subspace to this nocturne on the second-floor of the Mair House. It was one of the more supreme and mystic moments of my Halifax life. I just wish things turned out differently. I've always wished things turned out differently.

I'M NOT SURE how long I sat by myself on the floor but I remember the middle candle sputtering in its socket when Cyrus with a flashlight came bounding down the hall.

"Hey—" I held up the index cards. "These are amazing. I love these. We should do a whole book of these."

He was different now, under the pressure of some weird intelligence, and wrinkling into his face was an expression of extreme concern. "She's gone."

"Who's gone?"

"Aunt Emlyn."

"What—*no*. Why?"

"She took the car."

"She's driving? In this? Where'd she go?"

"Aubrey," said Cyrus. "She doesn't know how to drive."

I stared at him, trying to register that, for the first time in seven decades, since the day her brother was killed, Emlyn Mair was free in the streets of Halifax in the worst snowstorm in living memory.

THE MAIRS, THE MAIRS—what were they and why on earth? I have been collecting eccentric trueborn Nova Scotians my entire life but none compare, pound for pound, person for person, with the Titus Mairs of Tower Road. The Maritime provinces of Canada are saturated generally with peculiars—drunks, pundits, misfits, masterminds—but the Mairs were the oddest on record, functioning in the years of my childhood on an almost mythopoeic level. The family was Old Halifax—exotic, neurotic, highly alcoholic—at one time a group of great capital and smarts, the Mairs would become that glittering, decrepit, once-wealthy family where great-aunts collapse and sons die in madness. Clicking the lever of the Mair Family View-Master, shall we spin through some stereoscopic slides? A Matthew Mair begins these vanishing acts, disappearing at dawn from Devon in summer 1662, landing in the Royal Province of New York, and farmsteading near the town of Pelham. Skip a century to 1776 and in morning sun we see Jonathan Mair register with the King's Men and charge into the Battle of White Plains where, on the rebel side, his cousin Israel will be listed among the casualties. Jonathan will win that battle but lose the war—and also his fields, barns, stables, orchards, and right to vote—and in

November 1783 it's Jonathan the Exile who's evacuated from Lower Manhattan in one of Carleton's square-riggers. As an Empire Loyalist, he is granted two hundred acres of rocky woodlands in Nova Scotia, the only seaboard colony of the original fourteen to remain British after the Revolutionary War. Flickering through a pride of crofters—Wickham, Newton, Zephaniah—we rotate toward the industrialist Titus Mair who merits a reel to himself. Born in Five Islands, Nova Scotia, Titus Mair harvests the forests of the Bay of Fundy, ships lumber to the West Indies, molasses and rum from Havana, gypsum to Boston, flour to Newfoundland, salt cod to Baltimore, before relocating with his cousin Jedidiah to the region's capital. Halifax has swelled in a century beyond Cornwallis's citadel to comprise universities and hospitals, railways and redoubts, cotton mills and chocolate factories. It's a city of saltwater ferries and coal deliveries, where thousands of horses work the streets, but it's the sea that gives the city still its livelihood. Titus buys shares in and oversees the construction and management of a fleet of three-masted schooners—ocean-going, cargo-carrying vessels—and the Halifax Mairs sail on the floodtide of the city's expansion, optimism, and development. I think of old-time men like Titus Mair and Samuel Cunard and Alexander Keith as figures in a heroic drama, ranting and roaring about Hollis Street, representatives of Nova Scotia at the acme of its existence as a self-governing colony within the British Empire. Titus marries a woman sixteen years his junior, has with her six children, builds a great house on Tower Road, and from this noonday the prosperous Titus Mairs journey to points far-off and intercontinental, their wax-sealed letters exchanging a cavalcade of family news and historical event—Howland's record run from Marblehead, Ferelith's acceptance at Radcliffe, Merlin's Tibet Medal, Edwin's winter wedding, Emlyn's courtship and engagement. But as the era plunges on, and as the province's shipbuilding industry declines, never to recover, so, too, does the family's fortunes, its constituents becoming erratic with misadventure, and the Mairs begin to exeunt severally from the twentieth century. Edwin evaporates in the Halifax Explosion. Merlin is lost in the sinking of the HMCS Alberni. Miriam collapses during an address to the North British Society. And Ferelith Mair—the very name a dream of beauty—Ferelith Mair shoots herself dead in Boston for reasons never fully explained. Even before Miriam expires in a Kentville sanatorium, even before Howland goes missing off Point Pleasant Park, the common citizens of Halifax tend to think of the Mairs as a bunch of crumpled ruined millionaires in tennis flannels, the sort of curiosity who throws a loaded horse pistol off the Queen Mary before following it overboard. The family in mid-century conjures jitneys and howdahs and fops soused on Pimm's Cup, they're flimsy and shell-shocked and live within a sort of secret Halifax where history meets myth, myth meets fable, and fable suspicion and speculation. If they live at all. For Emlyn sees her family's presence in the city diminish over the decades. While the surname still evokes form and style, it no longer carries with it the heft of dynastic prosperity and, as we come to the end of the Mair Family View-Master, the properties and holdings of the family are much reduced, the remaining slides at twilight showing shipyards abandoned, wharves washed away, summer places empty. There are bays and harbours in Nova Scotia where you can find whole cemeteries filled with dead Mairs but to find any among the quick becomes a dimming proposition. Flashing to our last slide, we see there are but two, an orphan in a cashmere coat sprinting beside me in South Street's swirling snow, and the other, his aged aunt, some parasangs in front of us, loose in the night like a fugitive character from a Halifax game of Clue, her own desertion, I suppose, a kind of fated eventuality, simply the most recent in a long line of escape artistry.

THE CITY WAS IN A BLIZZARD, the weather in superflux, the sky electric with snow and lightning. Where Emlyn Mair was going—what she was trying to get to—I would never discover. I think, in her failing mind, in some magical thinking, she sought to return what once was lost to a place which once she'd known but of course whatever Halifax she knew had vanished from the world decades before. After some minutes following tire tracks filling up with blowing snow, we found the Mair family car, that purple tail-finned Mercedes, deserted on Barrington Street. It was wedged on a snowbank near the corner of Salter Street, the driver's door open. Close by stood a boy in a snowsuit with a toboggan. He described the scene from moments before—Emlyn swerving to avoid an ambulance, crashing over the sidewalk, foundering in the snowbank, the ambulance stopping, the paramedics taking her to emergency for observation.

Absorbing this information, Cyrus went to the vehicle. He found the keys in the ignition. He dropped to the street to study the undercarriage and saw the rear axle stuck in the frozen core of the snowbank. He started the engine, flicked on the headlights, and put it in neutral. He went to the front bumper. I joined him and together we tried to hoist the front end and rock the car backwards off the snowbank. Three times we tried and three times, with his first forward step, the hem of Cyrus's coat snagged under his shoe, trapping him in a squatting position. On the last effort, the sudden constriction sent him sideways into me, his forehead knocking into my jaw. I laughed, embarrassed, for it was one of those unexpectedly intimate guy-on-guy moments, a fusty pungency leaking from him, the odour of a man too many days in the same clothes. Cyrus swiftly stood only to just as swiftly slip off the curb and slide backwards down Salter Street. Coming to a herky-jerky stop, he struggled to regain his balance, snow tumbling from his shoulders, the hem of his coat snaring again under his heel. Shouting a vulgarity, he managed at last to stay upright. He bent over, trembling, his hands on his knees, staring sullenly at his snow-soaked shoes. There was a look in his eyes I'd not seen in some time, a no-way-am-I-going-to-lose-this-third-set look, and he spit, a stubborn sort of spit, as if he were daring the night to throw at him something else.

I began to shiver, violently, full of premonition, for I felt Something Complicated was nearing in the night and for some seconds I was aware of imminent calamity, as if a life might come undone in an instant. What made me follow this next line of inquiry, I'm not sure—although we were, after all, across the street from Saint Mary's Basilica—and of course it was, I felt, all along the real subject of the afternoon. "Here's a question," I said. "Have you talked to her?"

"Who?"

"Karin!"

"If you want to go to your wedding," said Cyrus, still staring at his shoes. "I understand."

"I don't think in this blizzard there's going to be any fucking wedding." I was watching him—monitoring him—very closely. "Because if you *are* thinking about it, it might not be the best idea."

"Karin—" Cyrus wiped his nose. "Gorgeous girl. Most beautiful anyone could imagine. The blonde hair, the glance, the wide-apart eyes like nobody else—"

"Sure, I admit she was the most beautiful ninety-ninth percentile babe. But at Queen's—"

"She went through a serious I-don't-want-to-be-pretty phase, yeah."

"She cut all her hair off. And went nuts. And now she's getting married?"

Cyrus jerked a shoulder, silent.

"Well, the guy can be nice. And he probably loves her."

"Probably thinks he does." Cyrus raised his head. "But he doesn't know her."

"Might know her soon enough."

"In his way. In his version."

"How else *would* he know her? What other version is there? It's still real."

"Is it?" Cyrus spit again. "Just his way. Believe me, I know who she is."

"From three years ago, maybe. But Cyrus—" I watched him soldier up the street and around to the back bumper of the Mercedes. "You can't live in the past."

"Can't live in—" He turned to me, fantastically alert. "That's what we're *doing*. Don't you get it? Where else is it?"

"Yeah, that's not crazy. That's not weird. You may want to pop a few more of your little pills there, buddy, because you've gone horribly insane." I watched him take off his coat and throw it down the steps of the Maritime Mall. "Returning to something like three years ago," I said. "You can't do it. It's not—it's a ridiculous hope."

"Hope—" said Cyrus, "is never ridiculous." Full of intention, he crouched behind the Mercedes and readied himself for a last almighty push.

"Are you deranged?" I screamed. "What—you're going to push a car out by yourself?"

The wind was changing, blowing up Barrington Street, in the direction Cyrus was about to push the car. Frustrated by his non-reply, I plopped through the snow, grabbed the back bumper with my bare hands, and set my shoulder beneath a tailfin. When Cyrus yelled, we shoved off and I was startled to feel the car advance. We charged forward, like linemen with a blocking sled, and the car came free of the snowbank—and our hold on it—and slid off the sidewalk and into the steepness of Salter Street. There it continued to drift sideways down the hill, a front tire bumping against a curb, the vehicle beginning a slow unpredictable rotation. Watching all this, we realized the car was likely to slide past Granville and Hollis streets toward the pier at the bottom of the slope. We ran headlong after it, managing to grab a bumper. I dug the heels of my loafers into the snow of the street, Flintstones-style, in an effort to stop the car from sliding onto the pier and into the ocean, an ocean at the moment in the full roar of high tide. The car juddered at the bottom, spinning through the dip of Lower Water Street, Cyrus falling to his knees—and I remember feeling perversely victorious to be the last man holding on—but when the back end swung wildly onto the concrete pier, I dropped off the merry-go-round. Shoving my freezing fingers into the pockets of my duffel coat, I watched the car bounce off a section of rebar and jolt to a stop at the end of the pier, one of its headlights still functioning, beaming up the hill, illuminating an infinity of whirling snowflakes. And Cyrus Mair.

He was silent, in a sort of reverie, watching snowflakes fall into the sea. There was a tremendous flash of lightning—the harbour full of spray and light—I was conscious of flooding depths, unstable boundaries, and incompleteness everywhere.

"Cyrus," I shouted, moving toward him. "Buddy, what's going on with you? Not sure I'm so keen on the whole get-hit-by-lightning thing."

"Everyone—" said Cyrus, "gets hit by lightning. That's how it starts." He was staring into the sea, his face sunburned in falling snow, his hair wet to his temples. "What's going on with me? That your question? This year, most of the time, I've actually been depressed out of my fucking mind. I kind of had this collapse. Back at Cambridge. This horrible thing with depression and other junk. And just the dread in my head and terror in my heart really kind of sucked. I didn't find that so nifty." Across the harbour, the lights of Dartmouth went abruptly dark. "Because the things that made me think I'm smart or special have fucked me up. That's been the single-most difficult thing in my life. That no one's really like me. That certainly became apparent the last little while. So, yeah, there were a couple years there when I sort of scared myself out of trying stuff. And avoided people. But I made the decision to come back. Whatever happens, I did choose that." His scarf fluttered wildly. "And to answer your earlier question. You wanted to know where the hell I've been? Africa. I woke up in Africa yesterday."

"Fuck off."

"Burkina Faso. Used to be called Upper Volta."

"Fuck off you were in Upper Volta. Doing what?"

"Went to a wedding. Went to a funeral. Mostly I was working." He saw me staring at him. "For McKinsey. The consulting company. They cherry-pick the scholarship students at Cambridge. Pay them a hundred grand to work in one-year placements."

"What kind of placements?"

"Denationalizing the Mexican phone service. Issuing debentures in Jakarta. I was part of a team doing a feasibility study for a gold refinery."

"*That's* where you were?"

Cyrus nodded. "Very Heart of Darkness. Very insane. But that was in another country and besides. Fuck it." At that moment, rather as if wanting in on the conversation, there came a smash of thunder from the sky. Cyrus waited for it to subside. "Amadu, the Zuber's foster kid, he and his sister live with their grandmother in a house made of mud. The family has six goats. They paddle around in a dugout canoe. They think Canada is a kind of grain—"

"You met the Foster Parents Plan kid?"

"Because that's what's stenciled on the sacks of food aid." Cyrus's scarf, flapping loosely, was blown from his neck in a blink. "It's kind of unreal the gulf between what we know and they know. This whole last month, I'm being driven to work in a limousine to an air-conditioned office and meanwhile the Burkina cabinet ministers? They don't even show up for the meetings. We have to take them out for a ten thousand dollar dinner just to be sure they'd be in the same fucking room for two hours." Wavering in a blast of wind, Cyrus fidgeted with his tie, tightening its knot into his collar. "And outside is the worst Third World poverty and filth. Industrial waste. Arsenic. Cyanide. You name it, the kids are running around in it. They're poor to the point of distended stomachs, infected eyes. Totally National Geographic poverty. And yesterday morning, I'm helping Amadu and his sister catch a fucking *aard*vark for supper—"

"I actually can't tell if you're being serious right now."

"But working for McKinsey—" He wiped the sleet from an eyelash. "I'm not sure I can do it anymore. Be a drone in middle management and finish the thesis at the same time. It's all been kind of surreal. Which is why—"

"Aardvarks?"

"I'm just trying to feel all this."

I remember Cyrus in this moment glancing fretfully up Salter Street—as if he'd begun to mistrust our position and guessed enemy operatives might be getting a bead on one of us—when his eyes relaxed with a sense of wonder as if he no longer cared about placements or phone calls or anything at all and I turned from Cyrus to look into the darkness for someone *was* moving toward us, slipping down Salter Street, and out of the wind and spinning snow in a wedding dress came Karin Catherine Friday, missing from her own service, a runaway bride in a December hurricane. A slam of wind filled her dress like a spinnaker—she was briefly gusted off the street—before she rejoined the earth, pitching forward, sliding in the snow down Salter, almost nosediving, before rebalancing and reaching to pull off an ivory satin shoe which, for whatever reason, she began waving above her head. She was shy, as if not sure what she was doing, but in her eyes showing she was willing, her veil blown sideways, wedding dress aglow in the shining headlight of the car. The effect was mesmerizingly female, a moment surreal beyond logic, it was as if I were looking down on this scene from above when I realized I *was* looking down from above for I'd been floated some distance above the pier by a flooding storm surge and swallowing a glop of saltwater I understood I was falling backwards into the sea so this is what it's like to drown I remember thinking as I fell into the ocean the sea sucking me deep down into the dark.

Death by Drowning

HOWLAND POOLE MAIR, LLB, KC, PC, fourteenth premier of Nova Scotia, husband to Vida (née Hendsbee) and childless when he lost the provincial election of 1953—H.P. Mair would return to private practice in Halifax at the age of sixty-nine. There is a black-and-white publicity photograph taken on the morning he gave the address at the opening of the Nova Scotian legislature on February 19, 1952—the opening that year delayed because of the death of King George VI—that, for several reasons, has gone deep into my memory. Not only because in dirty snow he is pictured in top hat and boldfaced cashmere coat, a coat of course I would know in later years as navy blue, but because it is the only image I've seen when he is unaware his picture is being taken and his hawkish face, turning with a smile toward the camera, shows a countenance uncontrived, his eyes in winter sun sparkly with an intelligence I connect with all the menfolk in his family as well as the assurance and conceit I would see firsthand near the end of his life. The coat was purchased on Jermyn Street, the suit, shirt, and tie on Saville Row, for he was a lifelong devotee of the patterns of the British Empire and old-school values of English perseverance, Christian heroism, and private alcoholism would set his tone and standard. His life moved toward some sort of epic grandeur, yes, but the romance would founder, turning tragic, and tawdry in its tragedy. I suppose a historical figure is open to multiple interpretations because the details of his life—and sudden death—support any number of interpretations, but I feel there *was* magic in the man and even the weirdness of his rise and fall scatters some strange magic of its own. I don't know. The intricacies and contradictions of the Mair family have proliferated for me over the years, which might say more about my wish for the subject to remain provocative, I know, than it speaks to some the-past-is-a-foreign-country or the-truth-can-never-be-known uncertainty principle. For these events occurred in a flux before my own days began and many of the lives described herein only briefly and peripherally extend into the beginnings of my own, H.P. Mair and Madeleine Zwicker being two of many strange gods born before me.

HE WAS, SIGNIFICANTLY, one of the few persons my father spoke of with considered respect. My father was a child during the Second World War and his experience of those years, and his understanding of the exigencies of those boys born ten years before, was something he never forgot—our one family trip to Scotland notable for a three-day detour to a Normandy cemetery where my father read in silent absorption the names of boys who graduated Grade 12 when he'd graduated Grade 3—and he tended to treat with deferential regard anyone who had been in the service. And because Howland Mair had served with the Royal Canadian Navy, on a Flower-class corvette, guiding convoys back and forth across the Atlantic, and was in the sea at Utah Beach, he more than qualified. "What H.P. saw over there," said my mother. "I don't know. He lost a brother in the war. Merlin. Drowned. He never talked about it. None of them did, really. You sort of had to guess the implications. Coming home wasn't always a whole new lease on life, you might say that." Given his naval and political achievements, as well as his family's social standing, Howland Mair would have been classed with an elite echelon of business folk in the province, white male grandees such as Robert Stanfield, Izaak Killam, and Cyrus Eaton, names superannuated now, but names in postwar Nova Scotia which would have commanded alert attention. "Remnants of the aristocracy," said my mother. "Faded grandeur. Your father loves that Old Money bullshit. H.P. talks about heated towel racks at the Savoy or Trumper's shaving cream and your father's over the moon with that junk. He thinks it's all strawberries and champagne. The Mairs, good God, they're all living in a dream world. But I don't know if H.P. had too many clients after being away in politics so long. Ask your father. But I think he was pretty much dead in the water till these young guys came along."

IN THE YEARS during and following the Second World War, Halifax was hectic but grungy, a jumble of warehouses, clapboard homes and grimy public buildings, its waterfronts haphazard with sea-craft—grey warships tethered along the Bedford Basin and Northwest Arm. "It was a shabby little city, a city of somber wooden houses in dark greens and heavy reds, a city of rusting cranes, of splintered and water-lapped jetties, a city ragged and yet ponderous in outline, worn stale and flat in detail." These lines are from the playwright Simon Gray, who is writing about the city he knew as an undergraduate at Dalhousie University in the 1950s. Such were the twin cities of Halifax-Dartmouth, and this was the municipality Howland Mair would have seen in 1953 as he sat in the law offices of Merton Mair McNab, gazing with fading eyes at the remains of the afternoon. He had been a two-term premier and his connections with the Liberal Party, especially at the national level—for he'd worked on Louis St-Laurent's successful re-election as Prime Minister—were not immaterial. And yet, though he was listed on the firm's letterhead as Senior Counsel, his situation was trending toward the ceremonial and his remaining clients, like him, were advancing in years. Where once he consulted on deals between the Bridge Authority, Dominion Steel, and the Halifax Dartmouth Port Commission, he now took anxious, worried phone calls from the widows of late colleagues, the wills for whom he administered pro bono publico. But, very notably, the year H.P. Mair returned to private practice was also the year Gregor Burr graduated law school. Free of education at the age of twenty-three, Gregor Burr started as an article clerk with Merton Mair McNab where he chose to present himself very much as a Young Turk, impatient with the ways and means of the firm's old boys, going so far in discovery as to suggest to a client an alternate plan of advocacy in front of the supervising lawyer. "It's not the sort of behaviour typically associated with an articling student," my father said later. "Certainly not in the presence of the client, no." My mother saw it differently. "Law firms back then, they were all stuck in a time warp. When your father and I were first married, I remember going out to buy a fedora. Men don't wear them now, but at the time they were all the rage. Well, he looks terrible in all of them and I have to ask why in the name of God are we buying this fucking hat when we barely have enough for cottage cheese? Your father was never one to stay on budget. But back then you *had* to have a hat, because you had to tip it to the senior partners when they walked into the elevator. That's the kind of environment it was and I don't blame Gregor for saying to hell with it."

Gregor Burr was transferred to the top floor, where, in a far corner, the Honourable H.P. Mair laboured in somewhat sinecured obscurity. At some point in the summer, the two would have spoken, the young buck and the senior statesman, and my father recalls seeing them together at The Halifax Club—Friday afternoons there full of cribbage and Rum-and-Cokes—and indeed Howland would sponsor Gregor for membership at both The Halifax and Saraguay clubs, as well as the Royal Nova Scotia Yacht Squadron, of which precincts he was an ex-commodore. It was at the Squadron that Gregor Burr was introduced to Ralph Fudge, a real estate developer, and here began a triumvirate partnership that would end in multiple allegations—the twisted legalities taking a number of lawyers a number of years to disentangle—but which, in the beginning, must have promised a glittering future. The nascent company was called Kingfisher Properties and its first development was a low-rise apartment building in Cowie Hill, the loans for which were rumoured to have been secured through Gregor Burr's management of party funds from the Liberal Party of Nova Scotia—through H.P. Mair's connections he'd become one of the youngest candidates in the province's history. The twenty-third general election in Nova Scotia was held in October 1956 and, although Robert Stanfield's Progressive Conservatives carried the day, Gregor Burr was elected to one of three downtown ridings for the Liberals, the victory party thrown over three floors at the Lord Nelson Hotel.

For a brief period in high school, during my time as an indiscriminate teenage joiner, I participated in Model Parliament and was invited to the final night of an adult leadership convention, also held at the Lord Nelson, where I was astonished by the loose, rutted energy of the midnight celebrations—grownups blitzed out of their minds in the hallways, bathtubs full of water and ice and floating cans of Schooner beer, Malcolm McCreery's father wandering the hallways drunk in a kilt and bagpipes and later making out with a Grade 11 girl in a stairwell—and I doubt the versions of these scenes in previous years were much different. "Oh Jesus," said my mother. "Those political parties—I wouldn't let Stewart go to them—people carrying on till four in the morning, Gregor organizing all these girls to be there. What I heard was, Gregor hires these professional girls and brings them to the Lord Nelson but doesn't tell the men anything. To the men, they're just women at the party, you know, secretaries and volunteers, the men thinking they're doing *so* well with these girls, the girls giggling and smiling, eyes a little wider than normal. 'Aren't you interesting?' 'You're so smart!' What a crock. But that's how H.P. meets this young thing. Madeleine. She was one of Milly's girls."

TO DESCRIBE THE FAMOUSLY PRIVATE Milly Rees, to explain the open secret that was Mrs. Rees's profession, to suggest What Milly Knew and Whom Milly Knew, requires a digression that is pertinent not only to 1950s Halifax, but to the entire province in the second half of the twentieth century. Put plainly, Milly Rees was one of the most fascinating careers in Halifax—ever. She was an exacting, mindful businesswoman who owned and operated multiple brothels in the city, and allusions to her, in the hotel lobby, on the street corner, in the dockyards, were ever-present. Milly Rees figures in Halifax's mythology much in the way Mayor Jimmy Walker does for New York or Mrs. O'Leary for Chicago or Rocket Richard for Montreal—singular personalities richly identified with a city's moral folklore. Much of what I know about Milly Rees I owe to an evening spent in the bottom of the Lord Nelson Hotel, in the now-vanished Lady's Beverage Room, in the company of a taxi driver named Murdoch Ryan. A NOTE OF PERSONAL HISTORY: In my younger and more vulnerable years, back when I was a crippled kid, I wheelchaired my way to school and back, unless the day was too icy or slushy or pouring rain, in which case I would call Regal Taxi. Given to my care was a voucher book of taxi chits, hundreds of which I would use during the years I wasn't able to walk. In this way I probably knew on a first-name basis more taxi drivers than any kid east of Montreal. Following my return to mobility, many of these drivers would remember loading me and my Petrie casts into the back seat and my wheelchair into the trunk, and so it was that in later years Murdoch Ryan would give me a honk-and-smile whenever his Mercury Monarch passed me on the street. I would wave back and in this way we preserved a familiarity that allowed for the prospect of taking him for drinks to ask about his motley career.

Now Murdoch Ryan was one of those men who look the same for decades and all the details I remembered as a kid—black-framed glasses, grey cowlicks Brylcreemed and side-parted, a pack of Craven A Menthols in a left slicker pocket, the semi-compulsive tapping of a foot—these were all wonderfully intact the evening we met in the LBR. He was happy to talk, the interview filled three microcassettes and was one of the favourites of the Common Room, and though he winked and glanced at me from time to time, he seemed, after five Jack-and-Sevens, to be mostly playing to the audience that was my girlfriend Gail, who was just out of high school and freshly tanned from a summer in the Naval Reserves. "Who—Milly? Milly *Rees*? This is Milly Rees we're talking about now? Why Milly paid off the politicians, she paid off the police, my God, Milly'd pay off the caterers at Camille's Fish and Chips if she thought it would do her any good. Smart lady. Hard-looking ticket, true, but fair. She had rules. She could be strict. But you always knew where you stood with Milly. Sixty years she ran that business. The place, the establishment she ran, this was the one behind Government House, Fifty-One Hollis, it had lines around the block during the war. 'I'm going to die at Fifty-One,' was what the sailors used to say, merchant marine and servicemen, before they went overseas. Some of those boys wouldn't come home, of course. But Milly, she was known all over. And in trouble with the law only once, if I remember right. In the last year of her life she got dinged for tax evasion. And how much money did she make that year? Three million dollars. In Halifax! All the money she made, Jesus. But she paid off those taxes. The mayor at the time, Porky MacPherson, he went to her funeral, God bless. Remember him? Oh, you do, do you, dear? But yes, I was one of Milly's drivers. Used to drive the girls around every week. Nice girls. Always dressed nice. Tipped pretty good. Some girls you'd see once or twice a week. Some you'd see once and never see again. But there was three I used to drive around pretty regular. Cee-Cee and Pearl and the one they called Maddy. Oh, I *loved* Maddy. A real sparkler. My God, they were living in an apartment on Jacob Street infested with three types of mice, mildew, you name it. Jacob Street's gone now, of course, torn down to make way for Scotia Square. But yes, usually you'd take the girls to whatever function it was, the event at the hotel or what-have-you—the Lord Nelson or the Sterling or one of the motels out there on the Bedford Highway. Sometimes you went right to the fellow's house and, you know, you might have to wait for the magic to happen. We weren't supposed to know the names of the regulars. They had code names for all the regulars. One fellow they called Mister Quickly. Another was Doctor Shubenacadie. There was the Blond Bomber and Reverend Gravy Train. A fellow called Lard-Ass I never met. Nope. Never did meet Lard-Ass. Huey Boy and Black Angus. Boner Fitzgibbon was one they all liked. The fellow you were talking about? I think they called him His Honour because he'd been in the government. Older fellow. He was the one who went with Maddy? My favourite of Milly's girls. And Milly knew everyone in the city. Everyone worth knowing. Smart lady. So what's next, dear? Another round?"

MADELEINE ZWICKER WAS a slim young woman with a slash of strawberry blonde hair. There is only one photograph of Madeleine from her young adult years, but to see it once is to understand why she was one of the more dazzling women a city might cherish. As she floated through the marble halls of the Lord Nelson in October 1956, coming into full view of the Honourable H.P. Mair, I think his thoughts for the evening, for himself and for the future, were luminously readjusted. That Howland Mair might have met one of Milly's girls is not so remarkable. That he seemed to wish to marry her was another affair entirely. "When he returned to his practice," said my mother. "People said he wanted a divorce. But Vida wouldn't give him one. People didn't really get divorced back then. They just lived apart, you know. Oh she'd be seen with her husband sometimes. She sort of tolerated him, I suppose. But the truth was they led separate lives. She lived in the Hotel Nova Scotian the rest of her life. With a bottle of Gordon's gin. So there was no love in his life for oh, ten years or so. People do strange things when that happens. They look for love, they think they find it, they can convince themselves of anything. Yes, he thinks the light's gone out of his life forever and then he meets this young thing from Ecum Secum. He was seventy-two at the time and she was twenty-nine. You do the math. They did the biology. Ha! It's funny now but at the time the city was scandalized. I don't think Vida ever spoke to him again. And Madeleine, what happened to her, well, that was tragic. I don't know how many times she ended up in the hospital. And H.P. of course he didn't think anything was wrong with her!"

THE SHIP THEY SAILED IN, the last from the Mair family shipyards, was the thirty-foot ketch *Serendip*. Toddling as a four-year-old in Point Pleasant Park, I remember seeing her moored off the backyard dock of H.P. Mair's house on Chain Rock Drive—a sleek, wooden anomaly among all the fibreglass hulls bobbing at the other buoys. On the day H.P. Mair disappeared in August 1968, the ship was seen in full sail, downwind on a dead run that took her out past Herring Cove, Sambro, and beyond. A week or so later, a small two-master was seen off Cape Hatteras flying the blue ensign of the RNSYS, but without a soul onboard. Nova Scotia has more than its share of ghost ships and maritime mysteries and *Serendip* would become another, sailing wide in vasty seas, without captain or crew, floating in and out of shipping lanes, drifting across the Atlantic, sightings made as far away as the Azores. She was seventeen weeks a derelict, weather-worn, sun-faded, finally found and steadied by the coast guard off the Canary Islands, two thousand nautical miles away. When she was towed into Halifax a few days after Christmas that year, there were some in the city who expected to find evidence of a bloody struggle or a suitcase full of body parts. There were no such signs. The ship was bare save for an ice bucket, a wicker picnic basket, a woman's shoe wedged into the planking of the starboard gunwale.

A YEAR AFTER MEETING H.P. Mair in the Lord Nelson Hotel, Madeleine Zwicker became pregnant, though it is unclear to whom she conveyed this intelligence, and it is possible, of course, that she did not know who the father was. For two centuries, unwanted newborns in Halifax had been abandoned by desperate mothers in stables, in cemeteries, in Point Pleasant Park. At the end of the Second World War, ten years earlier, there'd been a ghastly scandal at the Ideal Maternity Home, an unlicensed facility that sold infants—illegally—to families in New Jersey and New York. Babies who were unadoptable, *hundreds* of them, were starved to death and buried in wooden dairy boxes in a nearby field.

Madam Milly Rees would have been alert to public sensitivities to such stories, which is why she ensured that Madeleine Zwicker received proper medical care, Madeleine giving birth to a son in Delivery Room B of the Grace Maternity Hospital in November 1957. When no father was presented, and when Madeleine began to behave erratically in the weeks following her labour, Milly Rees installed the boy in her own house, giving him the surname of her then-boyfriend, a character named Dollar Bill Blomgren—a bootlegger about whom I've been able to discover very little—and so it was that little Vance Blomgren was raised and provided for by Milly Rees.

"That first child she has," said my mother. "Well, it's not the type of story you want to get around. Certainly not in those days. So Maddy disappears for a while. I'm not sure where she gets to. But a few years later she shows up again. Well, my God, H.P. brings her to the Nova Scotia Bar Society! I'm sitting there with your father, this was down at the Digby Pines, and H.P. comes out with Madeleine on his arm. When you're at these dinners, you know, you're sitting there for some ungodly amount of time, outside in the cold, the wind coming off the Bay of Fundy, lobster bibs flapping, and everyone's waiting for some asshole to finish his speech, but your father won't leave because how would that look? So Maddy and I, we go off for a cigarette, everyone smoked in those days of course, and we're joined by Tiggy and you remember Mrs. Ogilvie? Well, I'm not sure if they know who this Maddy woman is. To them, she'd be some common prostitute. But here she is tearing strips off all assembled. It was hysterical. I mean *funny*. Like manic funny. Well, manic-depressive. She'd be what's called bipolar today. Oh, the man was fooling himself. Thinking everything's going to be all right. Carrying on as if nothing's wrong. Throwing his life away for a kick of a girl."

The next winter Madeleine Zwicker conceived a second child and that autumn delivered a son—my great friend Cyrus Mair. "With that second child, I thought maybe he would've sent her to Toronto and set her up there. That's what Frank Tobin did. He had a girlfriend in Bedford for years, the travel agent with the scoop-neck sweaters. When she got pregnant, she and the little girl moved to Toronto. But H.P., I suppose he wanted them in town where he could see them. He must have really cared for her. I just don't think she was competent. And suffering from terrible postpartum. I had it with Katie. You feel overwhelmed. Terrible anxiety. Everything's hopeless. I don't know what kind of medication they had her on, but I remember seeing her on Spring Garden Road just out of it, pale as anything, not a thought in her head. Then she gets caught stealing those earrings from Mill's Brothers. Poor thing. What a sin. It was heartless how they treated her, the poor woman. That's who I feel sorry for in all this business. The men, they think only of themselves. That woman needed help—not to be jammed into some man's ideas for himself."

Not long after her arrest, Madeleine began the first in a series of stays at a sanatorium across the harbour. Founded as the Mount Hope Asylum for the Insane in 1858, it would become the province's largest mental health facility. The Nova Scotia Hospital or, as it was casually called in my childhood, "the N.S.," was often used as a threatening reference, kids everywhere hearing variations on a line like, "You keep acting like that and you're going to end up in the frigging N.S." The hospital is plainly visible from Halifax—an assembly of red brick buildings on top of hill and heath and overlooking Georges Island—and this was where Madeleine Zwicker was admitted for treatment in 1964. Diagnosed with schizophrenia, she was given a course of psychiatric drugs, experimental injections, and electroconvulsive therapy but to very little outward improvement, and the event of her second child—and Howland's death five years later—would result in a complete mental breakdown. The evening of the sailing accident, she was found collapsed on the Dartmouth side of the harbour, below the hospital, sodden, shivering, aphasic. Maddy Went Crazy—that's the Coles Notes to this story. She was deinstitutionalized and living in a group home on Vernon Street when first I saw her in the 1970s, by then one of the city's most recognizable street people, very much reduced in faculties, with a face lopsided, left eye sagging, one shoe tied to her foot with ribbon, the other in a ragged sock.

MY SISTERS TALKING: "I know who you mean—she was fricking psycho!—she fought Dobermans." "You used to see her on Summer Street when the Public Gardens opened in May. She'd be speaking in tongues, going from person to person, trying to sell her photographs." "I gave Crazy Maddy two dollars once and from then on it's like she was my best friend. When Jamie and I went to Thackeray's for my grad, she saw me through the window and barged right up to my table to ask for money. 'Make a deal with the lady?' She always used to say that. Remember?" I do—and I remember her wandering skittish the streets of Halifax, wiping at her cheeks, whispering into her coat sleeve, a plastic bag hanging from her coat's middle button, this bag a mix of breadcrumbs and crinkly old photographs. Her face, too, I remember—the sun-damaged wrinkles near her eyes, the tiny broken blood vessels of her nose, the missing-pigment splotches on her upper lip, all these features mystifying-terrifying to a child. But worse was the wince within her eyes which showed the pain of her own awareness and the distress such awareness brought her—as if in her mind she were participating in three different conversations, one happy, two sad, all painful. She would die a few years later, found inert on a ventilation grate on the south side of Scotia Square, in her coat pockets a mess of odd details—a cut-glass door knob, a near-empty bag of Peak Freans, a sprouting tulip bulb.

A NOTE OF MUNICIPAL HISTORY: early in the 1960s a bill was signed to expropriate and demolish one hundred and sixty-eight buildings and five city streets of old Halifax to make way for Scotia Square, at the time the largest commercial development in eastern Canada. Victorian Halifax was crumbling—Moir's Chocolate Factory, the Halifax School for the Blind, the South Street Poor House—all of these would be demolished before my childhood was done. Scotia Square marked the era of Halifax's great postwar expansion, and H.P. Mair and his partners at Kingfisher Properties were among those who would steer grimy, rusting Halifax toward six-lane expressways, cloverleaf interchanges, shopping centres—though these plans for urban renewal, population displacement, and high-density land use were not supported in all ridings. Gail Benninger, fresh from reading Jane Jacobs, would describe the ideas of H.P. Mair as "WASP ascendancy plutocrat bullshit," dismissing wholesale his rational planning as the prejudiced views "typical of that generation of white supremacist assholes." While I do think H.P. Mair wished the city to be storied, to be splendid, to fulfill the promise he knew in his gilded childhood, he was forcing a vision of grandeur on a city that, except for the dizzy expansions of its wartime years, had been in decline for almost a century. He reckoned on the city's growth and expansion, imagining an easy commerce of the old and new, but things are not always easy in Halifax, fewer are really new, and the city takes its time about its own evolution. Still, as a response to Scotia Square, he pursued a final development called Empire Plaza. It was an elaborate scheme that sought to preserve six pre-confederation buildings around what would become the city's largest business tower, home to offices, storefront shops, and a new royal conservatory of music. For this venture, Kingfisher needed an anchor tenant and what better and steadier than the provincial government itself? Just the year before, Gregor Burr had crossed the floor of the Legislature to join the ruling Progressive Conservative party, and the prospective deal, based on early conversations, seemed a given. This was the plan and the exploit and in 1964, when it was drawn up, Empire Plaza must have seemed a fitting capstone to the monument of H.P. Mair's life and career. But the fate of Empire Plaza, like so many developments in Halifax, was blighted—devised and ground-broken in a time of optimism, stalled and unoccupied in an economic downturn, its Office Space banners blowing to tatters. Kingfisher Properties would dissolve in a series of misunderstandings, accusations, and litigation. The suit, in the Supreme Court of Nova Scotia, Trial Division, was between Howland Poole Mair, plaintiff, and Gregor Oswalt Burr, defendant, and heard at Halifax on May 29, 1968, the plaintiff contending the defendant in essence directed him to believe the provincial government would be leasing the first five floors of Empire Plaza. "I think it's probably reasonable to assume," said my father, remembering the case and speaking in the studied tone he reserved for subjects whose complexities were sometimes the focus of unstable speculation, "that the interests of the three partners had separated some time before." My father, who would represent Gregor Burr in a variety of lawsuits, both civil and criminal, was exceptionally circumspect whenever one of his clients was discussed. In fact, my father spoke so seldom to any of us about what he did when he wasn't in our house, that the few times he *did* speak about his cases—or anything at all that actually mattered to him—I tended to respond with full attention, though pretending, for reasons I'm not sure I understand, as if I were only half-listening. "Very strange, Max," he said. "Very strange. Whenever you set up a deal between partners, whatever their personal relationship, even if they're related by marriage, it's best to have a separate lawyer, preferably at a different firm, represent each party. To have one lawyer do the deal for all three partners at Kingfisher was very odd. That H.P. would have exposed himself to such a misconstruction was very out of character. He may have had other things on his mind at the time."

"You *think*?" said my mother.

"Well, my sense was that his own finances were in some disarray."

"In some disarray? Stewart. Get real. He had an office building he couldn't fill, a legal bill he couldn't pay, a wife and mistress he couldn't support. He had his own house up for sale. The man didn't have a pot to piss in or a window to throw it through! She bailed him out. The sister did. Emlyn. Honest to God, the Mairs, I don't know, that family, they're not made for the real world. H.P. wants a conservatory, he wants expressways, I don't know where in the name of God he thought he was living. Cole Porter's New York, maybe. Cole Porter's New Glasgow, more like it. I know this building was supposed to be his legacy, but by the time he died, the things he knew, the life he knew, it was all disappearing. He wanted things done his way but that way was gone. The man was lost at the end. It's a wonder he lasted as long as he did."

THEY WERE ON AN EASTERN TACK, the wind from the northwest, the mainsail fastened, in the dazzle of an August afternoon. H.P. Mair was born at the end of the nineteenth century and mostly I have imagined his life in sepia tones, sometimes grey-scaled and indistinct, like the blackening Benday dots of a newspaper image, or the dark hues of a Steichen photograph, but, when picturing the events of his last day, I see the sequence in brash colours, like a film from the American New Wave. Colour 16mm shot on hundred-foot reels in a spring-wound Bolex, the image glinting with lens flares, a scene quickening as the motor sputters down, perforations of a reel-end flapping with random reds and yellows. The ocean is a saturated blue, the luffing sails burning white, and flashing into frame are further details—the scarlet of lipstick, a sun-freckled balding head, milky sunlight washing over the green bottle of champagne. A bottle of Veuve Clicquot was purchased earlier that day at the Clyde Street liquor store but it was not found onboard so let us suppose that Howland is at the helm, Madeline charged with evening drinks, fumbling with the bottle's foil wrapping, and as a burst of wind fills the mainsail she loses her balance, the bottle dropping and skidding along the deck, precarious on the leeward edge, Maddy sliding down to retrieve it—only to slip between boom and gunwale and vanish with the bottle into the sea, one shoe left behind, caught in the side planks. Howland points the boat into the wind—the mainsail for some moments loose and flappy—so to scan the surface of the water, calling her name, hearing nothing, then deciding to pursue her overboard as a second tempest fills the sails, sending the ship toward the open ocean. Halifax Harbour is never really warm, not even in summer, and the cold shock of water to a somewhat desiccated man in his eighties would be enough, it would do, the heart attack sudden, the drowning quick, dimming eyes staring into the sea's green darkness, plasma from his blood seeping into and filling up his salt-watered lungs, his body softly following the sinking champagne bottle more than sixty feet to the sea floor below. For twenty-one days, in five fathoms of water, Howland Mair lay, till the contents of his stomach—the beef tenderloin in wild mushroom sauce, the duchess potatoes, the Johnnie Walker Blacks—would generate gas enough to free his body from the mudded deeps, the bloated corpse breaking into daylight with the force of a popping cork. So long submerged, the Honourable Howland Poole Mair was almost unidentifiable, the skin of his hands wet-wrinkled, his face blistered black, his blue eyes lost to sea-bottom sculpin.

Tempest

MY MEMORIES OF MY LIFE underwater are few. I recall spinning upside down, seawater drenching my clothes, not knowing which way I was pointing. I was amid a confusion of warm and cold currents, brine flooding my nose, disorienting me, and I did not know which way to go. Opening my eyes, I saw nothing and simply tried to swim away from the colder water, knowing I would soon need to breathe. I tried to exhale a very small amount of air, but my throat in shock had contracted and even when, with a sudden surge, I found myself on the surface, I managed only a sucking gasp before plunging again in closing seas. Tumbling past something solid, a wharf piling or iron-edge, I raised my arms to protect my face but was bluntly struck in the nose. Then I was sinking in great pressure, my body forced into a geometry I did not fit. My fear I would not be able to register everything—my thoughts no longer coherent—became a panic I would soon black out. I kicked. I breast-stroked. I reopened my eyes. Lightning flashed in the sky above and toward this I struggled, finding myself, after an overwhelming urge to breathe, again on the ocean surface, and breathe I did, inhaling a mix of spray and wind. In between swells, I thrashed away from the suck of the tide before the ocean surf slopped me somewhere on Bishop Street, five boat-lengths downwind from where I went in. I crawled to clutch at a parking meter. My face was stung and throbbing—the smell of blood at the back of my nose a sensation weirdly nostalgic—and after a dazed moment I cast off my sopping duffel coat and shivered across Lower Water Street like a shipwrecked person. I'd fallen through river-ice as a kid and knew if I kept moving I'd be all right for some minutes. But I was in the middle of a storming blizzard, in some primeval Rupert's Land, snow smarting my eyes, winds so fierce I couldn't walk against them. It was Halifax's first December hurricane since 1862, category three on the Saffir-Simpson Scale, spawned somewhere off Africa, spun up the coast of Mexico, and making landfall on McNabs Island. Winds of seventy miles an hour blew snow through darkened streets, waves rose and broke over thruways, trees were splitting, thunder rupturing as if the sky itself was turning inside-out. I limped inland, my left foot slipping wet inside a slushing shoe. My suitjacket and pants were freezing, stiffening, making it difficult for me to move and, arriving at Government House and Barrington Street, I was stumbling more than walking when another flash of lightning showed some movement in the cemetery across the street. This was the Old Burying Ground, known to me since childhood because of a magnificent sandstone lion atop a triumphal arch, and blowing on one of the spikes of the cemetery's wrought-iron fencing was Cyrus Mair's blue cashmere coat. Some Samaritan must have found and draped it there. Purchased on Jermyn Street forty years before, worn by H.P. Mair in his office as premier, dormant for decades in drycleaner plastic, and lately worn by Cyrus Mair, here it was twisting in the wind like a drunk concert conductor, sleeves epileptic in the storm. It seemed to be signaling behind itself in the direction of Queen Street. I limped across the road, picked it off the fencing, and put it on. The item fit perfectly—I'd never worn it before—and, numbly fastening all its button, I sallied forth, deciding to generate some body heat, determined not to die at twenty-two.

Spring Garden Road was disorder at the first street corner—power cables snapped and sparking, telephone poles knocked down, maple trees blown over—and yet the panorama was oddly beautiful with sideways falling flurries, wind-whorled drifts, and very dark, looking much as it would have *in* 1862. I kept walking. Though my hands were dead cold, I pressed them hard against my ears to keep my head insulated from the storm. At Queen Street, the next corner, through the wind and sleet, I saw the lights of something below, the Infirmary Hospital, one of the few buildings in the city with lighted windows, and it became my beacon and guiding light. I staggered down the hill in knee-deep snow, my back in spasm from the cold, forcing myself toward illuminations that were to me a Shangri-La. Readers may be wondering what I felt to be so abruptly abandoned in the sea, like a common parricide, but I don't think I knew myself. Apart from a vague feeling of dissonance, I was mostly fixed on putting one cold foot in front of the other and sort of mindful of my responsibility to the fuller story, whatever that was, though it's just as true to say I still had a sense of not knowing which way I was pointing.

MY REFLECTION in the glass sliding doors of Emergency showed a shivering ghost—sallow face with bleeding nose and frozen hair snow-spangled—but I made a point to walk, in squashing shoes, as seriously as I could, as if I was very much on my way somewhere. Past the waiting area, in an interior hallway, I found a single bathroom with a locking door and went about my rehabilitation. I hung the coat on the opened door of the toilet stall. I shed my freezing clothes. I filled the sink and dunked my wrists in hot water and kept them immersed till I stopped shivering. I grabbed paper towels from the dispenser and wiped my face free of blood and blotted my thawing hair. In the sink, I rinsed my clothes, item by item, and tightly wrung them dry. My underwear and socks I heated under the wall-mounted hand dryer. On top of a wire shelving unit, beside a box of empty specimen containers, I found a stack of laundered hospital gowns. I dressed in two of them, the first facing one way, the second the other, using them like long underwear, before putting my own clothes back on. My clothes were damp, I was clammy, and in the mirror above the sink I looked greenish-pale but, if you squinted a little, you would think me bondable. I did notice, however, some gown-bunching at the trouser crotch point. I unzipped myself and dropped my pants. As I was pulling one of the gowns further down my thigh, I saw someone in the mirror lurch at me. This came as a jump-scare—for I was sure I was alone in the bathroom—and I screamed. My heart fluttering, I turned to see the coat had simply slipped off the stall door and fallen to the floor. Hopping over, as if I was in a very confined potato-sack race, I seized it and immediately felt something, a weight within the coat-bottom, between the silk lining and cashmere wool. Removing miscellaneous articles from a side pocket (flask, book, fountain pen, apple) I put my hand through a hole in the pocket-bottom and fingertipped my way within the fabrics, my hand closing around the hard edges of a smallish hardcover book. Pulling it out, I saw it was a page-a-day pocket diary. I was thinking it was the sort of thing a child might be given on her birthday when I realized a child *had* been given this on her birthday, in fact *I'd* given it to my sister Bonnie on her ninth birthday, for this was the page-a-day pocket diary swapped to Cyrus Mair some seventeen years before.

IT WAS FADED, timeworn, and kept tightly shut by a thick purple rubber band, the kind you might find around grocery store broccoli. I removed the rubber band. Inside the cover, on a gilt-edged front page, in kindergarten printing was the name Cyrus Francis Mair. The subsequent pages were worryingly dense with writings and ink-spills—as if an overzealous props department had been tasked to create the dream journal of an Unstable Outsider Artist—but I soon saw, after a section where pages had been ripped out, that the handwriting settled into a steady, adult-looking cursive. I flipped to a midpoint and then, standing in a bathroom of the Halifax Infirmary, somewhat scared I would be caught, quite literally, with my pants down, I began reading the diary of Cyrus Francis Mair.

> June 2. London. "Don't you dare put things in there about how I'm not as nice as other girls you went out with!" Karin sits across from me in The White Horse, reading a book and eating green grapes. Two in the afternoon and I've been thinking to make a proper entry in these pages for three months now. We meet next week Karin's father in Nice, a city she has been dreaming about for "billions of months." And something still to be remembered.
>
> June 4. A movie in Leicester Square where we walk the sloped aisle of a cavernous theatre amid smells of popcorn and throw-up, invisible to the couple kissing onscreen. In the tube to Parsons Green, we run down to the street, smelling the cotton of our clothes, the scent of an approaching storm, and a quick downpour on scorching asphalt as Karin's rain-spotted sundress covers in prickles.

June 6. "Put on your hat, Flippit! You'll get a sunburn on your head and have to stay in the bathroom puking all day." Before leaving London we stop at Piccadilly Hatchards for books. Karin gets a Woolf, me another Weil. Every time I think I understand her ("Attention is the rarest and purest form of generosity") she comes up with: "There is a reality outside the world, that is to say, outside space and time, outside's man's mental universe, outside any sphere whatsoever that is accessible to human faculties." Who says that? "Honeybunch," says Karin. "I love you to the moon and back but what are you doing in the window?" "Trying to figure out this book." "What's it about?" "The difference between what people think and what people are made to think." "Oh. That. This wine is for you, freak. Can I just say you smell so beautiful and look so beautiful with that white shirt and blue sky?"

June 12. Paris. Blood-damp towel on the empty bed. *Mrs. Dalloway* face down on the floor. A centime, a flip-flop. Postcards written to Zuber and McKee. The smells of the building itself, a hundred and fifty years old, and Karin sitting naked within a blowing curtain, all holding in place a river-breeze on a Sunday afternoon.

June 24. Gare Thiers. Michael Friday a no-show. Two hours waiting last night in the restaurant. Ridiculous. Not even a phone call. Karin silent, sullen. Apparently he's done this before.

June 29. Salzburg. Karin saddened so I speak to school kids and four-year-old Erin. "Does the sun know it's hot?" "Yes!" "Why?" "Because it's way high up in the air." "Does it have a birthday?" "No." "Who made it?" "God made it."

"Does it know it's alive?" "If the sun is God then it knows it's alive and can hear you when you say your prayers. And also my sister's." "Do you think God could be a girl?" "*No.*" "Why not?" "Because God's not a girl's name."

June 30. Karin troubled. More than a few times we've talked of families. She explains why her mother left her father and worries my growing up without parents has made for a "strange bouncing around." Then: "Sometimes I think you don't want me to love you." "When?" "Because everyone who's loved you has gone away. And I don't want to have thoughts you don't have and you do."

July 1. Break up in July under a wide open sky and I can no longer express in words what I am anymore.

July 8. London. Weird, recurring memory. A week before we split, on the train out of Rome, Italian men were giving Karin a terrible time. Hooting, grabbing. We were exhausted with travel, wary of being mugged, drugged. After she fell asleep beside me, I went to the bathroom to write in this diary. When I came back, two older nuns, disembarking at Siena, could not keep from staring at her. One of them, her eyes wet with tears, put her hands on Karin's face and kissed her awake. "Una ragazza cosi bella. Una ragazza cosi *bellissima*." Karin looking very Vermeer but in a too-dreamy-to-think state. And furious with me. "When I looked for you before, I thought you were gone. I thought you weren't going to come back. Cyrus, what if something happened?"

These last lines, as Fortune would have it, coincided with an urgent knocking on the bathroom door. I snapped shut the diary and replaced the rubber band. I did up my pants. I chugged what was left in the silver flask—about three shots of scotch—and emerged from what had been my own private dressing room and study carrel, choosing to avoid eye contact with the room's next occupant, a plump woman with a four-point cane who seemed a very buxom doppelganger of Sir John A. MacDonald. But on second thought, remembering it was a day of surprise guests but odd graces, I turned to smile respectfully at my fellow outpatient. But the door had closed, the lock-bolt spun, and I was pivoting away when I noticed the Trivial Pursuit card on the floor. I was happy to see it. For this item, like the blue cashmere coat, had developed over the night into a spirit guide of sorts and I gladly returned it to my pants pocket. Pleased with my service stop, I thought to check in with the front desk to see if any Mairs or Fridays, or elderly Siennese nuns, for that matter, had been admitted to hospital.

The waiting area was Standing Room Only, crowded with exhausted-looking interns, watchful paramedics, and assorted refugees from the extreme weather. The triage nurse was understandably reticent with me. She explained that, unless I was family, she could not disclose any information about recent admittances. But she did tell me, because the Infirmary's resources were at capacity, that ambulances in the last hour had been redirected to the Victoria General Hospital on South Street. I was moving to an exit door, and shoving it open against the storm, when my name was roared—rather as it would be during roll call at boot camp—back in the waiting area.

THERE UNDER fluorescent ceiling lights stood Bunker Burr, the day's best man. He wore a black tuxedo, a Boston Red Sox cap, and he was bleeding freely from his left eyebrow. There have been in these reminiscences more than a few allusions to the Burrs and now that one of the more exemplary family members has shouted his way onto the page it seems appropriate to set down a few essentials. The Burrs were fantastically confident, beautifully handsome, and carelessly rich. They were originally from the South, traced their line to Aaron Burr, and came to Halifax following the American Civil War. Though Nova Scotia's sympathies were mostly with the Union states, Halifax gave extended safe haven to a number of Confederate ships, among them the *CSS Tallahassee*, a steamer warship out of Carolina. The Burrs were likewise out of Carolina and, like the Loyalists before and the Draft Dodgers after, migrated north because of a war. Over the decades, they'd become a family of some means and influence in the city. They were sharp and ambitious—with a vast strength of will—and I'm not sure I can convey how potent such a party mix can be. It can be so diverting to consort with pretty, affluent people that you may not notice when their smiles tighten with competition, or when a racist joke is repeated, or when you sense they have in their hearts a determined inclination toward Money and Achievement and the Right Sort of Person. Because, for the Burrs, winning mattered. Before a family member's race or final, they held a pep rally, called Burr-Ups within the family circle, to maximize the competitor's mojo. Framed photographs of these team-building exercises, the family posed like a football team on their cottage dock, were conspicuously displayed over the fireplace in their Halifax house on Belmont on the Arm. They were a big noise in Halifax, to be honest, and represented the zenith of a certain sort of South End expectation—well-to-do husband-and-wife, three children, Labrador Retriever, house on the Northwest Arm, cottage in Chester, sailboats, ski trips, scandal. People *loved* to talk about the Burrs. Gregor and Tiggy were a storied socialite couple and their three sons were notorious on the highways and byways of the province.

MY MOTHER TALKING: "I don't know how Tiggy does it. They're in Toronto, Tiggy comes home, Gregor stops off in Ottawa to see his mistress. She'll say Gregor's seeing to some parliamentary matter. Or he's seeing a friend. That's what she calls it. A friend. Must be nice. Must be nice to live in that much of a dream world. He could've been a cabinet minister in Mulroney's government if he could've kept his dick in his pants. *Such* a sleaze bucket. My God, the Burrs, the Flynns, the Jessups. They don't read. They don't go to the theatre. There's always people in their homes. All they do is drink! Those people—I don't know how your father puts up with them—they've always got to do things in a group. Sugarloaf. Race Week. Always together. They don't know what they think about anything. They have no ideas. No inner life. Eli Brimmer. The Ogilvies. They all go skinny-dipping, you know. They're in their hot-tubs. They've all seen each other naked. They're so bored they don't have anything better to do. I don't know. People talk about the good side of the Burrs. I haven't seen it for a while."

I'd seen Bunker through the ages, the awkward stages, the dental braces, the paisley bandanas, the blond fringe tips. As a kid, I more than casually admired the brothers Burr for I keenly wished for *any* type of brother and to have an identity within a family of boys who raced in sloops and shells and giant slaloms seemed sterling to me. In my boyhood, my awareness of the world of older kids was gregariously mediated by the lives of Brecken and Bunker and Boyden Burr. They were lively, pubescent, autonomous, teenage jocks in tie-dye shirts, tennis shorts, falling-apart Tretorn sneakers, and their older teenaged lives were linked in my mind with the theme song from the television show *Room 222* and with Dennis Wilson, the drummer for the Beach Boys, whom they all closely resembled, especially as he was pictured in the stills for *The Pet Sounds* album, the sun-bleached hair swooping across the eyes. First-born Brecken was his father's favourite, the baby Boyden his mother's pet, and Bunker a case study in messed-up Middle Son Syndrome—hyper-competitive, highly erratic, and somewhat criminal. I admired perversely his wild compulsions and troubled history. He once threw a dinky toy and hit my sister Faith in her backyard playpen. At twelve, he chugged a bottle of Tabasco on a bet. At seventeen, Bunker sank his grandfather's Boston Whaler cranking whoopee turns in the open ocean, totaled his dad's BMW doing donuts in the snow, and wrapped his older brother's Kawasaki Z1000 around a service pole on the Hubbards highway on-ramp. Tribulations continued. The summer of freshman year, he served a commuted sentence on weekends for sucker-punching a bouncer at The Palace Cabaret. At twenty-two, with a roommate from St. Francis Xavier University, he tried to windsurf from Nova Scotia to Prince Edward Island, got blown out the Northumberland Strait, and had to be rescued by the Coast Guard. None of this fazed or dazed or much amazed him. Bunker Burr had immense self-possession, bulletproof belief in his own prospects, and at the first sign of complication he pressed for advantage. He could be selfish and hilarious and juvenile. But he liked people—his kind of people—and simply ignored details that didn't square with his version of the world. He had plans for himself and from these plans he would not be distracted. Besides, like his brothers, Bunker Burr stood to inherit half a million dollars from his paternal grandmother. For a few years playing tennis tournaments we were friends. I found him dope, he bought me booze. We partnered in doubles when Cyrus quit the sport, Bunker bouncing around the backcourt, thumping forehands, serving bombs, crushing match points.

We played the Nova Scotia Closed, Atlantic Regionals. At the Maritime Open we made the semis, beating the top seeds in fading sunlight, and that Saturday I was invited to the Chester cottage for supper. Chester is a seasonal life of sailing and golf and partying, full of great quantities of fizzing beer and tanned young people in pink shirts and plaid shorts and sockless deck shoes, a vacation town for the great washed and blowdried and wind-tousled. The Burrs in Chester sauntered over summertime grass to the Fo'c'sle Tavern with a kind of indiscriminate amiability—Canadian variants on Kennedy-style frat boys—and lived a life of shirts untucked, faded jeans, floating key chains. My memory of that dinner is vivid and blurry, a scene sequence of hot-boxing and sunburn, lobster leftovers and rhubarb fool, and Bunker's mom in an outdoor hot tub, clad only in a string bikini bottom, sitting with a blissful smile, nominally absorbed in a hardcover edition of *The Hotel New Hampshire*. "There they go," I remember her saying. "The men who make it all possible." Bunker and I swam blitzed out of our minds to the sailboats moored in the Back Harbour, climbing aboard and raiding cans of beer from *Wind Runner* and *Rum on the Rocks, Sundowner* and *Sticky Fingers*, wet jeans weighed down with our thievery and sinking us in tidal seawater. We drank on the shore past midnight, talking, riffing, dreaming on things to come. It was as close as we've ever been and since then we've always approached each other with the idea that we'd enter into some serious, marvellously fulfilling conversation but, seeing him now in the Halifax Infirmary, I wondered if that conversation was ever going happen.

"There he is!" Bunker strode over to me. "Prince of the city." He spoke with wonderful confidence and humour, as if it was only natural he was the one doing the talking. "How are you, brother? Haven't seen this clown in ages." He smacked me on the back and turned to a fellow with a crewcut sitting in the waiting area. This man wore a brown suit, had his hand wrapped in paper towels, and sat beside an opened magnum of champagne. He seemed drunk out of his mind but tried to look sober as he stared at the paper towels which, after he flexed his fingers, coloured with blood. Bunker introduced him as Dunc Chapman and I asked if he was all right.

"You kidding me?" said Bunker. "Dunc's the real deal."

"Everything—" Dunc Chapman smiled at me after a complicated burp. "Cancelled."

I asked if that meant there's no wedding.

"Is no anything." Dunc Chapman directed his smile toward his shoes. "City down. Storm."

"The storm—" Bunker made a strangely enlightened sneer, as if he was sort of happily disgusted, then turned to me with a winning smirk. "I know. Insane. It's insane out there. It's a fucking zoo. We got so boned by this blizzard. The whole city's totally boned." He reached for the magnum of champagne. "Bottom of Spring Garden and I'm seeing the Archbishop fighting his way into a taxi. How is *this* happening? Brutal. Just brutal. Taxi gets stuck in the snow and me and Dunc, we're pushing—how many cars we push out, Dunc? Fucking dozens. We fall I don't know how many times. Dunc slashes his hand there. That's going to need stitches. I pop a header and gash my head on a fucking bumper. I think we can keep going but it's like, 'It's over. You're gone. You're done, bud. Nobody cares what you think. Go get checked at Emergency.'" Bunker drank from the champagne, a ring on his hand flashing with reflected light. It was an X-Ring, a senior class ring from St. F.X., which meant he must've graduated and I remembered now he went through law school at UNB and was articling with his father's old firm, once called Merton Mair McNab but now, after amalgamation with firms in the three other Atlantic Provinces, rebranded as Merton Fortiers Chisolm Blades.

"Been quite a week," said Bunker. "At the stag last night, we got fucking wrecked. Just face-plant, re*tard*ed drunk. Flaming Sambucas. Montecristos. The whole bit." Bunker had missed a spot shaving, I noticed, and dark little bristles sprouted beneath a nostril. "It was like the night Dooder fell out of Dad's boat. Remember that? The boys were trying to remember who pulled Dooder out of the Arm that night. I said McKee'd remember. If anyone could." Bunker put his arm around me and swiveled toward Dunc Chapman. "McKee here's got the most phenomenal memory. This guy remembers *every*thing. Name of your imaginary friend in nursery school. Capital of Kamchatka. Maybe there's a blind kid in Calcutta who's better but the smart money's on McKee. He's got all the goop. Seriously." His arm still around me, Bunker slapped his hand against my chest. "And this guy's dad? The *lawyer's* lawyer. McKee's dad is easily the top litigator in the province. He's an icon around here. An icon."

"Right on." Dunc Chapman opened his eyes very wide, trying to focus on me. "Was your name again?"

"But Dunc here?" Bunker released me and shadowboxed at Dunc Chapman. "This fucking guy? Just made partner at Merton and his billable hours are ri*dic*ulous. I mean this year alone Dunc's billing twenty-two hundred hours." He mussed Dunc Chapman's crewcut. "You fucking high-baller. You're *king* of the zoo. You got due diligence up the ying-yang, brother. But you got to learn to kick back once in a while. Like last night after the stag, I take Dunc to the Liquor Dome. My Apartment, Lawrence of Oregano, you know."

At the mention of these nightspots, Dunc Chapman raised a fist to say, "*Hell*, yeah."

"Absolutely, absolutely." Bunker smiled. "Pretty target-rich environment. Where do these girls *come* from? I meet some chick named Courtney? Makes it three chicky-babes in three nights. Not too shabby. Done and done. What can I say? I'm on a roll." Bunker jingled some coins in his front pocket and turned to me with a friendly you-know-what-I-mean smile. "Because when you get that first one? Dunc?"

"Gotta smear—" said Dunc Chapman, making a great boozy grin. "Gotta smear that fuck all over you."

"Fucking right," said Bunker. "As long as it's done according to Hoyle." His mouth slightly open, Bunker allowed his head to roll around his shoulders, as if he was working a kink out of his neck.

While it's true a certain stamp of women were aware of Bunker—he was cocky and tall and immediately handsome—I'm not sure his was an appeal universally acknowledged. This didn't matter to Bunker because he would never accept a situation where a woman liked him less than he liked her and I remember when he asked Kelly Gallagher to his high school graduation—and she demurred—he never spoke to her again and simply behaved as if she never existed.

"But what about you, McKee?" asked Bunker. "What's up? Weren't you and your buddies writing a book?"

"Didn't happen."

"Didn't finish it? So where you coming from—The Seahorse? You and the other New Wavers." Bunker took off his cap, touched at his bleeding eyebrow, and turned to Dunc Chapman. "McKee was a punk rocker there for a while. Ran around with the lunatic fringe. Mohawks. Safety pins. The whole schmear. He was with this one little nut job. Kind of chunky. I don't know what she had stuck in her clit. But the *energy* he put into this girl. Jesus. I hope she's grateful. I hope she knows what you did for her." Bunker smiled again, his upper lip catching on one of his front teeth, making him look briefly like a simpleton. "Glad to see you put on your big-boy pants because I didn't think you were going to get anywhere with her."

Bunker meant, of course, Gail Benninger. Gail didn't really belong to the logic of Bunker's civilization. And this understanding was not really open to revision. It would not change—no matter how much evidence was created to the contrary—because Gail's possibilities were not convenient for him. Bunker needed coordinates and reference points that could match with his own interests, or his own self-interests, and, thinking about someone like Gail, he couldn't find any. To Bunker, Gail was merely an aberration, an irrelevancy. And me—what were my coordinates? I was restless with a few contingencies. I put my hand in my pocket, my fingers finding and closing around the soggy Trivial Pursuit card. The card seemed a forlorn little entity now, like an elastic band you might see in a puddle, and on impulse I brought it out. Contemplating its colours, I said, somewhat privately, "William Jennings Bryan—"

"What's that?"

I took the magnum of champagne from Bunker and chugged from it. "That's who pulled Dooder out of the Arm that night."

Bunker's instinct was to laugh, not so much with amused surprise as outright derision, and grabbed the magnum back. "McKee," he said. "Remember when we played the quarters of the open? Epic. Fucking epic. Dunc, you should've *seen* this guy. In the first set, McKee's on fire! Total beast mode. Swinging top-spin volleys from No Man's Land? Who does that? Running no-look overheads? Who even *tries* that? I was like, How is he *doing* this? Just killing me. Then in the second set tie-break, you're stumbling around, you're swearing, you're screaming. How many match points you have? One smashed racket later and—boom—you're gone. Thrown out of the tournament. The Full McEnroe. Done and dusted." Bunker pulled on his cap. "Too funny."

"Yeah." Letting go of the Trivial Pursuit card, I watched it drop, like a descending magic carpet, to the tiled floor. "I got boned. I got boned on that one. Totally boned up the old ass-crack there. Boned till my eyes popped—"

Bunker was smiling at me, assessing me, the better to process my deadpan remarks and suddenly, or not suddenly, but gradually and inexorably, standing there with Bunker Burr I felt an overwhelming sense of Halifax—a great interconnectedness of the Nova Scotian Open and Wednesday Night Races and the Headwall and LSATs and Connaught Avenue and Park Lane and the Palace and Liquor Dome and X-Rings and Kelly Gallagher—and Bunker Burr seemed sort of absurd to me, with his beliefs and misbeliefs, how he worked to secure connections through teasing and jokes and stories and when he swigged again from the magnum of champagne I found I couldn't look at him without feeling slightly sick.

I gazed instead at Dunc Chapman. He was passed out in his chair, bent over, slobber from his mouth dribbling into the paper towels wrapped around his bloodied hand. "Dunc and Bunk," I said. "Live from Carnegie Hall."

"From *what?*" said Bunker, befuddled.

"But Dunc's drunk—"

"You're a funny sort of fellow, aren't you, McKee?"

"And you're a lot of Bunk." I tilted my head. "So fun! But I'm done."

"Done with what?"

"Limericks." I stared at him. "And beurre d'arachide."

Bunker's expression didn't really change, exactly, but his smile shifted into a pressed-lipped sort of grimace and he put down the magnum of champagne. He tugged on his shirt cuffs. He touched at his cufflinks. He was bleeding again—a few drops splashed to the floor tiles—but he stood there, Bunker Burr, as if he knew what to do in every given moment, as if he knew what best served the city's interests, as if he knew his prospects were perfectly set. It was the reaction of someone who kept to himself a sense of his own future superiority and I knew, in Bunker's mind, in the family sweepstakes of the city, the Burrs would always win. They would be taken to be the victors and returning champions, no matter what the pursuit, no matter what the endeavour, and Bunker Burr was proceeding toward such a destiny as if it were already true. Staring at him in the Halifax Infirmary, I took a sudden dislike to Bunker Burr and I felt a charge of anger so unstable it seemed the anger of another person. What was said next I don't recall but I knew, as the champagne and scotch mixed in my blood, I had to get the fuck out of that waiting area and the next I remember I was running in the storm, scowling at insolent stop signs, swearing at idiotic trees. In my fury, I felt super-powered—and "Psychotic Break" might be a phrase appropriate to this part of the evening—and as I sprinted I began to think of myself as Super-Fast Running Man, or perhaps Drunk Guy Who Thinks He's Super-Fast Running Man, but whichever, I ran through the stormy streets of Halifax for no reason except I felt I had to *do* something. I don't know about you, but there are days after you've been flipped into the ocean, blown around by a hurricane, and forced to dress in stolen hospital gowns, when you feel *some* sort of direct and immediate action should be taken. I was taking it, I was running with it, and I tore in the blizzard into my own No Man's Land.

The warmth of my perspiring body mingled with the smell of the cashmere coat, provoking a sort of soggy woollen fragrance that seemed very personal to me and which gave me focus as I ran and followed westward a single set of snowplow tracks. I had more going on in my mind than I knew but mostly I was thinking about families and the city and cities over time and I remembered how I used to run this very street with

Uncle Lorne and I remembered the silent reading of the purple-faced boy and scenes with Sofya Benninger and dealings with Howard Fudge and a hundred other figures to whom I was connected by strains of life lived and thoughts sustained and I became strongly conscious of my former life and the various Aubrey McKees who put in appearances here and there in other people's lives and it seemed to me I was coexisting with earlier versions of myself—here escaping my sister's birthday party, there returning to an empty house—and as I ran a few cardinal ideas emerged in my mind about myself and Halifax and someone like Bunker Burr. Bunker Burr would always go to where he was envied and admired and he would become what was considered a success in Halifax, he was the very pattern of the place, a merchant prince through which the city might perpetuate itself, and I knew Bunker Burr was arrogantly himself just as Gail was furiously herself and Cyrus Mair strangely himself and so, perhaps, was *everyone* themselves but something inside me wasn't right, some disruption within me was growing, much more than the flang of feedback or a few misplaced notes. All my pursuits, common, personal, and trivial, seemed ridiculous to me and I felt, if this *was* to be a question of final belief, then there had to be something more. Either I wanted to be more than I was, or I wanted the city to be more than it was, and though I couldn't hold in my imagination what I wanted these to be, exactly, I knew very drunkenly, very extremely, very finally, that I was choosing not to care about Halifax anymore, I didn't see myself in Halifax anymore, I didn't see a future in Halifax anymore. With this conclusion arriving in my mind, directly between my eyes, as it were, I skidded to a stop in the snow, sucking air, exhausted, my race done. In memory, this sequence plays for me cinematically so suppose the camera has dollied in on me, finding in extreme close up my staring eyes, and audible offscreen is my huffing-and-puffing and the thunder of the storm, but as the camera rises up all diegetic sounds drop away and heard in the sound design are the faraway winds of a blizzard, and noticeable now are a few drifting synth-tones from the musical track, and with their advent the scene slows down, snow flurries loose in the air, rotating in real-time a moment more, before tumbling sluggish and time-bending into slow-motion, CGI snowflakes spinning and spinning in a widening spiral, a few ambient piano notes coordinating with their down-falling movement, and the camera gradually cranes up and away, looking down on a figure shrinking smaller and smaller in frame as we rise as high as the crane will allow, above the treetops and into the swirling snow—and with this bird's eye view the music shimmers between B minor and A major chords and we are about to slowly fade to black when somewhere out of frame sounds the first blast of an air-horn—a very triumphant overachieving D major—stopping cold the camera move. It isn't until a fire engine fishtails past me, and I begin to chase after the flashing lights of an ambulance, that I wonder just what in God's name is going on.

A FINAL SCENE: A HOUSE IN FLAMES AND TEMPEST. There is something to the spectacle of a house on fire, when all around is stormy dark and the place flames amazement—chimney bricks bursting into the night, shingles melting into creamy smoke, a thousand embers like confetti in the sky... Let me explain what happened not as I knew it then but as I came to understand it later, a last commotion between Mair and Friday, the final movement of the night, and the figurative coda to the symphonic work that was The Common Room. Some of what follows is conjecture because I wasn't there, I was on the outside, looking darkly in, but certainly all the planning, all the plane tickets and phone calls, the crammed briefcase, all of these were in service of some final escape and elopement. In my mind, I see a jumble of his clothes—suitcoat, shirt and tie—leading from the staircase to the third floor attic where, soaked through and almost hypothermic, Karin has collapsed in the bed. The house is dark, the rooms cold, and Cyrus rises up the attic stairs with a lighted candelabra, slush from his shoes pooling into puddles on the wooden steps. She is shivering as he undresses her, unfastening the fifty-eight pearl buttons on the back of the once-in-a-lifetime dress, peeling off the crystal-beaded bateau neckline of the bodice, stripping off the ivory-satin skirt. He removes the rest of his own clothes, clothes he's been in for days, and doubtless their looks to each other now have some shyness, Karin watching his profile, touching at his sunburned face, she in candlelight looking silver-pale, other-worldly. She stares at him full in the eyes and for him it would have been thrilling, calming—*everything*—to look again into the eyes of Karin Friday, to be at her side, faithful now to the theme and vision of his life. Six years they've known each other, true, but meanings change over time, and in these first minutes there would be for both some sudden newness overwhelming past familiarity, as moments past change into moments loving, moments that belong to their privacy and of course into further romantic intimacy I do not feel comfortable imagining myself. Whether or not they make love as some have daydreamed, I do not know and have never sought to discover—for these final stage directions there is no unanimously agreed-upon version—but Karin and Cyrus do fall asleep together, like lovers anywhere, really, with infinity on either side of them.

WHEN I ARRIVED on Tower Road, the air was full of ash and fire and the heat from the blaze could be felt across the street and my clothes, once sopping, were soon baked dry to my skin, sweat fresh on my face. The fire fighters were soaking the rooftops of nearby houses when someone smashed their way naked out of the windows of the first floor of the Mair House. It was Karin, I saw, bleeding, and getting to her feet, she fought disoriented against a fireman, trying to return to the house. It was lightning that hit the house and started the fire, just where it struck was never determined. It may have travelled toward the tallest point on the block, a Golden Pippin in the backyard, then into the ground, only to stream back up within millionths of a second to the first floor fireplace. There it set alight the flammable chimney-stuffs—dried droppings, nesting twigs—which burned and sideways-smoked because the chimney-tops were clogged with snow. Cyrus left the bed when the chimney materials first exploded and moved dizzily downstairs to Emlyn's bedroom, the site of the only plausible fireplace, to find the source of the smoke. He did not know the fire had started and spread from the floor below. He did not know Karin behind him would awake alone, dozy with smoke inhalation, and stumble all the way down to the first floor, finding the place in flames. Of course Cyrus returned to the bedroom for her, his face seen for a moment in the attic window—this my last-ever glimpse of him—before vanishing, as if responding to a cry within, but now, for a first time, there was no one in the house but him. Karin outside was being wrapped in a fire blanket—and finding her way *out* of a fire blanket—and falling to the snow and slipping as she ran toward the house only to be pulled screaming to an ambulance, screaming because the freshly broken windows had provided combustible air for the fire within and with a stunning whoosh the house enflamed, the volumes of its libraries, *Watership Down, Daisy Miller, Jack Harkaway*—as well as the wingbacks, pianos, photographs—all tinder for this great fire. I was witnessing something I never thought to see, everything was sort of unreal and hyper-realized at the same time, but my imagination was fighting the permanency of these events and when I rushed the house I was near enough to breathe its searing fumes, near enough to singe my eyelashes, near enough to sense a deeper fire within the flames, before I was seized by two firemen and frog-marched backwards. The pigeons, I saw, were flapping above the gables and eave-troughs, not wishing to leave their home, or each other, dozens of them fluttering panicked about the windows, many burning their wings and falling into the flames and as the top floors collapsed into the basement, I realized I was watching, finally and literally, the fall of the house of Mair—the great pith and moment of a family passing—there seemed an eerie music, a wailing sigh, as the place crumpled inward, sending into the night a confederation of sparks, and I was made to realize that my friend's time and possibilities, and all those he imagined for us, had ended, and so Cyrus Mair was dead.

I REMAINED ON TOWER ROAD for some time, well after the emergency vehicles left, for there were fires and sirens in other neighbourhoods now. I walked up the street, still wearing the blue cashmere coat. A few minutes before midnight, underneath South Street's only functioning streetlight, beside a parking lot which had once been the playground for the School for the Blind, where first I saw Cyrus Mair, I reached into a coat pocket and took out his diary. I removed its rubber band. From the back of the diary, from a hollow inside the paste-down endpaper, fell a folded personal letter. The moment had a strange, fifth dimensional quality and, as I located the letter in the snow, I stared at it dumbfounded, as if I didn't know what it was, or what it did, or even what side of it I was on. I picked it up. The letter, composed on pink onionskin paper in blue Magic Marker, was written some years before, a few months after its sixteen-year-old author met the addressee, and it seemed to have been read and reread, and unfolded and refolded, three hundred times since. I opened it. As snowflakes spun out of the sky and along the edges of the letter, the blue words leaking into each other in a smudgy palimpsest, I read the letter once through before letting its pages drop and blow down Tower Road. Afterwards, I felt no need to read anything else. Then I slipped the diary back into a coat pocket. I took off the coat. Before trudging away, I left it swinging from a fencepost in the whirling snow, knowing for a while the coat saved my life, maybe in the way this letter saved someone else's.

l'heure bleu
a new year's eve
un pneumatique

O MY OWN DEAR SWEET DARLING CYRUS MAIR

I am so sorry I dint get to see you again this evening on this your last night home even! Cuz my Mom dint tell me you was here til it was too late. You know, my Mom what's starting to get upset because of how she dint bring me upright and how I'm not as good a hostess as I could be and how I'm a delinquent because I'm starting to talk like you all the time. Oh pshaw and harrumph.

She dint tell me you came back bud when I heard your voice at the back door I ran downstairs to the landing but man I durst not go further. I was wearing only a slip! Barebum. All my Mom's party-men woulda seen ma décolletage. There was about 104 of them. I was thinking of snucking out but Mom's really had it with escaped orphans et les enfants perdues. I fought you mite fro rox at my winnow so I wend back into bed. A-waiting. I called your house bud Auntie Em said you weren't home yet. Where do you go? You are always disappearing, Cyrus of Persia! I guess I shoulda gone out and got drunk with the Common Room, right?

What a loofah. So I gave up on reading. Too tie-erd. It was pass one in the moaning. I fell a-sleep for a-while. It was quiet in the dark-of-night then. But now I'm awoked and just found and opened your note and think you are the nicest wonderfullest sweetest boy I know and you are always sea-prizing me, boyo! I jez never figgered that present box woulda come from you. The best magic ever! And I shall share these gifts with some youngsters because I know you would like that I can't believe how much I love that letter and plus I always love green spearmint leaves.

I think of the strangest things at the strangest times. Because now I feel all sad and Garfunkly and I know you hate it when these silly mushy wimpy sad sentimental feelings take me over bud how can I hep it? I can say I never felt so lucky-overjoyed-surprised as when you met me out of the blue at the train station. It was like I missed you but didn't know it and was never so happy to see someone

And I was thinking before I'd kissed all your friends but not you because I was always afraid you'd think I was a whatever and you never show things because I know who wants to be like a boyfriend-girlfriend and do all that boyfriend-girlfriend crap? But I remember what you say! Do you think I don't listen to you? Yes and yes and a thousand times geesh.

Because I know yer always understanding what everybody's thinking like the time you lent me your enchanted plum or when you took out my splinter & warmed my nude feet at Babba's bonfire on the beach and the spooning and the kisses and the hoojamaflip. I much prefer your calm talk to when you go bonkers and suffer from a spastic brain fever and maybe I don't always know what you're meaning but sometimes when you touch me I feel like I'm going to fall off a cliff

So now I miss you so much I burp all the time on account of it and I have a red spot on the inside of my nose because of it and I git all tingly innermost when I think of it and I miss you Cyrus Mair perfectly darling boy and bien sur I want to go to Europa Parigi, Firenza, Alpen, Muesli. And I will swim like a Turk in the land of Egypt. That is a promise and a promessa und der vogel ist das wort.

I have to get a new pair of trousers.

Please wear a hat.

But most important—don't you dare kiss Brigid Benninger!

And super apologies everything screwed-up tonight I am truly sorry about such predicaments but I am in love with you Cyrus Mair once upon a midnight.

Til soon!

Best love from

KARIN

ps I love love love those poems esp the line where the world lives and dies with each person all you need now is a rhyme for person!

Aubrey McKee

FOR MANY YEARS it would be the biggest event in my life. Maybe things in Halifax do not change so swiftly but things for me had changed forever. It was a grief that filled me. I could not control it. The confusion and damage I felt from this winter would last ten years or more and I would act it out in any number of personal relationships—this the accurate contention of my adult girlfriends—and certainly in the days and nights immediately following I was a mess, lurching from one bar to another, falling down, picking fights, slutting after strangers. There I am, plastered and getting bounced out of the Palace, and there I am again, driving drunk down Coburg Road to the closed-for-the-season Waegwoltic Club, speeding by the icicled gatehouse and swerving into the club's empty parking lot where I sit on the car's front bumper, in the wind and whipping sleet, downing what's left of a bottle of wine, drunk in my aloneness, watching the tennis courts fill up with snow.

WHEN SAINT MARY'S Cathedral Basilica re-opened in January, Karin Friday would marry Boyden Burr on a Saturday afternoon. I was invited, did not attend, but chose to visit the church later that day, slinking hungover into the rearmost pew for the third wedding service of that afternoon. This was a couple from Hantsport, a woman named Publicover, and I remained in my pew some minutes after the service was done and the hall was emptied. I wandered toward a white gladioli arrangement on a table fitted with a pressed white tablecloth. Somewhat inexplicably, someone had written on this tablecloth in red ballpoint pen the word "mood" with a line through the m. Why anyone would write on a newly-pressed tablecloth was beyond me. The action seemed repulsive in the extreme. Whichever—earlier that day Karin Catherine Friday took her husband's name and became Karin Catherine Burr. She would become known afterwards as K.C. Burr and then simply Casey Burr. We are, at the time of this writing, probably three phone calls away—I call my sister Carolyn who calls Trish Burr who calls her sister-in-law—but Casey Burr is pretty squarely gone from my experience. I don't know much about her present life. I imagine her as one of those women—perfect blonde highlights, year-round tan—you see springing out of a Porsche Cayenne with a cellphone to her ear and a tightening in her eyes. She lives now within the ten thousand families of Halifax, her life full of children's hockey and ballet lessons, March Breaks in Whistler, a bungalow in Bermuda—a signature cast member of The Real Housewives of the South End. I have been chastised by my sisters for my partiality to this rather petulant interpretation but in Casey Burr I have sensed a very stark, even slightly sociopathic, self-involvement so, who knows, maybe I am simply following her example. "Blondes don't always age well," was my mother's somewhat cryptic assessment.

THE HOUSE OF COURSE IS GONE. The address of 1121 Tower Road no longer exists. The Mair property, like the Moir's chocolate factory, like the Halifax Herald building, is no longer extant, its libraries, ballrooms, attics, rose gardens—and all the meanings they once implied—completely gone. Two days after the storm, I went to view the hurricane and fire wreckage. The street was a mess, the clogging street snow a cookie dough colour, trees blown sideways, heaved-up roots glazed with ice, sidewalk squares turned over. The property itself was a cindered shambles, a smell of burnt planking and blackened plaster, drifts of ash and snow crisscrossed with bicycle tracks where kids had ridden in soot and grime. Soon after, the ruins of the Mair house were razed and demolished, the entire acreage bulldozed. What stands in that location now, should you be walking down Tower Road, is a concrete apartment building, a shabby low-rise already deteriorating, iron fittings rusting, cement showing a crumbly, weathered aspect. "The times changed and they didn't," said my mother. "That family, they couldn't let go of the past. All of them. I mean it's a sin what happened. When you think of the darling little boy who came to Bonnie's birthday party. But who sends a four-year-old to live with a woman in her sixties? I swear that family has no sense! For all their brilliance, they have no sense. I found him one day out in the driveway. Where was the babysitter? And what in the name of God was she thinking? You never leave a four-year-old on their own. The poor child. Playing in the slush. Improperly dressed. It's a wonder he wasn't run over by a truck. And how they end up? With all those books and pigeons? It *is* a sin. A travesty. The whole thing's beyond belief."

THE MAIRS, THE MAIRS—what *was* their substance and how on earth? Maybe they were merely everyday transposable folk, as worn-out and done-to-death as those in any how town. Or maybe they were unique to Halifax. To think a last time on Wallace Stevens, and how he placed his jar in Tennessee to make the wilderness surround a hill, so, too, the Mairs seemed placed on Tower Road to make the city's history surround a house and street. In memory, the family seems a fantasia on Maritime themes—brilliancy, loss, nostalgia, decay—and the Mairs a medium through which the mystery and tragedy of Nova Scotia expressed itself. Note the past participle. The family is mostly gone. Although they'd long been important to Halifax's imagination of itself, and, for a few years following, the family would be recalled with baffled amazement—they that perished in seas and fire—but it wasn't long before the surname would drop from the news cycles of the city. I have a niece who claims she once saw a Mair, a gay, estranged, and renegade cousin named Augustus, whom Emma maintains she saw tumble down the ski slopes at Martock, but rumour is he moved away years ago. To be honest, even alive the Mairs seemed to be living in—to borrow the title of a book—a Vanishing Halifax. For each in their way wished to return to something that was already gone.

Howland Mair sought to create in Halifax a metropolis based on defunct ideals. Emlyn Mair—who would die in hospital a few weeks into January at the age of ninety-two—she was concocting for Cyrus a life from obsolescent glory. I think, in the way she felt accountable for her brother's death, she felt responsible for her nephew's life. So she made a stately project of the boy, sending him to boarding school, to Cambridge, planning to bestow upon the world a Cyrus. But her efforts were mostly a means to recover what she herself had lost. Seen this way, Cyrus seems to me an innocent scion, a kid flung forward into present-day confusions like a message in a bottle from the Edwardian past, expected to continue in a line of figures who have about them something of imperial exploit—Cyrus Mair, the living end-effect of the schemes and strivings of the Emlyn Mair Expeditionary Force—but I'm not sure this allowed for a boy to find his own way in the world. And, for Cyrus, how was the waning past repeated? I'm not sure it was. I feel he wished to return to the rush of First Love and all the possibilities that rush might mean. For him, Karin was perfect and peerless and he sought to identify himself with her in her best moments of sustained joy and self-possession—before the meanings of the adult world would really involve her and before her own self-involvement would really absorb her—and perhaps he pursued her a second time because he'd become infatuated with this very same self-involvement. I don't know. Maybe he just wished to be returned to the first time he heard the song. If I could identify the contradictions in the man, it would be the conflict between wanting to give to someone the open-ended freedom to infinitely develop as well as wanting to impose a structure of meaning on that someone as a way to organize his own understanding of the world. With most citizens, he was sufficiently isolated to be safe in such procedures but with Karin Friday I think he was suspended somewhere between Love and Reckoning and these variant feelings became for him a source of personal confusion. That's my pass at it. You have to believe in something. He certainly believed in Karin Friday. She was his context and system, his story and history, his exquisite truth and fiction.

As he recedes with the years, what remains of his too-brief life will linger in the subjectivities of those who knew him. Whether he was a crackpot who amounted to a lot of spilled milk or a poet whose medium was other people, I'm not sure, but he was probably the single-biggest influence on my young life and one of the most brilliantly unpredictable minds I've known. Strains and traces of his life and thought have followed me in this, my later life, he was certainly one of the voices in my head—and to think of all the people I would go on to meet and he would not! My emotionality would change, my response to the world would change, who I *was* would change—all these would distort and morph under the pressure of new realities, for I would enter a world of further spirits—but most of those to whom I would be drawn would have in them reminders of Cyrus Mair.

"He was so young!" Babba said to me recently, impulsively touching my wrist and squeezing my hand. "He was twenty-*two* years old. Do you remember how young that is? That's practically a baby. Think of it. Think what we were like back then." She shook her head, in her wince and manner conveying her still-palpable exasperation and sorrow. "There was just something so *frantic* about him. In such a rush, always. And I don't know if being smarter than everybody else was such a big advantage. Being super-smart, I'm not sure it's so helpful. I mean, if you let the universe inside your head like that, it can get pretty disturbing." I remember Babba gazing down in this moment, somewhat off the portside of her own elbow, before adding, "He'd been alone so much of the time, in boarding school, playing tennis, at university, and I know he read about everything in life. But I'm not sure he *felt* it. I'm not sure he felt as much as he read. Who could? I don't know. Sometimes angels come down to earth for a while. That's what I think."

TO REPRISE: life in Halifax is rich with connection and overlap, with shared lives and shared relationships. It's almost impossible to be discrete there. Everyone's life complicates with connection—though complicate doesn't seem to adequately convey the saturated, interrelated confusion of its lives. MY SISTERS TALKING: "Halifax is a small world." "Everybody knows everybody." "Life in the fish bowl." "Weirdness within weirdness." "And who's changing the water?" "I have never seen a place so obsessed with itself as Halifax." I do think of Halifax vast and big, rich and strange, changeless and changing, this mess of small eternities, and in my mind I've counted all the cracks in its sidewalks, seen all the tennis balls on its school rooftops, looked in the eye all its leading lights. But in its complexities of course I have moved only a very small part. These, my efforts, have been subject to my own prejudices, as well as the prejudices of my circumstances, but they are *my* efforts. And my mistakes. Whatever these recollections have been, they have been mine, for this was Halifax as I knew it, as I lived it and felt it, and this pattern of reminiscences, these feats of recovery, these acts of betrayal, have become *my* Halifax Book. I have done my best to recover these moments, to display them as best as I could, and to show the mysteries—and people—who were to me the city's truths.

SO I WOULD LEAVE NOVA SCOTIA. I remember the midwinter day Carolyn drove me the twenty-two miles to the airport. The sun was setting in the west, flurries scattering on salt-bleached highways, the colours of the world drained to desolation. As I flew back to university and a city that would claim me for many years, I glanced out the airplane window at the speckling lights of the twin-cities below. For other passengers, the city's constellations might seem, in Saul Bellow's phrase, a tremendous Canada of light, but I saw the gloom between the glimmer, the darkness suggestive of obstinacy and misperception, and I decided there was more to the world than what my hometown was interested in. Hometowns for a twentysomething can be like that. I could have just as easily looked down on Rochester or Pittsburgh or Raleigh. I may not have understood all of my thoughts, really, but I knew that in the somersaults of the next generations, no one would really know me or Gail or Cyrus. We'd be absent from the far future, from its conflicts and vocabularies, its further flux of circumstance. Vast and elaborate crimsons separate us from the people of the next few centuries and you wonder how our situations, lived somewhat erratically in their past, might offer any meaning to their lives. How odd to think that everything we know—dominions, virtues, principalities—will one day vanish from this curious adventure. Strange and strange, isn't it?

IN MY YOUNG LIFE, I'd been called many things, Kink and Mickey, Charles and Grub, Tudball and Harold and Max, but in the next few years, when my charms might be more my own, I had an idea to commit to some system of Aubrey McKee. For I knew I still had to make myself up.

END BOOK ONE